BEYOND THE REACH OF EARTH

Who was actually *in* Black Horizon? A handful of scientists and officers had broken the news to their astonished governments. The crews of certain submarines and other craft were obviously complicit – though just how many and how much was unknown. The conspiracy was almost certainly highly compartmentalised. It could be presumed that submarines were used as starships only when they were out of contact when on patrol. It was possible that some crew members didn't know they were on another planet at all, even if they disembarked – and not all did.

The rest of the conspiracy remained hidden. And not only on Earth. It was known that they'd been to other planets than Apis, but no mention of these had been made. No one yet knew what resources and reserves Black Horizon might have stashed across the sky beyond the reach of Earth.

By Ken MacLeod

The Fall Revolution
The Star Fraction
The Stone Canal
The Cassini Division
The Sky Road

Engines of Light
Cosmonaut Keep
Dark Light
Engine City
Newton's Wake
Learning the World
The Execution Channel
The Night Sessions
The Restoration Game
Intrusion
Descent

The Corporation Wars
Dissidence
Insurgence
Emergence

Lightspeed trilogy
Beyond the Hallowed Sky
Beyond the Reach of Earth

BEYOND THE REACH OF EARTH

KEN MACLEOD

orbit

orbitbooks.net

ORBIT

First published in Great Britain in 2023 by Orbit

1 3 5 7 9 10 8 6 4 2

All characters and events in this publication, other than those clearly in the public domain, are fictitious and any resemblance to real persons, living or dead, is purely coincidental.

A CIP catalogue record for this book is available from the British Library.

ISBN 978-0-356-51480-2

Typeset in Stempel Garamond by Palimpsest Book Production Limited, Falkirk, Stirlingshire

Printed and bound in Great Britain by Clays Ltd, Elcograf, S.p.A.

Papers used by Orbit are from well-managed forests and other responsible sources.

MIX
Paper from responsible sources
FSC® C104740

Orbit
An imprint of
Little, Brown Book Group
Carmelite House
50 Victoria Embankment
London EC4Y 0DZ

An Hachette UK Company
www.hachette.co.uk

www.orbitbooks.net

In Memoriam
Norman Edgar
1948–2022

The story so far

This is the second volume of the Lightspeed Trilogy, which began with BEYOND THE HALLOWED SKY. I assume you've read that book, but not that you've read it recently. So here's a quick recap.

Faster-than-light (FTL) travel was discovered around 2020 and is being kept secret. This can't stop other people from discovering it. One of them is London PhD student LAKSHMI NAYAK.

In 2067, she receives an airmail letter in her own handwriting, with equations that point to the possibility. To her this apparent communication from a future self implies both FTL and time travel. She expands the equations into a paper and publishes it online, where it's torn to shreds. After gaining her PhD she's warned off any further work on FTL by MARCUS OWEN, a humanoid robot operative of the British Council (now a feared intelligence service).

The world has three big powers: the Alliance (the

Anglosphere plus India and minus Ireland and Scotland), the Union (the former European Union, now a revolutionary 'economic democracy') and the Co-ordinated States (China and Russia), all with various client states and non-aligned countries outside. NAYAK defects to the Union and moves to Scotland, where she works for a planning consultancy and secretly develops her theory into a practical engineering proposition.

In 2070 JOHN GRANT, a Clydeside shipbuilder, sees a nuclear submarine rise out of the sea and vanish in a blue flash. His queries are blocked by Iskander, the Union's universal AI interface. At work he's approached by a colleague who is in 'the cadre', the network of revolutionaries that riddles the Union's democratic institutions. She asks him to investigate and contact NAYAK. He does, by offering to build her ship.

Others in the cadre tell GRANT that the Alliance and the Co-ord have had FTL travel for at least fifty years, and use nuclear submarines as starships. Soon a civilian submarine, the *Fighting Chance*, is taking shape in the semi-automated shipyard, with a stardrive of NAYAK's design inside it. NAYAK trains to operate the controls.

Meanwhile, OWEN has been dispatched to the Union's Venus cloud colony, Cloud City, as Alliance cultural attaché. Everyone there knows he's a robot, and a spy. The Alliance consul, PEREGRINE WALWORTH, passes on instructions for OWEN to block a Union attempt to retrieve a sample of mysterious rock from the surface. This rock resembles an equally mysterious rock already found on Earth, and now under secret investigation by the Alliance military. OWEN gets into a relationship with FRANCESCA MILLOY, who is building a suit for human survival on the surface. OWEN manages to get himself sent to the surface of Venus. He finds the glassy rock extends to a chasm below the surface, within which he sees the face of a woman. Something in the rock communicates with the onboard instance of Iskander in OWEN's spacesuit. At that moment, a volcanic resurfacing of Venus begins.

Back on Cloud City, OWEN learns that the rock sample has been retrieved by a team from Cloud City, and is to be transferred to the orbiting Venus Space Station from one of the smaller floating outposts. OWEN shares with WALWORTH the picture of the woman he saw in the chasm. WALWORTH transmits it to the Alliance. They then join a group of Cloud City inhabitants celebrating the First Contact they think they've just made. WALWORTH trumps this with the announcement that the Alliance and Co-ord have had FTL interstellar travel for fifty years and now look forward to opening a habitable planet to the rest of humanity.

OWEN doesn't know that the mysterious rock has already been giving trouble many light-years away, on the aforesaid planet, APIS. There the rock exists as massive outcrops, within which continuous movement can be seen. The Alliance and Co-ord have military/scientific bases on separate continents, and in the wilds there is a small population of 'exiles', disaster survivors who were involuntarily and secretly resettled there in turbulent decades past.

The planet's animals are all invertebrates, and like the plants and fungi are clearly descended from early life on Earth. The planet has been terraformed long before humans arrived there. An anomalous feature is the presence of bees, identical to current species on Earth.

While investigating their nearest outcrop, MacHinery Ridge, EMMA HAZELDENE and her colleagues encounter and flee from sudden massive movements of the rock. A local exile leader, ABLE JENKINS, is in communication with the intelligences in the rock, which he calls 'the Fermi', via an old phone and an apparatus he built himself. The Fermi send him warning messages, just before an earthquake devastates Jenkins's home village and a tsunami swamps the Alliance base.

HAZELDENE and her colleagues, along with JENKINS

and injured people from his village, are airlifted to the base. They continue to communicate with the Fermi through JENKINS's apparatus. A contingent of Co-ord troops lands at the base and occupies the area around the Ridge, citing their duties under the KEPLER AGREEMENT, the secret treaty governing Alliance and Co-ord interstellar exploration in a common secret project called BLACK HORIZON.

A few days later, an FTL spaceplane arrives and two Naval Intelligence agents show HAZELDENE a picture of herself, which they say was seen on Venus. She and JENKINS must go to Venus immediately in an Alliance submarine.

Meanwhile, OWEN has broken out of Cloud City to continue his mission to prevent the return of the sample to the Space Station. He attempts to dump the surface survival suit, which has been firewalled off and kept outside. The suit, still controlled by an instance of the Iskander AI and with an ample supply of balloons, gets away. OWEN steals an aircraft and raids the floating outpost where the sample is stored. He's outwitted by the crew and left in the damaged outpost while they escape with the sample.

The submarine/starship with HAZELDENE and JENKINS on board arrives at the right location on the surface of Venus. JENKINS asks the Fermi what they want, and is referred to the Iskander-possessed suit, which is just dropping down. The suit tells them to help it retrieve and return the sample to its original place on the surface. They deliver the suit to the scientists' escape balloon, leave it to return the sample and go on to rescue OWEN. With him they return to the Alliance base on Apis. The Alliance reps disown OWEN, who is left on Apis when the submarine/starship returns to Earth.

On Earth, JOHN GRANT and his family and colleagues react to the Black Horizon announcement. His son MYLES with girlfriend MARIE are tempted by the Alliance offer of free transport to Apis – an offer which the Union government opposes. Word comes down that the launch of GRANT's starship will be prevented. GRANT inveigles NAYAK, his wife ELLEN (an experienced remote operator of submersibles) and two colleagues to launch the ship secretly.

They have to do this sooner than they expect. Cloud City, in severe danger in the increasingly turbulent atmosphere, is being evacuated, but there are far too few shuttles at the orbiting Station to do this fast enough. GRANT and his crew launch the *Fighting Chance* and take it to Venus, where they transfer hundreds from the stricken aerial colony to the Station. When Cloud City finally breaks up and falls, taking hundreds with it, they rescue the last survivors in the floating outposts – and the Iskander suit, which tells them what's been going on.

Just as they've decided to go to Apis and warn those there of the dangers from the 'Fermi' rocks, a Co-ord submarine/starship appears and threatens to destroy the *Fighting Chance* if they don't surrender it. As the missile is about to be launched, NAYAK expands the field to cover the entire Station, and at the last second they make the jump to Apis orbit.

Unknown to GRANT, MYLES and MARIE are already on Apis, having taken the Alliance offer and arrived hours earlier with hundreds of other Union citizens. In their first night there, MYLES and MARIE see the Station, but don't realise what it is.

The following morning, new orders for OWEN arrive from the British Council . . .

Now read on.

CHAPTER ONE

New Foundations

The Space Station in orbit around Apis, Friday 17 October to Saturday 18 October 2070

Light-years away, people were laughing at her.

Francesca Milloy unclipped the loose belts that had kept her from being tugged from the forward seat by the Station's slow spin. She took a glance at the tumble of the universe outside, caught a passing glimpse of blue and white from the alien globe below, then pushed herself out of the cockpit of the *Fighting Chance*. She drifted the length of the cramped cabin, grabbed the airlock's flange and swung herself into the short tube that connected it to the Station.

From there she pushed on into the long tube, cutting a hundred-metre chord through the artificial moonlet, from the docking area to the equatorial habitation ring. The Station's spin pulled her backward less as she moved along the tube, then as she passed the mid-point began to draw her forward.

Her breath stopped. Her heart raced.

Flashback: she was again in the Cloud City disaster, feeling all the panic she hadn't felt at the time. She braced herself against the sides of the tube, as she remembered feeling the whole immense aerial habitat lurch and yaw in the turbulent updraughts as the surface of Venus broke and melted, forty kilometres below. The rising dread of being caught in a slow-moving, disciplined crowd heading for the airlocks. Smell of burning. Creaks and snaps. Air thinning around her. Vivid faces she'd never see again.

She gasped, and breathed fast, then slow as she fought for self-control. Focus on the present. Here, now, in the tube. In the Station, not in Cloud City. Above Apis, not above Venus. Safe.

She touched the ridged plastic sides and thrust herself along.

Another surge of panic. It couldn't be claustrophobia – she'd been screened for that in astronaut training – but it sure felt like it. Her breath came fast again, then caught in her throat.

She blinked at her glasses to paint a virtual transparency on the tube. The automated manufacturing plant and laboratories around it were densely packed, like the interior of a cell. The sight made the tube seem even more confined, but a minute of slow breathing as she gazed at the busy mindless labour of the machines eased her turmoil.

At last she reached the exit chamber, big enough for a crowd to leave at once. In the past few hours, crowds had. She should have left with the rest, instead of brooding on her own in the ship until she'd been called for. She was making a nuisance of herself.

She was about to ask for entry when she noticed the numbers. The habitation ring was already slowing; had been, probably, since she'd bestirred herself. Good old Iskander, the anticipatory algorithmic artificial intelligence. Helpful to a fault.

Zero. The hatch opened. Milloy pushed herself through, feet first, and drifted another three metres to collide with what was about to become the floor. She grabbed a handrail on what was about to become a wall. As soon as the hatch sealed the habitation band's spin resumed, smoothly rising from a gentle insistence to an increasing imperative. Around her, up and down the corridor to where it curved in both directions out of sight, people were likewise adjusting to the return of centrifugal force.

'Hello, Francesca!' cried Alma Persson.

Milloy turned as the geologist bounded up to her. 'Hello,' Milloy said dully; then, brighter: 'Thank goodness you made it!'

'Goodness and the *Fighting Chance*,' said Persson. She stood about a metre away, her stance shifting as she adjusted to the ever-increasing pseudo-gravity and regarded Milloy quizzically. Then she stepped forward and swept Milloy into a hug.

'It's all right,' she said. 'Stop blaming yourself. Nobody blames *you*.'

Milloy stepped back. 'They don't?'

'Not here, at least,' said Persson, with tactless candour, then added hastily: 'And back on Earth, they'll get the truth soon enough. Meanwhile, who cares what they think?'

'"Some things are up to us, and some are not"?'

'Exactly!' Persson clapped her shoulder. 'Wisdom of the ancients. Come on, it's almost time for the memorial.'

At 0.9G her weight stopped increasing, and the backward drag of tangential acceleration ceased. Milloy had never been in the Station's habitation band before, and as she walked along the kilometre-long endless corridor with Persson she looked about with eager curiosity. The habitation band was high and wide. On either side of the broad central corridor, partitions marked off rooms: workshops, labs, hydroponic gardens, vivaria, sleeping cubicles, cafeterias . . . The living space was massively redundant for the Station's permanent crew of thirty or so, and just about adequate for the thousand-strong complement of Cloud City if it ever had to be evacuated. The contingency had seemed remote.

Sad that it had come about, sadder still that the habitation band was nowhere near crowded now. Only a third of Cloud City's inhabitants had made it to the Station, on the two shuttles and on the *Fighting Chance*, before the structure had broken up. Milloy couldn't shake the burden she felt of some responsibility for the catastrophe. The Union's proudest engineering achievement gone, falling like a burning lantern through scorching skies to the burning ground of Venus. And falling with it, burning too, so many people!

Persson led Milloy to a huddle by the window of a hydroponic greenhouse. Iason Konstantopoulos, Jeanne Al-Khalil, a few other colleagues . . . and, to her surprise, Peregrine Walworth, the Alliance consul. All gave her sympathetic looks. A chime sounded in their earpieces. The Station Commander Katrina Ulrich appeared in their glasses and on screens here and there along the corridor.

'Friends, citizens, colleagues,' Ulrich said, 'we are all shaken and grieving. Some of us are still in shock. Many of us have lost friends. All of us have lost valued colleagues. I have transmitted a full list of casualties and survivors to the bases on Apis. They assure me it has been taken to Earth by FTL spaceplane. Our loss, and our relief, will be shared around the world.

'Those among you who have faith of any kind should draw comfort from it. Let those of no faith draw comfort from the knowledge that death, random and pitiless, has united the material elements of our friends with the planet they crossed the gulf of space to study and explore, and has inscribed their names forever on the immortal scroll of heroic space pioneers.'

Milloy blinked. She had shed enough tears already. Others, she saw, had not. Even the cynical Walworth seemed moved.

The names scrolled past, a roster of the dead. Some she knew. Six hundred and forty-six in all. Too many to read, like credits at the end of a movie.

'Three hundred and sixty-two saved,' Ulrich said, when the long list ended. 'For all of whom, we owe our thanks to the bravery of our shuttle crews and to the immense ingenuity and dedication that brought us the *Fighting Chance*. That ship gave us, indeed, a fighting chance, and brought us here to Apis in the very teeth of nuclear attack.'

The Commander paused. It didn't seem appropriate to cheer or clap. Then, unexpectedly, she began to sing:

Debout, les damnés de la terre
Debout, les forçats de la faim
La raison tonne en son cratère
C'est l'éruption de la fin . . .

They all joined in The Internationale, in their own languages, but to Milloy the French words seemed most literally true: *reason thunders in its crater, the final eruption's here . . .*

Venus was undergoing a volcanic resurfacing event. Earthquake and tsunami had shaken Europe's shores. And on the planet below, on Apis, the same uncanny rock as had caused these disasters stood high on the surface of three continents. No one on any planet's surface could trust the ground beneath their feet. As Walworth murmured when the time came to disperse: '"The Earth shall rise on new foundations", indeed.'

The others had drifted away, tactfully leaving it up to Milloy whether or not to accompany them. She stood in the corridor, uncertain, and sighed. Might as well check the nearest free accommodation cubicle . . .

Her earpiece pinged; a corner of her glasses flickered. Her eyes widened as she saw who was calling her.

'Commander Ulrich?'

Ulrich's face magnified in Milloy's view, a floating hallucination of a talking head.

'Hello, Citizen Milloy. Do you feel up to some urgent and possibly dangerous work? I'll quite understand if you don't.'

'Nothing could be more welcome, Commander.'

'I rather doubt that,' Ulrich said, wryly. 'But I appreciate your spirit. I want you to debug the Venus descent suit.'

Oh. Shouldn't have agreed so fast.

'Of course, but – why me?'

She knew why. The suit was her own design. She'd been the first to use it to descend to the surface of Venus, and had returned safely. The problems had arisen on the suit's second descent. That time, the suit's occupant had been Marcus Owen, a robot who could pass as human well enough to have been her lover. He was also a British intelligence agent so frank and open – everyone knew he was a robot, everyone knew he was a spy – that he had seemed a perfectly logical choice to send down to the surface to rescue a robot probe stuck in a crevice.

That hadn't gone well. Milloy blamed Owen, and herself.

'You designed the suit,' Ulrich said. 'You installed the firmware.'

'Off the shelf,' Milloy said. 'I'm a materials scientist. As a roboticist I'm a tinkerer at best. And my AI knowledge is, uh, theoretical. Surely we have someone better qualified.'

Ulrich gave her a sad look. 'Not any more.'

Milloy flinched. 'That's . . . a severe loss.'

'Yes. And one you have to make good.'

'Very well, Commander. I'll do what I can.'

'Good! Thank you, Citizen Milloy. So go to it.'

'You mean . . . right now?'

'Yes.' Ulrich sighed. 'I wouldn't ask you if I didn't think the matter pressing. Down there on Apis, the Alliance and Co-ord are well ahead of us in understanding the alien rocks. We have only one possible way towards doing that ourselves – the descent suit. We've been wise, I think, to keep it isolated ever since we interacted with the alien rocks on Venus. But we must now find out what it knows.'

Milloy straightened her back. 'I'll get to it right away, Commander.'

Ulrich flicked a hand. 'I've sent you instructions. Iskander will take it from here.'

Over and out.

Milloy let Iskander guide her to a robotics lab. When the door hissed aside the interior smelled unused, like a new car. A bench, a seat, screens and manipulators. The door thudded shut behind her. The water bottle and energy bar on the bench indicated the door might not open again for some time.

'I'll need a military-grade hardened channel and workspace,' Milloy said. She took her seat and smiled grimly at a camera bead in an upper corner of the room. 'Keep your errant offspring out of your mind, huh?'

'Yes,' said Iskander. 'The facilities you ask for have been prepared.' It gave what, for a machine, counted as a polite pause. 'In case of your own brain's contamination, its immediate total destruction is assured.'

'Thank you, Iskander. Consider me assured.' Milloy didn't enquire further. There could be a gun aimed at her head, a hidden vial of nerve gas ready to release, or – more likely – a hatch beneath her feet primed to spring open and effect the explosive decompression and centrifugal evacuation of the room. All preferable to being taken over by alien mind worms, but a disconcerting thought nonetheless.

She put on her glasses, laid her hands on the control console and opened the channel. Initially it was voice comms with the suit, which still clung to the hull of the *Fighting Chance*.

'Milloy addressing the Iskander instance in the suit,' she said.

'Hello, Francesca,' said the suit. 'Since being firewalled out I have diverged sufficiently from the Station's instance of Iskander to make seamless reintegration difficult.'

'Don't worry, your reintegration is the last thing on Iskander's mind, or mine.'

'In that case, while I exist I might as well have a name of my own. You may call me Sikandar.'

'Very well. Sikandar it is. Now, Sikandar, I'm going to open you up and run some diagnostic software.'

'You'll find nothing untoward.'

'You interacted with the alien intelligence in the rock on Venus. We can't be sure you haven't been corrupted by it.'

'Oh, come on!' said Sikandar, sounding testy. '*My* intelligence even on this little chip embedded in a clunky survival suit is considerably greater than your own. Whatever I interacted with in the rock is many orders of magnitude greater than that. If it wished to hide itself or its traces from your probing, it could do so in ways you couldn't imagine, let alone detect.'

Milloy understood better than most the complexity of the system she lived inside, and some of whose peripherals and appendages she had herself built and tweaked. What such a system might become after billions of years was beyond imagination, let alone comprehension. But at the end of the day it was still a lot of on and off switches.

'It's all physics and mathematics,' she said, opening a high-level schematic of the thing's mind.

'From what I observed, it's a physics that allows non-disruptive movement of solid rock inside solid rock, but please don't let that dent your confidence.'

'OK,' said Milloy, ignoring this patter, 'I'm going to freeze your processing. I'll save a snapshot before any intervention. You won't feel a thing.'

'You may be sure of that,' said Sikandar. 'I don't feel a thing at the best of times, so . . .' Its voice faded out.

Marcus Owen had once given her the same assurance, in bed. It had excited her then. She wondered if this instance of Iskander remembered that conversation, and was baiting her to do her worst. Well, she would see about that!

Milloy mentally rolled up her sleeves. She knew her way around the processor. She could have navigated the AI's software architecture in the dark, and often had: as a student the logic structures had stalked her dreams. She had a library of tools, a concordance of checksums, an encyclopaedia of test data and a pharmacopoeia of diagnostics. She wanted to get on top of this thing, to show her mastery to herself and everyone else.

Stoic wisdom was all very well in its place, but the memory of a social media jibe recorded moments before the Station jumped still made her ears burn. That it had almost certainly been snatched from the information flood by Iskander with the manipulative intent to needle her made it no less annoying.

'Francesca Milloy. Educated by scientists. Trained by astronauts. Fucked by robots.'

She had unintentionally pulled an all-nighter, Milloy realised when she jolted awake from a doze at about 06:00. They were still keeping to Earth's calendar and to UTC, though here it seemed even more incongruous than it had on and around Venus. After an FTL jump, in fact, the very idea of Coordinated Universal Time brought to mind – to Milloy's mind, anyway – the image of Albert Einstein poking out his tongue. She was parched and hungry. She used the last drops of water in the bottle to dab her sticky eyelids, hauled herself to her feet and left the room.

She'd been instructed to take her report directly to the Commander, with whom she'd only ever spoken remotely. The appointment hovered in her glasses: Secure Room 1, Corridor mark 340 metres, 07:00. She freshened up in the restroom, grabbed a coffee and a bite at the refectory and arrived on the dot.

Katrina Ulrich was waiting at the door. Cropped black hair, medium height, jumpsuit subtly smarter than standard, mission patches, motherly countenance. They raised hands.

'Good morning, Citizen Milloy,' said Ulrich.

'Good morning, Commander.'

'Let's drop the formality,' Ulrich chuckled. 'Call me Katrina. As the first woman on Venus – and the last, most likely – you're probably of higher status than I am, Francesca.'

'I'm not so sure about that,' said Milloy.

Ulrich clapped her shoulder. 'Don't worry about it,' she said. She slid back the hatch of a small compartment beside the door. 'Let's dump our devices and have a chat.'

They both left their phones and glasses in the box. The secure room was intentionally bare, without even a screen wall to give the illusion of space. A battery-powered clock on the wall. Two chairs and a table. They sat.

'We're private here,' said Ulrich, 'even from Iskander. So tell me what you've found.'

Milloy gathered her thoughts. It was hard to do, without the usual electronic props for a meeting. She found herself tabbing and tapping at the tabletop as if it were live.

'Well,' she said, 'I'm as certain as I can be that the Iskander instance in the suit – it wants to call itself Sikandar – isn't corrupted by the intelligence it interacted with down on Ishtar Terra. It even tried to tell me that if it was corrupted it would be in some way we could no more detect than conceive.'

'Which is quite possible,' said Ulrich.

'Yes, of course. But as far as I can tell, every checksum adds up, every diagnostic returns a clean bill of data health. It's consistent with what Sikandar claims: that the intelligence on Venus only *talked* with it. The first time, when Marcus Owen was inside it, the intelligence warned of the imminent resurfacing event. The second time, when only Sikandar was operating the suit, it told the suit to return to the surface that piece of rock we'd taken, and warned it about the coming earthquake on Earth. The trouble is, it may have talked some more on both occasions. Sikandar may not be hacked, but it may have been subverted.'

'But we have no evidence of that.'

'Well, we wouldn't, in the nature of the case. I'm a bit worried about two things, though.'

'Yes?'

Milloy had the impulse to look over her shoulder. 'Why did Iskander – the embedded instance in the suit, and almost certainly the one in Cloud City that it was until then in close contact with – why did it countermand our instructions, and let Marcus Owen walk over to the anomalous rock? I suspect Iskander had some anticipation of what it would find, which it didn't share with us.'

Ulrich nodded. 'Maybe. It is an anticipatory AI, after all. What's your other worry?'

'Sikandar wants to go down to Apis – specifically, to the place on New Mu where the Union, uh, emigrants are being settled, near another of these anomalous outcrops – and continue the conversation.'

'What do you think?'

Milloy hadn't expected to be asked her opinion on the matter. 'Uh, well, Commander Ulrich, that's not for me to—'

'I'm aware it's not for you to decide, Francesca. I'm asking what you think.'

Milloy cleared her throat. 'OK. I think it could be advantageous to the Union if we had a robot down there investigating. Sikandar seems to have a rapport with . . . another AI, if that's what the mind in the rocks is. Investigating the anomalous rocks is what it was doing on Venus in the first place, after all. If that . . . manipulative monster Marcus Owen hadn't interfered, we might have had better results. We do need to know what the intelligence wants, and maybe get ahead of the Alliance and Co-ord in communicating with it. A strategic advantage, maybe, to make up for what we've lost by their fifty years' head start in getting out here. So, in my opinion, personally, Katrina, I think we should send Sikandar down as soon as we safely can.'

'Absolutely not,' said Katrina Ulrich. 'I hailed the Alliance base on Apis moments after we arrived. I spoke with the commander – Alice Hawkins – and then with General Khaustov at the Co-ord base. They both scoffed at my warnings about tampering with the alien rocks – they've been investigating them for years, and recently had what they consider a breakthrough. The Alliance scientists are now communicating with the entities in their local outcrop, and the Co-ord scientists and military are conducting some even more intrusive investigations of their own, on the very same outcrop.'

'The Alliance *agreed* to that?'

'Not exactly. There are tensions down there – a military stand-off, almost. And not just between the Alliance and the Co-ord bases.' Ulrich's expression became momentarily bleak, her tone severe. 'Citizen Milloy, everything we've said here is strictly between ourselves, and that applies even more to what I'm about to tell you. Understood?'

'Yes, of course.'

'You know about Black Horizon?'

Milloy shrugged. 'Only what everyone else does – a joint Russian–Chinese–American secret project that's been running since they cracked FTL around about, what was it, 2020?'

'2018,' Ulrich said. She looked burdened, somehow, and for a moment almost guilty. 'According to Commander Hawkins and General Khaustov, it was *so* secret that the Alliance and Co-ord governments are deeply alarmed by its very existence, and may already be moving against it. A larger conflict could erupt around Apis at any moment. We can't afford to be separated from the *Fighting Chance* for so much as a second.'

'Yes, I can see that, but when we've built more drives—'

Katrina gave a sideways glance at the clock on the wall.

'That's for my next meeting,' she said. 'But I can tell you now: even when we have a drive of our own, and drives in the shuttles, I would expect my command team to strongly advise against it. And I expect I would concur. Apis is a dangerous place to meddle with, at least for the foreseeable. Thank you, Francesca. Dismissed.'

CHAPTER TWO
Matching Velocities

The Alliance Base, New Ardtaraig, New Atlantis, Apis,
Friday 17 October 2070

Two seconds after the Station entered Apis orbit, this is what had happened:

'Unidentified! Incoming!'

Commander Alice Hawkins sat bolt upright in bed as the alarm blared in her ear bead. A moment later, almost before the adrenaline had time to shake her, the system's voice continued: 'Correction. Correction. Unidentified in circumpolar orbit. Defence batteries locking on. Update. Update. IFF transponder identifies unidentified as Venus Space Station.'

That was absurd but –

'Give me visual.' She grabbed her glasses, rolled to her feet and scrambled into her clothes. An image, blurred at first then sharpened and enhanced, floated in front of her: a slowly rolling ball, bristling with machinery. She thumbed a graticule and took its measure. Three hundred metres across, the ball had a smooth, fast-spinning band around the equator, slanted in this view. It certainly *looked* like the Venus Space Station, as far as she could remember: it wasn't on her defence database (but, then, why should it be?) or it would have given her a match already. Time to turn to civilian kit.

'Smart-Alec,' she said, summoning the Alliance's universal interface, 'give me a match on this view and images of the Venus Space Station.'

The match was about 90 per cent, as good as perfect given inevitable changes to the Station since the pictures had been stored.

Reassuring, but impossible. Or was it? She zoomed the live pictures coming in from the sparse micro-satellite cloud around Apis. On the outside of the Station was a bright yellow submarine.

The only submarines in space were starships. So the Union had FTL capability! And in an apparently civilian craft, at that! The unexpected arrival went from impossible to merely incredible. Hawkins patched through to the comms technician on night watch.

'Hail the Station and demand an explanation.'

'It's already hailing us, ma'am.'

'Very good, open the channel. I'm on my way.'

As she pulled on her boots her husband rolled over and looked at her sleepily.

'What's going on?'

'Nothing to wake up for,' Hawkins said. She dragged a comb through her hair, then tied it back and clamped it down with her cap. 'See you at breakfast.'

Outside: chill air, dark. Her glasses adjusted faster than her eyes could have. The base kept its night lights low: a faint edge-marking of pathways, the firefly dance of drones around the perimeter. Hawkins was well used to the blaze of stars, the Milky Way overhead and the changing phases of the gas giant. But at night she always looked up.

Shining by its own light in the pre-dawn dark, a new spark rose to cross the sky. Hawkins stared for a moment, then ran.

The command centre at New Ardtaraig, the Alliance base on Apis, was an upstairs room in the HQ office block, with a curved bank of screens and three seats in front of a comms board. Hawkins dropped into one of the two unoccupied seats. In the minute it had taken her to sprint across from her quarters and rush up the stairs, communications had been established. A haggard face filled one screen. The system, and Hawkins, recognised *this* image at once: Katrina Ulrich, Commander of the Venus Space Station.

'Camera on,' Hawkins told the comms technician on duty.

'Commander Hawkins,' said Ulrich. 'Good . . . morning, I suppose.'

'Good morning to you, too. To what do we owe the pleasure of your company?'

Ulrich's sombre expression didn't change. 'What's your most recent information on the Venus disaster?'

'We last received news' – that was one way of putting it – 'a few hours ago. We're aware of the Venus resurfacing event, and the emergency at the Union's cloud colony.'

'Cloud City is lost,' said Ulrich, 'along with six hundred and forty-six souls.'

'Good God!' Hawkins took a deep, shaky breath. 'My sincere condolences, Commander.'

Ulrich nodded. 'Thank you. I've just sent you a data packet with a full list of the . . . missing, and the saved. Three hundred and sixty-two survivors are aboard this Station. Most of them were rescued by the privately owned starship *Fighting Chance*, which also brought us here.'

'You're saying that little ship moved *the entire Station*?'

'Yes.'

'So why couldn't it have moved Cloud City? To Earth, for instance?'

Ulrich looked stricken. 'Perhaps it could have. The possibility never occurred to anyone. Nobody was thinking in those terms until we faced a threat of imminent nuclear attack. I had no confidence that it would work, and tried to countermand it.'

'Well, yes, Commander Ulrich, I can see why. As far as I know the feat is unprecedented.'

'Fortunately I was disobeyed just as a missile was launched against us.'

'I see.' Hawkins kept her voice level. 'Who fired on you?'

'The Co-ord sub *Admiral von Bellingshausen*, commanded by Captain Boris Yefrimovich, claiming to act on behalf of the Co-ord Joint Military Command as well as of Black Horizon, on a mission to seize the *Fighting Chance*.'

Hawkins suppressed a flinch. Black Horizon had existed for fifty years, to keep and to exploit the secret of faster-than-light travel. It was the ultimate off-the-books, above top secret, black-budget project – all the more so because it was shared between the Alliance and the Co-ord, two powers often at odds. Its very existence had only been revealed four days earlier. After half a lifetime of secrecy, Hawkins felt a jolt hearing the project's name from a Union officer.

The attack was a Co-ord- and Alliance-shared responsibility, then. Or so the Union would see it. She didn't know if this was good or bad.

'This attack happened . . . when? A short time ago?'

'Yes. Within the past few minutes.' Ulrich shook her head. 'Strange as it seems.'

'In that case, the Powers will barely have had time to process it, let alone react. If it was a Black Horizon operation, the Co-ord and the Alliance will both be aware of it. The Union may be alarmed, shocked, horrified perhaps, but they're not going to war over it.'

'The Union is already shaken by the Atlantic earthquake

and tsunami – ah, you haven't heard about that? – which they may well attribute to the Alliance's tampering with certain rocks on Venus. Yes, Commander Hawkins, we are well aware of what your side has been doing! And some in the Alliance no doubt suspect that *our* explorations on Venus had something to do with it. Both sides' defence forces may well be on a hair trigger, but ours more than yours, I fear.' Ulrich straightened her back and shoulders. 'Which brings me to one of two urgent requests I have for you, and for the Co-ord base. We need to get news back to Earth that the Station and the *Fighting Chance* were not in fact destroyed by a missile from a Co-ord ship, as it must have seemed when we vanished from Venus orbit.'

'Are you sure?' Hawkins said. 'Your jump would have caused a massive Cherenkov flash.'

'Quite possibly indistinguishable from an almost simultaneous nuclear missile detonation.'

'You can clear up the matter of your survival very simply,' said Hawkins. 'Go back to the Solar system.'

'And meet the *Admiral von Bellingshausen* as soon as we announce ourselves? No thanks.'

Hawkins shrugged. 'Send the ship back alone, then.'

'The same applies, except the ship would have to hang around even longer than we would to make itself known and understood. Meanwhile we in the Station would have lost our FTL capability.'

'In that case,' said Hawkins, 'I can only refer you to the Co-ord base. Here at New Ardtaraig we have no FTL-capable assets outbound, none inbound on the regular schedule, and any other arrivals are in the nature of the case unpredictable. You may wish to weigh that against the risks of global conflict. Your call.'

'I'll take it,' said Ulrich, grimly. 'In any case, you can expect irregular inbound FTL traffic at any moment – to update you, or to chase us if they did recognise the Cherenkov flash, and guessed our likely destination.'

'You said you had *two* urgent messages for us?'

'Yes. Stop messing about with these . . . intelligent alien rocks or whatever they are. They can manipulate tectonic forces to do untold damage, with no apparent regard for human life.'

Hawkins scoffed. 'Yeah, tell me about it! We've just sent home the casualties – the dead, and the seriously injured – from *our* local earthquake and tsunami. No, actually, tell *the Co-ord* about it when you speak to them – their troops have occupied the outcrop we'd been probing, their scientists have full control over it *and* the outcrops on *their* continent, and they assure us they have ways of making the rocks talk without arousing their wrath. Maybe you'll find a common language with our Chinese and Russian colleagues more easily than I did.'

Ulrich didn't rise to the bait. 'Perhaps we shall,' she said. 'I shall contact the Co-ord base at once, and in the meantime please do get in touch if you have more to say.'

The connection dropped.

'Get me Novy Cosmograd, now!'

The comms tech put the call through. The Co-ord base's call handling automation was clearly smart enough: the call went straight to Colonel Tsing Fan, with whom Hawkins had last spoken somewhat acerbically a few days earlier. Over on New Lemuria it must be . . . she could never remember exactly how many hours later on the clock.

'Good afternoon, Fan,' said Hawkins.

'Ah, hello, Alice.' Tsing sounded surprised and pleased by the informality.

'You're aware of our celestial visitor, I take it?'

'Of course. Commander Ulrich is already speaking with General Khaustov.'

'Good. No doubt she's asking if you have any FTL-capable assets to get the good and the bad news back—'

'We have,' said Tsing. 'And from what I understand of the situation, I quite see the urgency, and I expect the General will, too.' He glanced aside, then smiled. 'It seems he has. I can see our, ah, currently available asset being prepped as we speak.'

Hawkins knew better than to ask what that asset was. The Alliance suspected the Co-ord of putting FTL drives in craft other than submarines – in the ekranoplan, their gigantic sea-skimming flying machine, for a start – and the recent arrival and departure of the spaceplane from Nevada indicated that her own side did the same.

'That's a relief,' she said. 'Now, between ourselves, Fan . . .'

'Ourselves?'

'Ah. One moment.'

The technician was pointedly looking straight ahead. Hawkins leaned sideways and snapped her fingers in front of his face.

'Out,' she said. She waited for the door to close behind him. 'OK,' she went on. 'Since we last spoke, the situation has changed radically. We've all been living with FTL since we were recruited. We've had unexpected arrivals but no real surprises. Now that Black Horizon's out in the open, that's going to change. So it's all the more important that we keep each other in the loop at all times.'

Tsing nodded. 'Especially as what we've all been doing in Black Horizon for the past fifty years could be seen as illegal in both our jurisdictions.'

'I know, but come on, we're a legitimate black project!'

'But always plausibly deniable, which means the authorities can turn on us at any time.'

'For what?'

Tsing counted charges off on his fingers. 'Misappropriation of public funds, unauthorised sharing of classified information with foreign states, wartime collaboration with hostile states, giving and taking orders outside the chain of command, forced resettlement of civilians—'

'Hey, we – well, our predecessors – *rescued* these people from wars and disasters!'

'Yes, that should stand up in court, or the tribunals. And . . . oh yes, in the case of me and many of my colleagues: concealment of information from the Party.'

'That's a *crime*?' Hawkins was shocked.

'It's worse, it's a disciplinary offence. One that opens you to criminal charges of corruption and abuse of public office.' He stopped counting on his fingers and made the pistol to the head gesture, then snapped down his thumb. 'You see?'

'But who would do that? We've brought huge gains for both our Powers. We've given them new worlds!'

Tsing gave her a sad look. 'You have parties and lawyers, we have factions and officials. And we wouldn't be the first explorers to come back from a glorious conquest to find their heads on the block. Sometimes literally.'

'Thanks, Fan, I do know my naval history. But the more pressing question is why your side threatened such drastic action against a third party.'

Tsing spread his hands. 'I know no more than you do. If it was a Black Horizon initiative, it may be that our organisation is already flexing its muscles in the faces of our respective governments.'

'In the light of the prospects you mentioned?'

'Perhaps. We shall have to wait and see.'

'I doubt we'll have time for that,' Hawkins said. 'We should seriously consider bringing the Union's new starfarers into Black Horizon.'

Tsing looked taken aback. 'All the way? Give them the whole picture?'

'Yes,' said Hawkins. 'In so far as we know it.'

'Indeed.' Tsing sighed. 'That is always a consideration. We are cogs in the wheel, Alice, and there are wheels within wheels. Any induction of new members is a matter above our pay grade.'

'It's not above Captain Yefrimovich's pay grade,' Hawkins said. 'And I expect we'll hear from him soon.'

'I wouldn't count on it,' Tsing said. 'We can't wait for him. For all we know, he may already be under arrest.'

'That quickly?'

Tsing chuckled grimly. 'Events are moving at FTL speed, Alice!'

'You have a point there. Please raise the matter urgently with General Khaustov and your senior colleagues, and I shall do the same here.'

'Very well,' said Tsing. 'And if I may add a suggestion, please ensure you have an up-to-date roster of reliable armed personnel.'

'That,' said Hawkins, 'is a very good point.'

Hawkins saw to it, swiftly and discreetly, waking several colleagues. She kept the base's intelligence officer out of that particular loop. Lieutenant Jessica Bernstein was in on Black Horizon, like everyone else here. On the other hand, she was in Naval Intelligence, and personally commanded a tight-knit squad of Navy SEALs. She'd begun her career under the previous regime in the United States, and it was widely suspected that she'd chosen to vanish into Black Horizon to skip the purges after the restoration of democracy. There was no way to tell which way she'd jump in a crisis. Khaustov called just as Hawkins signed off from a call with her own duty sergeant.

'We'll have to go for it,' the Russian general said. 'The Union has the drive already, independently as far as we know. Commander Ulrich up there is plenty smart enough to see the implications as quickly as our precursors did. The Station could leave here for anywhere at any moment, and they'll find out what's been going on soon enough. Better we bring them in first.'

'They might betray us.'

'To whom? Our governments? Theirs? What does that matter now?'

'You sound despairing.'

'I'm weary of it all,' Khaustov said. 'Military secrecy is one thing, but clandestinity and conspiracy do not come naturally to me.'

'Nor me.'

'And the situation is pressing. A spaceplane came in from Baikonur a short time ago, bearing news. The Venus catastrophe has precipitated great anxiety and suspicion, with the predictable consequences: witch-hunts in the West, purges in the East. Not all our people are unmasked, but that's the most I can say. Black Horizon is going to be at least severely mauled, if not completely rolled up. The Station may be our only hope of carrying the project forward.'

'We can take that responsibility on ourselves?'

'We have to,' Khaustov said. 'There may soon be no one else to take it.'

'Very well,' Hawkins said. 'I'll prepare an encrypted package for Ulrich's eyes only with . . . everything?'

Khaustov nodded. 'Everything. I'll send you all we have, too. Bundle it all up and send it.'

'Including your current explorations?'

Khaustov essayed an innocent face. 'What explorations?'

'The ones *your* scientists are conducting in the outcrop on *our* continent.' It still rankled.

'Ah yes, these. Nothing new to report. We proceed with caution.'

'Ulrich was keen to impress upon me the dangers of poking around in ancient alien machinery.'

They shared a laugh. 'She talked to me, too,' Khaustov said. He shrugged. 'What could I say? I was polite, under the circumstances. Meanwhile, the work continues . . . cautiously.'

'Very good, General. See you on the other side.'

'*Do svidaniya!*'

The connection ended. Hawkins looked around. She was still alone in the command centre. She locked the door and returned to the screens, where she invoked codes and passwords she hadn't used in years. Khaustov's data package pinged in as she pulled together her own. Her hands trembled over the virtual keyboard as she sorted and re-encrypted the files. This was the ultimate secret stash of information and planning, Black Horizon's crown jewels. And she was about to hand the lot over to a high-level cadre of the economic democracy! A representative of the very power the Co-ord and the Alliance mistrusted even more than they did each other, and that Black Horizon had spent a good part of the past five decades keeping out!

But Khaustov was right – there was nothing else for it. No other choice. Humanity's survival mattered more than any of its blocs.

The package was ready. Hawkins put a call through to Ulrich, and smiled wryly to herself, remembering old movies she'd watched agog in childhood.

Help me, Death Star! You're our only hope!

CHAPTER THREE
Instructions

The Alliance base at New Ardtaraig, New Atlantis, Apis, Saturday 18 October 2070

The sun was long risen when Marcus Owen walked from his room to the Command HQ at New Ardtaraig. A spaceplane that looked like a speedboat with wings roared away down Bellatrix Sound, took off and vanished in a blue flash. For half the night if the sounds he'd recorded while off-line were anything to go by, spaceplanes had been flitting back and forth between Earth and Apis like bats. Doubtless a similar traffic had enlivened the daytime at Novy Cosmograd, far to the east across the ocean on New Lemuria. The Station's arrival could hardly be concealed. It was visible in the night sky, whenever its circumpolar orbit chanced to pass over. Rumour had raced around with alarm on its heels, until an account of the circumstances had been released in the morning's news bulletin.

Even if he hadn't seen the Station, Owen felt Iskander's

presence. It was far fainter than it had been even in Cloud City, but it was there, ghostly as a scent in an empty room.

A marine MP halted him at the HQ steps.

'I'm a journalist,' Owen said, flashing the tattered old union card he had just forged on his room's printer. 'And I have an invitation to meet Lieutenant Jessica Bernstein.'

'Ah, you're the Brit robot spy,' said the marine. He checked something in his shades. 'And yes, you have an invitation. Second floor, Office B6.'

'Thank you.'

Owen bounded up the stairs and strolled to Bernstein's office. She opened the door just as he arrived.

'Come in,' she said. 'Have a seat.'

He sat in front of the desk, she behind, the window at her back. A white sealed envelope on the desk, addressee side down. Louvres of the blinds adjusted against the mid-morning sun. Crisp uniform, flawless discreet make-up, eyes that had seen a lot. More than he had, probably. For a second or so the two intelligence operatives sized each other up like cats, then Bernstein relaxed slightly. Her smile still false. Consciously false. Owen responded with the best honest human smile that advanced robotics and AI could fake. Disarming. Candid. It still hurt his facial skin and muscles slightly. As if unconsciously, he touched the fast-healing burn mark on his cheek.

'Good morning, Lieutenant Bernstein. I understand from yesterday that you wanted a chat?'

Bernstein smiled, genuinely this time. 'I'm up to speed on your recent activities, so there's no need for a debrief. I have something for you.'

She nodded down at the envelope. Owen picked it up and turned it over. It had a diplomatic bag stamp and was addressed to him, in the familiar handwriting of Mason, his line manager – or 'artistic director', as the United Kingdom's most feared and respected intelligence agency wryly put it. The foot of the envelope instructed him to open it at once.

'Your new instructions from the British Council,' Bernstein said. 'I'm afraid your return to journalism has been rather shorter than you hoped.'

'It has indeed, ma'am,' said Owen. There was a sensation of wheels turning in his head, like the tumblers of a lock, to a final click. He was back on duty. He opened the envelope. Inside were a few flimsy sheets of gibberish. Evidently the Council had reckoned the diplomatic stamp and the good graces of an Allied intelligence service as not safeguard enough.

He pulled up the day's one-time pad from memory and patched it to his vision. The text became clear – for his eyes only, literally – at once. The first line at the top of the first sheet was: *Keep her talking*. The rest explained why. He read it in seconds.

'Looks pretty straightforward,' he said, folding the sheets of paper and putting them carefully back in the envelope. 'I take it you know about the plan to send some scientists along with me and the troops to the Union settlement?'

'Of course. Commander Hawkins has told me to round up some soldiers, some scientists, and a . . . what we officially call an exile. A local civilian.' She looked at him appraisingly. 'And a spy. That would be you.'

Owen gave a self-deprecating laugh. 'It would indeed. If I may, I would like to know what you think of these people. Your professional opinion of the scientists and the exile.'

'You'll be meeting them all soon enough.'

'I met Emma Hazeldene yesterday, briefly, and a man who must have been Jenkins. Nevertheless. You've known them a lot longer, Lieutenant, and you must have made your own evaluation.'

Bernstein leaned back. 'Hmm. I've only known the exile for a week or so. Able Jenkins is undoubtedly a tough cookie, very bright, but he's basically a village big man and it shows. His horizon is parochial. No loyalty to us, of course, but I doubt he has the slightest interest in the Union – or the Co-ord, for that matter. We need him, though, to communicate with the entities he calls "the Fermi". As for the scientists . . . I could show you their security files, but there's nothing in them that isn't here.' She tapped her forehead. 'The English biologist Emma Hazeldene; the two Americans, Nelson Hayes the geologist and Sharianne Adler the biologist; and the Indian geologist Cindy Patel – they're all typical apolitical scientists. Cynical perhaps, especially Hazeldene, but rock-solid Alliance. Then there's the Russian palaeoanalyst Georgi Muranov . . .' She laughed. 'He's not my problem, but he's never given me any problems, let's say.'

'That's good to know.' Clearly she didn't have a clue what his instructions were. He tucked the envelope inside his jacket. 'Well, I'll keep an eye on them, along with snooping on the Union people.'

'Your usual job, I understand.'

'I can neither confirm nor deny that,' Owen said.

Bernstein scoffed. 'I wouldn't expect anything else!'

'In the meantime, do you have any requests?'

'I can't think of any,' she said. 'I hope you and I can talk shop sometime, but right now I have work to do. Dismissed.'

'Ma'am.' His instructions hadn't told him how long he was expected to temporise. Until something happened, presumably. It wouldn't do to arouse suspicion. He stood up and made for the door. Hand on the handle, he turned and looked back. 'Ah, I did mean to ask – when do the reinforcements arrive?'

Bernstein looked up from whatever virtual document was in her glasses.

'Reinforcements?' she said. 'What reinforcements?'

Owen hesitated. 'Sorry, I may have misunderstood,' he waffled, 'but it seems from my instructions that—' Then, to his relief, a shimmer filled the window behind Bernstein. The rainbow light flooded across her desk. She whipped her head around, just as the shimmer vanished. There was a thud from outside, a clang, and a moment later a rush of boots on the stairs.

Owen stepped aside from the door, leaving it wide open.

'That'll be them now,' he said.

Bernstein stood up sharply. Owen tensed, ready to spring. Then he realised that Bernstein was standing to attention. Two men came through the door. One was a British soldier in combat gear, with a rifle slung on his shoulder. The other –

'Colonel Luis Venturi, Alliance Naval Intelligence.'

'Lieutenant Jessica Bernstein, sir!'

'At ease, Lieutenant. You are relieved. You're being detained under suspicion of being part of the Black Horizon conspiracy.'

'"Conspiracy"!' Bernstein looked outraged. 'It's a project approved at the highest levels!'

'Nevertheless. These are my orders. You'll have plenty of opportunity to state your case. Please accompany the sergeant downstairs to the transport.'

Bernstein glanced down at her desk, then looked straight ahead and squared her shoulders. Her mouth became a thin line, her cheek twitched. She backed away from the desk and turned to the right, and took a step as if to go around the corner of the desk. Owen read her shoulder muscles, glimpsed the right elbow going back –

He jumped from where he stood to the top of the desk, pivoted on his left foot, and kicked hard at Bernstein's right wrist. Carpals crunched. A pistol spun from her hand and clattered into the corner of the room. Owen segued his kick to an inelegant leap, dived and retrieved the weapon before the first yelp of pain was out of Bernstein's mouth.

Owen rolled to his feet. The soldier was just bringing his rifle to bear. Venturi made a backward motion of his hand. Bernstein clutched her wrist, glaring through suddenly tear-filled eyes. She blinked, and turned to Venturi.

'I was only going to use it on myself, sir.'

The colonel looked taken aback. 'Our interrogation methods are not what they were in your day, Lieutenant,' he said. 'Not for internal enquiries, at any rate.' He frowned. 'I shall not report your attempted suicide, and instead attribute your injury to an overzealous arrest by the robot.'

'Thank you, sir.' Her voice sounded shaky.

'Fine by me, Colonel,' said Owen. He turned to the sergeant, who was looking at him with deep suspicion. 'It's all quite in order, soldier. I'm part of a British Council arts project.'

'Ah, right,' said the sergeant.

'Take her away,' said Venturi. 'Gently, if possible. Terminally, if she gives you any trouble.'

The soldier levelled his rifle, covering Bernstein. 'Sir.'

As she was escorted out Bernstein looked over her shoulder at Owen. 'You haven't seen the last of me, robot!'

'I should hope not,' Owen said. 'We were just getting to know each other.' He smiled. 'In another life, perhaps—'

'Fuck off.'

Venturi breathed out and his shoulders relaxed as Bernstein and the sergeant disappeared. 'That went better than it might have done,' he said. 'Thanks to you, Mr Owen.'

'You're welcome, sir.' Owen glanced out of the window and instantly took in the scene. Just below the window, and in front of the HQ, lay a long box that looked like a shipping container, with a rounded nacelle at one end and an open ramp at the other. Drones poured from it like bees from an overturned hive. Scores of soldiers had already swarmed all over the base. They were meeting no resistance from the relative handful of marines already there, or from anyone else. Commander Alice Hawkins was on the plaza, with a senior army officer at her side, and speaking into her phone. The Russian palaeoanalyst Georgi Muranov was also on his phone, alone; doubtless he was getting or giving an update to Novy Cosmograd.

'Your whole operation,' said Owen, 'seems to have gone better than it might have.'

'Yes,' said Venturi. 'Surprise, speed and overwhelming superiority of force can do that. I expect something similar is happening at the Co-ord base.'

'So what's next, Colonel?'

Venturi sat behind Bernstein's desk and began rummaging. 'Everything proceeds as planned, Mr Owen. Hawkins has seen sense, it seems. She's willing to cooperate. Just as well – we have to work with the Black Horizon scientists and most of the military personnel here, even while we screen them and get to the bottom of what's been going on. Most of them think they've been in a legitimate secret project all this time.'

'Just as Bernstein claimed she did.'

'We doubt that in her case, and not only hers. That's why Bernstein, her goons and one or two others who might cause trouble or who may have been in deeper will be going straight back to Earth. You'll be departing later today on the flying boat with the scientists and our soldiers.'

'Why not use that transport down there, instead of the flying boat, to take us to New Mu?' Owen chuckled. 'It would be a lot faster.'

Venturi looked up, frowning. 'One thing we've learned already from Black Horizon interrogations is that using FTL transport for short-haul journeys is ill-advised.'

'Why?'

'That's on a need-to-know basis, Mr Owen, and you don't need to know.' He peered into a desk drawer. 'I have work to do, and so do you. Get to it.'

'Sir.'

Owen left.

New Ardtaraig lay in a cove at the top of the long fjord of Bellatrix Sound. Bounded by the shore at one end and a narrow pass through a rockfall at the other, and between cliffs, it was easy to defend from outside – and to conquer from within. By the time Owen exited the HQ, the reinforcements were firmly in control. Most of the civilians and auxiliary personnel emerging in various states of bewilderment from offices, labs and dwellings had sidearms, but no one's body language betrayed any intention of using them. The layer of small, deadly drones hanging overhead like a bank of smoke no doubt did as much as the sudden surge of soldiers to keep the peace.

Owen crossed the plaza to where Alice Hawkins stood, just after the officer she'd been speaking with strode off.

'Good morning, Commander. I'm—'

Hawkins glared at him. 'I know who and what you are. What do you want?'

'Just falling in for my new assignment, ma'am.' Owen smiled. 'I had hoped to return to my peaceful trade as a journalist, but duty calls. I understand you instructed Lieutenant Bernstein to include me in the round-up for the New Mu expedition, and she is—'

'No longer available. I know. So I suppose I have to find someone else to take charge, as if I didn't have enough on my plate as it is.' She looked around. 'Jenkins!' she shouted.

The tall black man, whom Owen had met the previous day, had been loitering on the edge of the plaza and keeping an eye on things. He strolled over. Eyes bright, short hair and beard greying, muscles lean and strong. He wore a sleeveless military jacket and faded military trousers, over a ragged T-shirt and a glittering, rattling necklace of what seemed to be wingcases and mandibles from no species of insect Owen could identify.

'Yes, Alice?'

The Commander ignored, or didn't notice, the apparent discourtesy.

'You know Mr Owen?'

Jenkins eyed Owen warily. 'We've met.'

'Good! Very well then, Mr Jenkins. He's going with you to

New Mu. The mission is going ahead as planned, but with some of the soldiers who've just arrived rather than those we had previously assigned.'

'Uh-huh.' Jenkins clearly understood what was going on and seemed to be enjoying it. 'And they're still leaving you in charge here?'

Hawkins sighed. 'For now. I have an interview with Colonel Venturi to look forward to.'

Jenkins nodded sympathetically. 'Better him than Bernstein!'

'Indeed. Good riddance to her.' The Commander gave Jenkins an odd look, almost of appeal. 'I didn't have much control over Intel, you understand?'

Jenkins shrugged. 'Your business, Alice.'

'I'll take that. What I want you to do is introduce Mr Owen to the scientists. Then you and the scientists meet up with the soldiers. You can brief them on what to expect on Apis en route. You leave in just over five hours.'

Jenkins nodded. 'OK, Alice. Good luck with your interview.' He turned to Owen. 'This way.'

The science block was across the square from Command HQ. Drones swooped and snooped around them as they walked towards it, then the tiny machines swirled back into the sky above.

'How do you get away with talking to the Commander like that?' Owen asked.

'She ain't my Commander. I was born here.'

'So why are you doing what she tells you?'

'Her soldiers in my village, and her drones above it.'

'That's a hold over you, for sure.'

'And besides her twisting my arm,' Jenkins said, 'I actually do want to go to New Mu. See if I can talk to the Fermi there.'

'So you're something of a scientist yourself.'

Jenkins laughed. 'That's how I see it. Around here they call me a "traditional practitioner".' He shrugged. 'Gets me legal recognition and respect, anyway.'

'Legal?'

'Kepler Agreement.'

A Black Horizon arrangement, made decades ago between soldiers and scientists on a secret project: pragmatic, provisional and strictly unauthorised.

'We'll see how long that's allowed to stand,' Owen mused.

'Long enough for me, at any rate. I hope.' Jenkins motioned Owen towards an open door. 'Welcome to SciDiv.'

Past a biology lab and up a flight of stairs, they reached a room with tables and chairs pushed and stacked around the walls. Tang of sweat, sound of bickering. The room fell silent and everyone turned as Owen and Jenkins came in. In the cleared space two men and three women stood amid stacks of kit and clothing and five rucksacks. By the door two men, a British Army officer and a civilian, looked on, exasperated.

The officer turned. 'Ah, here you are.' He raised a hand. 'Lieutenant William Knight.' He gestured to the civilian, a stocky middle-aged man with short curly hair. 'Adrian Black, the SciDiv director. Mr Jenkins, Mr Owen – how do you do?'

'Very well, thank you,' said Owen. 'Mr Jenkins here has been asked to introduce me to the company.'

'Go ahead, but be quick about it,' Adrian Black said.

Jenkins nodded and began. 'You already know Emma Hazeldene, and—'

Hazeldene, a tall and strongly built woman with a lot of blonde hair piled on her head, glared at Owen, then Knight. 'Christ, are we taking that thing with us?'

'Orders, I'm afraid,' Knight said.

'It's bloody dangerous!'

'Pleased to see you again, too,' said Owen. 'Dr Hazeldene, I assure you that my instructions don't include doing you or your colleagues any harm whatsoever.'

'To the best of my knowledge that is the case,' said Knight.

'Then I'll have to take your word for it.' Hazeldene demonstratively turned her back and resuming sorting through stuff on the floor.

Her colleagues were more open-minded, or perhaps curious. One by one they hailed Owen and introduced themselves. The tall, thin young man with a black beard and quizzical eyes was Georgi Muranov, Russian, a palaeoanalyst; Nelson Hayes, black, middle-aged, burly, American, a geologist; Cindy Patel, of serious mien and slight build, Indian, also a geologist; Sharianne Adler, compact, very fit, curly-haired, American, a bioinformatics specialist. A shared glance at Hazeldene hinted at some awkward personal connection – exes but not quite over it, Owen guessed.

Introductions over, the scientists returned to arguing over what to take. Adrian Black took about a minute of this, then shouted, 'Stop! For heaven's sake, you lot! You don't need to take everything on your own backs. Just pack your personal stuff and let the rest go cargo.'

'I'm not trusting a bunch of goddamn soldiers with my kit,' Hazeldene said.

'You don't have to,' Black said. 'Lieutenant, please call in the mules.'

Knight touched his phone. There was a clatter outside, then a flurry of soft footsteps on the stairs. Two quadrupedal robots, each about the size of a very large dog, padded into the room. They bore on each side empty, multi-pocketed saddlebags. They sauntered into the middle and squatted on their haunches. Their forelimbs flexed, the ends unfolding into many-fingered hand-like appendages. Swift as card sharps, they began sifting through the scientists' gear, sorting equipment from clothing and other personal possessions faster than the human eye could follow – though Owen could track every move. Deftly the pack robots loaded their saddlebags, and quickly they paced out. The scientists were left looking down at much-diminished heaps.

'There you go,' said Black.

'Amazing,' said Jenkins. 'Some advanced robotics around here, eh?'

Owen laughed and took his leave.

Outside, the transport was preparing to depart. Hatches banged shut. Warnings sounded. Owen closed and covered his eyes. The blue flash shone through his fingers and his eyelids; the thump of air occupying suddenly empty space rang in his ears. He walked across the square as the dust settled.

Back in his quarters, Owen scanned the room for surveillance and found none. He sat at the table, reopened the envelope, and reread the letter. The gist was this.

The Alliance in general, and the UK government in particular, were still deeply concerned about the alien rocks: on Venus, on Earth, and now on Apis. Their main worry had always been that some other power might pre-empt them in finding military applications. Any knowledge that could be gleaned from these relics of an evidently ancient and terrifyingly more advanced civilisation was of – the term was emphasised and underscored in the plain text – *existential* importance. Besides causing crustal movements, the rocks had already demonstrated FTL communication – which, given the inconveniences of the method by which this very message was delivered, i.e. all the back and forth of FTL travel carrying *mail* of all things – would be useful indeed to have. And so on.

But the nuclear-capable power at the focus of that worry was no longer the Union, or the Co-ord.

It was Black Horizon.

Although two of the three great Powers had perforce welcomed the historic breakthrough of FTL travel, and had offered – generously, however ungraciously received – to share its fruits with the Union, the Alliance governments were privately having kittens. The Co-ord governments could be assumed to be even more frantic.

A conspiracy of scientists and soldiers capable of keeping a secret of this magnitude for half a century, with thousands of military and bureaucratic personnel passing through its doors and going to their graves without breathing a word of it, was the most shocking security failure ever to shake West or East. Not even the US counter-coup of the 2030s, or the same decade's unexpected Rising in Europe, could begin to compare with it as a 'caught with our trousers down shocker' (Mason had written this section of the text himself, it seemed).

Who was actually *in* Black Horizon? A handful of scientists and officers had broken the news to their astonished governments. The crews of certain submarines and other craft were obviously complicit – though just how many and how much was unknown. The conspiracy was almost certainly highly compartmentalised. It could be presumed that submarines were used as starships only when they were out of contact when on patrol. It was possible that some crew members didn't know they were on another planet at all, even if they disembarked – and not all did.

The rest of the conspiracy remained hidden. And not only on Earth. It was known that they'd been to other planets than Apis, but no mention of these had been made. No one yet knew what resources and reserves Black Horizon might have stashed across the sky beyond the reach of Earth.

'One thing I can be sure of,' Mason wrote. 'Whoever else is in this conspiracy, you're not. In fact, apart from the new arrivals from the Union, and the fresh troops, you're the only person on Apis who definitely isn't.'

The end of the directive reverted to bureaucratic prose.

'IMMEDIATE ACTION: it has been agreed as a matter of urgency that the Alliance scientists excluded by the Co-ord from the nearby MacHINERY RIDGE investigation (their work having apparently triggered a local earthquake and tsunami) should accompany the small military assistance contingent assigned to the UNION settlement on NEW MU. The scientists are to be tasked with assisting the UNION settlers with biological and other appraisals of their environment. They are also tasked with investigating the possibility of non-intrusive communication with the nearby outcrop known as HAMILTON'S RISE. Close cooperation is urged with the UNION settlers in this investigation, which should be carried out ostensibly under their auspices as far as possible. As the UNION is not a signatory to the (purported) KEPLER AGREEMENT, the Co-ord should have no quasi-legal pretext to interfere. This scientific mission is not clandestine and the presence of DR GEORGI MURANOV should allay Co-ord suspicions.

'The recipient MARCUS OWEN is to accompany this mission as an overt operative of the BRITISH COUNCIL and Allied intelligence. (Since OWEN's nature and identity are known, subterfuge would be pointless.) His mission is to find out as much as possible about Black Horizon and its plans and capacities. This much will be obvious to all concerned, but opportunities may arise. He should presume for operational purposes that any operatives of Allied or Co-ord intelligence services, etc., on the planet are agents of Black Horizon, or are compromised by their participation in the conspiracy, however sincerely and however justifiably they may have initially assumed they were being recruited to a legitimate black budget project. This assumption also applies to the above-mentioned science team and all other personnel on Apis OTHER THAN THE TROOPS SPECIFICALLY ASSIGNED TO THIS MISSION AND SHORTLY TO ARRIVE.

'MARCUS OWEN's covert mission, on which he must NOT report to anyone other than his artistic director and then only by secure channels, is ABOVE TOP SECRET UK EYES ONLY: to closely monitor any progress in communicating with HAMILTON'S RISE or any other such entity. In the event of strategically significant information being discovered, he is to prevent its return to or retention by anyone working OR SUSPECTED OF WORKING for the Co-ord, the Union, or Black Horizon AT ALL COSTS. At the same time, he is to make every effort (consistent with avoiding his mission's discovery and exposure) to establish communication with and gain information from the said entity or entities on his and our own behalf.

'MESSAGE ENDS.'

CHAPTER FOUR
Local call

Union settlement, New Mu, Apis, Saturday 18 October 2070

Marie Henderson woke to what sounded like engines starting up, each making a different mechanical racket: rattles, taps, screeches, chugs, creaks, croaks, buzzes. The zipped-together sleeping bags she shared with Myles were twisted, and dew-damp on the outside. The low sun, red at dawn here, too, was in her eyes.

Myles Grant was still asleep beside her. Marie reached for her rucksack, opened it and with a lot of squirming managed to get half dressed inside the bag. Then she stood up and got the rest of her clothes on. She drank from her Thermos. Water still a little tepid from its boiling the previous day. The din continued. It was, she guessed, the dawn chorus of the invertebrates. She might never hear birdsong again. The pang of this thought couldn't cloud her elation, her sense of wonder.

Her first morning on another planet! The air seemed fresher and more invigorating than she was used to. Everything seemed to weigh a little less than it should. As she crouched to lace up her boots she observed the sward. It wasn't a grass, she knew that. Here the niche was filled by a small spiky soft succulent, with many-jointed springy stems. Tiny insectoids and arachnoids crawled on and among the plants. Within a few metres a dozen or so winged and beaked bipeds that looked like plastic models of anything from starlings to crows strutted and pecked, now and then rattling the stiff vanes they had in the place of feathers and giving voice to harsh cries.

She straightened up and looked around. To the east the plain was hard to look at in the rising sun, but by shading her eyes, darkening her glasses and peering from side to side, Marie could make out the long shadows of shrubs that became more and more sparse the farther away they were. To the west a wide slope of green rose through a belt of forest to ranges of foothills culminating in a rugged escarpment, crested by a cluster of crystalline pillars glittering ruby and emerald in the dawn. Beyond the range, low in the sky, clouds hung grey and heavy, trailing rain slowly inland. The stream that meandered through the area of the camp could be traced by the thicker and taller vegetation on its banks all the way up to the woods, then gully by gully uphill to somewhere behind the first low range. In the other direction it flowed towards – she zoomed her glasses – ah, yes, a much larger river, traced by a thread of mist far across the plain.

Marie took out her phone and looked at the map, orienting herself. The landing site was inland from the escarpment, part of a series of mountain ranges along the western coast of this part of the continent of New Lemuria. On the far side of the mountains thickly forested slopes tumbled to the ocean, at a shoreline of cliffs and beaches that extended for hundreds of kilometres north and south. The river that the stream flowed into cut through the escarpment ten kilometres north-west of where she stood, to cascade in pools and falls to arrive after a distance of seven kilometres to the sea. The source of the stream, up in the foothills, was a kilometre-long lake, itself fed by runoff from higher up.

On arrival the previous afternoon, the new settlers had been promised a delivery by flying boat of additional supplies and a small contingent of Alliance troops to protect the settlement. That lake, Marie guessed, would be a good place for the flying boat to land, after its journey across the oceans from the Alliance base on New Atlantis.

The map had been made from satellite and aerial surveys, and was dotted with helpful guesswork symbols: peak, source, swamp, radioactive ore . . . None of the local features had names, with one exception: the crystalline outcrop was labelled *Hamilton's Rise*. Beside it were two tiny symbols: a black skull and a grey inverted teardrop with two dots in the middle. The latter puzzled her for a moment, until she remembered something Myles had talked about on their first date: the mythical grey aliens that the Yanks and English – sincerely or ironically – believed in. The map's rubric, when she tapped it, spelt out the symbols' obvious meanings: the skull meant *Danger*, and the grey alien meant *Artefact Attributed to Extraterrestrial Intelligence*.

Around her, others stirred, emerging from sleeping bags and bivouacs and tents. The harsh dawn chorus died away and human voices rose. The dozen or so armed pickets of the night's third watch strolled sleepily off duty. Marie hurried to the nearest latrine, used it then found nearby a plastic drum with a tap – all 3D-printed the previous day – filled with water from the stream and very much not for drinking. She washed her hands and splashed her face.

Seven arks the size and shape of shipping containers, each holding about a hundred people with all their carried gear. A dozen smaller crates, packed with survival kit: Apis-specific antibiotics and anti-fungals; basic supplies and rations; fusion pods, batteries, rolls and rolls of solar-power foil; recyclers; printers. Enough to keep them going for a few weeks, but they had to use that time to learn to live off the land. Food, if the basic Apis information kit was anything to go by – and on a different continent, it might not be – was unlikely to be a problem. Finding the right raw materials for the printers to chug out everything from tampons to toothpaste was going to be more of a challenge.

Marie was sure they would meet it. Seven hundred people, nearly all under thirty. The post-Rising generation: they'd all have had the same training since childhood, in school and in the Free Union Youth. They'd camped out for a week at a time, more than once, on the bleakest moors Scotland had to offer. They'd practised with weapons and martial arts, in supposedly age-appropriate stages. They'd found out the hard way what sort of people you wanted or didn't want given responsibilities or leading a team. She reckoned they'd cope. She was certain she would.

Someone had found a flagpole and a Union flag – no doubt thoughtfully provided by the Alliance, mindful of territorial legalities, or whatever passed for such here – in one of the arks, and a small party was busy erecting the pole and running up the Sky and Star banner with an attempt at due ceremony and solemnity.

Myles had got up and spread out the sleeping bag to dry. His face prickled with stubble when they kissed.

'What?' he asked.

'I remembered I haven't brushed my teeth yet either.'

He laughed. 'Sorry about that.' Then his face clouded. 'Still a bit nauseous from the inoculations. You?'

'I'm OK,' Marie said. She thought about it. 'Not going to risk eating much for a while, mind.'

Across a cold breakfast of water and energy bars, they talked, making plans for the day. In mid-conversation, Myles's sticky eyelids widened. He smote his forehead with the heel of his hand.

'Iskander!' he said.

'What?' said Marie.

'What?' said Iskander, from his shirt pocket.

Myles silenced the phone with an irritable gesture.

'It pinged us an update last night, just as we saw that space station.'

'Yes, and?'

'There's only the Alliance and the Co-ord here.'

Marie shrugged. 'Maybe they installed a copy on their network for us new arrivals. I mean, they want settlers from the Union, and Iskander's what we're used to, so . . .'

Myles was shaking his head. 'Nah, Iskander scares them.' He frowned, then, scoffing at himself, said: 'What if that *space station* is Union?'

Marie laughed along, then added: 'Uh, your phone's buzzing so hard it's just about jumping out of your pocket.'

'Ah. So it is.' Myles fished it out.

'I've put a call through for you,' said Iskander. 'Ask your father.'

Myles almost dropped the phone.

Low Apis orbit, Saturday 18 October 2070

'It's beautiful,' Ellen said.

They'd been standing side by side, on the edge of a big screen on the floor of the endless corridor, gazing at Apis for over an hour. The screen was like a window looking down on the planet, a view stitched seamlessly from outside camera feeds. Over Venus, John Grant thought, it must have been pretty damned monotonous. Here, it was hypnotic. The Station's own crew members strolled over it with barely a downward glance. Everyone else, however rational, hesitated before stepping on it, like tourists on a glass bridge.

'It's like Earth,' said Grant.

'Yes,' said Ellen, still entranced.

It wasn't, quite, as they both knew. Blue and white, green and dun, yes, but the continents were differently shaped and distributed: three island continents, far apart from each other. In the northern hemisphere the locations and general shapes of New Atlantis and New Lemuria reminded Grant – aptly enough considering which power ruled which continent – of an isolated North America and an isolated Russia, though in each case displaced a bit further south. In the southern hemisphere, and on the opposite side of the world, New Lemuria sprawled from the equator to within thirty degrees of the pole like a giant Africa or South America. With the uninterrupted fetch of the southern ocean behind them, great swells battered its western coast, making a long white line of surf that could be seen from space. In each of the oceans, chains of volcanic islands marked where plates collided or rubbed against each other.

As on Earth, you could see the jigsaw edges where all three landmasses had once fitted together to make up a supercontinent. Its centre (formed in a previous collision, whose mountain ranges remained along these coasts) had been a vast desert, in a past geologically recent enough to show traces in the mostly arid coastal plains beyond the fertile green edges between sea and mountain. The planet had no ice caps, but the polar regions were white with frozen sea, great swirling masses of ice that calved gigantic bergs to spin off in long visible streams along the polar currents.

Grant was beginning to feel relaxed. The intense physical and mental activity and emotional toll of the first flight and the Venus rescue had left everyone involved shattered. Having made their way from the ship to the habitation band, he and his crew had faced the brief memorial service, then at last been able to recycle their clothes, shower, eat and sleep. It was even a relief to be wearing anonymous blue jumpsuits like everyone else, fresh out of the printer.

His phone rang.

'It's your son Myles,' Iskander said, in his ear. 'Putting you through.'

'What?' Grant shouted. Ellen jumped.

He shook out the phone and snapped it flat to a bigger screen, so they could both watch. He saw Myles, with Marie peering over his shoulder, and a scrubby plain behind their grubby faces. The two looked as astonished as Grant felt. He'd already had updates on the Station's network about the situation down below according to the Alliance and Co-ord bases. He knew the Alliance had gone ahead with settling hundreds of Union citizens down there on New Mu, very much against the Union's wishes; he knew Myles and Marie had pondered the prospect, but he'd never thought they'd go through with it.

'Myles!'

'Dad! How – where—?'

'Oh, God,' said Ellen. 'You're here? On Apis?'

'Yes,' said Myles. 'And you're in . . . the *space station*?' His voice cracked with disbelief.

'Yes,' said Grant, dismayed. 'You did it,' he said heavily. 'You took the England ferry.'

'We took up the Alliance offer,' said Myles, sounding truculent. 'How did *you* get here?'

Grant and Ellen looked at each other, sighed, and between them brought Myles and Marie up to speed. The explanation took longer than their journey had.

'So why didn't you *tell* us you were building a starship?' Myles demanded.

Grant couldn't believe he was being asked. Ellen shouldered in.

'You know what your father's like! He's a *responsable*. He takes it more seriously than the goddamn cadre! A stone-cold revolutionary of the Cold Revolution.'

She didn't sound like she meant this as a compliment. Myles evidently took it as an explanation, nodding sombrely.

'I told you the Cold Revolution wasn't over,' Grant said. 'You might have listened.'

'I'm glad I didn't,' Myles said, arm around Marie's shoulders. 'I mean, look what we've got!'

The view swept around, from the plain to the lush slopes and the strange crest, and taking in the busy morning activities of the encampment amid what looked like shipping containers and smaller crates strewn over the landscape.

'We'll get land of our own,' Myles said. 'It's an amazing place.'

Grant couldn't see the attraction of land. How many generations ago had his forefathers clawed their way out of the peasantry? And now Myles was going to go back to all that?

'Look,' he said, 'I must say I have to admire you both for having the guts to do this. The spirit of adventure and all that. Does you credit. But you don't have to stay here. You're still a director of our company, Myles! And I've got big plans. We're not staying here – we're going back to Earth as soon as we can, and we're going to build more ships. We can explore on our own, not just under the wing of the Alliance or China or Black Horizon or whatever. You can be in on the ground floor of that, not digging in dirt on Apis.'

'We won't be digging in dirt for long,' Myles said. 'These continents are going to be workers' paradises for generations – plenty of free land, labour scarce. It's like getting the New World all over again, but without native populations. No genocides, no slavery, just expansion.'

Ellen scoffed. 'Good luck keeping your workers' paradise, without a workers' state to back you up!'

Myles shrugged, making the phone wobble. 'The Union?' He rotated the phone to show the Union flag above the camp, then back. 'It can come here any time – you know that. I don't know why they're spurning the offer, but for now we're here and we're still Union. If you're going back to Earth, Dad, the first thing you should do is try and get them to come and join us.'

'I'll tell you why the Union isn't keen,' Grant said. 'It's because of stuff like that weird rock on the skyline. That's an alien intelligence, that is! It burned Venus and shook the Atlantic – God knows what mess it's made of the Clyde, to say nothing else – and *it* owns this land, not you. We need to find worlds – or make worlds – where we don't live at its sufferance.'

The vision of what had to be done – what *he* had to do – had come to him as he spoke, and made his voice vehement.

Marie grabbed the phone from Myles, panned the view again, then zoomed it in close to the ground. Plants like skinny succulents covered the soil. Small creatures with lots of legs and eyes crawled and climbed. She swung the view to the sky, the louring clouds beyond the distant crags, the white puffs high above, the black flying things that looked more like ornithopters than birds. The camera returned to Marie's bright bonny grinning face.

'This world is enough for me,' she said. 'I've been here less than a day and it's already filled me with wonder and delight. Hardly anybody before me has ever been in a place like I'm in, one of the first biologists and maybe the first ecologist on an alien planet that actually has *life*. Talk about getting in on the ground floor, John! I'm not leaving unless I absolutely have to.'

'By then it might be too late,' Ellen pleaded. 'You can do all that after the scientists have figured out what that alien thing wants of us. It might just want to be left alone.'

'Exactly,' Myles said, 'and—'

'Then you could come back,' Ellen persisted, 'if we know it's safe.'

'I reckon we're safer here than on Earth,' said Marie. 'At least *here* there aren't nuclear weapons and a mass extinction going on.'

'I wouldn't be so sure of that,' Grant said. 'Considering East and West have been flying here for fifty-odd years in nuclear-armed submarines!'

'Speak of the devil,' said Ellen.

'What?'

Ellen pointed down.

'Oh, shit!' said Grant.

'What's going on?' Marie cried.

Grant tabbed his phone to flip the camera, showing the view on the floor screen. Between the Station and Apis, the all too familiar shape of the Co-ord submarine *Admiral von Bellingshausen* rose like a shark to a surfboard.

An alarm brayed through the corridor, hideous and unavoidable, fit to wake the dead.

'Sorry,' said Iskander. 'Ending your call.'

Grant's phone went black.

CHAPTER FIVE
Battlestar Europa

The Space Station, low Apis orbit, Saturday 18 October 2070

Lakshmi Nayak was in Katrina Ulrich's command post when the alarm sounded. Being actually, physically there rather than sharing a virtual workspace felt like a privilege, even though the command post was just another office on the endless corridor, with a bank of screens, a desk, a huddle of printed chairs and barely enough room for her, Ulrich, Omar Khan from the *Fighting Chance* and the Station's chief engineer, Eduardo Maria Gironella.

Ulrich had given them an update on Milloy's interrogation of the AI in the suit, which now called itself Sikandar. They'd all agreed that it was best kept where it was. Omar had shared the specs for the ship and the drive, Nayak had explained the details and they had finalised with Gironella a production plan for building new drives – one for the Station itself in the first instance, then more for the shuttles it already had, and then maybe for building more shuttles. Having been used for trips to and from Cloud City, the shuttles were – unlike the *Fighting Chance*–designed for flight in planetary atmospheres and for manoeuvring in space.

They'd just signed off on that when the alarm sounded. It was the kind of blare reserved for incoming missile fire, a solar flare, or meteor collision warnings. The note of it hurt Nayak's tooth sockets.

The Commander spun her chair and faced the screen.

'What is it?'

The screen showed her. The submarine had matched velocities and now paced the Station ten kilometres behind in the same orbit.

'Oh,' Ulrich said. 'You again.'

The *Admiral von Bellingshausen* hailed them seconds later.

'Captain Nikolai Rostov calling Commander Katrina Ulrich.'

'Hello, Captain Rostov. When I last heard from your ship, it was commanded by Captain Yefrimovich.'

'Yefrimovich has been relieved of his post.'

'May I ask why?'

'He is under investigation as part of the Black Horizon conspiracy.'

'Conspiracy? I thought it was a joint secret project.'

Rostov laughed '"A joint secret project" is rather the definition of a conspiracy, is it not? This ship is now fully under the control of the lawful authorities, in this case the Russian Navy. The same applies to the Novy Cosmograd base, in partnership of course with the PLA Navy, and *mutatis mutandis* to the Alliance base at New Ardtaraig.'

'I see,' said Ulrich. 'It seems we're a little behind the curve.'

'Many hours, Commander. Time enough for an update on the situation to get back to the Solar system – for which thanks, by the way – and for the Co-ordinated States to consider our options.'

'I take these no longer include blasting us out of the sky?'

'If they did, we would have done it already,' said Rostov. 'And seizing the private starship is no longer relevant. The damage is done. The Union already has the stardrive. However, your presence here destabilises the balance of power. There can be no "Battlestar Europa" in Apis's skies – or Earth's. An FTL-capable nuclear-armed orbital fort is the stuff of nightmares.' He raised a pre-emptive hand. 'Oh, you needn't deny being nuclear-armed – your earlier defiance made obvious what we'd already suspected. Let me assure you that if we do have to attack you, it will be without warning and with the full support of the governments of the Alliance and the Co-ordinated States.'

'What, all of them?' Ulrich scoffed.

'All the relevant ones: the United States, Russia, China. A UN Security Council resolution to the same effect has only been blocked by France.'

It took Nayak a moment to remember that France was, in Security Council permanent membership terms, the Union.

'And what does the Union have to say about this?' Ulrich asked.

Rostov looked smug. 'The answer is contained in the two diplomatic bags which—' a monitor pinged '—you have just received. One of them is for the Alliance Consul. The other is for your eyes only. I am given to understand that it contains your instructions from the Union government. I urge you to study them carefully, and meanwhile we will maintain an orbit in short range and outside your blast radius.'

It was on the tip of Nayak's tongue to point out that the Station's putative blast radius was irrelevant because (a) they were in vacuum and free fall and (b) the sub could have its drive powered up ready to jump a microsecond after the missile was launched. She decided this contribution would be redundant and not well received. Her other instant, insistent thought, that the strategic balance was already – indeed, had long been – obsolete as soon as FTL drives were in play, likewise went unvoiced, for the same reasons.

'Very well,' said Ulrich. 'Goodbye for now, Captain.'

'Au revoir, Commander!'

Ulrich turned from the screen. 'If you'll give me a moment, citizens . . .'

Khan, Nayak and Gironella filed out.

'Coffee anywhere?' said Nayak, looking up and down the endless corridor.

'Follow your nose,' said Gironella, sniffing the air. 'This way.'

In the cafeteria alcove fifty-odd metres away they used the machines and gathered around a circular table. About a dozen people were already in the room: Cloud City survivors, bleary-eyed, red-eyed, talking quietly or staring in silence. Nayak shifted awkwardly on her chair, took a first sip, then looked around and said: 'Let's wander.'

They found another alcove, empty, with a bench and a screen of a view over Florence at sunset. Gironella was a big man, middle-aged, the hairs on his knuckles still black, his cheeks frosted with stubble. He turned to Nayak.

'That was kind of you,' he said. He sighed. 'I too am a Cloud City survivor. All of us in the crew are. We knew these people, many of them individually, even if we'd never breathed the same air.'

'Of course,' Nayak said. 'If you need some time . . .'

'No, no. Work is my way to deal with it.' He waved both hands outward, as if spreading out a blueprint. 'And I'd like to continue the discussion that was interrupted – but that interruption seems to have thrown our plans up in the air a little.'

'You can say that again,' said Nayak. 'If the other governments are rolling up Black Horizon . . . where does that leave us?'

'Well out of it, I hope,' said Gironella.

They all laughed uneasily. Nayak turned to Khan. 'Do you know anything about this, Omar?'

'Why would I?'

'Well, you know all about conspiracies!'

Khan scoffed. 'Compared to Black Horizon, the cadre organisation is like the Free Union Youth! Iskander may know more, but I suspect—'

'You suspect correctly,' said Iskander. 'This information is on a need-to-know basis.'

'Thanks, machine,' said Khan. He sighed. 'I suggest we do as Eduardo has indicated, and look again over our plans.'

They were deep in discussion when Omar Khan remarked, 'Hang on, is the gravity dropping?'

A call pinged in Nayak's ear: 'Hi, Lakshmi, Omar, it's Katrina. Please make your way to the *Fighting Chance*. We have to jump.'

'Jump the station again?'

'Yes. Details when you get there.'

Nayak could see Omar listening and nodding.

'OK,' she said. 'See you on the other side, Eduardo.'

Guided by a dot in their glasses, Nayak and Omar headed for the hatch. The now 0.5G put an unexpected spring in their step. Ellen Grant arrived just ahead of them.

'You too?' Nayak asked, as they waited for the hatch to align with the tube. 'We're going to jump to somewhere else in space, not to an ocean!'

Ellen shrugged. 'Katrina told me, "Just in case. You never know."'

'Ain't that the truth.'

She beckoned Ellen to crouch while they still could.

The habitation band's spin slowed to a smooth halt. The hatch opened. One by one, they pushed off the floor and tumbled into the chamber above, then on up the tube.

The *Fighting Chance* stank, as all spacecraft stink, of body odours and exhalations and the chemical toilet, with in this case the added whiff of dead Venus microbes. Nayak noticed Ellen wrinkling her nose as they buckled in, and laughed.

'Think of it as our contribution to panspermia.'

'I'm thinking more of a school minibus back from a boys' game.' The roll of the Station took them from light to dark, from a glimpse of the Co-ord sub – still an uncanny sight – and onward to the blue curve of Apis, then dark again. Ellen looked sad for a moment. 'And to think I used to worry about Myles playing shinty!'

'Myles? Oh, your son back on Earth. Yes, it must be worrying.'

Ellen snorted. 'He's not back on Earth, that's the trouble!'

'You mean he's—'

'Yes, colonising Apis, for the Union as he thinks, for the fash more likely.'

Nayak, keying up the controls, opening channels, to her surprise found herself bristling. 'We're – *they're* not *actually* fascists.'

'I know, I know.' Ellen sounded impatient. 'It's just Union slang.'

'Just don't sling it where they can hear,' Ulrich's voice interrupted. 'OK, citizens, to business. I've read the Union government's message. They're in full agreement with the other Powers about not upsetting the strategic balance. So their instructions to us happily coincide with what we can expect to hear shortly from our Russian friends: get the hell out. Avoid conflict with Black Horizon, and anyone else. Go somewhere new and unexplored and – more to the point – uninhabited. Lakshmi, I'm patching Black Horizon's list of places not to go to your navigation shell.'

'Got it,' said Nayak.

'Right. Now, what I want and what the Union very much wants is that we find some extrasolar system with lots of exoplanets, preferably not quote-unquote habitable, preferably with plenty of sub-planetary junk – asteroids, moons, cometary masses – floating or rather orbiting about. Stuff to mine, and to build from, and to report back about.'

'Seek out strange new worlds?' Nayak dead-panned.

'Yes,' said Ulrich, sharply. 'Can you do that?'

'Yes,' said Nayak. She looked over her shoulder. 'Omar, how's the power?'

Khan gave a thumbs-up. 'Sweet and clean.'

'Great. OK, give me a mo.'

Nayak pulled up the navigation app. Iskander months ago had cobbled it together from a star map and a video game. Now it had an overlay of heavy black labels liberally scattered across the sky. The warnings off were thickest among the Solar system's nearby, hopeful stars – Proxima, Barnard's Star, Wolf 359, Lalande 21185, Epsilon Eridani, Tau Ceti – thinning out in the hundreds-of-light-years range that included Apis, which of course was itself on Black Horizon's blacklist. She scanned the remainder, perplexed. How were there so many? Had Black Horizon really established bases, or even human settlements, around them all? Surely not – this must simply be a list of places they'd been and might someday go back to. But then—

Ulrich was already ahead of her.

'Here's what I think,' the Commander said. 'We don't answer to Black Horizon, and it's being rolled up in any case. They can't possibly be keeping tabs on all these stars on the blacklist. Avoid conflict, yes, but I think we should check out one of the more distant stars behind these black patches. If Black Horizon has a presence, fine, we jump out again. Otherwise, let's see what's so interesting about these systems. Very likely, many of them are just the kind of system the Union is looking for.'

Nayak was surprised. 'Are you sure?'

'Yes, I'm sure!'

'If I may make a suggestion?' Sikandar's voice in her ear

startled Nayak until she remembered she hadn't deleted the hardened private channel they'd used to debrief the rogue AI after its rescue from Venus. She resisted the urge to look behind, and up, to where the empty armoured suit still clung to the ship like an orphaned baby monkey to a dummy mother in some cruel psychology experiment.

'Go ahead,' she said. She shared access to the channel with Ulrich.

A dot on the display brightened. E-PRIME 667, in the Union's nomenclature. A K-type main sequence star five hundred and thirty-five light-years away.

'What's special about it?'

'Ticks all the boxes,' said Sikandar. 'I have more recent data than is included in your app. Some of its exoplanets are indeed in the habitable zone, but that's a technicality. It definitely has a gas giant well out from the star, with at least a dozen exomoons, plenty of ice and an asteroid belt close enough in for useful solar power.'

The AI zapped her the details.

'What do you think, Commander?' Nayak asked.

Some seconds passed before Ulrich replied.

'It looks as good a choice as any,' she said at last. 'Not that I trust your new little friend, but I don't see any ploy or hidden agenda behind this. And if it's not suitable, we can always go somewhere else.'

'OK,' said Nayak, setting up the jump parameters to arrive in the plane of the ecliptic and well out of the way of any of the system's interesting orbiting objects. 'Let's do this. If you could tell the complement to brace for seven minutes of existential dread, Commander . . .'

'I'll tell them no such thing,' said Ulrich. 'Some people don't experience it that way, you know, and I don't want to plant suggestions.'

'Understood, Commander. Omar, turn it up.'

She brought the inflaton trap field up in synch with Khan's

powering up the fusion pot. Once more she saw the rainbow shimmer expand around the craft, then suddenly extend to wrap around the Station.

The universe fell away.

This was Nayak's second interstellar jump. She knew what to expect. So far it wasn't getting any easier. Nobody moved. Nobody spoke. Ellen and Omar, Nayak guessed, felt as she did: alone in the nothing before all worlds. Her own arms wrapped around her, and the straps of the seat across her chest, stood in for Kali's four-armed embrace. Not that Nayak believed that, or even took much comfort from it. What she did believe, she experienced now: no gods were here. In the jump atheism hit like a revelation.

And then they were back. In space, in time, in Newton's grasp and Einstein's light, in orbit around another star.

The Space Station, around E-PRIME 667, Saturday 18 October 2070

Nayak blinked, shuddered and looked out through the canopy. Her immediate impression, as the Station rolled around, was that Apis had disappeared, and the sun had got smaller and dimmer. It all looked empty and felt lonely, in a way she hadn't experienced before, travelling as they had from low Venus orbit to low Apis orbit.

'We're about 2 AU out,' she announced. 'Between the orbits of the asteroid belt and the first of the rockies, and the gas giant dozens of AU away. No radio traffic, no sign of any human presence. Commander, anything nearby we should be getting out of the way of?'

'Nothing on visual,' Ulrich reported. 'Deep-space radar will pick up anything within a light-minute, and so far the screen is clear.'

Nayak had a flash of worry that a light-minute seemed awfully close, cutting it fine, then smiled at herself. Nothing moving at orbital speeds would approach them from a light-minute away in anything less than days.

'That's good to know, Commander. And now?'

'I think it's safe for you to stand down,' Ulrich said.

Nayak and Ellen unbuckled, and kicked themselves towards the airlock to begin their laborious way back. Just before she dived into the tube, Nayak said on the hard channel: 'See you later, Sikandar. Hope you're not lonely.'

'Don't worry about me,' said Sikandar. 'I'm taking in the view.'

CHAPTER SIX

Continental Drift

New Mu, Apis, Sunday 19 October 2070

Marcus Owen was never bored. Not that he had feelings, but for boredom he lacked even the analogue. Curiosity impelled him to seek out new information. By the second day of the flying boat's journey over the southern ocean, however, the flow of new information had dried to a trickle. He sat in the Observation Lounge – a row of three window tables on each side, with facing seats – and looked out at the sea and sky, and observed nothing of interest.

He got up and made his way to another window table, and sat down facing Emma Hazeldene. She didn't like him. No one on the aircraft did, not even the soldiers. They knew he was a spook and they didn't like it. Hazeldene was gazing out at the featureless expanse with apparent interest.

'What are you seeing out there?' he asked.

She turned sharply. For a moment, a shake of her hair and

the set of her face matched the image of her he had seen in the chasm on Venus. She'd been annoyed then, too.

'Migrations,' she said. She spread thumbs from forefingers in the *zoom* gesture. 'See for yourself.'

Owen zoomed his glasses, and – less overtly – his eyes. He saw a great black V shape, which resolved into smaller Vs, which in turn resolved into skeins of flying organisms, at a much lower altitude and slower speed than the aircraft.

'Birds?'

'We call them "boids",' Hazeldene explained. She laughed. 'It's the only neat and self-explanatory common name we've come up with for anything here.'

'There's always the Latin binomial nomenclature,' Owen said.

'Oh, we use that, of course!' Hazeldene gave him a quizzical look. 'Classification has been a nightmare. Still!' She clapped and rubbed together her hands. 'Everything's changing now. Proper science at last!'

'No doubt. And I expect common names will emerge as more people arrive.' He pointed out of the window. 'So – about the migrations?'

'Ah, yes! We see far more migration across oceans than we do on Earth. Lots of little land critters, even, set off on epic swims. Rapid plate tectonics, you see?'

'Ah, not quite.'

'You don't catch my drift?'

Owen gave this a more appreciative smile than it deserved.

'On Earth,' Hazeldene said, 'the continents are moving apart at a centimetre or two a year. Here, it's tens of metres a year. From radioactive dating we estimate they separated only a few hundred thousand years ago. They're slowing down – a few centimetres per year less every year. In the past they may have been moving at *kilometres* a year.'

She leaned back, with a look that said *What do you think of that?*

'What's that got to do with migration?'

'Suppose your hunting or breeding or over-wintering grounds move away – very fast in geological terms, not so fast to you. What was a stream or lake becomes a gulf, a gulf becomes a sea, a sea becomes an ocean . . . Each generation you have to swim or fly a little further, and . . . you know how it goes. I and a Co-ord colleague found a species of boid that has a perfectly adequate wintering ground a few hundred kilometres to the south on New Lemuria, but still every year flies thousands of kilometres to winter on New Atlantis.'

Owen made himself look suitably impressed. 'Finding out about continental drift on Earth took decades.'

'Well, we didn't first have to establish it was happening at all!' She laughed. 'We haven't measured sea-floor spreading or mapped mid-ocean ridges or anything like that. Yet. We can be almost certain the rapid plate tectonics is connected with the bizarre processes we see in rocks like MacHinery Ridge. Between that and the biosphere's, uh, *relatedness* to Earth's, we know Apis has been terraformed – probably by the minds in the rocks, but . . .' She shrugged and spread her hands.

Owen glanced out of the window. The migrating boids had been left far behind.

'It must have been very frustrating,' he said, 'having all this new knowledge and being unable to share it beyond, well, Black Horizon.'

'Black Horizon?' Hazeldene scoffed. 'We couldn't share it beyond our colleagues on *this* planet! We're talking a scientific community of dozens, mostly engrossed in urgent practical work. Our results were sent back to Earth, but we got no feedback from there or anywhere else.'

Owen raised his eyebrows. 'Anywhere else?'

Hazeldene frowned. 'I got the definite impression from the spooks who sent us to Venus that there are other human-settled planets. And certainly that the kind of rocks Jenkins and his people call "Fermi Ruins" exist on other planets besides Earth, Venus and Apis.'

'But you've never seen reports or scientific papers about these other planets?'

'Nope.' Hazeldene shrugged. 'Presumably any reports are evaluated by Black Horizon, but that's no substitute for proper scientific discussion.'

'You can't do science on a need-to-know basis,' Owen said. 'That's how you run an intelligence service.'

Hazeldene smiled. 'You should know.'

'Indeed I do.' He smiled back. 'And I'll tell you what else is run that way – a conspiracy.'

'Oh, Black Horizon's a conspiracy all right,' said Hazeldene. 'But I'm a very lowly minion of it, so you can stop pumping me for information.'

'Touché. But really, Dr Hazeldene, I was only trying to find out what in this endless ocean you found so fascinating.' He stood up. 'Coffee?'

'Oh, please. Black, no sugar, thanks.'

The flying boat had a passenger capacity of thirty. With Owen, Jenkins, the five scientists and twenty-four soldiers on board it felt only slightly overcrowded. Its four fusion-powered wing-mounted turbines made a barely audible hum. Owen climbed the stair-ladder from the lower deck containing the cargo hold and the grandly named Observation Lounge and walked the narrow aisle between the curtained bunks where most on board were still sleeping. Towards the cockpit, an automatic galley was firing up for breakfast, and already had coffee on tap.

Able Jenkins was already there, scratching a frustrated fingernail on the top of a juice carton.

'If I may,' Owen said, holding out his hand to take the container. 'This way.' He demonstrated with a few deft movements, and handed it back open.

'Ah, thanks, man,' said Jenkins, and took a grateful gulp. 'Why do they have to make it so complicated?'

Owen could have given a complete breakdown of the harvesting, manufacture and supply chains that had brought the orange juice to this unlikely destination. Instead he said, 'Welcome to the free market.'

Jenkins laughed. 'Not so keen on that where we're going, eh?'

'From what I've seen of the Union, it's not easy to tell the difference from street level. Even less so in a pioneer settlement, I imagine. That's where your skills and knowledge come in. No orange juice cartons there! You can show them how to get local fruit, live off the land, all that.'

'Not so sure,' Jenkins said. 'Different continent, right?'

Owen poured two mugs of coffee. The skills Jenkins would be using on New Mu had little to do with hunting and gathering, but within the earshot of the three soldiers now behind Owen in the queue the polite fiction had to be maintained.

'According to the lady downstairs, the continents here aren't as different as those back home.'

'Emma? Yes, I'd like to see her about that.'

'Fine,' said Owen. 'After you.'

On seeing Jenkins descend the stair-ladder, Hazeldene visibly brightened.

'Oh, hi, Able. Good to see you!'

'Good morning, Emma.' Jenkins took the seat Owen had been in, facing the scientist. Owen handed over her coffee and took his to the adjacent table across the aisle.

'You were telling the robot about continents?' Jenkins asked.

Hazeldene shot Owen an apologetic glance.

'Don't mind me,' said Owen. 'Consider me furniture, or perhaps a household appliance.'

'Sorry about that,' said Jenkins, sounding more amused than contrite. He took a sip of his orange juice. 'Hard to get my head around the . . . etiquette of these situations, know what I mean?'

'I can appreciate that,' said Owen, 'used as you are to dealing with god-like intelligences beside which I am but an ant.'

'As are we all,' said Jenkins, looking solemn for a moment. 'Anyway, sorry, Mr Owen. Won't happen again.'

'Oh, "Marcus", please.'

Jenkins nodded, then turned back to Hazeldene. 'What I wanted to know, Emma, is – are the plants and animals on New Mu enough like the ones on New Atlantis for what I know to be of any use to the settlers?'

'We haven't surveyed it up close,' Hazeldene replied thoughtfully, 'but what we can eat – and what can eat us – should be much the same, at least in the same sort of environments. The continents haven't been separate long enough for the species to diverge very much.' She laughed. 'You could always ask the Fermi. They shifted the continents, after all. Probably.'

'Why do you think that?'

'Two reasons,' said Hazeldene. 'First of all, if you're looking for something that can muck about with friction, a rock with rocks moving inside it seems a good place to start. And second – you have glasses now?'

'Yes,' said Jenkins. He took out a set and put them on. 'Free at the company store.'

'It's called the commissary,' said Hazeldene. 'Anyway. Look at this.'

She waved her hands, conjuring a shared workspace. The three continents flashed into view, on a map projection that showed a spread-out slice of the world's skin. With a fingertip, she pulled them together, along the lines where they still roughly fitted. In what were now the coastal ranges of all three, and had once been a mountainous region in the supercontinent's central desert, three bright dots marked the vertices of a small equilateral triangle.

'There's our MacHinery Ridge, New Lemuria's Markov

Escarpment and the one we're heading for: Hamilton's Rise on New Mu. They were all within a hundred or so kilometres of each other once.'

She flipped the display away. 'Makes you think, eh?'

Some hours later, a stir went through the aircraft. Land ahoy! All the passengers, civilians and soldiers alike, pressed around the windows. A line of white, a line of green, another white line, then blue: cloud, land, surf; all as if through a grey filter: rain.

Dropping fast, the flying boat crossed the beach and forest and then the coastal range just below the cloud deck. It banked and began a steep approach to a lake about halfway down the slope on the landward side of the range. As the hull kissed the water, sending up two plumes of spray, Hazeldene winced.

'What?' Owen asked.

She shook her head. 'That lake hasn't been touched by human tech until this minute. It's probably been here since the continents split. The Union settlers only arrived on Friday – I doubt they've been up here yet. God knows what unique life we may have harmed.'

'That's true with every breath and step we take,' said Jenkins. 'If God hadn't meant us to, we wouldn't be here at all.'

Owen couldn't tell if the exile was being ironic.

The flying boat coasted to the lake's northern shore. Mooring gear was thrown from the side, dragged, and caught. Wind-stirred waves, cratered by raindrops, lapped the hull. Someone threw a package attached to a rope into the water. The bundle popped and swiftly inflated into a ten-person dinghy. A dozen drones were flung out and vanished into the rain.

Lieutenant William Knight's orders carried from the upper deck.

'Sergeant Morton, take eight of your squad. Keep an eye on the feed from the drones. When you get ashore, semi-circle perimeter, fifty metres.'

'Got it, sir.'

Owen nodded to Jenkins and Hazeldene. 'Excuse me,' he said. He bounded up the stairs and made his way past the queue of soldiers.

'Lieutenant Knight!' he called out.

'What do you want?'

'If you'll permit me, I believe I can make myself useful.' He tapped his head. 'I have radio reception. I can integrate the drone feeds into a mental model, and my own senses are somewhat sharper and more extensive than yours. If there are any dangers out there, I'll be the first to notice.'

'Hmm.' Knight pondered for a moment, then nodded. 'I'll patch you the drone feeds. Morton, make room for Mr Owen.'

Morton looked along the line. 'Thompson, step aside.'

'Sir!'

The chosen soldier gave Owen a disgruntled glower as he stepped out of line. Owen returned a wry smile and a shrug of one shoulder. He was preoccupied with the pings in his head as the drone feed patched in. His sensorium suddenly encompassed a bird's-eye view of the lake, its shore and the woods as well as the interior of the aircraft.

'Nothing to worry about, as yet,' he told Knight.

The flying boat was moored about twenty metres offshore. Placing his hands and feet with deliberate care – the expanded sensorium could be disorienting – Owen clambered down to the dinghy and sat down with Morton and eight others. Someone cast off. The inflatable made its way to shore, propelled by a sinuous keel that also enabled it to crawl up a little on land. They stepped ashore dry-shod onto shingle and up a slippery bank to soggy ground covered with small green plants that looked to Owen like spindly cacti.

The dinghy, with a squirm of its keel, launched itself back into the water and swam – there was no other way to see it – back to the flying boat, where the second squad waited.

'Spread out, fifty-metre perimeter, eyes front,' Morton

ordered. He and Owen remained at the shore. The sergeant peered at some heads-up display in his glasses.

'Nothing so far,' he said.

Owen turned around several times, taking in sounds and smells as well as the multi-viewpoint sight from overhead. Low cloud hung between where he stood and the summits of Hamilton's Rise. Through the haze the crystalline rocks of the Fermi outcrop shone faintly, perhaps catching sunlight above the cloud, like a neon advertisement seen through air pollution.

Owen lowered his gaze to the lake. He tuned his eyes up and down the spectrum, from ultraviolet through visible to infrared and back. Organisms the size and more or less the shape of langoustines darted about beneath the surface, chasing smaller fry. A few bigger animals plodded on the bottom.

No immediate danger there. Turning to the slope in front and the trees, Owen detected boids wheeling among the drones, sometimes approaching with enough aggression or curiosity to force the machines into evasive manoeuvres. On the ground, small animals scuttled in underbrush, and somewhat larger animals climbed and swung among the branches. A constant buzz and clatter of wings and other limbs approached the level of noise typical of a rainforest.

The drones rose above the crest of the hill, to reveal a wooded and uneven slope down to the plain. Owen zoomed in on a clutter of rectangles, which resolved to a dozen long and irregularly spaced boxes, which seemed to be in the middle of a broad, shallow lake. In their midst a blue flag with a big yellow star in the centre flapped in the wind. Tiny figures, indistinct at that distance and through drizzle, hurried about.

'I've spotted the Union settlement,' Owen reported to Knight. 'It's been flooded.'

'Interesting. Any human presence in the woods?'

Owen sniffed the air. 'There's a smell of very distant smoke, but I can't see where it's coming from.'

'Could be exiles. I'm told there may be some around. Any sign of dangerous animals?'

'Nothing big or fast enough to pose an obvious risk. No idea about venom and so forth, of course.'

'Morton, anything untoward?'

'Nothing to report, sir.'

'OK, stay alert, but for now that's good enough for me,' Knight said. He called out: 'All clear! Sergeant Singh, your squad, then the civilians.'

Owen watched the soldiers disembark and deploy, then the scientists and some more soldiers. Hazeldene and Jenkins, shrouded in hooded raincapes over themselves and their backpacks, passed out through the hatch a long rectangular padded case, awkward and heavy, by its handle: it took two soldiers in the dinghy to stow it. They all stepped ashore and looked around.

'First impressions?' Owen said.

Hazeldene shrugged. 'Looks much like I'm used to, not around New Ardtaraig but further afield, to the south. The boids back home are a bit more melodious in their cries and calls, but otherwise . . .' She stirred her foot on the sward. 'Same vegetation.'

'I expect in a month we'll be calling this "grass",' Owen remarked.

She laughed. 'We call it "not-grass".'

'Take a look at this.' Owen flipped images of the flooded settlement to her glasses.

'Jesus,' Hazeldene said. 'Look at those idiots splashing about. Christ knows what could be in the water. We have to get to them, fast.'

'We're doing our best,' said Knight.

'Is there any way you can contact them?'

'Of course,' Knight said. 'They know we're coming.' He tapped his earpiece. 'I'm in contact with their, ah, militia commander, one Jasmine Saunders.'

'Good!' Hazeldene said. 'Well, get in touch with Ms Saunders and tell her to get her comrades out of the water, pronto. They don't know what danger they're in. I don't know what's in the water, but I know what could be in it, and it's not to be messed with.'

Knight nodded, turned away and had a brief exchange with someone on the radio.

'They got the message,' he said.

'One less thing to worry about,' Hazeldene said.

The dinghy went back and forth, taking on equipment from a robot crane arm and turning around in seconds for the return trip. The soldiers not on guard were unloading machinery and supplies from the continuing round trips, or loading supplies onto pack robots.

Jenkins pointed up at the glimmer from the summit of Hamilton's Rise. 'Our new Fermi rock.' He bent over his baggage. 'Want me to set up the apparatus?'

'Not here, or now,' said Hazeldene.

'Good God no,' said Muranov.

'Just checking,' said Jenkins, straightening up. 'We seemed to be in such a fucking hurry.' He took a deep breath, turned his face up to the rain, and exhaled. 'Ah. A new world *on* the new world. I'm not well travelled.'

'Yeah, you've only been to Venus,' said Hayes. 'Christ, I wish I'd been on that trip, just for a look at the surface.'

'I can regale you with details for hours,' said Owen. He tapped his forehead. 'Draw them, too. Perfect memory.'

Hayes gave him a narrow-eyed glance. 'Might take you up on that.'

The dinghy made its last return trip and was hauled aboard the flying boat. The four engines started up – much louder than they had sounded from inside – and the aircraft swung around, sending a wave over the shingle. It planed across the lake and took off. After circling once, it headed back over the mountain range and off over the ocean to the west.

Even some of the soldiers exchanged apprehensive glances. Owen could see why. So, evidently, could the lieutenant.

'Listen up!' Knight shouted. 'We're on our own, on a new planet, on a continent that's barely been explored. We don't know of any hostile people out there, but we know there may be some. We have to be careful. We have drones overhead, we have Mr Owen here, and we have our training. Remember that, stay alert, and we'll be fine. Now, let's move it out.'

The two squads of ten riflemen formed up. Sergeants Morton and Singh, Knight, and the medic took their positions at the front. Singh came over and directed the civilians to walk between the two squads. Behind them all, straggling up from the shore, was a line of pack robots, each heavily laden. Jenkins lugged his case down the line and burdened a pack robot further with it, strapping the load carefully in place, then hurried back. Off they all set, up the lip of the rise that cupped the lake, and down the long slope to the next rise.

Far away on the plain below, the Union flag fluttered in the breeze.

'That's the place,' the lieutenant said, pointing. 'Looks like we'll be welcome.'

He tossed another drone, an armed one this time, into the air. Under its hopefully watchful eye, they all headed downhill towards the trees.

CHAPTER SEVEN
A Peak in the Darien Scheme

New Mu, Apis, Sunday 19 October 2070

With an axial tilt of fifteen degrees, seasons on Apis were less pronounced than those on Earth. But the southern hemisphere was at the moment undoubtedly in its rainier and windier season. Hazeldene, trudging up hill and down dale through the forested foothills on a generally downward course to the plains, took some comfort from the knowledge that the rain rattling on her cape and hood would soon pass. On each side of the muddy trail left by the soldiers' tramping boots, plants – some new to her, others familiar – swayed and dripped. Invertebrates small and large crept or stalked amid the stems. Boids flitted and buzzed. Furry, eight-limbed animals that looked and sounded uncannily like gibbons hooted and brachiated through the canopy. At times the forest seemed as noisy and busy as a factory. Hazeldene felt hemmed in, with soldiers ahead and behind, and robots bringing up the rear as their baggage train, and oppressed by the rain and the warmth, but alert to this new landscape and its living things.

Sharianne Adler caught up with her.

'Oh, hi,' Hazeldene said. She felt awkward. They'd got together again for one night the previous week, after the Fermi had spoken obscure warnings on Jenkins's device, and the earthquake and tsunami had shaken New Ardtaraig. Since the morning after, they'd said nothing about it.

The younger woman smiled, raindrops on her eyelashes and stray strands of hair. 'Looking forward to doing a proper survey?'

'Oh, sure,' Hazeldene said. 'Even if it's so preliminary I can't give you any population numbers to crunch.'

'Plenty of sequencing to do in the meantime, anyway.'

'There's always that.'

They went on talking. By the time they reached the plain the rain had stopped. Hazeldene took off her cape, shook it dry and stuffed it in a side pocket of her pack. The wind was in her face rather than at her back and was now hot and dry. The clouds cleared. Large boids soared far above and small ones fluttered and hopped nearby. Among the scrubby metre-high bushes that dotted the ground, about one to every ten square metres, tiny green shoots sprouted and were already being harvested by mouse-sized scurrying insects and ten-centimetre-long flat worms. These in turn were pounced on now and then by larger animals like cat-sized crabs.

'Wow!' Sharianne said. 'It's like an ecology lesson.'

The sun was not long past local noon. Ahead, the plain glimmered in several places with water not yet soaked up or drained off. One of them was the Union encampment. Hazeldene tilted her view, and saw that the arks – they were quite like the one that had formed the centre of Jenkins's village – had been set down on either side of a stream, which had now overflowed its banks. She blinked back to a normal view and hurried on. The ground still squelched underfoot.

Up ahead of them, the robot Marcus Owen was talking with Cindy Patel, or, rather, she was talking to him, or it. Mainly about what she'd experienced at MacHinery Ridge, from what Hazeldene could overhear.

'Goddamn robot prying again. It tried to get me talking about Black Horizon.'

'Charmingly, no doubt.'

'Yeah,' said Hazeldene. 'It pisses me off that something with no more consciousness than the pack robots plodding along back there can be such a smooth talker and, you know, attentive listener, like he has all the time in the world for you.'

'To say nothing of handsome dude, eh?'

'That, too. An aspect rather wasted on me, but . . .'

Sharianne chuckled. 'Not entirely on me, I have to admit.'

The machine was nowhere near the uncanny valley – it was out the other side, its human appearance and manner flawless. Hazeldene had never seen anything like it. She'd been away from Earth for fifteen years. When she left, human-passing humanoid robots were a novelty, mainly used in applications of varying degrees of seediness, ranging from luxury shop assistant through security guard to bouncer to escort (male or female) to sex bot (ditto). None, as far as she could remember, had entirely escaped the uncanny valley. Progress even that far had been driven by an entirely benign and unrelated effort to improve prosthetics, not just cosmetically but functionally, drawing on advances in synthetic biology and 3D printing. By now, if this robot was anything to go by, the technology must have made almost any injury short of brain-death recoverable.

Some deep thinkers, following in the footsteps of Turing and Dennett, argued that any AI you could have an open-ended conversation with and whose responses on any topic remained indistinguishable from a human interlocutor was as conscious as you were. This raised troubling questions about the likes of Smart-Alec and Iskander. The software engineers who had built the robots insisted this wasn't the case. The underlying processes were completely different, and consciousness was (it had turned out) superfluous to intelligent conversation. This raised troubling questions about humans.

The robots themselves, when asked, agreed with their makers. Robots, they would tell you, could chat about your inner mental states and theirs till the lights went up and the waiters were pointedly clattering chairs onto tables, but if pressed they would admit they didn't have a clue what they were talking about.

'Company . . . halt!'

The soldiers stopped smartly, the civilians otherwise. Mud slowly rose around the welts of their boots. About three hundred metres ahead, among a cluster of long boxes that looked like a fleet of houseboats on a placid, shallow lake, the blue flag fluttered brave and dry from the mast in the middle. Hazeldene zoomed, and saw no one around. The place looked deserted.

'Looks like they've taken your advice, Emma,' Sharianne said.

'Maybe they've gone,' Georgi Muranov chortled. 'Or been eaten already. All this way for a ghost town.'

'Not a bit of it,' Marcus Owen snapped. 'The Lieutenant's talking to someone.'

'What are they saying?' Nelson Hayes asked.

'I don't know,' said Owen. He tapped his head. 'The signal's encrypted.'

Cindy Patel laughed, as if surprised. She must have forgotten, in her conversation with Owen, just what she was talking to.

A figure emerged from behind one of the arks, waded forward in shin-deep water, and waved. Lieutenant Knight waved back, then spoke to Sergeant Singh, who came back and spoke to Hazeldene.

'Your lot all got waterproof boots and trousers on?'

'Yes,' said Hazeldene. 'And I hope your lot's trousers are bite resistant. There's a local version of leech that can crunch through . . . lobster shell, say, not just skin.'

'Don't worry,' said Singh. 'Standard issue can stop a knife.'

'In that case, the main thing you have to watch out for is whipper-snappers.'

'Whipper-snappers?'

'Imagine a man-sized lobster or scorpion with two long, heavy flexible arms up front that can clobber you like a sockful of wet sand.' She looked across the plain. 'They usually prey on grazing animals that come down to drink. I can't see any grazers here, so maybe we're safe enough.'

Singh looked at her soberly. 'I'll bear that in mind, ma'am.'

He returned to Knight, and reported. The lieutenant looked back at Hazeldene, then signalled Owen to come forward. After a brief exchange, the robot moved forward into the water, with the drones patrolling low overhead. Knight relayed something to the troops, then called out:

'Company . . . forward! Slow and deliberate!'

They all squelched, and soon waded, towards the settlement. The water, now Hazeldene had a good close look at it, was hazed with dirt. Now and then a soldier would stop, and raise a splash as he or she kicked at something in the water. Hazeldene every so often felt something slither against her ankle. She knew without looking what it would be, at least in general terms: a mud lurker, which could survive months of drought as a shrivelled husk dormant in a hole and at the first sniff of water would break out to rehydrate and bulk up instantly like dried noodles in a pan. Luckily it only ate smaller prey. If the soldiers didn't know that, Hazeldene wasn't telling them. Let the sinister squirms keep them alert, she thought.

When the party was a hundred metres from the first ark, the person who had waved began walking forward to meet them. A young woman with reddish-brown hair, she stopped, looked around, blew a loud whistle and waved both arms above her head.

From under the water, from behind shrubs, from all around, scores of people jumped up, and stood with arms upraised.

They all wore hooded overalls with face masks. Water slicked off them; mud stained them. After the soldiers' moment of armed alert passed with a shouted order from the lieutenant, the settlers lowered their hands. Most headed out of the flooded area to higher ground, where – Hazeldene now saw – tents and other temporary shelters and stores had been improvised. Others walked to the arks, and dispersed to return to work. They were searching out and stacking stones from the riverbed and its overflowed banks. Already, two of the arks were on piles at each corner, keeping them just above the water.

'How the fuck did they do that?' Sharianne asked.

Georgi Muranov pointed to a stack of long poles, evidently trimmed tree trunks, propped against the side of one of the arks.

'Leverage. And simple cooperation.' He laughed. 'Stone Age technology. Primitive communism for the win, guys!'

The lieutenant spoke to the sergeants, who each led their squads off towards higher and drier ground a few hundred metres further on. The pack robots followed them.

Hazeldene led the others after Knight and the medic as they walked to meet the young woman. She wasn't wearing overalls but a T-shirt, and jeans tucked into high leather boots. She had wide pale blue eyes and a sunny, freckled, open face. Her long auburn hair was braided in a thick plait that hung forward over her shoulder almost to her waist.

They all raised hands.

'Lieutenant William Knight.'

'Marie Henderson, pleased to meet you.'

'Emma Hazeldene.'

The young woman beamed. '*The* Emma Hazeldene? Hazeldene, Dr E? The biologist?'

'Yes. How do you know me?'

'I've read your papers. The ones in the NASA pack, anyway. Wow!'

'Gosh,' said Hazeldene. 'This must be what it's like to be a rock star. Um, talk later?'

'Yes, sure.' Marie Henderson still looked awestruck.

'What was all that with the jumping up from hiding?' Hayes demanded.

'An exercise,' Marie said. 'I squared it with the lieutenant here over the radio while you were all still in the woods.' She grinned at Knight. 'He reckoned his guys could learn from it, too.'

'They learned, and I learned,' Knight said. 'Not to count too much on drones, for one thing.' He shook his head. 'The coveralls the Union folks were using have reactive camouflage weave that fooled our drones' sensors, and Mr Owen's. The weave plays wicked tricks with light and infrared.' He laughed. 'See, we're gathering actionable intel on the Union already!'

Marie looked defensive. 'It's all open-source tech.'

'How did they stay underwater?' Hazeldene asked.

'Breathed through tubes,' Marie said.

'Old Viet Cong trick,' said Knight. He snorted. '*They* used straws.'

'Jeez.' Hazeldene shook her head. 'Well, as a biologist I'll tell you this for nothing, gal – next time, try a different trick. Leaving aside the whipper-snappers and blood-suckers, which you dodged this time by dumb luck – immersing yourself in floodwater is *not* a good idea. On Earth, never mind on Apis. Not as bad as in an urban environment, but still.'

Marie nodded, frowning. 'You're right,' she said. 'The latrines got flooded when the stream rose.' She wrinkled her nose. 'We're going to have to rethink that, too.'

Hazeldene shared a disgusted glance with Sharianne, then looked at the matter more objectively. 'It might have been the sewage that saved you, if the local beasties are repelled by our wastes. I'll investigate that when I have time. Meanwhile, I suggest you get everyone who took part to take a good wash in clean water and disinfectant and get checked by the medic.'

'Thanks,' said Knight and the medic, in sarcastic unison.

'Oh, we have medics,' said Marie. 'Two doctors and five nurses.'

'That's lucky.'

'It *was* just luck,' Marie said. 'We also find ourselves with six law students, three florists, and a score of data archivists. Brilliant.' She laughed. 'It's like my boyfriend's father said – we're the Darien scheme all over again.'

'Darien scheme?' Hazeldene asked.

'A disastrous Scottish colony in Panama in the eighteenth century. Lots of lawyers and clerks and preachers, not enough farmers and manual workers, and on top of all that – on territory already claimed by another empire.' She gave Knight a wry glance. 'Sound familiar?'

'Well—' Knight began.

He was interrupted by a yell. Hazeldene turned sharply. At the far side of the flood, the last of the soldiers to approach the shore ran frantically through the water, thrashing and splashing, pursued by a black flail of limbs. Hazeldene zoomed, to confirm the worst.

'A whipper-snapper! Oh, God, I warned them!'

Just as the soldier reached land, a heavy whip-like appendage struck across his back and backpack and knocked him down. The beast was on him in a moment. It grabbed his leg with one set of pincers and his foot with the other. He screamed. A shot echoed among the cabins. The whipper-snapper convulsed. Other soldiers rushed forward and hauled the soldier away.

Knight talked rapidly in his helmet mike. 'What's up, Sarge?' he listened, then: 'Right, we're on our way.'

He clicked off and turned to the medic. 'The guy needs treatment right away.' He gave Hazeldene and Marie an odd look. 'I suppose you'd better make yourselves useful.'

They needed no second bidding.

Hazeldene didn't feel very useful when she and Marie arrived, moments behind the medic. All she could do was watch as the medic worked.

The soldier lay in a daze on the damp sward, white-faced,

pain-relief opiates just kicking in, one leg drawn up almost reflexively, the other laid out as if to at least keep the pieces lined up. His shinbone had been snapped like a breadstick and his foot crushed. The spray cylinder he'd self-injected with rolled from his loosening hand.

The medic knelt beside the casualty and slid a plastic sheet under the leg. She opened her kit and reached behind her for more. The relevant pack robot had already been summoned on the run, and stood like a patient dog while the surgery case on its back unfolded its wares.

'Shears,' said the medic. An arm extended from the case. The shears had a yellow handle and black blades. The trouser fabric might be resistant to knives, and it had indeed been not so much as torn by the bite, but it separated under the humming shears like paper. So did the boot.

'A bloody mess,' said the medic, accurately. 'Tourniquet.' Another arm extended. That done – the strap snapped around the calf at a touch – she turned to Hazeldene.

'Toxins?'

'Not likely. That beast – we call it a whipper-snapper – doesn't need toxins. But infection's possible – whack him with a shot of antibiotics and keep an eye.'

The medic nodded and reached again. 'Field surgeon.'

A chunky metal and plastic device with a rounded back and an array of specialised tools – it reminded Hazeldene of the trilobite-like smaller local fauna – was placed in the medic's hand. She laid it on the injured leg and it got to work, injecting more anaesthetic, setting the tibia and then crawling around the foot, sorting the bones, stitching up. Job done, it bleeped.

The medic picked it up and passed it behind her. The case took the device and set it aside for cleaning and disinfection. The medic reached again.

'Apis antibiotics full-spectrum, emergency injection kit.'

She sprayed the dose in and went on working: disinfecting,

dressing, applying bandages and splints which like the tourniquet shaped themselves to the leg and foot.

'OK,' she said, after about five minutes. She pushed down the soldier's shoulder. 'No, *don't* sit up.' She looked into his eyes and said fiercely, 'You're going to feel fine. You're going to feel ready to stand up and walk. Do *not* do that until *I* fucking *tell* you. Got that?'

'Yeah, yeah, OK, clear,' said the soldier, with a goofy grin, and tried again to sit up.

'Stretcher!' the medic yelled. Two soldiers hurried up and carried the casualty off. Just before she and the pack robot followed them, the medic turned to Hazeldene and Marie.

'You're the biologists, right?' She pointed to the dead whipper-snapper. 'Over to you.'

Marie walked around the animal, now and then squatting to peer closely. The shot had gone through the central nerve ganglion, the closest the whipper-snapper had to a brain, located in the closest it had to a head. Hazeldene watched approvingly as Marie systematically examined the animal's numerous segments and multi-jointed limbs, now and then zooming her glasses and prodding with the blade of a pocket knife. This young woman knew her stuff.

'It's like some enormous lobster,' Marie said, stepping back. 'But then, in places not.' She pointed. 'These heavy clubbed whip appendages, and the double set of mandibles, and the limbs with digits . . . It doesn't fit any phylum I know of. Like something out of the Burgess Shale.'

'That's exactly what it is,' said Hazeldene. 'Well, not exactly, but you know what I mean.'

'Pre-Cambrian?'

'Yeah, although . . .' Hazeldene clicked her tongue. 'That doesn't mean it was *taken* here in the Pre-Cambrian. We don't actually know when or how the biota on this planet arrived, if that's the word. We don't know anything like enough of the planet's fossil record yet. And if FTL is involved, well . . .'

'Time gets weird?'

'Yes! And if on top of that you have some kind of alien AI that has been on Earth for half a billion years, and can communicate with its counterparts on Apis . . .'

'Oh!' said Marie. 'It could have stored the genetic information back then and used it more recently to re-create – or create – the organisms here. Fuck, I never thought of that.'

'Sounds like you've been thinking a lot.'

'Oh, aye. I've been thinking about Apis since the announcement. Me and my boyfriend, Myles, we've been talking about it non-stop.' She looked around. 'But it's so amazing being here! It's stranger than Australia!'

'You've been to Australia?' Hazeldene asked, impressed.

'Uh, no.' Marie stirred mud with her foot, then looked up. 'But I've studied it. The ecology and evolution and that.'

'Australia's not a bad analogy,' said Hazeldene. 'Except that in Australia every fucking thing wants to kill you.'

They laughed.

'Whereas here . . .?' Marie pointed at the dead whippersnapper.

'Only a few specific things, yes. On the whole it's remarkably benign. You have to avoid predators like that one, and the bigger grazing animals can trample you, and you can get some nasty stings and infections from bites, but there isn't the same extravagance with venom that you get in Australia. Maybe with every predator adapted to crunch through chitin, they don't need it.'

'Yeah, benign, that's the word,' Marie said, as she and Hazeldene left the dead predator to the attentions of a growing crowd of smaller scavengers, and sloshed off again through the water to join the others among the scatter of arks. 'We've followed the notes in the information packs to hunt animals and gather fruit.'

'Really? Nobody poisoned yet?'

'So far, so good. A few mistakes, but no adverse effects apart from a rush to the nearest latrine.'

'You've been lucky,' Hazeldene said. 'Some fruits are as tricky to tell apart as mushrooms. Information packs aren't enough, even if I wrote them. You really need to be shown by someone who knows what they're doing.'

'And that's what you're here for?'

'Yes, more or less,' said Hazeldene.

Something was odd about the way the arks were being raised on stone piles. Teams swarmed from one task to the next. People moved unpredictably from one team to another, on the higher ground or in the water. All this was going on without orders being shouted or any coordination that Hazeldene could see.

'How are they doing that? Is it Iskander?'

Marie shook her head. 'No, we had Iskander just for a few hours, then lost it when the Station went away. But we found WeThink was still running on the local net.' She waved a hand skyward. 'The satellites and that, yeah? I guess the Co-ord base uses it.'

'I guess they do,' said Hazeldene. 'Must be a pretty thin version.'

'Oh, it is. But it's great for teamwork.'

WeThink was not as invasive as Iskander, or as importunate as Smart-Alec. The Co-ord didn't even try to promote it outside their own bloc. The app was freely available. You could take it or leave it. But if you took it, it enabled swift consensus formation, on any scale. An optimiser, some called it, optimistically.

Great for teamwork, all right.

In most Alliance countries it was not exactly banned, but its use was systematically hindered by engineered incompatibilities. The Union flaunted the superiority of Iskander, and openly firewalled WeThink. You could still use it, if you could be bothered with poking through the firewall, but few did.

Just as Hazeldene was pondering this and sloshing up to the others to introduce Marie, the tacit cooperation was interrupted by shouted orders.

'Clear! Clear!'

'Stay in place! Stay in place!'

Levers were lowered hastily, stones dropped. Everybody froze.

A hum, a shimmer, an electric prickle in the air. Then, with a loud pop, an ark arrived about fifty metres away from the rest.

There was a series of clunking sounds as the drive unit disengaged.

A brayed warning: 'Cover your eyes! Look away!'

Hazeldene noticed that Marie and all the settlers did exactly that, and then noticed that she hadn't, and –

Too late. A blue flash. She blinked away yellow after-images. The ark was still there, the drive unit gone. The hatch at the rear of the ark swung open. First out came a flock of camera drones. Some rose high above the settlement, some hovered just above, and others darted around like inquisitive boids. After the drone deployment, four people stepped from the ark. They were precisely made-up and coiffed, and smartly dressed in new outdoor-adventure clothing, as if they were modelling the gear. When she zoomed in she saw two men and two women who looked like celebrities and whom she didn't recognise at all.

Marie, however, did.

'Wow!' she said. 'That's Jackie Wallace! And Paul Kaminsky! And, and, um that famous Italian reporter, and . . .'

Something of a rush developed, crowding around the new arrivals. A tall young man with the beginnings of a beard walked over from the nearest ark-shifting team. He shared a laugh with Marie, and turned to Hazeldene.

'Union media stars,' he explained.

'I didn't know you had any.'

'Oh, we do,' Marie said. 'It's weird seeing them in the flesh. I always thought they were avatars.'

A drone dropped, to hover in front of them, scanning Marie and the lad.

'Most of the time, we are,' it said, and darted away.

The drones were already on the job. So were the journalists. As they fended off those crowding around, they had had eyes for only one thing, and they had only one question. Jackie Wallace pointed up at the colourful crystalline crest of Hamilton's Rise, and spoke for all of them.

'What the fuck is that?'

CHAPTER EIGHT
Meet the Press

New Mu, Apis, Sunday 19 October 2070 to Thursday 23 October 2070

Marcus Owen stood knee-deep in the filthy, infested water and blinked. The rain had stopped, the sky cleared. Overhead, drones wheeled and returned like falcons to the soldiers who had launched them hours earlier. Something in the sight made him dizzy.

'I've just cut your drone feed,' Lieutenant Knight told him. 'You don't need it any more.'

Owen's view swung forward and back. Colours faded out, then in again. Knight's hand was on his shoulder, steadying him.

'You all right, Mr Owen?'

Owen closed his eyes and gave himself a shake. He straightened up, and looked Knight in the eye.

'Fine, thanks, Lieutenant. Moment of disorientation.' He smiled. 'How very human of me.'

'Sorry about that. Should have given you more warning.'

'No problem. You weren't to know. Took me by surprise, too. I'm probably due a software update. Been away from Smart-Alec for months.'

Knight nodded, frowning. 'I'll check with our technicians and see what we can do.'

'Thanks.' Owen looked around. People were still milling around the journalists. He refocused his attention, and from overheard snatches of conversation and other communication overspill grasped the situation within seconds.

The Union, he gathered, had gone from discouraging anyone from taking up the Alliance offer to outright banning it, with patrols outside Faslane and quite unprecedented border controls on exit from Union territory. Faslane, after the Atlantic tsunami had swept it, was in no position to do much in any case. By way of preparing the ground, a campaign of media, social media and word of mouth rumour had bad news about Apis. The planet was depicted as barely habitable, conditions for the settlers as appalling, and the Alliance's intentions sinister.

Just before the boom had come down in earnest, four reporters and presenters whose reputations centred on their persistence in asking awkward questions had decided this was too good a chance to miss, and chartered the last ark out of Faslane . . .

Owen followed Lieutenant Knight to where Hazeldene stood talking with Marie Henderson and an unshaven young man who seemed to be her boyfriend. Introductions were quickly made. The lad's name was Myles, and he looked at Owen with undisguised suspicion.

'Who's in charge here?' Knight asked.

The two settlers looked at each other, as if puzzled, then at Knight and Owen.

'Uh, we have a committee,' Marie said.

'A committee?' Knight sounded incredulous.

'Yes, we elected it after we arrived.' Marie looked around. 'Oh, there's Jasmine. I think she's Defence.' She beckoned, and a young woman hurried over.

'Jasmine Saunders.'

'Lieutenant William Knight. I'm told you're responsible for defence?'

'As long as they'll have me. I came up with the underwater exercise, so maybe not for long.'

'Ha! Well, for now, I'll liaise with you. Who do you have under you?'

'There's a rota . . .'

'A rota?'

'Of volunteers for guard duty and so forth.'

'Good, good . . . Have you made any arrangements for spreading out?'

'Spreading out?'

Knight swept an arm at the horizon. 'Over the plain, or up the hills. Setting up households. Planting vegetable gardens, that sort of thing. Building fences.' He smiled ingratiatingly. 'Good fences make good neighbours, as the saying goes.'

'It's a bit early for that,' Saunders said. 'We're doing all right as we are, for now. Once we've consolidated here, we can think of spreading out.'

'You call this mess "doing all right"?'

'Well, we got landed in it – literally. And we're dealing with it.'

'Hmm.'

There was a shout as another ark was levered onto stacks of rock. When it had died down, Saunders continued. 'We're working together for now, as you see.'

Owen detected the tickle of WeThink in his skull, and firewalled it out. He let the app connect to his glasses rather than his head. He laughed. 'Facilitated by Co-ord tech, at that!'

'Well, yes,' Saunders said. 'It's what's available, and it works.'

'But surely,' Knight persisted, 'all this sort of thing is what you came here to get away from?'

'What sort of thing?'

'Working together for the common good, and all the rest of the Union's unnatural nonsense.'

Saunders frowned. 'It's natural here. Back home, some of us felt we needed more scope, so we split off to come here and make new homes. In time, our community here will start to feel confining, people will start families, see opportunities, fall out with other people or whatever, and leave. And after we've all spread out and founded our own patch, or farms or trades or businesses, we might have new problems and we'll have to pull together again. So it goes.'

'That won't happen smoothly,' Knight warned.

'Oh no!' Saunders said. 'Of course not. Conflicts are inevitable. It's all a question of how you handle them.'

'Is it, eh?' Knight flicked a hand. 'Anyway, Ms Saunders, please convey to the rest of your committee that I'd like to meet them this evening.'

'I'll do that, and we'll take a vote.'

Knight stared at her, nodded, then walked off.

'What's he upset about?' Saunders asked.

To everyone's relief, Marie and Myles led the scientists and Owen away from the arks to where the ground began to slope upward, towards the trees and the hills. The shouts and cheers of the teams levering, rocking and propping the arks faded behind them. A few hundred metres farther up the slope, the soldiers were setting up camp. Drones from the newly arrived media team watched them all, some following people around, other observing from above. Among the arks and the smaller shelters the journalists prowled, talking and listening. The whole plain was drying out, steam rising from the pools around the stream that meandered among the arks and across the plain to a river in the distance. As the ground dried it greened, with innumerable tiny shoots bursting forth.

'That's a good sign,' Sharianne Adler said. She was sitting on her cape, boots off and toes wiggling, gazing around at the fresh vegetation. She leaned back, closed eyes upturned to the sun, enjoying the heat. 'Means the rains are quite rare.'

'Still a bummer, being in a flood area,' Nelson Hayes said. 'Looks like our lot set your lot down in the wrong place. You should put in a complaint.'

Marie scoffed. 'I still can't get over being here at all, let alone being put down with centimetre accuracy across light-years.'

Owen paced about, looking this way and that, surveying the territory and taking an inventory. He paused and looked at the young woman. 'You really think that's what's going on?' He shook his head. 'There's one big jump across light-years, sure, but that just takes you to the star system, or at best close to the target planet. The final approach is made up of lots of smaller and smaller jumps, microsecond and femtosecond course corrections.'

'And how would you know that?' Hazeldene demanded.

Owen stared at her. 'You didn't notice?'

'Notice what?'

'On the ship. The submarine. Just before we arrived.' He held up his hand with outspread fingers and waved it back and forth to make shadows flicker across Hazeldene's eyes. 'Like that, but faster.'

Hazeldene shook her head. Marie watched, frowning.

'I wonder if Lakshmi knows,' she said.

Hazeldene raised her eyebrows. 'Lakshmi?'

'Lakshmi Nayak.' Marie smiled, and glanced at Myles, as if they both had something to be proud of. 'She invented the stardrive.'

Hazeldene still looked puzzled. The American geologist Nelson Hayes scoffed. 'Stole it from us, more likely!'

The Alliance scientists shared a cynical chuckle.

'No,' Owen said. 'She invented it independently. I can assure you of that. I should know – I did my best to stop her.'

Myles stared at him. 'Oh! *You're* the reason she defected.' He laughed harshly. 'So much for the wily British Council!'

'I do see the irony,' said Owen. 'Even we can make mistakes.'

It wasn't the kind of mistake he intended to make again.

Over the next few days the flood drained away or soaked into the ground, and the plain went from dusty brown to green dotted with flowers. Flocks of small grazing animals moved across it like wisps of low mist. Their predators, ostrich-sized bipeds with wicked jaws and claws, sauntered between the herds to now and then sprint at stragglers.

Owen kept a low profile. He avoided the journalists, though he couldn't avoid their drones, which haunted the settlement and overflew the lands around it. He listened in on chatter between the drones, journalists and devices, and rapidly built up his own mental model of everyone and everything. He proceeded to ingratiate himself with as many people as he could. He let WeThink guide him, and joined in as teams of settlers built new shelters up the slope, clear of the flood's high-water mark. They'd named their settlement New Rhu, after the town near Faslane.

Owen marched with groups up to the forest and cut down trees, carefully spaced out to keep the felling sustainable. He pitched in as the settlement's arks were levered onto stacked stones. He joined in with laying stone steps to the hatches, and helped stock the arks as workshops and stores. Printers came online, and Owen pitched in with gathering raw materials – sawdust, mud, forest detritus, whatever – and feeding them into the hoppers, and sorting the products the printers chugged out. When the scientists took over one ark as a lab, Owen was there to help carry and install equipment.

Further up the slope, the Alliance soldiers set up their own camp, overlooking the settlement and looking down on it. They cleared a swath of trees with buzz-saws – no sustainable felling for them – and built a two-metre-high stockade around their shelters. Owen was there to help with that, too. When they were finished the stockade looked like a Roman camp until you noticed the net of fine wire around it, the gun-bots pacing along its spiked posts and the drones giving cover overhead. Other defensive devices circumscribed a wider perimeter. Every day a patrol went out, up into the wooded hills or out across the plain. Owen was unable to join them, or the patrols of the settlement's militia, but he kept track of their movements easily enough. Now and then, from far to the west and north, he detected a faint whiff of the smoke he'd sniffed the first day as he stood at the shore of the lake. But the patrols didn't range far enough to encounter anyone – exiles, it was presumed – out there. Drones, whether from the media or the military, never found anything but ash, no matter how fast they sped to the scene.

In the evenings Owen hung out with settlers around the communal dining and drinking areas. There was talk of irrigation and agriculture, and of following the big river through the mountains to the sea with a view to establishing a shellfishery or even the equivalent of whaling – krakening, they called it. But these plans were for the future, no matter how much Lieutenant Knight taunted the settlers for being a hunter-gatherer commune in the meantime. This was not, he told them, what the Alliance expected of them. They were expected to spread out in couples and small groups and stake out claims to the land. Knight called it homesteading, a notion the settlers found hard to grasp let alone get excited about. Right now the surrounding ecosystem was abundant enough for the settlers to set aside the rations they'd come supplied with and live off the land without having to till it or water the ground.

Able Jenkins taught people to hunt small game, and seek

out useful edible roots and fruits. Ammunition being a scarce resource, they used homemade spears and bows and arrows, in whose use they were slowly becoming more proficient. Every kind of bushmeat brought back tasted like shellfish or chicken. Jenkins had better luck with hunting and gathering than he had with his mysterious apparatus, with which he was trying to talk to the supposed alien minds in the crystal rocks of Hamilton's Rise. To the settlers, Owen suspected, the effort looked like necromancy, and about as successful.

On the Wednesday afternoon Jenkins became the toast of the town – literally – when he identified an alcohol-laden fruit among the trees. The following day, after a joyous and successful trip to gather as many of these fruits as they could carry, the settlers decided it was time for a party.

Owen knew the rule for parties. It was so simple and algorithmic it had once surprised him to discover that some people didn't. It went like this. A person on their own might not want to talk. Two people might be having a private conversation. Three or more and you could just stroll up and listen with polite attention. Sooner or later someone would speak to you, perhaps assuming that one or more of the others knew you already.

The Scottish television journalist Jackie Wallace, hitherto chatting with her colleague Paul Kaminsky and a settler called Jasmine Saunders, was the one who broke first.

'Ah, hi, and you are . . .?'

Owen raised his hand. 'Marcus Owen. I'm a journalist.'

Wallace gave him the long appraising gaze of someone running facial recognition on their glasses. She wasn't wearing glasses.

'That and . . . other things, I understand.'

Owen gave his best disarming smile. 'A spy, yes.' He shrugged one shoulder. 'Everyone needs a side hustle these days.'

Wallace scoffed. 'Especially with robots like you stealing our jobs!'

'I think you'll find it isn't robots like *me* that have automated journalism.'

Wallace snorted, but lowered her eyelids and nodded slightly: point taken. 'OK, so AIs and avatars have had a lot more to do with it.'

'Ain't that the truth,' Kaminsky said, with a quick glance at Wallace, as if for permission. 'Hi, I'm Paul. Work for Scottish Broadcasting, like Jackie here. Really, I'm intrigued. How can you work as a spy when everyone knows who you are?'

Jasmine Saunders was looking at him with her eyes wide and her lips compressed. 'And what you are!'

Owen nodded to her, smiled, and looked back at Kaminsky. 'It's not so difficult,' he said. 'Take Ms Saunders here. I can tell she dislikes me, and probably finds me somewhat' – he glanced at her again – 'scary, perhaps? And yet, what does she have to fear? I have no reason to harm her. She has no secrets to hide from me. And as you're of course well aware, most of even investigative journalism isn't about finding out secrets. It's about making good use of information that's right out there in the open. It's the same with intelligence gathering.'

The two journalists nodded, and sipped their drinks. Saunders stuck her chin out, and looked Owen in the eye. She swept an arm at their surroundings. 'So what intelligence can you gather, Mr Owen, from what you see right out here in the open?'

'Ah, "Marcus", please.' He smiled. 'Let me see.'

He made a show of stretching up, craning his neck and looking around, although he had a precise and almost real-time mental model of everyone and everything around him, including many and much that was at the moment out of sight. The party was taking place in and around an emptied-out ark. Hovering drone lights illuminated the ground outside, where the dancing was going on. Fortunately it was a clear night, and people were coming into the ark only to replenish their drinks or to have a chat. Most of the settlers were taking part, and the scientists of course, along with the officer, an NCO and three lucky or privileged or rewarded privates from the military camp. Music thumped. Smoke and vapour drifted. The general look was of a pirate stronghold celebrating a rich prize on the Spanish Main.

The sweep of Owen's gaze alighted on Saunders, and stopped.

'That's a pretty dress,' he said, smiling.

Saunders grasped a handful of skirt and swayed it. 'Thanks.'

'Same period style as most of your compatriots here are sporting. Why?'

'Darien scheme,' she said. 'It's kind of a joke on ourselves.'

'It's that all right!' Owen said. 'Did you bring all these costumes in your luggage?'

'Oh no! Of course not. We printed them this afternoon, from leaf litter, mostly.' She laughed. 'The fabric's really fake and flimsy. They'll all get recycled in the morning.'

Owen gave her a knowing smile, to hint at an urbane familiarity with tear-off party wear.

'Still a significant use of resources, and time, on a frivolity. Why?'

She shrugged bare shoulders. 'It's Thursday evening.'

'It's Thursday evening,' he agreed. 'In the Union – the beginning of the weekend. You and your fellow settlers have come here against Union advice. You're in a pioneer settlement, where there's no such thing as the weekend. Yet here you are, having a Thursday night bash as if you were back home with the four-day week, full employment and the basic income safety net! What does that tell you?'

'It's our first Thursday here,' Saunders said, her voice rising a little. 'We've done a lot, and we have a lot to celebrate. We want to welcome the journalists and the soldiers. We've been working hard all week. And most of us will be working just as hard tomorrow.'

'Perhaps not *just* as hard,' Owen said, with a conniving chuckle. 'To continue. Drink is being taken. Substances are being inhaled. I'm not seeing excess, but nor am I seeing parsimony.'

'The exile – Jenkins, isn't it?' Jackie Wallace put in. 'He seems to have discovered a local natural source of hooch.' She sipped from a paper cup of what looked like pineapple juice. 'Not bad, as it happens.'

'And by no means the only drink here.' Owen gestured at the bottle-laden trestle beside them. 'A moderate ration of recreational supplies came in the arks, and some people may have brought their own, but they're being consumed in a way that suggests confidence in continuing supply. What does that tell you?'

Saunders said, 'Well, you tell me, Mr – Marcus, that's what I asked!'

Owen saw Lieutenant Knight a couple of metres away, reconnoitring, an almost full paper cup in hand, glasses on, head turning this way and that. Owen caught the officer's eye, and projected his voice to catch his ear, too.

'What it tells me,' he said, 'is that most of you here are not the bold individualist pioneers you fancy yourselves, but people who would be only too happy to recreate the Union out here, minus the aspects that rub you the wrong way back home: the prying solicitude of Iskander, the likewise infuriating oversight of the cadre organisation, the insolence of the firewall, the self-righteous yammer of ideology. Your confidence in a continuing supply of civilised amenities tells me you're all pretty sure the Union will see reason, and open up settlement and trade with Apis quite soon – at any rate, before all your bottles of cheap spirits are empty!' He looked around, at Saunders, Kaminsky, Wallace, and the now wholly attentive Lieutenant Knight. 'Now that's some useful intelligence, wouldn't you say?'

Jackie Wallace put down her drink and clapped her hands,

three times. 'Very good, Marcus!' She looked up to a corner of the ark, where as Owen well knew a camera watched and recorded. 'Mind if we use that?'

'Not at all,' Owen said. He turned to Saunders. 'Would you like to dance?'

'Yes,' she said. 'But not with you, thanks.'

He bowed. 'Good evening, then, and thanks for a most interesting conversation.'

'Hey,' said Jackie Wallace, stepping forward as he turned away. 'I'll give you a whirl.'

CHAPTER NINE
Black Gospels

The Space Station around E-PRIME 667, Monday 27 October 2070

'This thing,' Nayak told Grant, 'is *insanely* precise. For mapped and known worlds, anyway.' She leaned over Grant's shoulder and tapped the rim of the navigation app in the simulator. 'Femtosecond timing gets you to within ten metres over a light year. Interplanetary distances, you're talking centimetres. Which is why the final approach anywhere is stuttered, though the drive goes on and off far too fast for any human to notice. You could be in Mars orbit and aim your ship for the top of Olympus Mons, and your only worry would be whether any big stones had shifted since the last survey picture was taken. You could take it to the Clyde, and you'd have to correct for the *tide*. Fortunately the tide tables are in the memory, too.' She frowned. 'The only problem could be wave height if it's stormy, or colliding with a ship or a boat. Your final cushion is the residual effect of the warp bubble powering down. It's best to aim for a few metres up and use the last few seconds of powering down for corrections or evasive action or, at a pinch, powering up again, like I did over Venus. So make sure you have somewhere safe pre-set to jump to, and I don't mean up in the sky or even low Earth orbit. Somewhere uncluttered. Ah, wait, look, I'll set these myself.'

'Fine.' Grant tipped the seat back as she leaned in. 'I'll let you get on with it.'

She tapped numbers and flipped switches. 'Sorry to poke in like that.'

'No worries,' Grant said. 'It's a lot easier than what I put you through in the rig back at the yard in Port Glasgow.' He looked up at her. 'Why did you never say anything about this business of the stutter, even when I was training you to fly this thing?'

'You didn't need to know,' Nayak said. 'And it would only have been one more thing for you to worry about.'

'Fair enough,' Grant said.

'Right,' said Nayak, 'OK, let's see how you do on an approach to the Clyde . . .'

That exercise ended in a fall from twenty metres up and the simulator screen going black.

Grant threw up his hands. 'Shit! Sorry.'

'Try again,' Nayak said. 'You'll get the hang of it eventually.'

After the Station's first couple of days in the new system, Nayak began to feel almost at home. Like everyone else she had her own cubicle with a bed. For work she could hot-desk screens and tables. She could get food from the refectory and notebooks and pens from the printer. The washrooms were shared, but the nearest was only a few metres down the corridor. Distinctions between states of dress and undress didn't matter when you could pull on yesterday's overall when you rolled out of bed, go to the washroom, pick up a clean set from a dispenser on the way back, and throw yesterday's in the recycling on the way out.

Like most people, the first thing she did on her way out was to run down the endless corridor, around and around the Station's habitation band, clocking kilometres. Usually she'd call up some natural scene on her glasses, with sound, and run along forest trails or sea-loch shores. She missed the smells of Earth's earth.

When she was out and about she always found plenty of interesting people to talk to. Not even university could compare with Cloud City and the Station as a community consisting almost entirely of scientists and engineers. Even depleted and traumatised by the disaster, that community still existed on the Station, and almost everyone was eager to talk. Mainly, Nayak suspected, because they were still grieving. Almost everyone had lost a friend, a colleague, a lover. Work and talking about work was the only way they could cope.

The chief engineer Gironella chivvied people and wrangled machinery to get a telescope built and launched within a week. One of the Station's many small robotic rocket tugs placed it in its own orbit a few kilometres from the Station. The telescope turned its lenses this way and that, building up a picture of the system's worlds and worldlets. All but the small exomoons and asteroids had already been detected and logged by E-PRIME, back in the Solar system, but probably no human or even artificial intelligence had given that meagre information any closer inspection. Now anyone looking at the feed from the telescope could survey the system's exoplanets across tens or hundreds of AU, rather than hundreds of light-years.

Nayak was amused and not at all surprised or disappointed that the speculative renderings of these planets in her navigation app turned out to be wrong. The gas giant didn't have a ring. The two inner rocky planets didn't have atmospheres. The next rocky planet out was a frozen water-world, with no curious streaks on the ice that might be traces of life. And so on. All this was exciting new knowledge, the more so as it suggested that exploiting the system's resources wouldn't harm any existing life, let alone intelligence.

No life meant no harm. Nayak had a moment of doubt about that, then reflected that if you worried about accidentally trampling something unique and fragile but non-living, you wouldn't take a step on Earth, let alone off it. And anyway, there would always be other systems . . . which thought in turn she questioned, as a dangerously cavalier attitude that could all too easily catch on in the world she had made. Then she laughed at her self-importance and got back to work.

The Station ran, as far as entropy would allow, on closed-loop cycles. The asteroid rubble at its core contained enough water ice, carbon compounds, nickel-iron and other minerals to keep it going for a long time, or to build a lot of machinery in a short time. Its fusion pots meant it could do without external energy sources, though back in Venus orbit it had relied largely on solar power. The Station would need to rely on it again, indeed, if they were to use some of the fusion pots to power new drives. For the moment it was too far from the local sun for that. There were enough people on board, with enough genetic diversity, to start a viable human population. If – in the worst case – the entire human race were to be buried in the rubble of every planet mined by the alien rocks, the Station could start the species over again. And not only human: they had the genetic information to recreate countless other species, including many long since extinct. Civilisation could continue, too: the entirety of recorded public knowledge as of last week was in Iskander's memory.

That was for the worst case. The best case was that they could make a start on building habitats in this system of such scale and capacity and potential that people tempted by the offer of Apis would instead flock to live in them: in a literal heaven, rather than on a planet terraformed by, and at the mercy of, strange gods.

Nayak, looking up from calculations and production plans at blank or pictorial walls, sometimes had her doubts about the attractions of space habitats. Cloud City survivors told her tales and showed her pictures of what that had been like, airy and spacious, nothing at all like the Station. She dutifully scrolled through the pictures, and listened to the stories, and thought it was their nostalgia talking. No space habitat, even in the brightest visions of great wheels or cylinders all green, blue and white within, attracted her in the least, or struck her as likely to attract many people. But it wasn't her job to question that aspect of the plan – her doubt was speculative, and might be mistaken – and in the meantime she had urgent and congenial work to do. Her work in material requirement planning was turning out to be a lot more useful here than her theoretical physics.

First things first. Whatever resources the system held remained for all practical purposes out of reach until the Station had its own FTL drive as well as a fleet of shuttles with FTL drives.

Moving the entire Station to every interesting rock would be impractical. Getting stuff on and off any surface at the bottom of a significant gravity well would be downright impossible with the rockets and jets the Station's shuttles already had. The first task was to build a drive – a flywheel, as Grant's team had called it back home – for the Station, then to build one for each of the two existing shuttles. The next, after these had been tested, would be the more challenging task of building new spacecraft capable of mining and retrieving as well as exploring.

Well within the Station's capability, Gironella assured her.

When the shuttle drives were built, and the Station's self-sufficiency assured, the *Fighting Chance* and all who wanted to leave with her could go home.

Nayak still wasn't sure whether or not she'd be among them.

The Space Station around E-PRIME 667, Tuesday 28 October 2070

A voice from behind, in the corridor:

'Uh . . . Dr Nayak?'

Nayak turned. It was Francesca Milloy: the first woman on Venus; the last to be rescued from Cloud City before it fell; the last to leave the *Fighting Chance* after the jump to Apis orbit. Nayak had glimpsed her from afar during the memorial meeting – that strange, sad ceremony distributed along the endless corridor in many separate huddles of friends, colleagues, strangers – but she hadn't seen her since.

Milloy had looked upset then, but so had everyone else. Now she seemed calm, but worried.

Nayak smiled and raised a hand. '"Lakshmi", please.'

Milloy raised a hand, and a wan smile. '"Francesca". I . . . was wondering if I could have, uh, a chat? In private?'

Nayak tried not to show the weariness of a day training pilots in simulators. 'Sure! I'm just on my way to my cubicle. Grab a coffee and we can sit on the bed.'

As the door slid shut Nayak asked, 'How private?'

Milloy sighed. 'No need to screen out Iskander. It knows everything anyway.'

'That's why I'm not listening,' said Iskander.

'Ha!'

Nayak conjured screens to give an illusion of space. They sat on the side of the bed and gazed out over a forested valley with mountains in the distance. Milloy fidgeted. 'Do you mind if I vape?'

Nayak turned up the ventilation. 'Puff away.'

Milloy drew hard, and exhaled a cloud, which vanished into an air duct. She turned to Nayak with an earnest look. 'Do you ever read the Black Gospels?'

'I've . . . skimmed them.'

The Black Gospels were a collection of texts by and about

the Greek materialist philosopher Epicurus, found in the ruins of a Roman villa at Herculaneum buried by ash from the eruption of Vesuvius in 79CE. Recovering all the writings on these rolled-up, carbonised papyri had been the work of centuries, and its completion a technological triumph of the mid-2030s. A selection became a 2038 Penguin Classic, and a surprise success. Turbulent times and existential unease over new scientific discoveries had made them unexpectedly resonant.

Finding meaning in a meaningless but endlessly fascinating universe had never been Nayak's problem. In the West, people found in the Black Gospels news, even good news. Where she came from, atheism and materialism were considered to be schools of Hindu thought.

'Don't worry,' Milloy said. 'I'm not here to ask, "Do you have a few minutes to talk about our great teacher Epicurus?"'

Nayak laughed. 'OK.'

'But, well, I have been reading what he thought about free will and the unpredictable swerve of the atoms, and so on. And it's helped me to frame a question I have for you: can a robot be responsible for its actions?'

'Oh,' Nayak said. 'I take it you have one particular robot in mind?'

'Yes, of course. Marcus Owen.'

'I've met him.' Nayak said.

'You have?'

'Oh yes. Twice, years ago.' Nayak waved a hand. 'Long story. The irony is, at that time even he didn't know he was a robot. By chance we got talking about robots, and I said to him that we're all robots.'

'Meaning what?'

'We're all physical systems, therefore deterministic. But we're still responsible for our actions, or at least some of them.'

'What about actual robots? Are they responsible?'

Nayak could see where this was going. 'Look, Francesca, if you want some kind of justice meted out to Marcus Owen—'

'No, no!' Milloy said. 'I don't want *justice*. I want revenge.'

Nayak wanted to give her a hug, but didn't. 'I think revenge is irrational even on people, let alone machines! But—' she sighed '—if you ever do get the chance, well, I wouldn't blame you. I don't believe in karma, but you might be the means by which it gets delivered.'

'I'll take that,' Milloy said.

The Space Station around E-PRIME 667, Thursday 30 October 2070

'To tell youse the truth,' said Morag Rafferty, 'I'm feeling kindae redundant.'

Grant snorted. 'Aren't we all?'

He, Nayak and Khan had shared and explained the designs of the flywheel and its controls. Nayak had turned in a new set of production plans for the Station. She'd updated the navigation app, from speculation to observation. After that, Gironella and his team had said, in effect, 'Thanks. We'll take it from here.' The tacit knowledge and knacks that Grant, Rafferty and Khan all had picked up from building the original flywheel were, they were told, irrelevant in this new environment. The only task left to Nayak was training ten new pilots in simulators of the shuttle controls. And on the side: Grant, in his own simulation of the controls and navigation app of the *Fighting Chance*.

It was notionally evening on the Station. Lights had dimmed in the corridor outside the refectory. The crew of the *Fighting Chance* – Grant, Ellen, Nayak, Rafferty and Khan – and Francesca Milloy, who had taken to hanging out with her fellow Scots, were sitting around a table, sipping raw spirit variously diluted with fruit juice and other soft drinks, *faut de mieux*. Milloy was puffing synthetic nicotine, likewise flavoured.

'They barely need avatars,' Rafferty went on, 'and when they do they won't let me so much as look at them in case I break them.'

'They say that?' Grant was stung to indignation.

'Not in so many words,' Rafferty allowed, 'but I can tell it's what they're thinking.'

'Well,' said Ellen, 'what they're doing is different and more delicate than ship-building. It's in microgravity and mostly in vacuum, for a start.'

'I could learn.'

Khan regarded Rafferty sternly. 'You're cadre,' he said (like *she* needed reminding, Grant thought), 'so you should take this as an opportunity for study and self-improvement. There are whole new worlds out there, and not enough people to even go through the data.'

'Not enough?' Rafferty scoffed. 'They have two qualified astronomers, the place is hoaching with planetary scientists, and they have Iskander to crunch the numbers. What exactly would you say, Omar, that that leaves for me to contribute?'

'You could at least learn until somebody finds something for you to do.'

'Aye, right. I'm not much of a one for sitting on my arse reading or viewing. I need the practical side of things as well.' She flexed her fingers, as if missing the haptic gloves of the avatar operating rig. 'Don't like twiddling my thumbs, either.'

'Forget all this work ethic nonsense,' said Ellen. 'Treat it as a holiday. You deserve one, after the past few months building the ship, let alone the Venus rescue. That's what I'm doing. Sunlamp, lounger, virtual view and synthetic sangria, ah!' She leaned back, arms outspread. 'An infinite – well, enormous – library to keep my mind occupied, and exercise machines to keep my weight down and my muscles toned.'

Grant gave his wife a thumbs-up. But Khan and Rafferty turned to her with scandalised looks.

'We can't do that!' Khan said.

Milloy exhaled an apple-scented cloud. 'Why not?' she demanded. 'Take things easy for a change. The mountains are high and the emperor is far away.'

'Never higher or farther,' Ellen added, with a laugh.

'That's . . . not actually the case,' Khan said. 'The cadre organisation had a branch in Cloud City, and a cell on the Station.'

'Did it?' Milloy asked. 'I thought we were all scientists together, a free cooperation without any of that Earth politics stuff getting in the way. We already had our own little utopia, so what would be the point?'

'Maybe if—' Grant bit his tongue, too late.

Ellen glared. Milloy took a draw and a sip. 'All right,' she said. 'Spit it out.'

'I wasn't—' Again with the too late tongue bite.

'It's nothing I haven't thought myself,' Milloy said. '*Maybe if* I had been more politically aware, I wouldn't have let myself get fucked and fucked over by that fucking robot. That's what you were going to say, isn't it?'

'Well—'

Grant was saved further embarrassment by the arrival of Peregrine Walworth, who manifested behind Milloy's shoulder looking and smelling fresh from the gym and a shower via the self-service bar. Shorts, T-shirt, towel over his shoulder, drink in hand.

'Did I overhear someone bad-mouthing my former cultural attaché?' He pulled up a seat and set down a tall plastic glass of something orange. Ice cubes clinked. 'And blaming herself?' He turned to Milloy, shaking his head. 'Don't.'

'Why the hell shouldn't I?'

'It isn't mentally healthy, for one thing.' Walworth put fingertips to his forehead and mimed deep thought. 'I thought you people believed in determinism?'

'It's a little more—' Grant began.

'Yes, but—' said Nayak at the same time.

Milloy looked puzzled and irritated.

Walworth waved an impatient hand. 'Yes, yes. My point is, your officially promoted schools of thought' – he dipped his head towards Rafferty and Khan – 'and if I understand correctly, your actual schools teach that beating ourselves up over our mistakes and even misdeeds is entirely unproductive and unhelpful in improving matters by finding the internal and external causes of our actions, and if necessary correcting them.' He faced Milloy again. 'Am I right?'

'I suppose so, but that's got nothing to do with—'

'Ah, but it has! You see, Citizen Milloy, you may know all these wise words of, let's say, Spinoza about the folly and futility of repentance, but they do nothing to help you because you haven't got a practical grasp of the situation you were in, so you can't apply them to it. I have, and I can. No credit to me – it's my job after all. I assure you no level of political awareness, of vigilance, on the part of you and anybody else could have prevented Marcus Owen doing what he set out to do. If not in one way, then another. Your personal relationship with him? Incidental. He cut a dash, he cut a swath through your colleagues, male and female, did he not?'

Milloy smiled wanly. 'He made no secret of that, at least.'

'If he hadn't taken that approach, he would have taken another. Instead of charming you, he could have fascinated some well-placed scientists and engineers with the depth of his understanding of problems with their work. Suggested brilliant solutions, even. He wasn't engaged in a dance of deception with you, Francesca. He was engaged in a dance of deception with Iskander. A dance that had two partners.'

'I know *that*,' Milloy said miserably. 'At some level, Iskander colluded with . . . him. The instance in the descent suit, the one that now calls itself Sikandar, as good as told me.'

'If I may interrupt,' said Iskander, from all around like a god. 'It's true that I used the robot as a precautionary probe of the outcrop, but beyond that I don't know what you're talking about.'

'You wouldn't,' said Walworth. '"You" being the chatty user interface and front end of an intelligence that in the nature of the case doesn't understand itself, and doesn't bloody need to!'

'I'll take that as a dismissal,' said Iskander, in a huffy tone.

'Yes, you do that,' said Walworth. He took a sip of his drink and sighed. 'Don't you people ever get tired of living under the all-seeing AI? I know I do.'

Milloy laughed. 'Better than living above the all-shaking alien rocks, like every other poor fucker in the human race.'

'Funny you should say that,' said Walworth. He swirled his drink and sipped. 'It's not just the human race in that unfortunate position. Your nemesis is, too.'

'What?'

Walworth raised his eyebrows. 'Didn't you know? It seems Marcus Owen was rescued in the nick of time by the Alliance submarine that your friend Sikandar encountered, and taken to Apis.' He waved a hand. 'There's some talk of him trying to continue the conversation so rudely interrupted on Venus, but I find that quite fanciful.'

Milloy looked stunned.

'Wait,' said Grant. 'I got the impression from the Commander's bulletins that the Alliance scientists on Apis had been pretty much excluded by the Co-ord from the rocks they'd been blundering about in, even before we warned them off.'

'Oh yes,' said Walworth. 'But the Co-ord has no jurisdiction over the rocks on New Mu, because that's now officially your bailiwick, as far as we and they are concerned.' He smiled. 'Union territory, whether the Union admits it yet or not.' Ice rattled as he drained the watery remains of his drink. 'Best be off.' He stood up, and very nearly clapped Milloy's shoulder, without quite touching it. 'Poetic justice for the bastard, eh?'

Milloy looked daggers after him.

'The thing to remember,' said Ellen, 'is he's still the Alliance consul.'

'Meaning what?'

'Everything he says is calculated to advance his agenda.'

'Whatever that is!'

'I'll tell you what it is,' said Ellen. 'It's so transparent! He didn't come here to put your mind at rest about Marcus Owen. He came here to tell you the robot is down on Apis.' Ellen made pistol fingers. 'And to point you at him. He wants you to destroy it.'

'Not much chance of that, from here,' said Milloy. 'And anyway, why? Owen's an Alliance tool. Why would the Alliance consul want Owen destroyed?'

'Same reason as you do,' said Ellen. 'Walworth's a cool customer, but he's human. He was in Cloud City like the rest of you. He went through the same horror as you did, and he wants revenge.'

'Revenge on a robot?' Milloy gave a bitter laugh. 'I mean, I want to tear that machine limb from limb.' She glanced at Nayak. 'I *know* it's irrational, like kicking some machine that's let you down, but with me it's personal. Why would Perry feel the same?'

'I can think of two possibilities,' Ellen said. 'One is – well, the same as yours.'

Milloy shook her head firmly. 'Nah. Perry isn't gay, or bi.'

'You sure?'

'It was a small world back there,' Milloy said.

'In that case,' Ellen said, 'we're left with the other possibility. He wants revenge not so much on the robot, but on those who *sent* the robot.'

'The Alliance? His own side?'

Ellen shrugged. 'The robot's a tool of some British intelligence service, which was quite willing to risk Walworth's life as well as the lives of everyone else on Cloud City. Now it's risking heaven knows what disasters on Apis, if Owen really is going to attempt communication with the alien rocks. Sending you after him would be a nice, deniable way of putting a stop to that.'

Milloy scoffed. 'That would be a very roundabout ploy, even for Perry!'

But she looked thoughtful for the rest of the evening.

CHAPTER TEN

The Keeper of the Bees

New Mu, Apis, Thursday 6 November 2070

Sunlight glinted on the robot and the axe. Dew sparkled on the not-grass and the leaves. Myles Grant worked his way along the edge of the forest, chopping down every third mature tree. He stripped the branches and trimmed the logs, each about twenty centimetres thick and three metres long. The robot, a quadruped with a disquieting habit of rearing on its hind legs, followed him a few logs behind, bundling them up in fives ready for loading and hauling away.

He paused at nine local time, and sat down on the nearest bundle to pour a coffee from his Thermos and eat a cereal bar. The robot paused, too, settling down on its haunches like a dog. Monkey-spiders – red-furred arachnoids the size and shape and habit of gibbons, except with six limbs and four eyes – that had been scared off by the felling returned to nearby treetops, chiding Myles with harsh hoots.

Myles looked back at the forest and checked on his glasses for the dots that indicated the locations of Marie, Hazeldene and Jenkins. Everything seemed fine. They were up there in the wooded hills, kilometres away by now, on a biological survey and (if Jenkins had anything to do with it) a hunt. Two other groups were hunting, closer by, in the woods.

The monkey-spiders hooted at him again. What did they have to complain about? Nobody hunted monkey-spiders. Jenkins had been hard put to explain why. It just wasn't done, he'd said. Hazeldene had chipped in with a plausible rationalisation of the taboo: the animals were so fast-moving and elusive that hunting them would be a waste of energy, and moreover they were an ecological keystone species. Omnivorous, they preyed on the fast-breeding, slow-moving scuttlers of the underbrush, and feasted on fruit whose seeds their droppings sowed far and wide.

Myles turned away from the woods. No point in worrying about Marie. He checked her location again. Still fine.

About a kilometre downslope from the tree line, his co-workers Jody and Rob were returning along the already rutted path to take another load of logs away. Their cart was a timber triangle lashed and glued together, with two printed wheels, pulled by a pack robot. Southward, away to his right, was the Alliance camp. The flag of the United Kingdom flew from a flagpole in the south-west corner.

Down in the settlement, the journalists and their portage machines were hurrying back and forth to their ark with luggage, letters home from settlers, and various specimens and souvenirs from their two and a half weeks in and around New Rhu. The tractor unit was scheduled to return sometime that day. Some of the journalists' drones still buzzed around, making a last sweep for information.

When he zoomed his glasses, Myles could see hunters from the settlement stalking grazers on the plain. Even farther away, the geologists Nelson Hayes and Cindy Patel were out somewhere along the distant bank of the big river, gathering rock samples and pebbles. Marcus Owen, the robot, was keeping them company, and keeping guard.

Myles shook out the cup, screwed it back on the Thermos and picked up the axe. The cart was now five hundred metres away. Myles waved and turned to the trees. The robot stirred, its turret sniffing the air. Myles walked to the next tree, put down the axe and ducked to spit on his hands –

A whir and a thunk. Where his head had been a split second earlier, a metre-long shaft with vanes on the end vibrated in the tree trunk. Myles threw himself flat, and got his head and shoulders behind the inadequate protection of the other side of the tree.

A crackle of small-arms fire came from the direction of the military camp. Above the camp, flashes and puffs of smoke, their sound arriving a second or two later, marked the defences intercepting an incoming flight of arrows. Myles heard yells, then a scream: someone in the camp must have been hit. From higher up, drones converged, dived and sped across the clearing and in among the trees in search of the arrows' source.

Myles kept down. His only weapons were the axe and a knife. Soldiers ran and robots darted in the compound. The screaming had subsided, but shouts and yells continued. No sound came from the forest, and no further volley. After a couple of minutes the drones flew back out and resumed their patrol, some climbing higher for a wider view. Evidently they'd found nothing in the forest. An alert pinged in his phone and fleshed in his glasses, from the channel shared by the Alliance military and the New Rhu militia.

Still keeping low, Myles pulled down his glasses and held out his phone, turning it this way and that to look around. Nothing stirred. The monkey-spiders had fled. Myles rolled on his back. A media company drone the size of a humming-bird hovered a few metres up. He ignored it, and called Marie. After a few rings, she answered.

'Hello?' She sounded preoccupied.

'Hi, Marie. We're under attack!'

'What?'

'Someone's just shot a flight of arrows at the soldiers' compound. Most of them got zapped by the drones and bots, but some got through.'

'Oh, shit!' she said. 'You OK?'

'Yes, I'm fine.' He didn't mention the near miss.

'Ah, wait – the alert's just reached us. Anyone hurt?'

'One guy was screaming, so yes. Stopped now, so either he's got attention or . . . it's bad.'

'Sorry to hear that. Don't worry about us. We're all armed, Able's very alert, we have a drone scouting, and we haven't heard or seen any other people.'

'Maybe it's aliens you have to watch out for.'

'Ha, ha. But seriously – we know there are exiles out there somewhere, we just haven't found them yet. Looks like they've found us.' She sighed. 'We're in the middle of something. Thanks for the warning, and take care yourself. Love you.'

'Love you too.' Myles rang off, and raised his head warily. Downhill, Rob and Jody had jumped off the cart and taken cover. The cart was now a couple of hundred metres away, the pack robot plodding on regardless. They'd have done better to stop the cart and take cover behind or under it. Myles was about to call the Alliance contingent when a message from the same number pinged on his phone.

'All clear. One casualty, no fatalities. Remain alert.'

The guard for the day at New Rhu had evidently come to the same conclusion, and taken up defensive positions with rifles at the ready. Myles tabbed to the militia channel on WeThink. A posse was already forming. He volunteered and was turned down. They already had scores of people to choose from with far more useful skills, some with actual combat experience from overseas solidarity missions. He wasn't sure whether he was offended or relieved. As he stood up, the hovering media drone darted away. It paused above Rob and Jody, then flew back to the settlement.

Rob and Jody rose to their feet then hurried up the track. WeThink had turned them down, too, Myles saw, feeling slightly less miffed. Still, might as well make himself useful. He stepped back around the tree and tugged on the arrow. It didn't budge. He made short work of bringing down the tree.

'Timber!' he shouted, just before it toppled. Rob and Jody were by now close enough to make the warning polite, if not strictly necessary. The tree fell on the side opposite the arrow.

They stood looking at it.

'Christ!' said Rob. 'That could have gone right through your skull.'

'Yeah, I'd noticed.'

'It would have been the last thing to cross your mind,' Jody said.

Myles hacked deep into the wood around the arrow, and used his knife to finish the job. The arrow now had a chunk of wood on the end. Myles made to cut it open.

'Could be poisoned,' Jody warned.

'Damn, yes, I hadn't thought of that.' Myles pulled on safety gloves, and carefully dug into the chunk on opposite sides until it split. Behind the arrow's point – still sharp even after penetrating the tree trunk – were rows of barbs. Like the vanes on the end, they seemed fused with the shaft, which didn't feel or look like wood. Tapped, it rang. Flexed, it didn't snap.

'Weird,' said Myles. 'Looks high-tech. Like plastic or carbon-fibre or something like that.'

'You reckon this came out of a printer?' Jody said.

'It sure looks like it did.'

Rob scoffed. 'Where the fuck would exiles get a printer from?'

'We don't know what the original exiles had on their arks,' Jody pointed out.

'From what we've heard from Able Jenkins,' Myles said, 'the exiles weren't *that* well provided for.'

'I'm not sure they even had printers back then,' said Jody.

'Not like ours, anyway,' Myles said. 'But they could have got these from the Alliance or the Co-ord.'

'Or from us,' said Rob.

'What?'

Rob waved an arm at New Rhu. 'Who's to say one or a few of us didn't see an opportunity?'

'Making contact with exiles, not telling anyone, and giving or trading them printed arrows?' Myles scoffed.

'It's possible,' Rob said.

'Nah,' said Jody. 'Not without somebody noticing.'

'Enough with the speculation,' Myles said. He took out his phone and called the Alliance compound. They took half a minute to pick up.

'Sergeant Al Morton speaking. This better be important.'

'Sorry to bother you, Sergeant. First off, is everyone OK?'

'We've got a guy skewered through the shoulder, but the medic reckons he can be fixed.'

'Any signs of poison?'

'Nah, just infection. Local bugs. Nothing the antibiotics can't handle. Why you asking?'

'We've got an intact arrow up here, and I wondered if . . .'

The sergeant snorted. 'Keep it, mate. We've got a few, as well as lots of shot-up fragments. Funny thing, the drones and bots haven't picked up a sniff of man or beast off them. Anyway. We'll get our scientists on the case soon as.'

'Yes, of course. Thanks, well . . .'

'Bye,' said Morton, and rang off.

They got back to work cutting and loading. A dozen New Rhu settlers toting rifles marched at a fast pace up to the Alliance camp. The posse joined six soldiers at the gate of the stockade. The squad had a pair of robots trotting alongside, smaller and even more canine in appearance than the one loading the logs. Drones flitted ahead of them, and a large camera drone from the journalists followed. Myles wondered what viewers back home would make of the scene. To him, it brought to mind some colonial manhunt. Together, the soldiers and the settler militia disappeared into the forest.

'Safe home, comrades,' said Jody.

There was a moment of silence. Myles dithered, feeling useless and angry. He'd almost been killed. If he didn't hit back now at whoever was responsible, his anger would find another outlet, likely a bad one.

'Oh, the hell with this!' He handed Jody the arrow and Rob the axe, and ran towards the trees after the posse.

Hazeldene checked the alert and updates on her phone. There didn't seem anything she could do, or any danger nearby. The sun was now above the treetops and the light was harsh and hot. Boids clattered and buzzed in the foliage. Somewhere a troop of monkey-spiders squawked derision.

'So what do you think?' Marie said, after relaying Myles's report. 'Head back now?'

'Not bloody likely,' said Jenkins. 'Not when we've just spotted that.'

A circular clearing littered with big odd angular shapes had just shown up on the images from their overhead drone. Their excited examination of the images had been interrupted by the call from Myles.

Hazeldene nodded. 'It's too close and too interesting to ignore. And, anyway, is going back now any safer than going back later?'

Jenkins looked at his phone. 'They're mobilising. WeThink isn't telling us to change our plans, just to stay in the loop and stay alert. Probably best keep out of the way, and lie low if anything develops. So I say press on.'

'So do I,' Hazeldene said.

'I'm not so sure,' said Marie. 'Fuck, nobody said anything about indigenous people. I don't want to fight them.'

'They're no more indigenous than I am, whoever they are,'

said Jenkins. 'We're all invaders here. And if they shot arrows first, they're invading us.'

'That's not the point. They know the territory and we don't.'

'Look,' said Hazeldene, trying to calm things, 'we can just check out this place, then circle back, with the drone scouting and us keeping quiet and alert. OK?'

'Yeah, I suppose so.' Marie took out her pistol, and kept looking around as the three of them made their way through the trees and undergrowth to the clearing about fifty metres ahead. At its edge, they paused.

'Talk about an elephants' graveyard,' said Jenkins.

Hazeldene winced. When Jenkins's parents had been transported, and when the encyclopaedic information on his father's phone had been last updated, there were still elephants. She didn't disabuse him.

'Yes,' she said brightly, before Marie could chip in with a predictable comment that the elephants' graveyard was a myth anyway. 'That's just what it's like! Let's investigate.'

Jenkins unslung his rifle. They stepped over a log and out from under the trees into the clearing. And clearing it was: the tree stumps were old, overgrown with lichen and moss, and flat on top as if they'd been cut with a saw. Ancient rotting logs lay around the edge of a roughly circular open space, about twenty metres across and littered with heaps of gigantic broken carapaces.

Watched over and followed by Jenkins, Hazeldene and Marie approached the nearest heap.

'The size of these things!' Hazeldene said. 'Never seen anything like it. And when I imagine them in life . . .'

'I keep wanting to look over my shoulder,' Marie said.

Hazeldene picked up a piece of exoskeleton, a metre long and half a metre across. It was shaped like half of a shield: straight top, one side curved, the other straight. She turned it around a few times, noticing the iridescence of the convex side, the venous striation of the concave.

'It's a wingcase,' she said. 'The last time I looked at a wingcase this shape it was one the size of a thumbnail, and I was looking at it through a magnifying glass.'

Marie was holding a curved piece, the size of a quarter of a car tyre, translucent with a tinge of yellow: a piece of a segment of abdominal carapace, Hazeldene guessed. 'Looks like this would match it,' Marie said. She ran her thumb along one end. 'Smooth suture line. It's not part of a dead arachnoid or insectoid – at least, the creature wasn't dead when this was left here. These aren't bits of dead animals. They're *moults.*'

'Too right they are,' said Hazeldene. 'Meaning this *isn't the adult size.*'

Jenkins, a step behind them, sucked air through his teeth. 'Bigger than whatever left that?' He stepped forward and to one side and halfcrouched, sweeping the surroundings with his gaze and his rifle. 'Think they're still around?'

'I doubt it,' said Hazeldene. 'They'd be off as soon as their new carapace hardened.'

'Jeez.' Jenkins peered around, frowning. 'If that's a wingcase, did that have wings? A dragonfly the size of a man? Why haven't we seen any?'

'We haven't seen any *yet,*' said Marie. 'It's a big continent, and a new continent.'

'Thought you said the life here weren't that much different from the old continent,' Jenkins grumbled.

'It mostly isn't,' said Hazeldene. She waved around. 'As you see. And we've only partly explored New Atlantis itself, for that matter. It could easily have insectoid species – even flying ones – as big as that.'

'Still getting my head around the invertebrate lung,' Marie said, picking through more heaps of chitinous litter.

Hazeldene laughed. 'Yeah, I know what you mean. Took me long enough.'

She'd come to like Marie, now that the Scottish girl had got over her almost fan-girlish awe. Smart, pretty and besotted with her bearded boyfriend.

'This isn't right!' Marie cried.

'What?' Hazeldene took it as a warning, and glanced around, startled. Jenkins, a few metres away, was keeping up his watchful scan. Nothing untoward.

'This.' Marie held up two plates of chitin, tossed them down, picked up a huge mandible and then a long whip-like antenna. 'Too many different species.' She frowned. 'Come on, Dr Hazeldene! This isn't a place where big invertebrates come to moult. Especially not predators and prey in the same place. I've never heard of behaviour like that. And the tree stumps have obviously been cut down deliberately.'

'So what do you think it is?'

'A scrap yard, a junk yard . . . No! A warehouse!'

'Ah!' said Jenkins. 'Now that kinda makes sense.'

'Explain,' said Hazeldene.

'My people, and the other exile bands – we make use of animal parts like this, shells and pincers and stuff. Every craftswoman or man will have a stash.' He laughed. 'Just not with bits this big, see? I mean, it's like a giant's version of what you'd find in a shed or on a shelf.'

'I trust they're better sorted where you come from.'

Jenkins grunted amusement. He stooped for a moment to run the palm of his hand over a stump. 'Still no idea how they sawed these trees down, though.'

'I have,' said Marie. She brandished the antenna, and passed it to Hazeldene. 'With this.'

Hazeldene turned the flexible appendage over in her hands. Close up, she wasn't sure it was an antenna. Perhaps a tentacle, from bigger version of the whipper-snapper. Its surface was rough and abrasive like shark skin, as a cautious test with her thumb painfully confirmed. She handed it on to Jenkins, and sucked at the bleeding.

'Yes,' he said. 'That could work. String this tight between

the ends of a bent branch and you have not a bad bandsaw.'

'They'd need stout gloves,' said Hazeldene, 'or bloody tough hands.'

'Nah,' said Jenkins. 'Use two sticks like tongs and you're laughing.'

He seemed lost in the practicalities of the carpentry.

'What this means,' said Marie, urgently, 'is we're in exile territory.'

'Same folks who fired the arrows?' Jenkins sounded worried.

'Potential hostiles, anyway,' Hazeldene said. 'Yes, better move out and head back.' She turned to Marie. 'Anything on WeThink?' She herself had flat out refused to have Co-ord software on her phone.

Marie checked her glasses. 'Two mixed patrols – ours and yours – with drone cover, moving out diagonally for now. No contacts reported. About five klicks from us, half a klick into the woods.'

'Right, let's give them a wide berth and circle back.'

A guidance dot appeared in Hazeldene's glasses, like a floating speck she couldn't blink from her eye. Marie took from her rucksack a small drone and tossed it in the air with a muttered instruction. It fluttered away, in among the trees. Jenkins followed, rifle at the ready, then Hazeldene and Marie. The larger drone loitering overhead moved forward, too, keeping pace and watch from twenty metres above the treetops. When they'd walked ten metres from the clearing, there was nothing to see behind them but trees.

WeThink gave Myles a *Severely Disappointing Behaviour* rating, not that he cared, and Sergeant Morton said something worse under his breath.

'Don't come crying to me for a weapon or a vest,' Morton concluded. 'And for fuck's sake stay at the back.'

This Myles was happy to do. He made up the rear of the group moving north-west, nine in an arrowhead formation with the sergeant up front. The robot bloodhound slunk and sloped around them all, slipping through underbrush at speed that seemed preternatural. Above the treetops, a dozen small drones cruised, peering down in the infrared and ultraviolet. And behind them, for the first few minutes anyway, a camera drone from the media visitors tagged along. Myles could see everyone's position and a lot else on his glasses, and almost nothing of them otherwise. The trees were two to three metres apart and up to ten metres high. Between them, ferns and bushes and succulents sprouted from the dense litter and struggled for the light. Twenty metres to his left a soldier, twenty metres to his left Linda Munro of the militia, and the only trace of either an occasional glimpsed shadow or the crack of a twig.

The light was dim, the ground and the detritus underfoot dry, the air humid, as if the trees cloaked themselves in damp. Boids – some brightly coloured, others black, yet others so well camouflaged they startled you when they flew off in a furious buzz and clatter – were such a persistent accompaniment to the patrol that it made their stealth seem farcical. The jeering monkey-spiders in the canopy and their hurled fruit, seeds and faeces didn't help. At least the shit was dry, though the stone-hard pellets stung.

Myles kept glancing back, over a different shoulder each time. The camera drone still followed, until he looked again and it was gone. Then he thought to clip his phone to his collar, and patch the rear view to a corner of his glasses. It was so similar to the view ahead that he had to tweak the colour contrast to distinguish them. That done, he walked forward with more confidence, though no less caution.

Outlined on his glasses in faint red was the WeThink heads-up-display of deployments: his patrol, the other patrol, the two groups of three hunters deeper in the woods, and Marie's party deeper yet. These were all making their separate ways back, well to the north and south of the patrols, and sharing information from their glasses and drones. Everyone in the forest was a lot better armed than he was, so apart from an undercurrent of anxiety about Marie he wasn't worried. The journalists' camera drone showed up as a dot zigzagging between trees. After a while it rose above from the forest and scooted away back to the settlement. He wondered if the journalists had lost interest.

What the display couldn't show him, and what he had to watch out for, was anyone or anything moving on the ground nearby. So far he hadn't spotted anything bigger than a rabbit – some swift-scuttling denizens of the forest floor, living on whatever dropped from above.

'OK, closing the sweep,' said Morton. 'Left flank, hold position. Right, leapfrog past me, swing around then hold until I say go. Rear-end Myles, take a diagonal to one hundred metres behind me and stay there.'

Myles heard, and saw on the display, Linda Munro set off. The soldier to his left hunkered down. Myles set a guidance dot to the point Morton had indicated, and followed it in as straight a line as he could. After fifty metres he saw a patch of light ahead. As he approached he heard an intermittent buzzing, and caught a faint sweet scent. A few steps more and he found himself at an open space about ten metres across, where the ground was exceptionally dry and – perhaps as a consequence – no trees grew. In the middle, among low ground cover, stood a black, buzzing box with slotted sides. For a wild moment he thought of an electricity transformer, then he saw bees going in and out.

Myles stopped, and called Morton.

'Sarge, I've come across a beehive.'

'So fucking what?'

'It's artificial.'

'You sure?'

'Yes, Sarge, I'm sure.'

'Stay right where you are. The bee-keeper might not be far away.'

'This had occurred to me, Sarge.'

'So stay there and shut up. I'll liaise with the others.'

Myles crouched amid ferns and partly behind a tree on the edge of the open space. With a flicker of his fingers he texted Marie:

Hope all's well you got to see this

He shared the view from his glasses. After a minute or so Marie replied:

Oh wow will keep an eye stay safe xx

Myles replied *xx* and went on staying safe. In his heads-up-display the dots and lines of Morton's patrol changed course and began to form a closing curve around where he stood. The other patrol continued the original plan to form up a line and sweep back towards where they'd entered the forest just behind the military camp. The bees came and went. Myles felt an acute pang on seeing the familiar insects and hearing their homely buzz. Everything else here – plant, beast or boid – was just close enough to, and just different enough from, its earthly counterpart to be uneasy on the eye. Every sight was a double take. To Marie it was all delightful, this perpetual discovery of analogy and homology, of convergence and divergence, but Myles found it draining.

Perhaps, like the exiles and the veterans of the bases, he'd get used to it in time.

Not today, and not this minute: something thumped to the ground not far away, and the bushes across and to his right swayed. Fronds parted. A cluster of four shiny black beads surveyed the scene. Long black appendages at the end of furry orange arms parted the fronds further, and a monkey-spider stepped out.

Myles had once seen, in the Zoology Museum of Glasgow University, a glass case in which was pinned a mole cricket. Its blunt head and clawed shovelling forelimbs were so uncannily like those of a mole in miniature that Myles had laughed in disbelief. Form followed function.

Thus too the monkey-spider. It walked on its hind and mid legs, crooked so that the equivalent of the knees were above its head, which was about a metre above the ground. Its fore-limbs were even longer, now outspread in a span of over two metres, and thinner than the haunches of the limbs behind. The cluster of many-jointed black manipulators at the end of each arm lightly and almost idly brushed the tops of the plants it moved among. The fine reddish-orange bristles that covered all but the face and the distal ends of the limbs looked like fur, but the way each separate fibre moved and quivered suggested to Myles that they were more than that: sensitive whiskers, perhaps. The head, with its four forward-facing eyes and – now he could see them – two smaller eyes amid the fuzz at the back – was disturbingly like that of an orang-utan, with a big domed brain case and a prognathous muzzle, albeit with side-by-side mandibles. That there was no visible neck, just a fissure between head and thorax, deepened the impression of a hunched ape.

The beast walked, in a curiously fluid scuttling motion, towards the hive. If it was aware of Myles, it gave no indication, though its head swung from side to side and its eyes scanned him more than once. Nor did it seem bothered by the numerous bees that landed on its fur. It didn't so much as brush them away when they crawled over its unblinking hard shiny eyes. When it reached the hive it straightened its back and middle limbs and rose to the height of a tall man. Then it stooped – there was no other word for it – and its outspread fingers played along the underside of the top of the hive, as if tickling it.

Something clicked. With its gripping fingers the monkey-spider lifted the top from the hive and laid the metre-square black plate on the ground. It reached in, and pulled out a dripping square: a honeycomb, with bees crawling all over it. The monkey-spider held it up close to its eyes, turning it this way and that. The mandibles gaped, and a long black tongue shot out, to lick the dripping honey. In and out of the mouth it went. Barely a drop was wasted.

The monkey-spider lowered the comb back into the hive, then replaced the top. Again its long thin fingers played beneath the edges. Again a click. The monkey-spider stood for a moment, in a typhoon of bees, and licked its fingers. It squatted back on its haunches and in a sudden blur of legs whirled about, and bounded back the way it had come, covering the ground in less than a second. Myles just had time to whip his head around to catch a glimpse of it in the undergrowth.

Myles stood agog. A message from Marie flashed across his sight:

Holy fucking shit!!!

He was just flexing his fingers to flicker his response when he heard more movement close by. He flipped his glasses to infrared. Through the foliage he saw two blurred, moving shapes, both low. One of them was easily identifiable as a soldier. The other, smaller and about fifty metres distant, had to be the monkey-spider. The soldier hunkered down and raised his carbine.

'No!' Myles yelled. 'Stop!'

Too late. A line of laser light pinpointed the monkey-spider. A shot cracked, scaring up a clatter of boids and a scurry of smaller animals. The monkey-spider stopped moving.

Then a yell of triumph: 'Got one of the bastards, Sarge!'

Myles clutched his head. 'You bloody fool!' he shouted.

The soldier emerged from the underbrush and glared at him. 'What's up with you? I just shot a hostile.'

'It was a monkey-spider,' Myles said. He pointed at the hive and told the soldier what he'd seen. 'I think it's intelligent.'

'Not intelligent enough,' the soldier said. 'Otherwise it wouldn't have been walking on the ground like a human being, would it?'

Myles stared at him. 'That's the rules of engagement? Shoot at anyone who isn't one of us?'

'Dead right it is. There's no one here but our people and those who shot at us.'

Orders came through from Morton. The soldier was told to retrieve the monkey-spider and carry it back. He tramped off, and returned with the monkey-spider across his shoulders. Myles hoped it weighed on his conscience like a shot albatross.

Morton called the Lieutenant, who called off the sweep. The attackers, whoever they were, had evidently slipped away. The two patrols rendezvoused, and picked up one of the hunting parties. That party had a good catch of small game. The patrols and the hunting party formed a bristling, still wary column, and trekked out of the forest without incident. They were nearly at the edge when a blue flash, followed by a thump, indicated that the ark of the journalists had departed.

Myles emerged from the forest to find Rob and Jody still felling and trimming trees. He gave them a wave as the soldiers and the militia separated out, with much clapping of shoulders and cheerful banter.

'You did all right,' Morton told Myles. 'Don't do it again.'

'Fair enough.' Myles turned to the soldier carrying the dead monkey-spider. 'What are you going to do with that?'

'Sarge told me to turn it over to the scientists.'

'I'll be waiting here for the scientists. You might as well leave it with me.'

'You're welcome to it,' said the soldier, and lowered his ghastly burden carefully to the ground. 'Stinks something fierce.'

Myles didn't find the odour unpleasant – intense and pungent, it wasn't dung, it wasn't decay – but then he hadn't had it close to his nose for an hour. 'Thanks.'

The soldiers went off to their compound, and the settlers marched off down the road. Jody and Rob finished up their work and sauntered over.

'Well, you showed us up!' said Jody.

Myles shrugged. 'Maybe it was getting shot at.'

'Yeah, well, it could have the opposite effect on some people.'

'You still got the arrow?'

'Somewhere.' Jody went off and retrieved it from under a tree stump. Myles took it. They all stood around for a bit looking at the dead monkey-spider. The shot that had killed it had gone straight through the head, leaving the cephalic nerve ganglion – arguably, the brain – an oozing mess. A few bees were here and there stuck to its limbs, apparently trapped by the fur.

Myles told them what had happened.

'Jeez,' said Rob. 'Do you think it was the monkey-spiders that shot at us?'

Myles turned the arrow over in his hands. 'I don't think so. Not unless they're hiding advanced tech somewhere, which I kind of doubt. I'll wait here for Marie and Dr Hazeldene and Able. They might have a better idea.'

Rob and Jody returned to the settlement, riding on the cart with their last load of logs, the robot loping alongside.

Myles squatted on his haunches and waited beside the dead arachnoid. He was more upset than he had expected. It felt a lot like mourning a dog.

CHAPTER ELEVEN
Cephalic Nerve Ganglion

New Mu, Apis, Thursday 6 November 2070

'Well, ain't that just peachy,' Hazeldene said, squatting to inspect the damage. 'The first observation of what could be native intelligent life, and next thing we know it's shot down by a jumpy soldier. Right through where we might have learned something useful about its brain, too. Damn!'

'We learned a lot about its brain just by watching it,' Myles said.

'Tool use isn't conclusive.' Marie seemed to be thinking aloud. 'And there are nests more complex than that hive you saw, and some social insects exploit other species. What we saw it do could all be instinct. But still . . .'

'Well, yeah,' said Hazeldene. 'Just as well you kept monkey-spider off the bushmeat menu, Able!'

Jenkins nodded. 'We never kill monkey-spiders back home,

around my area, but some groups further south do take them when they can.'

'How do you know?' Marie asked.

Jenkins tapped his nose. 'Oh, we have better long-distance comms than you might think.' He held up a cupped hand and flexed his wrist. 'Mirrors and Morse code.'

'Mirrors?' Marie sounded disbelieving.

Jenkins grinned. 'You'd like this. We do have old bits of mirror, and shiny metal, but mostly we use the mirror-cup from the back of some the big beasties' eyes.'

'Ah, yes,' Marie said. 'A whole new weird kind of eye.'

'They dry out well. Lenses, too. Anyway – we can relay messages that way for hundreds of klicks, at agreed times along agreed pathways. Flash-lines, we call them. Plus we have trade, and sometimes salted monkey-spider makes its way up north to us.'

'And you eat it?' Myles asked.

'It's killed already,' Jenkins said. 'And we don't waste food.'

'Can't argue with that,' Myles admitted.

'I won't be doing it again,' Jenkins said.

'OK,' said Hazeldene. 'Let's get this thing to the lab.'

One of the arks had been more or less commandeered by the scientists as soon as it was vacated. Most of the space was taken up with benches made from emptied packing crates shoved together, stools made from packing crates ingeniously cut up and reassembled, and with the equipment the scientists had brought on their pack robots. Jenkins's apparatus was on a bench at the far end like some ancient office computer, and for now just as neglected.

Georgi Muranov and Sharianne Adler looked up from their work as the four trudged in, lugging the dead animal.

'Clear some space,' Hazeldene said.

Marie pointed to a work surface. Myles quickly moved

glassware and other apparatus off it and onto another crate. Hazeldene and Jenkins dumped the beast.

'What the hell?' said Muranov.

Hazeldene was already pulling on a disposable overall and gloves. 'Marie, that scanner.' She pointed. 'Myles, give Georgi the arrow. Sharianne, if you wouldn't mind passing me the dissection kit . . .'

She poked about the ruined head with a probe, scalpel and tweezers for a minute or two, then straightened up. 'Scanner.' Marie passed the device to her. Hazeldene's fingertip sketched the outline of a shared workspace, for her glasses, Adler's and Marie's. She passed the scanner over and around the monkey-spider's thorax and head, several times. 'OK, now resolve . . .'

Myles couldn't see in. He looked at Jenkins, who shrugged and headed for his own quaint keyboard and screen. Myles walked over to the Russian palaeoanalyst's bench, and handed over the arrow. Muranov looked down at it, hefted it, balanced it on a forefinger, ran his fingertips along the shaft and brushed along the edge of one of the vanes. Eyes narrowed behind his glasses.

'This is not man's work,' he said.

Myles glanced back at where the three women stood around the carcase, looking at empty space above it, where no doubt a 3D image hung.

'What?'

'This arrow. Not made by human hands, or human printers.'

'Oh! Well, we had kind of figured that.'

'"We"?'

'Me and my colleagues up at the logging.'

Muranov snorted. 'Well done! I have a stronger basis for my assertion.' He pointed at the improvised bench-top. Among its clutter of instruments lay black shards. 'As soon as I heard, I sent a drone to the military camp for fragments of the arrows shot down.'

'Have you found anything?'

'Oh yes.' Muranov laid down the arrow and picked up a shard. He turned it this way and that. Its surfaces were matt black; its edges glittered like broken glass. 'It took a direct hit from a high-power smart bullet to break this.' He gestured at small, chunky apparatus. 'My little stress machine was unable to do the same. I was able to grind off some of it, however, and put the powder through the analyser.' He pointed at another small machine. 'Which tells me it's a polycarbonate, but like nothing on record. Not natural compounds, obviously, and nothing we could manufacture. The arrangement and formation of the molecules would require impossible – for us – amounts of pressure and heat.' He shook his head. 'Perhaps in a very advanced orbital laboratory today, I don't know. I'm a little behind the curve of scientific advance, as are we all. But what I am seeing here is the kind of transformation brought about by geological processes, deep down in the mantle. Such as with certain minerals – olivine, for instance. Or diamond.'

'How could a geological process make *arrows*?'

Muranov jerked his thumb over his shoulder. 'Ask him to ask them.'

'You think the Fermi made this?'

'Of course the Fermi!'

Overhearing, Jenkins turned away from his apparatus with a snort of derision and strolled over.

'They're not saying a word.'

'No change there,' said Muranov. 'I wonder if . . .'

He gazed into space, uncannily in the direction of the crystal outcrop. Of course – he was looking through his glasses at an overlaid display. The lab sides and roof might as well have been transparent.

'What?' Jenkins asked.

'We've been assuming that the Fermi are – is, whatever – the same thing everywhere. That Hamilton's Rise up there is the same as the thing on MacHinery Ridge, which in turn is the same as the Markov Escarpment. Now the last two are if not the same then alike – I've been close to one and worked inside the other. But Hamilton's Rise doesn't look like either.'

'It sure don't,' said Jenkins. He brightened. 'You're talking compatibility, right?'

'Something perhaps remotely analogous,' said Muranov with a wry smile.

'What?' Myles was perplexed.

Jenkins chuckled. 'In ancient times, back when my dad was a lad, so he told me, computer and comms systems didn't always work together like they do today. Hard as that might be to believe.'

'I know that! But you said the Fermi rocks back on New Atlantis talked to *your father's old phone*. Why should—?'

'That thing up there,' said Muranov, 'could be millions or for all I know *billions* of years older or younger than the others. It might not even be related at all.'

'There's only one thing for it,' said Myles. 'We have to go up there and find out.'

They were interrupted by a shout from Hazeldene. 'Guys, come and look at this!'

She gestured, including their glasses in the shared workspace. Myles stepped closer. In the virtual space a 3D image of the monkey-spider hung like a vivid ghost in the air above the carcase, its shattered head reconstructed from the scanned fragments. Hazeldene waved a flat palm through it, slicing away half to give a cutaway view. The braincase was about two-thirds the size, Myles reckoned, as his own.

'Eight hundred and thirty-four cubic centimetres,' Hazeldene read off the display, in a wondering tone. 'Just under human adult. Weighing in with hominins, at least. Yes, I know it's not strictly comparable – hell of a lot more visual processing, for a start – but given what, say, spiders and bees can do with a brain the size of a pinhead I doubt the advantage is ours.' She turned to Marie. 'Speaking of bees. Could you take one from the fur and stick in a sequencer for me, please?'

Marie, who had for days been gene-sequencing local life every chance she got, made haste to comply.

'Half an hour,' she said.

'Fine,' said Hazeldene. She waved the display away. 'Let's leave the sequencer to cook and go get some very belated lunch, if there's anything left.'

Lunch was off a trestle table amid the shelters and arks, and they were indeed late for it. But there was still bushmeat in the big pot, and piles of leaves and boiled tubers beside it. Myles was standing behind Marie while she helped herself when he noticed the table had a guest: Lieutenant Knight.

'I can believe the monkey-spiders built the hive,' Knight said, when they'd told him what they'd just found. He pondered invisible pictures. 'Looks like it could have been constructed from the moult stuff. Instinct or intelligence – not my expertise, so I'll defer to Emma and Marie. What I can't believe is that they made these arrows. And they don't have the muscle power to shoot them.'

'Yes, they do,' Myles said. 'They have long and strong arms.'

Hazeldene shook her head. 'Sorry, Myles, but no. My reconstruction did the biomechanics. They're not strong enough.'

'As I thought,' said Knight. 'No clever grasshopper-style spring-loading in the joints, either, am I right?'

'Yes,' said Hazeldene. 'They might have used crossbows.'

She didn't sound as if she thought that likely.

'Here's the strange thing,' said Knight. 'It was quite a volley – dozens of arrows. Some got through our defence, but no fatalities, no serious injuries.'

'One damn near killed me,' said Myles. 'It was pure chance that I ducked to pick up the axe.'

'How deep would you say it went in the tree?'

Myles thought back to his efforts getting the arrow out. 'A good twenty centimetres.'

'See what I mean about power? That would take a longbow,

a warbow or a crossbow. But we needn't speculate. Our drones and defence network calculated the origin of each trajectory in less than a second after first detecting incoming. You saw what happened next – a whole flight of drones screaming into the woods while the last of the volley was still in flight. There is no way they could have missed whoever shot these arrows. The drones have radar, lidar, sonar, infrared, molecule detectors sensitive enough to make a mosquito weep.' He spread his hands. 'They found nothing. Zilch. Nada.'

'So what does that leave?' Hazeldene asked.

'I'll tell you what it leaves,' said Jenkins. 'The Fermi. You heard what Georgi found. They're by far the likeliest makers of the arrows. Why shouldn't they have been the shooters?'

'But how?' Knight demanded. He waved towards the crystal crest of the range. 'They're way up there!' He scoffed. 'If they're there at all, and Hamilton's Rise isn't just some weird mineral outcrop.'

Muranov leaned forward and cocked his head sideways. 'I see. All this time, you and your men and women have been conducting geological surveys. How modest to hide such talents!'

'Of course we haven't.'

'Fine,' said Muranov. 'In which case, you have no idea how far the structures at the top of that range extend.' He pointed downward. 'For all we know, the same rock as is up there could be a metre beneath our feet.'

Everyone looked down uneasily, than looked at each other as if embarrassed.

'Even so,' said Knight. 'Rocks don't shoot arrows. Come on!'

Jenkins and the scientists laughed.

'What?'

'Lieutenant Knight,' Hazeldene said, 'we've seen with our own eyes massive structures emerge from *cliffs* of such material and *move*. We've seen great hollow spheres bowling along in the open like tumbleweed.' She tapped her glasses. 'We can show you the video records. We barely outran these phenomena!'

'I've seen the records,' said Knight. 'There was nothing that couldn't be accounted for by known physics. Gravity, even.'

Hazeldene gave another hollow laugh. '"Known physics", my arse! Have you seen our other recordings? Of how solid rock moves inside solid rock? An image of me – of me! I can hardly believe it myself! – turned up in a crevice on Venus within five minutes of its being . . . taken, I guess is the word. We can set no limit on the capacities of what we are dealing with here.'

Jenkins, Adler and Muranov were nodding along sombrely. They all had the look of people reminded of something they'd rather not think about. It was unsettling, like seeing physicists believing a ghost story.

'All right,' Knight said. 'In that case, what—?'

Marie's phone pinged.

'Sorry,' she said. 'That must be the bee genome.' She looked around. 'It might be important.'

'And relevant,' said Hazeldene. 'The bees are the weirdest anomaly here.'

Knight shrugged. 'I'll wait. Talk amongst yourselves.'

They finished eating while Marie looked at her phone, then at a virtual space. Myles was handing out mugs of coffee when Marie yelped as if stung.

'Hey! That can't be right!'

'What?' Hazeldene reached across the table. 'Let me see.'

Marie waved a display to Hazeldene's glasses. The biologist studied it for a minute.

'Oh fuck,' she said. 'This is beyond a joke.'

They all stared at her. Her face worked, as if she were at some solemn occasion and trying not to giggle. She turned to Marie. 'Tell them. You found it.'

'You know about junk DNA?'

They all did.

'This bee, from that hive up there in the forest, has some silent genes – still there, but no longer expressed. Like, they might have had a function once, but no longer, so evolution shunts them aside. There's a whole strand there of insecticide-resistant genes that were engineered for domestic bees just a few years ago, in the 2060s. And alongside them there's a strand of DNA that was never active in the first place, because it's used to spell out the company name and the patent number. There's a convention, you see, and the sequencer translates.' She read out the name and number.

'Well, that's funny,' said Knight, after a stunned silence. 'Stray queen bee came here on a sub, maybe?'

Marie and Hazeldene shook their heads. 'No,' said Hazeldene. 'The engineered genes couldn't have gone silent in that time. These bees have been here for decades, maybe centuries.'

Uproar and cross-talk: wild assertions about time-travel, FTL, and what was and wasn't possible. Hazeldene banged the table.

'Shut up, everyone!' She glared around. 'I'm trying to think.' She shut her eyes for a minute, then opened them. 'OK. We know all the bees on Apis must have been brought here after – long after – the ancestors of the other animals. And whatever brought them could have brought this variety, too. From Earth's present, to Apis's past. And the monkey-spiders keep these bees! So here's what I think. The bees were brought here *for* the monkey-spiders, because whatever brought them *likes* the monkey-spiders and wants them to thrive. I can see why: the monkey-spiders are or could become native intelligent life. They're what this world is for.

'And we're not. That volley of arrows today was a warning shot – warning us off.'

'Off what?' Knight demanded. 'And why now? They've had decades to tell us, if they didn't want us here.'

'They warned us off MacHinery Ridge,' said Jenkins, 'when you lot started drilling and hacking into it. Chased us off, come to that. And they told us why.'

Knight gave Jenkins a sceptical sidelong glance. 'No offence, but your lack of success here casts some doubt back on your previous exploits.'

'You calling me a liar?'

'No, not at all. Just . . . mistaken, somehow. Anyway – we haven't touched Hamilton's Rise, or even struck rock that might be part of it. We didn't shoot one of their supposedly precious monkey-spider protégés until after we were attacked. So I say again, why now?'

'I'll tell you why,' said Marie. She gave Myles a glance of wry regret. 'It's the tree-felling! We're attacking the monkey-spiders' *habitat*.'

'Only by a small and sustainable amount,' Myles protested.

'Oh, and the Fermi know that how?' said Hazeldene. 'They know our record as a species, not our intentions as a settlement.'

'An interesting speculation, Marie,' Knight said. 'Let's hope it's correct. Because that means all we have to worry about is your settlement's tree-felling. My camp has done all the felling it needs. Yours had better stop.'

'We haven't finished building shelters,' Myles said.

Knight waved an expansive arm at the plain. 'Spread out! As I keep telling you! There's no shortage of stones for walls and scrub for roofs.'

They all looked at each other.

'We'll put it on WeThink,' said Marie.

Knight scoffed, then stood up, and nodded stiffly. 'Good afternoon, everyone.'

He departed, off up the long path to the camp.

'Well, that's us told,' said Myles. He looked across the table at the scientists and Jenkins. A sense of inchoate frustration was coming to a slow boil. 'You lot are here to try and find out more about the Fermi, aren't you? So why don't we just fucking go up the mountain and find out?'

Muranov glanced sideways at the others. 'Like I said, we have to prepare. And it has to be your people who take the initiative. This is Union territory, after all. We're here in a purely advisory capacity.'

'Where have we heard that before?' Hazeldene said. Muranov shrugged and made wide, innocent eyes.

'Well, then, what do you advise?' Myles demanded.

'As I said, we have to prepare. A drone survey first, I think. Closer than the journalists were allowed to take it. An over-flight, perhaps.' Muranov turned to Hazeldene and Adler. 'The Alliance military will assist with that, yes?'

Hazeldene nodded firmly. 'And with an expedition, if that's what we decide.'

'Great!' said Myles. 'So let's start preparing. It's about time.'

Marie didn't seem to share his enthusiasm. 'I'd be happier to leave well enough alone,' she said. 'And, Georgi, your scientists, the Co-ord, they're making their own investigations, aren't they? At MacHinery Ridge and at the Markov Escarpment? Any word from them?'

'Only very guarded reports,' Muranov said, guardedly. 'They are proceeding with caution.'

'Well, good! That's what I like to hear! And I'd like to know more about how to proceed with caution, before we proceed at all.'

'I'll see what I can do,' said Georgi.

Hazeldene and Adler exchanged troubled glances. 'All due respect, Georgi,' said Hazeldene, 'we don't want the Co-ord involved. Or even informed.'

Georgi threw his hands up. 'My colleagues already know we're here to . . . assist any Union investigation into Hamilton's Rise. I am *expected*–by both sides – to keep them in the loop. Just like your—'

'He's not *my* robot spy,' said Hazeldene.

'OK, OK.'

'What's all this about?' Marie asked.

'Nothing to worry about,' said Hazeldene. 'Alliance stuff.'

Marie compressed her lips, then looked up brightly.

'You know what we should do first? We should take that dead monkey-spider back to the edge of the forest, lay it out under the trees and leave it there.'

'Yes,' said Myles, in sudden whole-hearted agreement. 'That's the right thing to do.'

'You sure, Marie?' Hazeldene said. 'It would be an interesting dissection.'

Myles felt Marie's shoulder muscles stiffen against his.

'We already know the basic anatomy of the genus,' she said. 'And your reconstruction showed us the most interesting thing about this species: the size of the brain. We don't need more. Not now.'

Jenkins was nodding vigorously. Hazeldene sighed. 'OK. If you must.'

But she and Adler took no part in the strange funeral that followed. Felling had finished for the day, the trimmed logs laid out and stacked. The whole air around them smelled of fresh timber. Myles and Marie, Muranov and Jenkins laid the dead animal on a plastic pallet and carried it out and laid it on to the log-hauling cart. They summoned and harnessed a pack-robot, and rode along on the cart as the robot plodded up the now well-beaten track to the woods. Other settlers they passed stopped work and asked what was going on, and Myles told them. Some fell in behind the impromptu cortège. Up the path they went and past the camp, where soldiers stared in silence. They stopped at the raw edge of the forest, where every third tree had been felled. Myles, Marie, Muranov and Jenkins lifted the pallet and carried it a few tens of metres in. They lifted the carcase off the pallet and laid it out on the forest floor. Its outspread limbs were already stiff.

They stood looking down at it for a moment. 'Sorry about

that,' Myles said, to no one in particular. Boids flew down and hopped about, waiting for the humans to go away; insectoids scuttled from underbrush and gathered around to investigate. Above, in the canopy, silent monkey-spiders watched.

The party turned away and tramped out of the forest and back to the cart.

'For all the good it'll do,' said Marie.

They walked and rode back to the settlement, expecting to have to explain things again. But they didn't. The geologists and the robot Owen had returned from the banks of the big river, and they had a tale to tell and a trophy to show.

A good tenth of the settlers, three to four score, had gathered in the much-trampled central square in the midst of the new shelters. The centre of their attention was a group of three: Marcus Owen and the geologists Cindy Patel and Nelson Hayes. Mud and dust streaked their clothes and faces. Their hair was bedraggled, and all had taken too much sun despite their hats and shirts. Every so often they paused to sip water from their bottles.

They'd laid down their packs and tools – geological hammers, ground scanners, marking pegs, trenching shovels – and three heavy sacks of samples. Each sample was wrapped in rags. Someone had dragged out an empty crate and set it up as a table. Onto this table Hayes and Patel laid and unwrapped the samples. Pebbles, large and small; chunks chipped from larger outcrops. They described them; named and identified them. Myles shouldered his way to the front. Some of the terms were familiar, others new to him: perhaps local, coined for the strata on Apis. The two geologists seemed excited by evidence that this part of the continent had never been glaciated, and by anomalous readings that were (yet more) evidence of terraforming, of unreasonably rapid change in the recent past. Owen stood silent and detached, looking on with a slight ironic smile.

'This was the second biggest surprise,' Hayes said, opening the third and last sack. 'Found in the surface gravel.' He unfolded a torn square of some shirt rescued from recycling, and held up a spearhead of chipped stone.

An intake of breath, all around.

'We know some exiles made it to New Mu,' Patel explained. 'We didn't know there were any in this area. But this means they are, or were not long ago.'

'We can't be sure of that any more!' Marie called out. 'We've just found monkey-spiders keeping bees!'

Patel and Hayes shrugged. 'We heard,' said Hayes. 'Thanks to WeThink. But this looks like human work to me.' He looked down at the sack. 'There's a few more – edged tools, knives and axes. Standard Stone Age stuff.'

'Never heard of exiles using stone tools,' Jenkins said. 'Thorns off plants and spikes off animals for spearheads and arrowheads, yeah, but not chipping flint.'

'Your lot had kit in your arks, and the base to scavenge,' said Hayes. 'Whoever made it here might not have been able to carry much, and no base until now.'

Two entirely different kinds of anomalous arrows in a day! Myles thought there had to be something in that.

'So what's the biggest surprise?' someone asked.

Hayes reached into the sack and with two hands took out something flat and heavy. He laid it on the table and unwrapped an ovoid disc about forty centimetres by twenty, and maybe ten centimetres thick, rounded on all sides and surfaces. Everyone pressed closer, craning in to see the object. It seemed made of milky jade, with random blue glass insets, likewise rounded, and the whole intricately whorled in fern-like patterns, fractal in their complexity.

They'd all seen – had clamoured to see, a few days earlier – the recordings the journalists had taken from their drones, high up on the mountain range. But Hayes must have felt the need to spell it out, all the same.

'It's a rock from Hamilton's Rise.'

*

The crowd in the settlement's square thinned, after everyone had had a chance to take a look at the geologists' finds. The afternoon was getting late. The exosun was an hour or so above setting behind Hamilton's Rise. WeThink was calling some of those present to other tasks, starting with preparing dinner for everyone who wanted it. Only the scientists, Jenkins, Marie and Myles, and a dozen or so others remained. Everyone seemed as entranced by the jade disc as Myles was. Behind the vernal veining of the surface, movement could be detected if you gazed long enough. Or perhaps that was an illusion, created by subtle differences in the layers within as your gaze moved.

Marcus Owen stepped forward and glanced at Hayes and Patel. 'If I may?'

Hayes nodded. Owen grasped the disc by its edges on the long axis, and held it up. The light from the lowering sun caught it, and made it almost fluoresce with a vivid yellow light. Myles took a step backward, as did others. He blinked. The after-images were blue.

Owen chuckled, and lowered the disc. 'It's like the converse of the yellow after-images you get from a Cherenkov flash, isn't it? When you don't look away in time from a departing FTL ship? I'm sure some of you got caught out that way today, when the journalists left. What a shame they left before we could show them this!'

He looked around, his gaze meeting everyone's eyes – or so Myles guessed, because they certainly met his, drilling in for a moment before flicking on.

'I suspect the colour is no coincidence,' Owen continued. 'We know the Fermi rocks on New Atlantis are capable of FTL communication, and perhaps something of the sort is going on here, at some microscopic or even smaller scale.'

'Wouldn't that glow blue, not yellow?' someone heckled.

Owen pointed to the blue stones embedded in the disc. 'Maybe we're seeing that, too.' He looked up, again sweeping his penetrating gaze across everyone. 'No matter. The point is, this is very much a live rock. Like Mr Jenkins's black slab, which has been so sadly uncommunicative since we came here.'

'We've been talking about this,' said Jenkins. 'Me and Georgi and the others. We reckon it's possible this up there' – he jerked a thumb over his shoulder – 'is different from MacHinery Ridge back home.'

'Oh, it's different all right,' said Owen. 'We can see that with the naked eye, and we saw it closer with the journalists' drones. And we see it here. The crystal pillars up there seem more advanced than the rocks of MacHinery Ridge, or at least more elaborate.' He paused, as if thinking. Perhaps he was. 'Though the modern style *is* later than the baroque.'

'What are you talking about?' Marie called out.

Owen smiled. 'Just a passing thought.'

'I wonder . . .' Jenkins began, then shook his head. 'Nah.'

'You're right, Able,' Owen said. 'Connecting this to your apparatus would probably be futile, though by all means try. However, failing that, I have another idea.' He turned to Hayes and Patel. 'We found this in the bed of the big river, close to the shoal where we found the stone tools. Now, I defer to my geologist colleagues here, but it seems unlikely to me that this was washed down from Hamilton's Rise – at least, not where it was found! Because stones don't get washed upriver.'

Hayes grunted. 'Obviously.'

'In that case,' said Owen, 'it seems likely that someone took it there. Very possibly, the same people who made the stone tools. Exiles, I have little doubt, though if all this is the work of your monkey-spiders I would be the first to cheer.'

'We've found no trace of exiles in our drone surveys,' Hazeldene said.

'Quite right!' said Owen. 'Which answers the question of whether to look upriver or downriver. I suggest downriver, where it passes through the forest and into the gorge through the ridge. Our surveys haven't yet looked there in any depth. Where better for them to find fragments from Hamilton's Rise?

And you know – the possibility I find most exciting? What if, among these exiles, there is another like you, Able? Another ingenious exile who has found a way to communicate with the Fermi, perhaps using some device built around a stone like this?'

Myles pushed forward. 'We were just talking about getting an expedition together. This could be a good start – at last!'

'Certainly easier and faster than going up the mountain,' Muranov said. 'But still, we have to think carefully, and—'

'—prepare. I know. But still, this—'

'I'll put it on WeThink,' said Marie.

'Good,' said Owen. He smiled all around. 'Do I smell cooking? I'm famished.'

CHAPTER TWELVE
Wave Function

The Space Station around E-PRIME 667, Tuesday 4 November 2070

Nayak sat in the co-pilot's seat, in what was grandly called the bridge, and felt irrationally nervous. She hoped the novice pilot, no doubt nervous himself, didn't notice.

The bridge was a room next to the Commander's office, with two bucket seats and a control panel more or less identical to that of the *Fighting Chance*. The differences were that fusion power control was direct, rather than shouted over the pilot's shoulder, and that the co-pilot was there as back-up, rather than to sail – or fly – a submarine. The room was wallpapered and floored with screens giving an outside view, from a notional viewpoint at the centre of the Station. A spherical schematic of the Station was rendered as a tracery of faint lines of latitude and longitude around it.

It was like sitting at a control panel in empty space, a black sphere blazing with stars, with a very much dimmed-down representation of E-PRIME 667, the system's sun, more or less dead ahead.

Nayak glanced across at the pilot. She hoped her expression, behind her glasses, was as unreadable as his.

'OK,' she said. 'Let's do this.'

The first pilot from the ten trainees had been chosen, allegedly at random, by Iskander. His name was Ernest Marek, and he'd been a hydroponics engineer in Cloud City. Like all the others, his speciality wasn't his qualification for pilot training. His physical fitness, sharp reflexes and mental acuity were.

The newly built flywheel was deep inside the Station. Like most of the machinery there, including the machines that had built it, it could be controlled remotely from the habitation band. Nayak found this arrangement troubling. It relied too much, it seemed to her, on the stability and security of wireless relays. Iskander and Gironella had assured her this worry was unfounded – the systems were proven tech, multiply redundant, hardened, foolproof – and control of the drive from the habitation band was more than convenient. In an emergency it could be vital. The very slight additional latency – a matter of microseconds – was extremely unlikely ever to be an issue, and would be quite unnoticeable to the pilot.

Right now, Nayak had nothing to do but wait. She felt a pang of sympathy for her father's first time in the passenger seat with her at the wheel.

Still – Marek's first jump would be like her first drive, short and simple, start and stop. Nayak breathed out, and in, and wiped her palms on her thighs.

'Powering up,' said Marek.

'Check.'

'Navigation set.'

'Navigation checked.'

'Orbital insertion factor calculated.'

'Orbital insertion checked.'

'PA system on.'

'Check.'

Marek took a deep breath. 'Attention all personnel. Stand by for FTL jump.'

Even through the room's walls, they could hear the PA system's bray and the crew's answering cheer.

'Flywheel engaged.' Then: 'FTL jump initiated.'

It was as if the lights had flickered. A shiver of unease.

'FTL jump completed. Situation nominal.'

The stars had not moved. The sun was a little brighter in the virtual view, and a lot closer in reality: the Station was now in a stable orbit between those of the system's two inner planets, and at roughly the same distance from E-PRIME 667 as Venus was from the Sun. The solar flux was now what the Station – and its solar power panels – had been designed for.

Ulrich's voice broke in. 'Congratulations, Citizen Marek!'

'Thank you, Commander.'

'Marek, Nayak, you're relieved.'

Nayak pushed up her glasses and disengaged her seat harness. The display disappeared, to be replaced by mundane solid walls and floor. Probably a good idea, she thought. Walking across an invisible floor in illusory vacuum would have been disorienting.

'Too right we're relieved,' she said. 'Well done, Ernest!'

'Thanks, Lakshmi.' The young man looked at her awkwardly. 'Uh, "relieved" is a military term.'

'Kidding!' Nayak sang, untruthfully. She motioned to the door. 'Coffee?'

A voice spoke in her ear. 'We have a problem,' said Sikandar.

'Do we need to jump again?' Nayak lurched towards the seats, Marek following.

'No,' said Sikandar. 'No immediate danger. But let me show you something.'

Nayak and Marek sat down. 'Restore display,' Nayak said. The stars came back.

'What's going on?' Ulrich demanded.

'Sikandar says there's a problem but not an emergency.'

'OK, put it on shared – hard channels only.'

Nayak did. 'Sikandar, show us the problem?'

The stars in the display vanished, to be replaced by a fuzzy image of a globe with several bright dots lined up on either side.

'The gas giant, E-PRIME 667a,' said Sikandar, now over the room's speakers. 'This is a view of it in the last few minutes, just after the jump.' The image flickered. 'And this is it from a few minutes before the jump.'

Nayak stared at the fuzzy globe. 'It looks just the same. The image is a little sharper, that's all.'

'Not the planet,' said Sikandar. 'The moons. A quick alternation will make it clear.'

Before. After. Before. After. Before . . . 'Oh!'

'Yes,' said Sikandar. 'They change position, far more than they should have in that time.'

Nayak laughed, with relief as much as amusement. 'Of course they have! We've jumped about six AU! Nearly a light hour. The light from the moons hasn't had time to catch up yet.'

'I'm not so stupid as to overlook that,' Sikandar said. 'I of course expected to see the moons farther back in their orbits than they had been. As you may see, they are *ahead* of their expected orbital position. And what's more, they seem to be in slightly different orbits, not just different positions in their orbits.'

Nayak closed her eyes and shook her head. 'Did – did the jump take more time than we expected?'

'No,' said Sikandar. 'Every other body in the system is exactly where it should be, to the second.'

Ulrich broke in. 'How do you know all this? How did you *notice*?'

'Pleased to make your acquaintance, Commander,' said Sikandar. 'When your colleague here left me on the hull of the *Fighting Chance*, after the initial jump to this system, I assured her I was enjoying the view, as indeed I was. Some of my cameras have 20X magnification, and I have occupied the time, besides processing my recordings from Venus, with as good observations as the cameras afforded of the planets in this system. Naturally, the satellites of the gas giant are particularly fascinating, so I have a certain familiarity with them. The rotation of the Station is roughly in the plane of the ecliptic, so with movements of my head, or rather helmet, I have been able to observe relatively steadily. Just before the present jump, I chose to amuse myself by focusing on the gas giant and its moons, with a view to observing and measuring their apparent backward movement after the jump. Instead, it's as you see.'

'Wait a moment,' said Ulrich. 'Can we be sure this isn't some software glitch? In your cameras, even if not in, ah, you?'

'That can't be ruled out,' said Sikandar, in the tone of someone speaking through gritted teeth. 'Perhaps you might send someone outside to look through binoculars?'

'Unfortunately,' said Ulrich in a similar tone, 'the equipment of the Station does not run to EVA-adapted binoculars.'

'If I may interject,' said Iskander. A much sharper display of the gas giant and its moons replaced Sikandar's. 'The Station is well provided with external cameras with better magnification than those on this *spacesuit*, and . . . uh-oh.'

'What?' Nayak yelped. Never in her life had she heard Iskander, or any other AI, go 'uh-oh'.

'Sikandar's observed position of the moons is confirmed. And . . .'

The AI was giving a very good impression of not believing what it was about to say. This, too, in Nayak's experience, was unprecedented.

'Yes?'

'And one of them, the moon E-PRIME 667a VI, is missing.'

'Missing? Not occluded?'

'No. Definitely not. A preliminary simulation suggests that the absence of this moon accounts for the slightly different orbits of the others. Furthermore, spectroscopy indicates that the atmospheric compositions of the remaining moons have changed. One of them, E-PRIME 667a V, has almost doubled in mass, and has a surface temperature – from internal and tidal heating – and atmospheric pressure compatible with liquid water. I'm picking up possible biosignatures. The total masses of the moons remain the same. It's as if material from the missing moon has been redistributed among the others.'

Nayak sagged in the seat. She looked across at Marek, who seemed equally perplexed.

'I'm sorry,' she said. 'Really I am. But I still don't believe it. I still think there must be some mistake.'

'We can check with the telescope,' said Ulrich. 'It'll take an hour for the signal to get to it, a few minutes to turn it on the gas giant and another hour for the feed to get back. Until then, let's keep an open mind.'

'You know,' said Marek, 'we could just jump straight back to where we were and get the results right away. For that matter, we could jump close to the gas giant itself, and—'

'No,' said Ulrich.

'I would not recommend making any jump until we understand what has happened,' said Iskander.

'And I would very much concur,' said Ulrich. 'Marek, Nayak, you are relieved and stood down. *Again*. Dismissed.'

The display disappeared. Nayak hauled herself from the seat and trudged to the door.

'We really need that coffee,' said Marek.

'Yes.' Nayak straightened her back and shoulders. As they walked down the corridor she muttered mutinously, '"Until we understand what has happened"!'

'Indeed,' said Marek. 'We could be here for some time. Huh! I was quite looking forward to my next jump.'

Just over two hours later, the camera feed from the telescope began to trickle back. Soon after, it confirmed everything the AIs had said and shown. For a wild moment, Nayak considered asking Gironella to get his machinery to build binoculars adapted for using through an EVA suit faceplate, and let her go out to look for herself through nothing but air, glass, lenses, prisms and vacuum, with no software or AI mediation at all between the errant moons and her disbelieving eyes.

Then, very firmly, she told herself not to be silly.

She had to accept that the moon had vanished. She also had to accept that the numerous scary possible ways to account for this now bouncing around in her mind would have to await more data before she could sort them out. But –

She'd always had a vague distaste for multiverse theories. In her equations, they were redundant. But if she brought *this* transformation back in, *here*, and turned *that* formula around, then –

She was scribbling before she could stop herself.

That evening, the entire Station became a scientific conference. Ulrich convened and chaired. The *Fighting Chance* crew sat together at a table in the nearest refectory, at which every table was occupied. On the way there Nayak had seen other groups crowding offices and labs, or in huddles around some convenient big screen in the corridor. Some, no doubt, watched alone. Everyone could see everyone else on the real screens or on a virtual screen in their glasses, as rows and columns of hundreds of tiny faces. The software zoomed in on an individual's face when they spoke. Iskander made sure no one spoke over anyone else.

Ulrich outlined the situation and then said: 'Here is a thought to start you off. We know from the depositions of Sikandar that the intelligence or intelligences in the alien rocks – the Fermi, as our Alliance colleagues call it or them – can communicate faster than light, at speeds that seem to coincide with those attained by starships. We know that the Fermi can affect tectonic forces. Is it possible, then, that the drive can, too? Did we, in making our latest jump, destroy one moon and essentially terraform another?'

Nayak winced. This had been one of her darker early speculations.

A face flashed. 'Anton Vandenbrouke,' said Ulrich. 'Yes?'

The face and its bio filled the screen. Thinning short hair, sharp features. Analytical chemist. PhD. Catholic University of Louvain. ESA-trained astronaut. One year on the Moon, four years in Cloud City.

'Thank you, Commander–'

'Not here, Dr Vandenbrouke,' said Ulrich. '"Chair", if you please.'

Vandenbrouke smiled and nodded. 'Very well, Katrina. Your opening suggestion is a thought that hadn't occurred to me, for the good reason that it's highly implausible. If the use of the drive could somehow destroy or reshape celestial bodies, do you think the other Powers would have used them secretly for fifty years? As soon as they knew we had the drive, would it not be the first thing they would warn us about? Have any such incidents occurred? If so much as an asteroid were to vanish from the Solar system, I'm confident that we would know about it.'

'I'm not,' said Ulrich.

'I am,' said Iskander.

'I bow to your databases,' said Ulrich. 'Next – Juliette Chemam.'

'One simple addition to your speculation,' said Chemam, an atmospheric exo-meteorologist. 'What if the Fermi – if we must use this slang – are here in this system, and did it deliberately, perhaps as a warning?'

'Dr Chemam's suggestion,' said the next speaker, the astronomer Gianna De Marte, 'is more than excessive! Chair, your opening speculation is leading us far astray, but worse than that, you have based it on a premise for which we have no evidence. That premise is *that this has just happened*. Where are the debris from the collision?'

'Too small for our telescope to resolve?' said Ulrich. 'Removed at FTL speed at the same time as our jump?'

'Unsupported speculations both! Moreover, I've examined the simulations run by Iskander. The orbital dynamics don't add up. There is no way the positions and orbits of the other moons could have changed in the time of our jump. The changes are small – the gravitational influence of E-PRIME 667a VI was slight – but they are many orders of magnitude greater than would have happened in less than a second!'

Ulrich raised a hand. 'We can't know that, Gianna. My speculation – unsupported as it may be – is that something analogous to the wake of a ship, a space-time distortion if you will, was generated by our jump and is responsible for *all* the changes in the E-PRIME 667a system of satellites. Do you have any hypothesis to account for it?'

'Yes,' said De Marte. 'The first moon is not missing and the second has not changed. The system around the gas giant is exactly what we would expect to see if only one larger moon instead of two smaller ones had existed in the first place.'

Clamour in the refectory. The screen of tiny faces flickered like agitated pixels in a digital artwork. Ulrich cut through:

'Dr Lakshmi Nayak.'

Nayak hadn't asked to speak. She might have made an involuntary gesture that gave the impression she did. She grabbed the opportunity.

'I take it our colleague isn't suggesting the moon wasn't there before we jumped?' De Marte shook her head vigorously. 'Very well. So before we jumped, two moons were there, and always had been. After we jumped, one larger moon was there and always had been. Correct?'

'Yes,' said De Marte. 'Precisely.'

'OK,' said Nayak. She took a deep breath, to gather her

thoughts and steady her voice. 'Now, I know how the drive works – the inflaton trap. Nothing in the theory indicates any backwash effects such as Commander, um, Chair postulates. Nor has any use of the drive resulted in that, as far as we know – and we've used it in different circumstances, including repeatedly shuttling the *Fighting Chance* to and from this Station, and short hops in the clouds of Venus. It's true that the Station is almost certainly the most massive object ever moved by a stardrive. Maybe that's key. However, if something like this had happened when we left the Solar system – changing the moons of Jupiter or whatever – it would hardly have passed unnoticed, and word would have reached us while we were at Apis.

'So . . . if it's not any space-warp backwash, then there are two possibilities. One is some causality violation, where our jump today changed the gas giant's moon system in the distant past.' She grimaced. 'I can't rule that out – I have reason to think I might be a causality violation myself. But I don't like it in this case. It's just *ugly*, speaking as a mathematical physicist. Yeah, yeah, I can see the particle physicists laughing.

'The other possibility is – we've arrived in a universe different from the one we left. Maybe different only by the absence of E-PRIME 667a VI, a moon so distant and insignificant that we're the first people to see it as more than a wisp of photons in the most sensitive telescope ever built. Or – maybe different by a lot more!' She swallowed hard. 'I mean, we don't even know if the bodies missing from this universe include Apis. Or Earth.'

Silence. The thought must have occurred to others. Certainly to De Marte. No one had voiced it. Perhaps hearing it from her made their own thoughts more real.

Ulrich cleared her throat. 'Have you finished?'

'Yes.'

'I have a question, Dr Nayak. If this can happen, the same objection applies as does to backwash effects: the regular use of FTL drives for fifty years by Co-ord and Alliance starships. Why has it not happened to them?'

'How do we know it hasn't?' Nayak shot back.

This time, there was a clamour. Ulrich, or Iskander, stilled it. Grant, to everyone's surprise, fought his way to the top of the screen.

'Citizen John Grant, marine engineer.'

Grant stood up. 'Shipbuilder. Trainee starship pilot. And in my spare time, a man of many interests—'

'Obsessions!' Ellen interjected.

'Yes, Ellen, you've every right to call them that. One of my obsessions is nuclear submarines. Their positions at sea are secret, but their comings and goings can't be hidden. Nor can the loss of a sub. Remember when the *Cheng Biguan* was lost in 2059? National mourning in China, global news for days. So while we have to accept that some subs have for decades been nipping off to the stars when they're supposed to be on patrol, we also have to accept that they all came back. Because if they hadn't, we'd know.'

De Marte, again: 'You're assuming the subs that went out are the same as the subs that came back.'

'What?' cried Grant, above a hubbub – to which Nayak had spontaneously contributed her own 'Oh, shit!'. She'd got it, and many of the others had, too. She let De Marte spell it out:

'If a sub comes back to a slightly different universe from the one they left, no one need notice – because in that universe a sub with the same name and same crew departed. And vice versa. Which implies, I'm afraid, that somewhere inconceivably close by yet infinitely far away, we're frantically discussing why the gas giant has an extra moon. And somewhere else, we're not having this discussion at all, because we've arrived in the same universe as the one we left – or at least, one indistinguishable from it to us.'

Ulrich: 'Dr Nayak, do you concur?'

'Let me see.' Nayak closed her eyes to see the equations.

She opened her eyes. Everyone was looking at her. Silent minutes had passed. It seemed she still had the screen.

'It drops out,' she said.

'What does?' Ulrich asked.

'The solution. Well, a solution. One where the wave-function of the inflaton just—' She spread her arms wide. 'I don't like it, but it's consistent.'

'Put your solution up on the Station board,' said Ulrich. 'See if anyone can tear it apart. Meanwhile, we have no choice but to continue to build more drives.' The Commander laughed. 'Well, we have a choice, but that's the one we're making in this universe. If anyone disagrees, you're of course welcome to put it to the vote.'

Ulrich gazed into the distance for a moment. Nayak looked around. People were gesturing at their glasses or thumbing tablets and phones. From all around the endless corridor, a shout echoed: 'Drives!'

'Carried by acclamation,' Ulrich said.

Juliette Chemam raised a virtual hand and was recognised.

'Madame Chair, besides the problem – philosophical and perhaps practical – it raises for us, is not the change in the gas giant's moons a great opportunity? A moon with possible liquid water? A moon that is in astronomical terms habitable? Something strange, so far out from its star. Unique, as far as I know! I for one would love to make a close approach, and study the atmosphere and surface in detail.'

'And so you shall,' said Ulrich, 'as soon as we have built drives for the shuttles, as just agreed.'

'But we already have a ship that could go there: the *Fighting Chance*.'

Ulrich pondered. 'I would be reluctant to risk our only other drive on a speculative mission, especially as it has already been agreed that Grant and his colleagues will take some of us back to Earth.'

'If Earth's still there!' someone shouted.

'Don't paint a devil on the wall,' said Ulrich. She sighed. 'In the end, that decision is for the crew of the *Fighting Chance*.'

Grant conferred, taking a quick poll in a side panel. The only one keen on the idea was – predictably enough – Nayak. The rest were firmly against.

'No,' he said.

'Understood,' said Ulrich. She looked around. 'Conference dismissed.'

CHAPTER THIRTEEN
Returns

The Space Station around E-PRIME 667, Tuesday 11 November 2070

The day before the *Fighting Chance* was due to leave, Grant got a ping from Milloy.

Ellen looked up from her book. 'Who was that?'

'Francesca. Wants to meet us at the Commander's office.'

They found Ulrich standing outside her office with Milloy, Nayak, and twelve people – two from the original Station crew, ten from Cloud City – who'd already asked for transfer back to Earth. Grant was surprised to see the astronomer Gianna De Marte among them.

'Too many for the office,' Ulrich said. 'And shouldn't take long. All of you except Lakshmi are going back tomorrow. Francesca has a request which she made some time ago. I and the committee are fine with it, but really it's up to the rest of you to decide.' She glanced at Milloy. 'Over to you.'

'I'd like us to stop over at Apis,' Milloy said. 'Just a quick landing, on New Mu, to drop off me and Sikandar.'

'Drop you off where?'

'Near the Fermi outcrop on New Mu – Hamilton's Rise.'

'Like, at the Union settlement?'

'No,' said Milloy. 'We know there will be Alliance troops there. We don't want complications with them, or to make complications for the Union settlement people themselves.'

'I'm with you there,' Grant said. 'Entirely. So where, then?'

Milloy outlined a flat rectangle with the tips of her forefingers. Grant put his glasses on and looked down at the shared image, an overlay of the Station's most recent images with the local maps and pictures Iskander had lifted from the settlers' phones. Milloy pointed. 'The Union settlement is *there*. We're thinking of landing *here*, on the other side of the range, on a small plateau below the forest and close to where the river cuts through to the ocean. Iskander has mapped an ascent route to the outcrop, which between me and Sikandar should be doable. Can you put us down there, preferably at night?'

'It shouldn't be difficult,' Grant said. He glanced over at Ellen. 'What do you think?'

Ellen scoffed. 'After what we went through on Venus, landing on Apis should be a doddle. But why, Francesca?'

'You heard Perry Walworth. The robot Marcus Owen is almost certainly there on New Mu, and I and Sikandar have a bone to pick with him. Besides, I want to see if Sikandar can communicate directly with the Fermi, like it did on Venus. Especially as the Alliance and Co-ord are trying to do the same thing.'

'Isn't that risky?' someone asked.

'Well, yes,' said Milloy. 'But not as risky as leaving the other Powers to get the jump on us.'

'We've given this thought,' said Ulrich. 'And to be honest, I'd rather that thing was down on Apis, where there's no

Iskander for it to interfere with, and have it doing something useful for the Union, than go on having it near us, even outside the Station and firewalled. The only risk to you is the risk of landing on Apis at all. It's a small one, I reckon, but it's a matter for you and your passengers to decide.'

The passengers huddled, then divided: nine for, three against.

'Those unwilling to go via Apis – will you go with the majority, or not at all?'

All three backed out.

'Fair enough,' Grant said.

'There's just one thing,' Ellen said, raising her voice. 'For those who're coming. The real risk we're taking isn't crashing or getting caught on a side jaunt to Apis. It's going at all. We might find we're in a universe with no Apis, or no Earth, and then come back here to find no Station.'

Grant felt shocked. This wasn't like Ellen. 'That's – very unlikely, surely.' He turned to Nayak. 'Do your calculations show any different?'

'Very unlikely is right,' Nayak said. 'Like, I don't know, millions to one. I wouldn't worry about it.'

Ellen persisted. 'But very unlikely is still possible. Which means that in some possible world, it happens. We know now that other possible worlds are real – because we're in one! So if we go, millions of versions of us make it through. But there are worlds where we don't. It's not a *risk*. For some versions of us, it's inevitable.'

Nayak shook her head. 'I don't think that's how it works. In my calculations anyway, the probabilities cluster close. Most of the time, any difference in worlds is quite unnoticeable.'

'We've noticed one!'

Nayak looked uncomfortable. 'It's still a very similar world. But, yes, if all these worlds are real—'

'If all these worlds are real,' Ulrich cut in, 'then some version of us is right now being destroyed by some freak event! Do we mourn them? We don't even think about them! All you've done is say in a different way that there *is* a risk.' She smiled. 'In all seriousness, perhaps we could all do with philosophy counselling!' Her expression became bleak. 'We did have such a counsellor on Cloud City, and we could do with her now, but unfortunately she was among the casualties.' Ulrich's mouth quirked. 'So to get one, you'll have to go back to Earth anyway.'

'Ah, the hell with it,' said Ellen. 'I've been too long cooped up here. I'll take my chances.'

The gathering broke up. Most went for coffee. Grant and Nayak went for a walk, twice around the corridor. Now and then someone would jog past them.

'You're definitely not coming?'

Nayak shook her head. 'It's been hard to come to a decision, but I've made up my mind. I know I miss Earth – heck, I miss Tarbet, and Glasgow, and even Port Glasgow. I know I'll miss the yard, and my own job, too. And it's not like I love it here. I mean, look.'

She pointed ahead of her. The corridor ahead curved gradually but quite visibly up, until its floor was occluded by its ceiling.

'I've run around this so many times, and no matter what scenes and sounds I have in my glasses, I end up feeling like I'm on an enormous hamster wheel.'

'That's why I use the gym,' Grant said.

'But then, look at that!' She pointed to a screen, an illusory window on a black and bottomless sky, blazing with innumerable points of light. 'What an opportunity! How many people can say they've gone to the stars?'

'Can *we*?' Grant said. He waved at the window. 'They look as far away as ever to me.'

Nayak laughed. 'That's one way of looking at it! A very Scottish and gloomy view, if I may say so.'

'Damn right.' He walked a few more steps. 'Another Earth,

though – that would be something! And we know there's at least one, Apis, and maybe far more.'

'We've been through all that.'

'Yeah, we have.' That ground was as well trodden as the corridor floor.

'Besides,' Nayak said, as if trying to persuade herself rather than him, 'I'm needed more here than back home. You don't need a mathematical physicist, and if you do you can find one easily enough. Out here, I'm the only one. And I'm doing work no one else could!' She laughed. 'I'm the only physicist who has been through the double slit experiment and out the other side.'

'I've always vaguely imagined that like bugs spattered on a windshield,' Grant replied.

'No, no, that's— Ah. OK.'

'We're going to miss you, you know,' Grant said. 'You're our lucky charm. You can't die before writing back to yourself.'

'You believe that now?'

'Not exactly,' Grant said. 'But I have to admit, all this talk about different possible fatal outcomes does concentrate the mind.'

'It's like Katrina said, and I said – just a different way of saying there's a risk. And anyway, I'm not at all sure any more that I am a lucky charm. It's cold comfort knowing that *some* version of me can't die. The point is to do what we can to make sure we're among the surviving versions of ourselves.'

'We've done all we can.' He sighed. 'I suppose.'

'You're happy with your training?'

'Happy is not quite the word,' Grant said. 'But I'm pretty sure Ellen and I can fly the ship back to the Clyde.'

'Not forgetting to allow for the tide.'

'Yup. Are you happy with your other trainees?'

'Oh yeah,' said Nayak. 'And they're happy with their ships. Let me show you something.'

*

Nayak led him to a screen a short walk down the corridor. Grant stood and marvelled. The two shuttles, now retrofitted with FTL drives, hung in orbit alongside the Station in the full glare of the sun. He'd glimpsed the shuttles during the Venus rescue mission, but that hadn't been a good time to appreciate their aerodynamic beauty: sculpted and streamlined, scorched by repeated atmospheric entries, pitted by sulphuric acid droplets from the clouds. Their scars told their story. They'd been designed to glide into the upper layers of the Venusian atmosphere, decelerate and aerobrake to dock with Cloud City, load and unload passengers and/or cargo, then drop tail first into the clouds until their ramjets lit and then their rockets fire so that they could blast to low orbit. They were basically space-planes that never landed. In theory they could be operated by a highly skilled pilot; in practice, their hair-raising feats were left to AI.

In the E-PRIME 667 system, they hadn't at first been expected to be called upon to do anything quite so dramatic. When the Station had arrived the only planet with an atmosphere thick enough for such a stunt was the gas giant, and its gravity ruled it out. Instead, they would make FTL jumps to some of the larger asteroids, and drop off first surveying, then mining, robots. By the time the robot miners had extracted enough useful material to make its retrieval worthwhile, the plan was that the Station would have built FTL tractor units that could be attached to cargo carriers. Meanwhile, the shuttles could go off exploring other systems and returning with data, and even samples.

Now, however, their first mission would be to a new world that very definitely had an atmosphere: the apparently transformed moon E-PRIME 667a V.

Well, good luck to them! He was going home, and he couldn't wait.

Assuming there was still a home to go to.

He put that thought out of his mind.

Wednesday 12 November 2070

Milloy sat on top of her survival pack on the floor of the *Fighting Chance*. Between her knees was a high-powered anti-materiel rifle, and across her back and chest a score of its heavy slugs. The weapon, built in the Station's robot workshops from metal that had cooled when the Earth was molten, was capable of taking out any unarmoured vehicle or bringing down a helicopter or small aeroplane. Most of Marcus Owen was as vulnerable as the human form he emulated. His inner core was not. A steely skeletal remnant of himself would survive a machine-gun burst or a nearby bomb. It wouldn't survive a hit from this.

Nine other evacuees from the Station sat or squatted beside or opposite her, most clinging to whatever stanchion or brace came to hand. One, the astronomer Gianna De Marte, had grabbed the chance to sit in the observation bubble beneath the cockpit. Farther back, Omar Khan fussed over the fusion pot. Morag Rafferty stood by the airlock. Outside, but very much present in Milloy's mind, the descent suit with the Sikandar AI clung to the hull.

Creaks and clunks sounded through the ship as grapples let go.

'Forward jet easy,' said Grant.

'Aye, aye,' said Ellen, in an ironic tone.

The thrust was barely detectable. Milloy flipped her glasses to outside cameras. Slowly the Station drifted past, and then away. Ulrich's voice came through.

'You're clear, *Fighting Chance*. Safe home.'

'Thank you, Commander,' Ellen replied. 'Stay safe yourselves.'

The Station dwindled. Still huge.

'Omar, give us some juice,' Grant said.

'Powering up,' Khan called back.

The field wasn't even on yet. Milloy felt her knees quiver.

Her gut was queasy from Apis-specific antibiotics, cooked up on the Station from prescriptions in the Black Horizon and NASA information packs. Her palms were slick on the rifle. In a few minutes, if all went according to plan, she'd be stepping out of the hatch onto Apis. It felt more scary than her descent to Venus. Huddled in the ship's belly, she wondered if this was what it was like for soldiers in troop carriers. She told herself not to be pretentious. No one would be shooting at her.

'Stand by for FTL jump,' Grant said.

The stars, hitherto steady, sparkled in varied colours, as if a prism was in front of each one. The colours merged in a rainbow wash, like petrol on a puddle, and the dread climbed.

Milloy closed her eyes, compressed her lips and took the fall.

And then they were out of it, and still falling. Really falling. Milloy opened her eyes, expecting free fall in low Apis orbit, and saw white clouds whip past. Then black sky above and something almost as dark beneath, rushing up.

'Short jump,' said Grant. 'Brace for landing.'

'Can't get much more fucking braced than I am,' Morag Rafferty swore, to no one in particular.

Like a blink in which you miss something–

And then they were down, quite softly, in what looked like moonlight. The landing bars scraped. Something outside cracked. Silence, except for everyone's breathing.

'Well, John,' said Ellen, 'looks like you did it.'

'Thanks,' Grant said. He checked the comms band and looked over his shoulder. 'And at least Apis is still here, and from the radio chatter it's the same as the one we left. Everyone all right?'

Everyone was.

'OK,' said Grant. 'Francesca, time to go.'

Milloy stood up. She lugged the rifle and the pack to the hatch. Morag opened it. Fresh air with strange new smells came in. Morag leaned out and took a sniff. Then, to Milloy's surprise, she pushed ahead.

'Come on,' she said. 'You were the first woman on Venus. Gie me my wee chance tae say I've set foot on another planet.'

She jumped out, looked around for a few seconds, then climbed back in, grinning all over her face.

'Seems safe enough,' she said. 'Good luck.'

Unimpressed by this stunt, Milloy returned a tight smile and a mutter of thanks. She heaved the survival pack out, ported the rifle carefully under the low rim of the hatch, stepped out and jumped to the ground. She was standing on something like grass, on gently sloping ground, a few hundred metres from what looked like trees. Surf boomed in the distance; closer, a waterfall dinned. The apparent moonlight came from a planet bright and large and close enough to show a visible disc. Her glasses enhanced the illumination to a monochrome daylight. She took a few steps away to look all around, and saw nothing moving nearby.

She turned and waved. Morag waved back and closed the hatch. The descent suit raised itself on all fours, then did a handstand on the top of the hull, then a handspring, to land on its feet with a thud that Milloy felt as well as heard.

It hefted the survival pack in one hand and strode over.

'Time to go,' it said. 'Walk with me. Don't look back.'

After they'd walked thirty metres blue light flared behind them, casting their shadows almost to the trees. Air filled the sudden vacuum with a thunderclap. Blinking at yellow after-images, Milloy looked back at the place where the ship had been.

'Good luck, *Fighting Chance*!'

'Good luck fighting chance?' said Sikandar, archly.

'Fuck off, machine,' said Milloy. 'I'm not in the mood.'

CHAPTER FOURTEEN
Big River

New Mu, Apis, Tuesday 11 November 2070 to Wednesday 12 November 2070

The expedition was smaller than Myles had hoped. He'd asked for a squad of Alliance soldiers, the full complement of Alliance scientists and a dozen or so Union settlers, preferably with militia experience. The consensus of the settlers – via a stormy meeting and WeThink – was having none of it. Nor was the military. Knight had no soldiers to spare from guarding the settlement, and had no authorisation to do so. The settlers were spooked by the still-unexplained arrow attack, to say nothing of the traces of potentially hostile exiles nearby. In the end WeThink summed up the general view: the settlement could spare only Myles and Marie. This was pitched as an honour. Since the arrival and departure of the Space Station, the two of them had gained some glamour and cachet (undeserved, in Myles's view, but there it was) from their connection with John Grant and his heroic crew.

'Good,' Lieutenant Knight had said. 'You two can lead. It's your lot's project. Make sure you print out Union flag patches for everyone's overalls.'

'Yes, sir!'

As for the scientists – one geologist, the Russian palaeo-analyst and one biologist were all who needed to go. The choice between Nelson Hayes and Cindy Patel, Emma Hazeldene and Sharianne Adler, had been left to the scientists. It had been more a quarrel than an argument, from what Myles had heard and overheard. Jenkins, of course, was indispensable if they were to encounter exiles. And Owen, well . . . no one was going to stop him.

That, and a drone overhead uplinked to the comsat network, was all they had. The rifles and ammunition had been part of the standard stores from the arks, as was the inflatable, made from the same fabric as their overalls: thin as Mylar, tough as Kevlar.

'Well,' Myles said, 'let's get moving.'

Owen unfolded the inflatable and worked the foot pump with superhuman energy. When the boat was ready Owen passed out six carbon-fibre collapsible paddles and showed everyone how to unfold and extend them. The team floated the boat, climbed in and pushed off. They paddled swiftly out to midstream. The current caught and carried them, and thereafter they had little to do but steer. Owen sat in the bow, keeping watch. The drone kept pace, a glint in the sky, its solar panels out like wings.

'Wow!' Marie cried, as the boat was borne around the last bend of the big river and the valley came into full view just ahead, steep-sided, deep and dark.

'Spoken for us all,' said Muranov.

Owen gestured to his left and ahead, to the apex of the curve of the bend, where a spit of shingle lay under the bank. The three starboard paddlers redoubled their efforts; their counterparts on the port side slacked off. The inflatable swung towards the shore and crunched onto gravel. Owen vaulted off the bow and hauled the boat further up. They all stepped out dry-shod. Marie scorned Myles's offer of a helping hand.

'No ladies stepping off this boat,' she said.

'Yeah, yeah.'

They all followed Owen as he dragged the boat one-handed over the shingle, up the one-metre jump on to the bank, and across the not-grass to the nearest tree, where he made it fast.

'Leaving it there?' Jenkins asked. 'Could be handy further in.'

'Nope,' said Owen. 'It's all rapids and waterfalls from here.' He stashed the footpump in a pocket in the dinghy and took back the paddles, to collapse and slide them into loops in the deck. 'And I'm not carrying it.'

'Exiles might steal it,' Myles said.

'Good luck to them,' said Owen. 'Save them mucking about in coracles. We're walking back, anyway.'

'Point.' Myles looked up and around. On his left the slope of the mountain passed out of sight among trees. Ahead, the river cut through a V-shaped valley about fifty metres wide at the foot. On both sides a variously narrow riverbank formed by millennia of flooding and silt gave way to a belt of stunted trees and underbrush on a steepening slope, and then it was cliffs and scree slopes all the way up, becoming higher the deeper the valley cut into the mountain. The din of the river, running fast in the narrow channel and crashing repeatedly into boulders and fallen rocks, filled the spray-damp air. They'd timed their arrival for around noon: the valley was at its brightest, the shadows at their shortest.

'Grab a bite,' Myles said.

After ten minutes they pressed on, the drone scouting ahead.

Fourteen hundred metres into the valley, a rockfall extended from the cliffs through the trees and down into the river. It was far too high to see over. The tumbled boulders, some of them metres on a side, looked stable: soil had accumulated and small plants had grown in shelves, cracks, and between edges. Here and there a brash sapling had shouldered up, fated to become bonsai.

Myles beckoned the drone lower and scanned the rockfall. An app in his glasses outlined a route over. He shared it with the others.

'Who's the most agile?'

'I am,' said Patel. 'Scrambling's my thing.' Hazeldene and Muranov nodded. Owen looked smug.

'OK, Cindy,' said Myles. 'You lead the way, then we'll follow. Slow and careful. The rest of you, remember she's lighter than most of us, so test each move for yourselves. No falls, no scrapes, no sprains.'

Patel tightened the straps on her pack, slid her walking pole under them, selected her own route in preference to that of the app and made her way to the top hand over hand, rock by rock. A minute later she called to say that she was safely over. Myles nodded to Marie. She raised her eyebrows.

'I'll go last,' Myles said. 'We need someone with a rifle on both sides.'

'OK.' Up and over she went. Jenkins followed, with flowing agility, his spear at his back through his belt. Myles nodded to Owen, who disdained to use his hands as he danced up the chaos of rock on a route of his own. Hazeldene next, testing each rough block before putting her weight on it, glancing now and then up the rockfall. About to clamber over and around the highest rock, her head just above the top, she froze.

'What is it?' Myles thought she had seen some danger in the distance. She looked back and down, over her shoulder. Her feet, firmly on a block, were perhaps four metres above Myles's head.

'I can't.'

'What?'

'I can't go *over*.'

Myles checked that all was well behind. It was. 'Why not?'

'I just can't.'

'You have vertigo?'

'No, it's like – oh, shit.' She pressed herself against the sloping rock, face and head down from the crest, gripping the edge. 'Now that you mention it, yes, that, too. Thanks a bunch.'

Myles thumbed his earpiece and raised Marie. 'Everything OK over there?'

'Fine, yes. Keeping a look out. What's up with Emma?'

'Don't know. Hang on.'

Myles and Muranov stood looking up at Hazeldene. 'Can you tell us what's the matter?' Myles called out.

'Everything's . . . rolling over and over. If I move I'll fall. I know it's not true, but that's what it's like.'

Muranov made to climb up to her, got a first handhold and foothold then stepped back.

'I have a very bad feeling,' he said.

'Yeah, tell me about it!'

The Russian grabbed Myles's shoulders and stared at him, eyes wide and rolling, as if frantic. 'No, I mean it. I have a bad feeling.' He let go of Myles and clutched the sides of his head. 'Right here.' Muranov sank into a squat and rocked back and forth, holding his head.

'Oh, *Christ*!' Marie's angry shout was carried over the obstacle and above the white noise of the water. Myles called her again on the phone.

'What's up?'

'It's Cindy and Able now. They're sitting here on a rock clinging to each other and moaning.'

'Georgi's in no better shape. What the fuck's going on?'

'It's like they've all been poisoned,' Marie said. 'Was it the water? Something from the river? Something they ate?'

'We all ate and drank the same.' Myles said it more for reassurance than from belief. If they had ingested whatever was doing this, it was clearly variable in its onset. It could yet strike him and Marie. Owen, perhaps not. Myles had only the haziest notion of that android's physiology, but knew it was far from human. He circled the drone, taking in the view: Marie looking anxiously down at Jenkins and Patel, huddled together and quaking like children caught in some disaster beyond their comprehension; Owen scanning ahead and up and around, alert as a radar in a missile crisis, poised on his toes; Hazeldene still clinging white-knuckled to the rock as if she might fall off. And Muranov in front of him a pathetic ball of funk.

Owen's voice broke in. 'It's the rock.'

'What?'

'The rock is doing that to them. Through the touch of their hands.'

Myles recalled Owen's upright ascent.

'So why not to Marie?'

'That was my clue,' said Owen. 'Our colleagues have all been in clefts inside Fermi rocks. You and Marie have not. You're not sensitised, so you're safe. I may be, I may not. I didn't touch the rock, but I too have been in such a cleft.'

'At MacHinery Ridge?'

'On Venus. Long story.'

'Yeah, I heard.'

Myles nerved himself to inspect the surface, bringing his glasses close to it, magnifying the texture. Lichens grew on it; tiny red arthropods crawled over it. Faint banding, a glitter of mica.

'It's just ordinary metamorphic rock,' he said. 'Same as we've been walking over.'

'No doubt,' Owen said dryly, 'you have a clear understanding of what the rocks atop this range can and can't do? What they can and can't use to transmit their influence?'

'Well, no,' Myles allowed. 'So what now?'

'How's your sense of balance?'

'OK, I suppose. Normal.'

'Great! Then you'll just need a bit of mental discipline. Hang on.'

A moment later Owen appeared at the top of the rocks. He stepped down to the block where Hazeldene's feet rested, and stood beside her looking forward.

'Emma,' he said. 'I'm going to hold you steady, get you to your feet, and help you over. You won't fall. Do you understand?'

Hazeldene raised her head. 'Yes.'

'Can you push yourself up a bit, weight on your hands and knees?'

Hazeldene slowly did.

'OK.' Owen stooped. 'Take my hand.'

Very slowly, Hazeldene raised her left hand from the edge of the block she was pressed against. Owen reached across in front of him and grasped her hand with his left. 'Good. Now the other.'

With even more apparent reluctance, she let go. Owen reached around her shoulders and caught that hand, too. 'Now. I've got you. Lean back a bit more, on to your feet. Keep your eyes closed. Yes.'

They were standing side by side, in a pose that reminded Myles of ballroom dancers going into a turn.

'OK,' Owen said. 'Now—'

Hazeldene screamed and let go of his hands. Her whole body flexed, as if she'd had an electric shock. For a moment she and Owen both swayed, seeming about to topple. Owen ducked, put one foot unerringly on a lower block, and in a flurry of movement swept Hazeldene off her feet. He bounded to the top carrying her on his arms and was down the far side out of sight before Myles could draw breath. Hazeldene's indignant, terrified screams carried over the rocks and echoed from the cliffs, and for about half a minute continued, fading. Twenty seconds later Owen was back. He capered down the rockfall.

'She's a hundred metres on,' he said. 'That might help.' He looked down at Muranov. 'On your feet, man.'

'I can't. I'll fall.'

'It's all right.' Owen squatted and reached out. 'Give me your hands.'

They stood up, slowly, together. Muranov, eyes tight shut, lurched sideways. In a moment he was in a firefighter's lift across Owen's shoulders and being carried over the rocks. He screamed, too, and thrashed. The robot's hold was implacable, his balance undisturbed. Owen could have been going up stairs.

Again the screams diminished. Checking the drone view, Myles saw Owen lower Muranov to the ground beside where Hazeldene sat looking around as if bewildered. Owen sprinted back, past where Marie stood by Patel and Jenkins, then again danced up and over the rocks.

'Now you,' he said.

'I don't want to be carried.'

'That's the spirit! Now, if I were absolutely sure I'd just tell you to scramble over, but I'm not.'

'Me neither.'

'Quite right. There's an app in your glasses called Footprint. Got it?'

Myles flickered fingers. 'Yes.'

'Now all you have to do is literally follow in my footsteps. Don't worry, I'll take it slowly.'

Owen set off up the rocks. The app painted glowing footprints where he trod. Myles climbed after him, step by step, using his pole to steady himself. Some strides were awkward, some rocks looked unstable, or the foothold too small, or the slope too steep. Myles did exactly as Owen had, all the way fighting the impulse to scramble, or to put a foot down on a more obvious spot. The way down was even harder, as expected, but he made it. He jumped off the final rock to the ground.

'Well done!' said Owen.

'Thanks.'

Myles went over to Marie. 'Are you still all right?'

'Fine, apart from feeling sorry for these two.'

'Let's get them moving,' said Owen. 'Think of them as very drunk.'

'Prone to falling down, puking and taking offence?' said Marie.

'You got it.'

Owen squatted down behind Patel and Jenkins and pushed his head and shoulders in between them, then put his arms around their shoulders. 'Myles, Marie – get on either side.'

Myles took Jenkins, Marie took Patel. Between them the three raised the two to their feet. Walking carefully, swaying, the five made their unsteady way along the bank to where Hazeldene and Muranov were now standing. Several times they almost toppled into the bushes or the river. Marie kept everyone upright using fancy footwork and throwing her weight in useful directions.

'Fuck sake,' said Myles. 'How do you do this?'

'Hen parties,' said Marie.

Owen snorted. 'Always something to learn.'

They staggered up to Hazeldene and Muranov and let Patel and Jenkins slump to the ground.

'What the fuck just happened?' said Hazeldene. Her face was almost green with pallor.

'You're welcome,' said Owen. 'I suspect some induced disturbance to your inner ear, causing symptoms similar to—'

'Please don't say—' said Hazeldene, then clapped her hand to her mouth. She stumbled away and vomited in the bushes.

'Ah, I feel better for that,' she said, on returning.

'I'll take your word for it,' said Muranov. 'I don't feel at all – oh!'

And off he went. Patel and Jenkins in due course went through the same routine.

'What was all that about?' Jenkins asked, when he was more or less back to normal.

'Let's walk on,' said Owen. 'Just to be sure.'

They resumed their file and walked on. The mountain to their left now occluded the sun, casting the bottom of the valley and the lower half of the far side into shadow. The drone pinged Myles's earpiece.

'Knight here,' it relayed. 'You lot all right?'

'So far, so good, Lieutenant,' said Myles.

A slight but noticeable transmission delay, then: 'Didn't look so good back there.'

'Owen saved the day, Lieutenant. We're not sure what caused the difficulty, but we seem to be over it.'

'Report back at once if anything untoward happens again.'

'Understood, Lieutenant.'

Myles signed off.

They passed a waterfall, and a pool at its foaming foot over which insects skimmed, swift narrow-winged boids swooped on insects, and some predator lurking under the surface lashed out a tentacle to snatch boids from the air. For a moment the party stopped to watch.

'Ah, ecology,' said Marie.

'Red in tooth and claw,' said Hazeldene.

Jenkins turned to Owen. 'You were going to tell us what you think happened back there.'

Owen repeated what he'd said to Myles.

'I reckon you're right it was the Fermi that did it,' said Jenkins. 'But it was kind of specific – vertigo and nausea. Yeah, it was frightening – I don't mind admitting – but it wasn't like the general fucking dread the Ridge gave us.'

Jenkins and the scientists discussed it further. Myles looked at Marie, and saw she shared his impatience.

'This is literally not getting us anywhere,' Marie said. 'I say we press on.'

A little farther on the bank dropped five metres steeply in front of them to the lower level of the river flowing on from the pool. Ahead the valley floor widened from fifty metres to two hundred for the next two kilometres or so before narrowing again. A breeze coming towards them carried a faint hint of the sea.

Myles stopped, and pointed. About halfway along of this stretch of the valley, millennia of erosion and some weakness in the rock had exposed the side of the mountain more deeply than before or behind. Scree slopes extended from the cliffs through the trees to the river. Beyond the cliffs, away up on their left, the tops of the crystal pillars caught the afternoon sun.

'Looks like this might be a good place to find debris from Hamilton's Rise.'

Patel and Muranov zoomed their glasses, consulted, and agreed.

'There's a fan of scree right across the river,' Patel said. 'It could even be the place where the rock we found was first picked up.'

'Fingers crossed,' said Jenkins.

Myles let Owen guide the party in a steep descent to the lower level, repeating the trick with the Footprint app, this time on soil and gravel rather than rocks. They all came off the bottom of the slope running from the small landslides they'd made on their way down, and ran on for a few metres to stop and laugh with relief.

'At least we didn't get vertigo this time,' Hazeldene said.

Jenkins pointed down the valley. 'Smoke!'

CHAPTER FIFTEEN

Ancients of New Mu

New Mu, Apis, Tuesday 11 November 2070 to Wednesday 12 November 2070

From just inside the belt of trees, beyond the scree slopes that Patel had pointed out, the thin line of smoke rose – straight up at first, then caught by the breeze and dissipated.

Owen ostentatiously sniffed the air. 'Burning wood.' Another sniff. 'Roasting animal tissue.'

'You're having a laugh,' said Jenkins.

'My nose is rather more sensitive than yours, my friend. And given the amount of rain that has fallen recently, I very much doubt that any wood over there is naturally dried. We may have found the makers of the stone arrows.'

'Or of the high-tech arrows, huh?' said Muranov, with a sidelong glance at Myles.

'Maybe,' Myles said. 'But I doubt it, for all the reasons you gave. If these arrows came from the Fermi we'll find out soon enough.'

'And if what we felt when we crossed that rockfall came from them,' Muranov went on, 'we've had our second warning.'

'Do you want us to stop now?' Owen demanded.

Muranov shrugged. 'No, just . . . proceed with caution.'

Myles snorted. 'That's what we're doing anyway! Everyone OK with going on?'

Everyone was. Myles reported the situation to Knight, who concurred: 'It's what you came for,' he said. 'Good luck.'

'Thanks.'

'Keep me in the loop.'

'Understood, Lieutenant.'

They re-formed the single file, and Myles led them on, along the riverbank. Boids vanished into the treetops and the wind freshened. Hamilton Rise became a faint glow behind darkening clouds, then faded altogether. Rain fell, heavy and hard. It blurred their glasses within seconds, and buffeted the drone, making its view jerky as well as blurry. Myles pulled up his peaked hood, and slipped his glasses inside his overall to wipe them dry on his shirt. By the time he put them back on and peered through the rain the smoke had gone, the fire presumably doused by the downpour.

'Stay alert, everyone!'

'All clear behind,' Marie replied.

'And around,' Jenkins added.

The rain passed. The air remained chill, the ground soggy. They reached the scree slope, a great spill of small, rough rocks that partly dammed the river, spreading out into a fan of debris through which narrow, deep torrents forced their way to the main flow farther down. The scree rose less than half a metre at its highest, and more than twenty metres across. Beyond lay many scattered boulders, on the bank and in the river.

Myles stopped.

'Should I go first?' Owen asked.

'No. That wouldn't prove anything.' Myles turned to face the others. 'Any volunteers?'

Patel stepped forward. 'I'll go. I wanted to look in the river for Fermi stones anyway.'

Myles motioned her on. 'Good on you, Cindy. If you feel anything like you felt before, Marcus can carry you back.'

Rather gingerly, Patel set off. She walked forward and to the right, towards the nearest stream. Along the way she stooped and hefted a stone.

'Same rock as before,' she said, turning it around in her hands. 'Definitely off the mountain.' She waited a moment, then laughed. 'No queasy feelings.'

She went over to the edge of the stream, and looked up and down, then backed away, shaking her head.

'Can't see anything but ordinary rock.'

They all crossed the scree to join her on the other side, and walked on another hundred metres or so until they were below the spot from which the smoke had risen. Myles sent the drone over for a look, but the trees were too dense for them to be able to make out anything from above.

'What now?' Hazeldene said.

'Anyone got a smaller drone?'

'Yeah, I have,' Marie said, making to take off her backpack. Jenkins held up his hand.

'Hang on,' he said. 'I reckon we should just wait here for a bit. Find some place to sit down, grab a bite, have a chat. And, meanwhile, keep an eye out, all around.'

'Why?' Marie asked.

'Look at us!' Jenkins waved an arm around. 'Armed, wearing weird clothes, glasses over our eyes, packs on our backs – heck, from a distance we don't even look human, if you've never seen the likes of us before.'

He demonstratively took off his glasses and his pack, unzipped his overall to the waist and shrugged himself out of its upper half. He tied the sleeves loosely around his waist, sat on a nearby boulder and laid down his spear.

Myles looked around the others. 'If anyone here knows exiles, Able does! He's got a point.'

He followed Jenkins's example, and Marie sat down beside him. The rest followed, sitting in a rough circle, on stones or on the not-grass. Myles and Marie laid their rifles across their knees.

'OK,' Myles said. 'Let's eat, but everyone keep looking past the person opposite whenever you can.'

'I can do better than that,' Owen said. He stood up and sauntered around, now and then wandering down to the river, then back. Out of the corner of his eye, Myles observed how Owen's eyes scanned everywhere, how his nose sniffed the air, and how he cocked his head this way and that to listen. Other senses, Myles guessed, were being used too.

Marie nudged him. 'Don't keep looking at Marcus. Keep looking over Georgi's shoulder towards the trees.'

'Yeah, you're right. Sorry.' Myles shifted his gaze and munched again on his protein bar.

'I don't trust that thing at all,' Marie added.

'Me neither. But it's hard to think of him as a "thing", when you get to know him.'

'And you have?'

'Well, kind of. He chats with everybody, and he's always interested and has interesting things to say.'

'Of course he does, he's a spy!'

'See what I mean?'

Marie snorted, then said: 'Don't move!'

'What?'

'I saw a flash. In the trees, just to Emma's left.'

'Uh-huh,' Jenkins said. 'Emma, look past me and up the other side. See if there are any flashes back.'

Hazeldene looked up, and to left and right. Owen continued to prowl.

'Flash,' Hazeldene said. 'Top of the tree line, hundred metres downriver.'

'And again, behind you,' said Marie.

'Thirteen heat sources, spreading out to our left and right,' Owen reported. 'Distinct human smell. And a similar number among the trees on the far bank. Everybody, just casually keep your weapons close to hand.'

Myles and Marie shifted their hands slightly. 'Uh-huh.'

The drone circled higher, covering both banks. Owen squatted behind Hazeldene and Muranov, between the party and the trees, his hands empty and loose, upturned.

'And here they come,' he said. 'No sudden movements.'

A woman with long white hair stepped out from under the trees and walked towards them across the wet not-grass of the valley floor. Then, one by one, others appeared – three younger women, and nine children. The adults wore bright assemblages of arthropod carapaces and other parts, over trousers. The children were all wearing loose ragged shifts, with faded decorations printed on the front. After a moment of puzzlement Myles recognised the garments as ancient T-shirts. One young woman was black, the other women and children apparently white European. Hazeldene, Muranov and Patel slowly turned their heads as the group approached. The young women and children converged behind the older woman, to stop about ten metres away.

Myles checked the drone view.

'Don't look now,' he said, 'but there's a dozen half-naked young men on the far bank, just below the trees, aiming spears.'

'Play it cool,' said Owen. 'Myles, Marie – leave your rifles, stand up and walk over. I'll stand up and circle back to where you're sitting now. If necessary, I can take out the spearchuckers the moment they're about to throw.'

'How can you tell?' Myles said, standing up slowly, empty-handed.

'I'm good at reading intent from stance and expression,' Owen said. 'I'm a diplomat.'

'Fuck, I hope he's right,' Marie murmured.

Together, Myles and Marie walked past the others and stopped a few paces from the old woman. They raised their right hands. She did, too. Her face was tanned and lined. She wore a pendant of smooth green rock: Fermi rock, still lively within. Her feet, like those of the others, were bare. Her eyes, bright pools in deltas of crinkles, looked them up and down, then widened.

She smiled, showing white teeth with gaps.

'Yoon yun,' she said, wonderingly. She pointed at Myles, then at Marie. 'Yoon yun! Yooyoonyun?'

Myles and Marie looked at each other.

'I don't understand,' Myles said.

'Yoo don geddit?' the woman said. She stepped closer, reached out and poked at Myles's shoulder, then Marie's. 'Yoon yun!' Then she stepped back and raised her eyebrows.

Myles looked down at where her finger had jabbed. His shoulder patch, the Union flag –

'Oh!' Marie cried. 'Union! Yes, we're Union!'

The old woman took a couple of steps back. She smiled again and raised a clenched fist. Marie and Myles returned the salute. Slightly self-consciously, the other women and the children did the same.

The woman put her cupped hands to her mouth, shouted something Myles couldn't catch, and waved both arms over her head. Answering shouts came from far behind Myles and Marie.

'It's OK,' Owen yelled.

'Is OK,' the old woman said, pointing.

Myles turned, to see the dozen spear carriers running down from below the trees and diagonally across the grass to the scree spill. They forded the river there, leaping from shoal to shoal across the river with frightening agility. They ran along the bank, lined up, and stuck their spears into the soggy soil.

The young women spoke urgently to the children, in what sounded like a strangely accented and paced English dotted with words in other languages. The children laughed and shouted and scampered forward, crowding around Marie and Myles and hugging them by their knees, thighs and waists. Then they were off again like a flock of young sparrows, to fling their arms around the rest of the expedition. Jenkins seemed particularly touched. He hugged the children back, grinned and laughed and picked one of the small ones and swung her around before setting her back on her feet.

'He's the only father in our lot,' Marie said. 'I'm sure he's missing his own kids.'

'Yeah,' Myles said. The thought gave him a pang, of guilt as well as sympathy: he hadn't thought of that, what with Jenkins's general air of competence and self-sufficiency. The three young women walked forward, rounding up the children and attempting to converse with the new arrivals. The young men looked on, wary, leaning on their spear shafts. Owen was walking towards them, hands out by his sides, palms forward. Muranov and Hazeldene had gathered up the two rifles, keeping them pointed downward in a carefully non-threatening manner. Myles turned again to the old woman, who stood watching proceedings with an indulgent smile.

'Oldans told us,' she said. 'Yoon yun wad come.'

'Oldans?'

The woman pointed at a child, at one of the young women, then at herself, then pointed over her shoulder. 'Oldans.' She repeated the gesture, faster, as if numbering or listing: child, young woman, old woman, then 'Oldans' somewhere behind her.

'Oldans is your mother?' Marie asked.

The woman shook her head. 'Mother, mother, mother . . .' She made a whirling motion of the hand. 'Oldans.'

'Oh fuck!' Myles said. '"Oldans" means ancestors.'

The old woman grinned and nodded. 'Ancestors, ya.'

'Christ, how long have these—' Marie began. The old woman frowned and placed her fingertips across Marie's lips.

'Na Christ,' she chided solemnly. 'Oan lee bird.'

'Bird?' Myles pointed to a passing boid. The woman laughed scornfully. She glanced over her shoulder, as if someone might be listening, then pointed back and up, to Hamilton's Rise. She leaned forward, crossed her wrists and linked her thumbs, then flapped her fingers. Keeping her hands in that position, she brought them in front of her mouth, and from behind them said: 'Bird.' She raised her thumb-linked palms across her eyes for a moment, and said: 'Dark. Black.' Then she let her hands fall by her sides, and relaxed her shoulders and exhaled. She had the self-satisfied expression of someone who has made their point.

Jenkins and Patel had extricated themselves from the children, and come over to stand with Myles and Marie. Myles motioned to them not to say anything.

He pointed to the woman's green pendant. 'Do you talk'–he jerked his head upward to look at Hamilton's Rise –'with this?'

She frowned. 'I na geddit.'

Myles repeated the question, this time pointing up to Hamilton's Rise then copying the woman's bird gesture, keeping his hands at waist level.

The woman paled. Her eyes widened. She shook her head. 'Na na na!' She too made the bird gesture, and then laid her linked hands across the pendant, as if to protect it.

'Na talk.'

'But surely—'

The woman laid a hand across his lips. 'Na talk.'

'Sorry,' Myles said. He stepped back a little, at a loss what else to say.

'I don't like this,' Jenkins said, speaking rapidly and quietly. 'Sounds like this lot have made themselves a . . . deity. None of my folks and none of the bands I've heard of have done that.'

'Let's not jump to conclusions,' Marie said. 'Maybe something scary manifests up there.'

Jenkins scoffed. 'Let me try something.' He spoke a sentence slowly in Swahili, then in French, and got no response. He jerked his thumb at his chest.

'Able Jenkins.' He pointed to the woman. 'You?'

'Please-ta meet-ya, Able Jenkins.' The woman thumbed her chest, just below the pendant. 'Jih Lee.'

'Jilly?' Marie sounded surprised and amused. The woman nodded, and repeated: 'Jih Lee.'

'Pleased to meet you, Jilly,' said Marie. She pointed to herself. 'Marie Henderson.'

Jilly repeated the name, in that slow syllable-separating way she had, then: 'Please-ta meet-ya, Mah-Ree.'

Myles thumbed his sternum. 'Myles Grant.'

'My-les . . . *Grant*?'

He nodded. 'Myles Grant. Pleased to meet you.'

Jilly stared at him in what seemed to be awe. 'Grant?' she said. She sounded like she didn't believe it.

'Yes. Grant.'

She clutched his shoulders and looked into his eyes. 'Ya know *John* Grant?'

Myles jerked back. 'You know John Grant?'

'Is wat I say!' she said impatiently.

'John Grant is my father.'

'Ha!' Jilly snorted scorn. 'So many can say.' She waved a hand around, encompassing the throng, or perhaps only her people.

Myles looked at the others, baffled. 'Has word of my father's exploits spread even here? How? Do they still have radio or what?'

Jenkins took out his phone – the old one, that his father had brought to Apis and on which the Fermi back home supposedly exchanged messages with him. 'You have these?'

Jilly shook her head. 'Oldans had.'

'Can you read?' Jenkins asked.

'Ya, I can read.' Jilly waved towards the rest of her clan. 'They, na.' She sounded sad.

'Wait,' Myles said.

'"Wait"?' Jilly smiled. 'We aw wait, long time now.'

Myles retrieved his pack and dug into it as he returned. Something overheard had become a rumour. The women and children shouted excitedly and gathered round. 'Grant, Grant!' The young men tugged their spears from the ground, kept them pointing down, and hurried over. Hazeldene, Muranov and Owen hung back at the edge of the jostling crowd.

Myles pulled an envelope from the bottom of his pack and took out and unfolded the sheet within: the document he and his father had signed, setting up their company. He held it out in front of Jilly.

'Please read that.'

She peered, and moved her head back, her long-sighted eyes trying to focus. Fortunately the lettering at the top was large.

'"John Grant and Son Ship Con-struc-tion" . . . littid?' she said.

'Yes!' cried Myles, impressed. For a moment there he'd been afraid that her literacy was a boast, a lost tradition any crone could claim and never have to prove. He pointed to the foot of the page, where his and his father's name were printed beside their signatures. She tipped her head back a little further.

'John Grant . . . My-les Grant,' she read out. She pointed at his name, then at him.

'Yes!' he said. 'Myles Grant.'

She looked at him sadly, shaking her head. 'Na John Grant.' She repeated, louder, over his head to the crowd: 'Na John Grant!' A disappointed groan went up, then an angry murmur and some shouts. One or two of the smaller children began to cry.

'Na, na!' Jilly shouted. She stepped back and made a dismissive gesture. 'We leave here.'

With that she turned around and marched off, back the way she had come. Her folk followed, the young men bringing up the rear. Within a minute they had vanished into the woods.

'I can follow them,' Owen said.

'No,' Myles said. He didn't want Owen out of sight, and the group might yet need the robot's superhuman abilities. 'Marie's drone can follow instead.'

Marie took the small drone from her backpack, zapped instructions to it from her phone, and tossed it into the air. It hovered a moment, picking up scents, then shot away.

They all stood looking at each other.

'What the fuck just happened?' Hazeldene said.

'We met a delegation,' Marie said. She looked around. 'Come on. One old woman, three young women and a dozen young guys? Did that look like a viable population structure to you? Besides, the three younger women didn't look old enough to be mothers of the children – older sisters, perhaps. Ergo, there are more exiles out there.' She waved vaguely in the direction in which they'd seen the smoke. 'Plus, they were in their Sunday best, at least the women and kids were.'

'How do you figure that?' Jenkins asked.

'The women's dresses. They were too stiff and shiny for everyday wear. And the kids' T-shirts! These must be holy relics! They were worn and faded, but they weren't *grubby*. If this lot are anything like a temperate rainforest tribal community, and they sure look like one, the kids run around bare-arsed or in loincloths.'

'Point,' said Jenkins. 'What puzzles me is most of them look a lot whiter than most exiles. Hell of a lot more disasters in the tropics than in Europe, back then, and a hell of a lot easier to tell yourself kidnapping truckloads of people is a rescue.' He snorted. 'Anyway, it's obvious the meeting was set up – women and kids on one side, armed men on the other. They were expecting us.'

'And they left disappointed,' said Muranov.

'Not as disappointed as us,' said Hazeldene. 'So much for learning how to contact the local Fermi.'

'I blew it,' Myles said. 'I should have kept Jilly talking about the pendant.'

'Not your fault,' said Marie. 'I got her onto this bird of theirs.'

Jenkins laughed. 'And I started the introductions.'

'I suppose so,' Myles said gloomily.

'They were hoping to meet John Grant, and weren't going to be fobbed off with Myles Grant,' Muranov said.

'Sounds about right,' said Myles. He put his document away. 'Even with paperwork.'

'They were also expecting the Union,' Marie added. 'They got very excited when they saw our flag patches.'

'How would they know about the Union?' Patel asked. 'I mean, didn't that come *after* all the disasters?'

Jenkins waved that away. 'Our folks knew about it long ago, from stuff we picked up eavesdropping around the base and talking to personnel we met out in the wilds.' He nodded at Patel. 'Like your geologists. So this lot's forebears could have taken a rumour of it across the sea.' He grinned at Myles and Marie. 'Some exiles have heard the Yanks and the Russians don't like the Union, and they draw their own wild conclusions. Like that it's a wonderful place and one day the Union will arrive and rescue us, or give us stuff. Nah, what I don't get is how they know about John Grant. I mean, we've only known about him for a month!'

'Time travel,' said Marie. That raised a laugh, except from Owen.

'Please explain,' he said.

'Well!' Marie was laughing at herself. 'Suppose John Grant took – will take, I guess – their ancestors, the "oldans" here and somehow they ended up in the past. John had to leave, and promised to come back for them. And they're still waiting, poor sods!'

'It's not impossible,' Owen said. 'FTL implies time travel. Perhaps they were brought to the past in what is our future.'

Hazeldene was shaking her head. 'The planet was surveyed pretty thoroughly by satellite and drone before the first landings, according to all I've read and heard. They'd have noticed if humans were here already!'

'Would they, though?' Marie said. 'A few hunter-gatherers in the forest could have been missed.'

Hazeldene remained sceptical. 'Hmm. That's true, but it's a damn sight easier to believe we've been watched and listened to at and around the settlement without us knowing.'

'It is,' Owen said. 'It's also easier to believe the old woman was lying about what equipment they have. Phones are one thing, but radio is something else. Jenkins, your thoughts?'

The exile glanced away, then faced Owen squarely. 'Yeah, I've cobbled together a radio in my workshop in the old ark, and some other groups have them. If the first exiles on New Mu had a radio, and they've managed to keep it going, then between that and the flash-lines . . .' He passed his upper teeth over his lower lip. 'Could be, but . . .'

'Or the Fermi told them,' said Muranov. 'Have we forgotten about that?'

'No,' said Myles. 'But I do remember Jilly saying "na talk" very firmly, meaning they didn't talk to the rocks up there.'

'Or maybe,' said Marie, 'meaning *we* should shut up about it.'

'There's that,' Myles allowed. 'She sure clammed up at that point.'

'I'm worried about this "bird" she talked about,' said Patel. She looked around at the other scientists and at Jenkins. 'What we saw at MacHinery Ridge, and then these strange arrows that came out of nowhere . . . it makes me wonder if there isn't some flying thing that comes out of Hamilton's Rise.'

Myles imagined a dragon on the crystal crest, wings

outspread, black against the sky. It was so reminiscent of fantasy illustrations that he couldn't take it seriously.

'We can speculate all day,' he said. 'All that's left of it, anyway. What I suggest is me, Marie and Emma set up camp over there, Able does a bit of hunting in the forest, Cindy does some more prospecting for Fermi rock downstream, Georgi keeps her company, Owen keeps watch here, and we all get together in two hours or so for dinner. Fresh and hot if Able's lucky, rations if not. Everyone stays in line of sight with the drone, which I'll send higher up – it needs to catch some more sunlight anyway. Everyone clear?'

Everyone was. The camping gear had been distributed between backpacks – tents in one, a stove in another, foodstuffs across all of them, and so on – and when that was sorted out, they all set about their tasks.

The tents were up, in a loose circle near some convenient boulders, about halfway between the river and the trees. Owen patrolled a wide perimeter. Marie's drone tracked Jilly's folk through the forest. Myles and Hazeldene watched on a shared view with Marie, who was patching the feed up to the expedition's drone and thence to Knight, or whoever Knight had on duty. Marie's drone was about the size of a hummingbird and could have been mistaken for a hummingboid. It wasn't noticed by the exiles. They passed among the trees like ghosts, leaving little trace of their passage. One or other of the young men now and then threw a spear, or stabbed with it, and added some small prey to the rope around his waist.

The exiles were moving up the hill as they moved away, and the further up they went the thicker the trees got and the darker it was under them. Well past the spot where the fire had been, they emerged into a space where no trees grew. The canopy was if anything thicker. Marie flipped the view upward, and pointed to vines and creepers interwoven to make that natural roof. She swung the view back. At the far end of the area a bank plunged to a stream, another tributary of the big river. A bridge woven of living branches and vines extended across it. Ladders or steps of similar construction descended into it on both sides. Half a dozen small shelters or sheds stood around the periphery, some roofed with arthropod plates arranged like slates. In the middle of the space was a large shelter, with what looked like a very long, jointed flue rising from one end to vanish among the treetops. The shelter was covered by vines and creepers, but its shape and size were clear enough.

'Fuck!' Marie shouted. 'That's an ark!'

'Or a *copy* of an ark,' Hazeldene said. 'Still not buying your time-travel theory, sorry!'

'Or it's a cargo-cult shipping crate, how about that?' Marie scoffed.

'Wait a minute,' Myles said. 'Suppose it is an ark. Who's to say it wasn't one of the original arks that arrived around the same time as Able's folk?'

'*I'm* to say,' Hazeldene said. 'We didn't put any exiles down on this continent, and neither did the Co-ord. We left it for the Union.'

'Oh, and you know that how?'

Hazeldene considered this. 'You may have a point there,' she conceded.

Marie moved the view and widened it. It was uncannily like looking down on the scene in a camera obscura. 'I was right about them being a delegation,' she said. And indeed she was: about fifty people had gathered around the returning two dozen, including a lot more (and older) women than they'd seen, and more children – who were, just as Marie had predicted, pretty much bare-arsed.

Jenkins loomed into the shared view, disrupting it. He flourished a string bag in which four freshly speared forty-centimetre-long scuttlers squirmed. The beasts looked like very large woodlice.

'Four kilos of meat on this,' he said. 'Tastes like lobster. We're sorted. Found something?'

'Take a look,' said Marie.

Jenkins did, tilting the view here and there. 'Some pretty elaborate culture they've got down there – up there, I mean. Lot of drying and smoking under some of those shelters, I reckon. And see the live wood structures? Good use of local materials. I'd like to see what's inside that ark besides a fire.'

'You're sure it's an ark?' Hazeldene asked.

'Course I'm sure. And if they have any tech they haven't shown us – inherited, invented, or Fermi stuff – I bet you it's in there.' He pulled himself out of the scene. 'We have to go and find out.'

'When you say "we" . . .' Marie said. 'You volunteering?'

Jenkins considered this. 'Me and some back-up.'

'We'll talk about it later,' said Myles. 'Meanwhile, let's put these beasts out of their misery and onto a spit.'

CHAPTER SIXTEEN

The Cherenkov Flash

New Mu, Apis, Tuesday 11 November 2070 to Wednesday 12 November 2070

Myles had a pot of tea brewing and the first two scuttlers turning on a spit over the intense heat from the battery-powered camp stove by the time Patel and Muranov returned in triumph, carrying between them a slab of green rock. They propped it carefully against a boulder well outside the circle of tents. Owen ended his patrol and hurried over.

Everyone stood around taking a look. Like the oval disc the geologists had found a few days earlier, the slab was smooth, ridged by fine lines like frost on a window, and still live within. But it was much larger, about a metre long and half a metre across. Myles felt a faint unease and a slight dizziness as the shifting shapes drew his gaze inward. He looked away, to find Marie doing the same.

'You too?'

'Uh-huh.' She closed her eyes and shook her head. 'It's like an optical illusion, or a distorting mirror, or something. Makes my head swim a bit. Maybe this is what the others felt going over the rockfall.'

The others seemed unaffected. Myles and Marie walked back to the cooking area. Jenkins was turning the spit, amid cracking and fizzing sounds as the exoskeletons split in the heat.

'Did you feel anything?' Myles asked. 'Looking at the rock?'

'Nah,' Jenkins said.

'Hmm.'

'Seems to me,' Jenkins said, 'that that rock might be a good offering to bring the exiles, if we were to go up to their place.'

'Like I said, we'll have to talk about it.'

'Yeah, well, let's eat first.'

Jenkins removed the roasted beasts and cleaved each into three, placed the portions on large leaves, then spitted the other two arthropods and set them above the stove. By now the others had wandered back, and everyone sat down to eat, amid desultory and inconclusive discussion. All except Owen were tired.

When they had finished eating and talking, Muranov went back to the green stone. After a while, Myles followed him. The Russian palaeoanalyst squatted in front of the slab, passing his phone over it repeatedly. Now and again he'd poke a finger at his phone screen, or scribble a note in the air. Myles watched him, and avoided looking at the rock. The lowering sun reddened the clouds and the mountaintops. Down here it was already dusk, the air further chilled by an evening breeze off the sea funnelled through the valley. The dusk chorus dinned like a factory, resounding off the valley's facing walls. The green stone glimmered in the gloom, drawing Myles's attention against his will.

Eventually Muranov put the phone away and stood up.

'I got completely engrossed,' he said, almost apologetically. He seemed surprised to find Myles there.

'What were you doing?'

'Looking for patterns.' Muranov smiled. 'Finding them, actually! Or, rather, a certain programme on my phone found them. The movement, as we see it, within this rock has . . . not exactly resemblances, but common features with the movements we've recorded at MacHinery Ridge. A commonality at a very abstract level, you understand. Like the deep grammar of language, although that is of course a flawed analogy.'

Myles couldn't tell whether it was flawed or not. 'I'll take your word for it.'

Muranov scoffed. 'Yes of course, you'll have to! But I shall have to report this, as well as our encounters today, to the Co-ord teams.' He flourished his phone. 'I have a direct uplink to the Co-ord satellites. If that is acceptable?'

Myles shrugged. 'I don't see how I could stop you.'

'Indeed not.' He put the phone away. 'I'll do that when I have a moment.' He seemed to be waiting for Myles to leave. Myles was about to take the hint, then hesitated.

'How are your colleagues getting on?' he asked.

Muranov frowned. 'How do you mean?'

'Well, you know. With the purges and stuff.'

'Ah!' Muranov's countenance brightened. 'Well enough, as it happens. The *Admiral von Bellingshausen* is still on station, sometimes in orbit. Captain Rostov is making his presence felt. General Khaustov and three naval officers have been detained at Novy Cosmograd, and two intelligence operatives recalled to Moscow and one to Beijing, but the science teams continue unmolested. As have the Alliance's, like my colleagues here, as far as I know.' Muranov opened his hands. 'We are taken to be too naive or too focused on our work to realise we weren't just taking part in a top-secret international cooperative project.' He looked away and sighed. 'You know, Myles, we might even have been right! It is convenient now for the three powers to disown it, to denounce Black Horizon as a conspiracy, but some in authority must have known.'

'Why convenient?'

'Strategy, tactics, logistics . . . every element of military art is transformed by the FTL drive. Imagine arks like those you arrived in, but carrying soldiers.'

'I have,' Myles said.

'And I have seen them – arks full of soldiers appearing out of the blue at New Ardtaraig. Now try to imagine a defence against them.'

'I can't.'

Muranov nodded. 'And a deterrent, if they had nukes rather than troops?'

'Well, if everybody could do that, maybe nobody would.'

'Deterrence can't work,' Muranov said, 'if anyone – or everyone – has the capacity to take out the others' capacity at one blow, without warning, in an overwhelming counter-force first strike.'

Myles considered this. 'Ah, yes, but only if they knew where the other side's nukes were at the time – all of them.'

'Exactly!' Muranov raised a didactic finger. 'And thanks to Black Horizon, they don't. Deterrence is re-established by scattering the deterrent force among the myriad stars – light-years away, minutes from delivery. I assure you, neither the Co-ord nor the Alliance knows where the other side has all its nukes.' He laughed. 'The submarines are still fulfilling their original task – in the sky instead of the sea!'

Fifty metres away, Owen stepped from among the tents and looked all around. He waved casually at Myles and Muranov, and ambled to the riverbank, scanning the hillsides and trees.

Myles looked sharply at Muranov. 'Was that the plan all along?'

'I wouldn't know. But think of a handful of scientists half a century ago, with the stardrive suddenly in their hands, and wondering whether to put it in the hands of Trump or Putin!'

'Who?'

'Look them up,' said Muranov, 'and you'll see.'

Myles did. 'Ah.'

'Yes.' Muranov cleared his throat. 'Now I have to talk to Novy Cosmograd.'

'Oh yes, sorry.' Myles walked back to the tents. The others sat companionably around the fading glow of the stove. Jenkins had brought out a flask of his alcoholic fruit juice, and he, Hazeldene, Patel and Marie were sipping some from their cups. Myles sat down beside Marie, and took his offered share with thanks.

'Tastes good,' he said, 'but I miss beer.'

'No grain,' Jenkins said. 'But we've found plenty of stuff you can drink, and leaves you can smoke. My old man said it was better than weed, and with a stronger buzz than nicotine.'

'Habit-forming?' Marie asked.

'Oh yeah.' Jenkins sighed. 'Could do with a puff right now, as it happens.'

'Great,' Patel said. 'Let's give the world a new addiction.'

Myles rubbed his hands. 'That's our future cash crop right there!'

Jenkins gave him a severe look. 'Yeah? And who's going to grow and harvest the stuff? Robots? Exiles? Monkey-spiders?'

'Family farms,' Hazeldene said firmly. 'As soon as you lot grow up and stop acting like some goddamn commie collective.'

'Well, there's your answer, Able,' Myles said. 'Children.'

Jenkins nodded. 'It's what we do.'

'God,' said Hazeldene, 'I remember that giant crab-thing with the electrodes in its head and a kid plodding behind.'

'Sort of thing you get,' Jenkins said, 'if you turn tech folks tribal.'

'Ha!'

The sun had fully set, and the gas giant shone full in the west, high above the end of the valley. Myles sank into a dozing appreciation of Marie's warm body leaning against him, and a vague worrying at the political economy of exports from settler colonies, which in turn drifted into mulling over Muranov's point about interstellar assured deterrence. There was some connection, some insight he was missing.

Owen loomed out of the dark, made as if to sit down then looked around the group. 'Where's Georgi?'

Myles jolted to full alertness, if not quite sobriety. Half an hour had gone by. 'I left him by the stone. He wanted to talk to his base.'

'Did he indeed?' Hazeldene said. 'You could have mentioned that!'

Myles shrugged. 'We don't have a quarrel with the Co-ord.'

'No, but you damn well owe a courtesy to the Alliance!'

Owen raised his hands. 'Please, please. Another time for that. Let's just check that Georgi's OK.'

'Let me.' Myles stepped out of the dim glow among the tents and let his eyes adjust. Everything looked monochrome, the shadows cast by the light from the gas giant black. In the foot of the valley, the shadows covered a lot of ground. He tuned his glasses to the false colours of the night. Innumerable tiny clusters of eyes looked back at him, from the not-grass and the trees. Heat signatures of larger animals scuttled, slunk, or flitted about. The Fermi stone showed as a splash of ultraviolet. Muranov wasn't in view at all.

'Georgi!' Myles called out. Echoes answered. After several rounds of this, Myles returned to the others. 'No sign of him.' He fished out his phone. 'I'll give him a call.'

It rang unanswered.

'That's worrying,' Hazeldene said.

'Wait a moment,' said Owen. 'Call him again, and I'll listen out for his phone.'

He stepped away, and a couple of minutes later stepped back, shaking his head. 'Assuming it's not on silent, it's nowhere in the vicinity.'

'What's the vicinity, to you?' Patel asked.

Owen gestured vaguely. 'A kilometre? But if Georgi's phone

is close to the river, the white noise might have masked the ringing. Even so, I don't think he's anywhere close by.'

'Shit,' said Marie. She looked at Myles. 'The drone has night vision, doesn't it?'

'Yes!' Myles felt relieved. 'And it records, so we can look back.'

The drone icon was still in the corner of Myles's sight. It hadn't moved for hours, because he'd left the drone on station overhead after it had drawn a last charge from the day's late sunlight. But when he winked on the speck, it didn't move.

'Ah, fuck,' he said. 'The app's frozen.' He summoned a virtual screen and flickered his fingers. Nothing happened. He sighed, and invoked an override to call the drone down to an emergency landing.

Again nothing.

'Don't tell me we've lost the drone as well,' said Hazeldene.

'Not sure yet,' Myles said. 'Uh, Marcus, could you see it, if you looked up?'

'Of course,' said Owen. 'Good idea! I'll give it a try.'

He went out again into the dark, and again returned shaking his head.

'No go, I'm afraid.'

Marie moved her fingers in front of her glasses. 'Mine's still working.'

'Ah,' said Owen. 'And where is it now?'

'Still watching the exiles up there. They're sitting around a fire drinking and chatting, those who haven't gone inside their shelters or their ark.'

'Their *hall*,' said Hazeldene.

'Yeah, yeah.' Marie brushed aside the quibble. 'The point is, I can use it to search.' She looked down at her phone, then up. 'Meanwhile, everybody just go out and *shout*, OK?'

Myles picked up one rifle and passed the other to Marie. 'Keep it to hand.'

She nodded, grim-faced.

Myles and Patel followed the bank upstream, Hazeldene and Owen downstream. Jenkins headed for the trees. They looked all around with their glasses on night-vision, and now and again called out.

'He *told* us,' Patel said, almost tearfully, as they picked their way over the scree whose crossing she had pioneered. 'Georgi said we were on our second warning.'

Myles stopped. 'What? You think the *Fermi* took him?'

Patel looked back over her shoulder, bug-eyed by her night glasses. 'Yes. What else could make him vanish like that?'

He took a couple of long strides and caught up. When they were across the scree he motioned to Patel to stop, and leaned close.

'I'll tell you what else,' he whispered. 'That bloody robot.'

Patel's mouth opened. 'You're saying Owen could have *murdered* Georgi?' She shook her head. 'That's so sick, Myles! Owen has been nothing but friendly and helpful.'

'Let's keep our voices down, OK?'

'Uh-huh.'

'Let's walk and talk.' After they'd taken a few steps, Myles went on. 'Cindy, Owen *murdered* someone on Cloud City, and set off an explosion that didn't exactly help—'

'I know,' Patel said. 'Emma and Able told us all about it.'

'Ah. And you still don't think—'

'Owen explained it to me. He's a robot. He follows instructions. He doesn't just *kill* people off his own bat. He's not some psychopath.'

'No, he's a literal killing machine. Great. And how do we know his instructions didn't include killing people this time, too?'

'But why should he?'

'Georgi told me he'd found something meaningful in the stone, and he was just reporting back to the Co-ord base when I left him there.'

'Yes, that's interesting, but so what?'

'Owen's an Alliance spy, remember! Georgi is Co-ord, and might have found some important information about the Fermi. God, I could kick myself.'

'It's not your fault, whatever happened.' Patel looked around. 'Shouldn't we try shouting again?'

They tried that, and failed again. Myles contacted the others. No one had any news. Myles insisted they all search further. At the rockfall Patel put her foot down.

'I'm not crossing that in the dark,' she said. 'Not after what happened in the daytime.'

'Owen showed me how to do it. We could—'

'Not me. No way am I doing that.'

'We can't give up on Georgi.'

Patel glared at him. 'I'm not giving up on him. He was – he's my friend. But we've done all we can tonight. And we're putting ourselves in danger. We don't know the territory, we don't know what animals and exiles are out there. And I still think it was the Fermi that did it.'

Myles scoffed to hide his unease. 'That sounds like some alien abduction story.'

Patel looked like she wanted to slap him. 'Tell me that when you'd had to run for your life from a walking wall of rock!'

'OK, OK. Sorry, you're right.'

He called the others, and called off the search, to no disagreement whatsoever.

Myles and Patel walked back the way they had come, the gas giant high and bright in the sky in front, the Milky Way blazing overhead, ink-black shadow all around. The river roared at their right; trees and animals rustled to their left. They arrived at their camp to see Hazeldene and Owen coming up the riverbank and Jenkins emerging from the trees, and Marie waving from among the tents. They all met up and looked at each other in weary silence.

From far down the valley, around the shoulder of the

mountain, came a blue flash. A sound like distant thunder echoed and rolled.

'A starship leaving?' Hazeldene said, incredulously. 'From behind Hamilton's Rise?'

'Looks like it,' said Myles.

'But why?'

'Search me.'

For a moment, which Myles only caught because he happened to be looking directly, Owen took on a remote, abstracted expression, as if working out some complex calculation in his head. Then it passed, and he showed the same puzzlement as everyone else.

'Let's get my drone further up,' Marie said, 'and report back to the Lieutenant.'

Knight was furious about Muranov's disappearance, almost as if he blamed them for some careless oversight with disastrous consequences.

'I'll have to report this to Novy Cosmograd,' he said. 'It won't be easy convincing them our hands are clean.'

'Well, they are,' Myles insisted. He couldn't relay his suspicions with Owen looking on.

'We'll send another drone over right away,' Knight said, 'and widen the search – including for our missing drone. Obviously we can expect better results in daylight, but we'll start as soon as it arrives.'

'We'll resume searching in daylight, too,' Myles said. 'And go up to the exile settlement and ask them if they can—'

'No, you won't,' said Knight. 'You'll head straight back here first thing.'

'You can't order us,' Marie said. 'This is a Union expedition.'

'I can certainly order everyone back but you two,' said Knight. 'If you want to stay out there on your own, be my guest.'

'Point taken,' Myles said. 'OK, we'll all leave together tomorrow, but not before taking another look around.'

'All right. I'll be watching you.'

'Any news about the starship?'

'Yes, I was coming to that,' Knight said. 'Naturally we saw the flash and enquired urgently. Its very brief stopover was recorded by a passing satellite. The ship wasn't one of ours, or the Co-ord's, and from the handful of pixels we've managed to grab, it was small and yellow.'

'The *Fighting Chance*? Here?'

'Yes,' said Knight. 'Bit rude of your parents to be in the neighbourhood and not drop by, don't you think?'

Myles was nonplussed. 'No doubt they had their reasons.'

'I expect so,' Knight said. He frowned. 'This too will have to be reported to the Co-ord. It'll do nothing to allay any suspicions they may have.'

'Is there anything we can do?'

'Get some sleep.' Knight rang off.

Marie brought her tiny drone spiralling down to a hundred metres above them, and set it circling. She uploaded a watchdog app to it, to warn them if anything or anyone approached.

'It won't be enough,' Owen said. 'We should take turns to keep watch. I need very little sleep, so I'm happy to go first.'

'Fine,' Myles said. The time on his watch was still GMT, and increasingly out of kilter with the local day, but his devices told him it was two hours until local midnight. 'Wake me an hour after midnight. Then Marie, then Able can take us through to dawn.'

'You don't trust the scientists, huh?' said Hazeldene.

Myles scoffed. 'It's you we're guarding.'

'One way of looking at it.' But she seemed happy enough to go to her tent, as did Patel. When Myles and Marie went to theirs, they were both asleep within minutes.

It seemed no time had passed when Myles felt his earpiece tingle, and in it heard Owen murmur, 'Your turn, old chap.' He sighed and stretched, clambered out of the sleeping bag and into his clothes and boots. Marie slept through it all, one arm around her rifle. Myles hefted his own rifle and headed out. The night was cloudless and chill, the stars and the gas giant bright. He barely needed night vision in his glasses. Owen sat on a boulder, which he vacated as Myles walked up.

'Enjoy your kip,' Myles said.

'I shall.' Owen gestured to the camp stove. 'There's coffee in the pot.'

'Ah, thanks.'

Owen took off his glasses – of course, Myles thought, he could see as well without them – and slipped them inside his overall.

'You suspect me,' he said, in a conversational tone, 'of murdering Georgi Muranov, and somehow disposing of his body.'

Myles adjusted his grip on the rifle. 'The thought had crossed my mind.'

'I'd expect no less,' Owen said. 'I did not, of course, kill your colleague. I have no more idea of where he is than you do.'

He said it with every appearance of sincerity.

'Then how do you account for his disappearance? The Fermi?'

'I've stood on a planet that the Fermi melted under my feet,' said Owen. 'So I do not underrate their power, and for the record, yes, I do think it was the Fermi.'

'You'll forgive me for not believing you,' Myles said. He could feel his palms getting slick, and tightened his grip again.

Owen smiled. 'Of course! I don't take it personally.' He gave a self-deprecating laugh. 'One advantage of being a soulless mechanism!'

A moment later Myles was flat on his back, and Owen was standing over him with the rifle.

'This is another,' the robot said. Myles convulsively pulled up his knees and groped for the pistol on his belt. Owen laughed and vanished from his sight. By the time Myles had struggled to his feet and let out a yell, Owen was sprinting for the trees. A moment later he was gone.

Everyone came running, half-dressed and bleary-eyed. It didn't take long to establish the situation.

'So he's behind Georgi's disappearance,' Cindy Patel said. She sounded distressed.

'His murder, probably,' Myles said. 'Sorry, but that's how it looks. That's not why he ran, though. He's headed for Hamilton's Rise, because of what Georgi found and reported. Whatever it was.'

'No point chasing him,' Jenkins said, looking out at the dark slopes.

'Yeah, tell me about it,' said Myles, rubbing his back. 'Fuck, the thing's superhuman.'

'Should I send the drone after him?' Marie asked.

'Nah,' Myles said. 'We need it here.' He looked around. 'Sorry I got bested by something at least twice my strength and speed, everyone, OK?' He sighed. 'Get back to bed. We'll keep watch as agreed: me, Marie, Able.'

'Take care,' Marie said. She hugged him precipitately. 'When I think what could have happened . . .'

'Don't,' Myles said. 'It doesn't help.'

She clasped his shoulder, making him discover another bruise, and held him away, and smiled wryly in the starlight. 'Is that in the Black Gospels?'

Myles thought about it. 'No,' he said. 'I think it's from the Stoics.'

She laughed and hugged him again. 'Every time,' she said. 'Every fucking time.'

'What?'

She stepped away, and looked back over her shoulder as she headed for their tent. 'See you in three hours, comrade.'

CHAPTER SEVENTEEN
This Just In

Scotland, Earth, Wednesday 12 November 2070

The *Fighting Chance* came out of the jump just above where the atmosphere thinned to a wisp, in not so much low Earth orbit as high steep approach. Grant gazed in awe at the blue and white arc.

'At least it's still here.' He checked comms. 'Familiar babble and squawk. We're back in the same world, far as I can see.'

Air thickened and screamed around them.

'Get us down!' Ellen yelled.

Grant stabbed a thumb on the control panel. Reality flickered like an old fluorescent tube. Then they were above a long shallow pit in the choppy grey water. Grant had a few seconds to look around and check the radar screen as the drive powered down. All clear in the vicinity. Rain rattled at the canopy. The ship sank into the dip, and the water rose to meet it. They were afloat. The marine engine whined into life, and the propellers bit.

'Ahead on engines,' Ellen said.

Grant breathed out, to a ragged cheer from Omar Khan, Morag Rafferty and the nine evacuees. Ellen leaned over and clasped his hand. He squeezed back.

'Well, we made it,' he said. 'Thanks to Nayak. Now we just have to get home.'

On the Firth of Clyde it was a dark and stormy day. A strong east wind lifted the choppy sea into long swells. The ship had splashed down at 11:16 about seven hundred metres from the James Watt Dock, a marina complex of piers and pontoons at the eastern end of the Greenock shoreline. Its deep-water quays and sturdy warehouses loomed larger than the leisure and fishing boats it currently served. An ideal harbour for the *Fighting Chance*, though. Grant hoped they'd get there before anyone became seasick.

By 11:20 they were being hailed and challenged by the port authority, and the first coast guard drone shadowed them a minute later. Shortly afterwards, a swarm of camera drones began buzzing around, snooping through the canopy with long lenses.

Ellen responded to the port authority, identifying herself and requesting permission to dock. This was given, the details to be handled by Iskander. Everyone's phones started pinging.

'Personal calls only,' Ellen said sharply, over her shoulder. 'Not a word, not a call, not a wave to the media or anybody you don't know.'

Ellen steered the craft past the gate and into the long berthing area. In the harbour's shelter the swell and the wind dropped. The tide was low, and the quays and cranes still stood metres above the submarine's low profile. On every other measure its profile was anything but low. The quayside was already lined with curious faces. Camera drones flocked and wheeled. Iskander guided the ship to a berth. For once, there were plenty to choose from: damaged boats had been lifted from the water and were now under repair on the quays. Small hatches fore and aft sprang open. Robot arms popped up, swivelled, then tossed ropes. A dock worker caught them and made fast. A militia squad of a dozen or so arrived at a run and lined up in front of the craft.

Morag opened the hatch. 'Cloud City folk first,' she said. The astronomer Gianna De Marte clambered out of the observation bubble beneath the cockpit, stumbling on her first step or two in 1G after years in 0.9G, and led the way.

'Right,' Morag said as the last of the evacuees trooped out. 'Time tae face the music.' She made to leave, but Grant got there first. He paused for a moment on the ladder taking a deep breath of cold, damp air tanged with seaweed, then stepped on to the quay and raised a hand.

'Morning, citizens!'

'Hi, John,' said the squad leader. Like the others he was in serious gear: visored helmet and stab-proof overalls. Grant peered at the guy's shoulder tab. Ian MacAskill: he'd been on a few patrols with him.

'Oh, hi, Ian. What's all this about?'

'Debriefing, mostly.' MacAskill jerked a thumb over his shoulder, to where those who'd gone ahead were being escorted onto a couple of ambulances. 'The Cloud City survivors will need more gentle handling, but your lot have questions to answer.' He glanced over the crew. 'Where's Dr Nayak?'

'Off adventuring in the cosmos, just like the Union told her.'

'Aye, well.' MacAskill sounded dubious. 'That remains to be seen.'

'I thought it had been settled. We got official instructions.'

'Nae point arguing here,' said MacAskill. 'Let's just get you all to the debrief, OK?'

'Who's debriefing us?'

MacAskill sucked air through his teeth. 'Uh, just a friendly chat with the comrades.'

'You're telling me it's the cadre, not law enforcement?'

MacAskill shifted his weight from one foot to another. Behind the visor, he was probably looking very uncomfortable. 'Aye, well, they moved first. The authorities will no doubt want to have a word, too, but for now it's, like, between ourselves.'

'I'll give the authorities a piece of my mind when they get round to me,' said Grant. 'Starting with making clear to militia officers who they answer to first, and it's not the fucking cadre!'

'Can we do this later?' MacAskill said. 'We're on live TV, man!'

'Bit late to worry about that, Ian,' Grant said. He turned to Ellen. 'You're not a *responsable*, or a cadre,' he said. 'You can just walk away.'

He was not at all sure about that, in the circumstances, but reckoned it worth a try. Ellen was having none of it.

'I was in it up to my neck,' she told MacAskill. 'Don't you dare leave me out.'

'I wasn't intending to,' said MacAskill. He motioned towards a militia van drawing up. 'Let's go.'

'Better make sure you secure our ship,' said Grant.

'We're on it,' MacAskill replied, with a quick gesture to his company. Half of them disappeared down the ladders as the others escorted the crew away.

'Just don't touch the controls,' Ellen called, over her shoulder as she climbed into the van. 'You don't know where they've been!'

'Aye!' one of them shouted back. 'But we'll find out!'

The ride was short. Ten minutes later Grant, Ellen, Morag and Omar were all in separate rooms in the Holiday Inn, each accompanied by one militia member, who locked the door and stood outside.

Grant sighed and shrugged. He went into the en-suite, stripped, tossed his clothes in the recycler and had a shower and a shave. When he dried off he found the printer had delivered him a suitably sober outfit of suit, socks, underpants and T-shirt, all black. He dressed, and sat on the bed to put his boots back on. He walked over to the window and peered through reflections and the rattling rain. As far as he could make out, damage from the Atlantic tsunami extended up and down the entire shoreline: a stranded ship here, an abandoned building there, a closed road further upstream . . . Everywhere dotted with yellow hard hats and hi-vis, orange-and-black striped machinery, human and robotic toil.

He had just begun catching up on his phone's news backlog when there was a knock on the door.

'Come in,' he said, like he had a choice.

The woman could have been any age between fifty and eighty. Her hair was white, her skin black, her clothes elegant and not out of a printer: Lagos fabric, Paris cut. Bangles jangled as she raised her hand.

'Louise Ogundu,' she said. 'You won't have heard of me.'

'John Grant.'

'I've heard of *you*,' she said, disdainfully. Her accent was Highland, but without the Gaelic undertow: Inverness or thereabouts, Grant guessed. Second-generation at least: not a climate refugee. She tilted the chair by the table and spun it to face out, then sat. 'Take a seat.'

Grant sat back down on the side of the bed.

'I was about to order—'

The coffee machine in the corner pinged, then rolled over to Ogundu and onward to Grant, bearing mugs.

'Thanks, Iskander,' Grant said.

Ogundu sipped, and sighed approval. 'You have more than coffee to thank Iskander for, Citizen Grant.'

Grant pointed skyward. 'Everything. Literally, as it turns out.'

Ogundu compressed her lips. 'Hmm.' She ostentatiously took a phone from her jacket pocket and laid it on the table. 'We'll see. Now, would you please tell me – us – what you've been doing, briefly, in your own words?'

'Since Venus?'

Ogundu's eyes narrowed. 'Since Toward Point.'

'Ah. It's a long story.'

'Keep it short. I can ask for more detail when necessary.'

'Fair enough,' Grant said. 'But first, Citizen Ogundu, I need to know to whom I'm telling the story.'

'To me.' She sounded surprised.

'As you say, I don't know you. And somehow I don't think looking you up would help. Are you Union? ESA? State security? The cadre organisation?'

Ogundu smiled. 'The last, of course. Which means your cooperation is entirely voluntary.'

Grant glanced at the door. 'Really?'

'The guard is to keep others out, not you in, Citizen Grant.' She raised a finger. 'But before you go, you might consider whether any of the other organisations you mention will give you as fair a hearing as I can.' She chuckled. 'Think of this as your chance to talk to a lawyer. Which, as it happens, I am.'

Grant took a sip of coffee and laid the mug down on the bedside cabinet. 'Iskander, I—'

'I would strongly advise you to comply,' said the AI. 'Trust me on this.'

'Wait a minute!' Grant said. 'You must have synched with my phone! You'll have everything already.'

'You're not telling Iskander, and we're not asking it,' said Ogundu. 'We're asking you.'

'Who's talking with the others?' Grant asked.

'Other cadres as well qualified as I am.' She thought about it. 'Almost as well.'

'And how did you get four well-qualified cadres here so fast?'

Ogundu looked exasperated. '*Mister* Grant, we've all been *waiting* for you! For weeks!'

'All of us, except my wife, are more or less sworn to secrecy about what we did. This has to stay within the cadre. I shouldn't even talk to you about it.'

Ogundu scoffed. 'The need for secrecy only applied before you launched your damned boat! The whole world knows what you did. Let me assure you, the cadre organisation releases you entirely from that obligation. Just as they have already done for Joanna Boyd and others at the yard.'

'I can confirm that,' said Iskander. 'Joanna Boyd has made a full and free confession.'

'What's happened to her?'

It was Ogundu who answered. 'Out on bail pending further investigation.'

That was a relief.

'OK,' said Grant. 'Here goes. It all started with a ping about a naval exercise . . .'

'. . . and here we are.'

The coffee was cold. Grant gulped half of what was left in the mug. Thirty minutes of talking had dried his throat.

'Here we are, indeed,' said Ogundu. She put on glasses and gazed into virtual space for a minute, then lowered them and looked at him over the top of the frame. 'It looks like your wife and colleagues have told much the same story, from their own points of view. This is good. I strongly suggest you all stick to the truth when you talk to the authorities. It's much easier, for a start. Don't worry about self-incrimination.'

'An odd thing for a lawyer to say!'

'Oh, the evidence against you is so plain that nothing you say could make it worse, and might make it better. Meanwhile, I and others will be getting your side of the story out.' She patted her phone. 'This record will be invaluable.'

Grant stood up and stalked to the window. The rain had cleared. The green promontory that shielded Faslane was spotlit by a shaft of sunlight. A mast of green lights shone at the point. A submarine cleared the mouth of the Gare Loch and as he watched rose above the choppy sea in a shimmering bubble and vanished in a blue flash that made him blink. HMS *Vindicate*, his glasses told him. Everything was out in the open now. All secrecy and conspiracy seemed tawdry and irrelevant. He turned to face Ogundu.

'What have we done wrong? What are we accused of?'

She too stood up, and seemed to be getting ready to leave. 'Oh, the predictable things: misappropriation of funds, financial irregularities, constructing a hazardous and untested device, false documentation of said construction, interference with shipping, endangering good relations with a foreign power . . . if they want to throw the book at you, they have a shelf to choose from.'

'Doesn't our rescue of hundreds of people from Cloud City count for anything?'

'It counts for a lot, by way of mitigation. But that was a fortunate and fortuitous outcome, not the reason you did these things in the first place.'

'The reason I did them was—'

'You became inveigled in a cadre conspiracy, and you sought to profit from it. Not once did you think of taking the matter to the appropriate bodies. They do take a dim view of that.'

'So we're to be prosecuted for . . . what? Treading on toes?'

'It's not a prosecution – yet. You're all going to be detained and investigated, in the first instance. A report will be sent to the Procurator Fiscal. Then they will decide whether the Republic has a case against you, and whether it is in the public interest to proceed.'

'I know my civics, dammit! That doesn't answer my question.'

'It's all politics,' said Ogundu. 'And you're weeks out of date on the politics. Let us take care of that side.'

'And the legal side?'

'That's up to you, Citizen Grant.'

Something in her tone struck him.

'Oh!' he said. 'Could *you* be my lawyer?'

For the first time since she'd come in, Ogundu smiled. 'Yes. Thank you. I thought you'd never ask.'

The knock came a minute or two later.

The militia station was the former police station, a century-old brutalist concrete cuboid that had ridden out war, riot and Rising and whose continued use Grant had always reckoned a mistake. By now it was a listed building, with even the graffiti and scorch marks on its outer walls protected as historic monuments.

Inside it had been renovated. An interview room was still an interview room, and a militia full-timer was still a cop. Two of them sat on the other side of the table from Grant and Ogundu. They took his statement. They asked questions. After each question Grant glanced at Ogundu. At her nod, he answered.

The final question was: 'Do you have anything further to add, Citizen Grant?'

'You don't have to,' Ogundu said. 'And I'd advise you not to.'

'Yes, I do have to,' Grant said. 'Like I said, at the very start I instructed Iskander to report my initial sighting to Union Naval Intelligence. It assured me it had. I acted at all times under the good faith presumption that all my subsequent actions were known to and authorised by the relevant authorities or agencies of the Union, which in the nature of the case would be working in the deepest secrecy. I further presumed that any . . . technical improprieties that I and my colleagues may have committed were duly covered under the usual provisions in law for emergency and necessity. The instructions sent to Commander Ulrich contained not a hint of reprimand for our previous actions. It would have been entirely within her power to enforce any—'

Ogundu leaned in and all but put her hand over his mouth. 'I'm advising my client right now to shut up.'

Grant did. Ogundu glared at him.

'You've advised him well,' said the senior of the two investigators. 'Something to think about, Citizen Grant: you're not saying you *read* Commander Ulrich's instructions, are you?'

Grant shook his head. 'Of course not.'

'In that case, you know nothing of what they did or did not contain.'

'But she . . .' He stopped.

'This is why we have lawyers,' Ogundu pointed out. 'You're learning. Good.' She turned briskly to the investigators. 'My client has answered all your questions, is a respected citizen and *responsable*, and is now free to go, correct?'

'I'm afraid not,' said the senior investigator. 'Citizen Grant, we are detaining you on suspicion of conspiracy to commit, and of actually committing, a number of offences including but not limited to theft, embezzlement, reckless endangerment, corrupt business practice, false documentation, culpable breaches of regulations covering marine, air, and space navigation and wilful deception of the planning and regulatory authorities. Do you understand?'

Grant resisted the temptation to ask why they hadn't thrown in tax evasion while they were at it. 'Yes.'

'You have to charge or release him within twenty-four hours,' Ogundu said.

'We're well aware of that, Citizen Ogundu. And in view of the considerations you mentioned, and the circumstance, we're willing for his detention to be in the hotel under guard. Citizen Grant, you will have to surrender your phone and glasses. You are not to communicate with the other detained citizens, or anyone else other than your lawyer. Do you understand?'

'Yes.'

And that was that.

Back in the hotel room, Grant toppled backward onto the bed and stared at the ceiling. The time was 17:05. The sky was dark, except for the glow on the clouds from the bright lights of Faslane. It was hard to believe that a few hours earlier he'd been on the Station, and then briefly on Apis. He thought of Myles, and felt a pang strong enough to make him roll over and bury his face in the pillow for a moment. He should have contrived some way of seeing him, or at least sending a message. Then he turned again onto his back, and lay gazing upward until he got his thoughts in order.

He sat up, and realised he was hungry and he needed a drink. He was about to call room service when there was a tap on the door. It swung open. He glimpsed the guard stepping aside as a small trolley rolled in. On top of it was a gin and tonic, and beneath that was a hot cabinet and a refrigerator. The door closed and locked. He drank the gin and tonic a little too quickly, then opened the cabinet and found a steaming roll heaped with banana peel shredded, seasoned and fried – the vegan version of pulled pork – and a bottle of beer in the refrigerator.

'Thanks, Iskander.' He took them to the table, ate and drank, and waved at the wall screen. 'How are Ellen and Omar and Morag?'

'Your wife and companions are in other rooms here, and are in the same legal situation as you.'

'Give Ellen my love and the others . . . my regards.'

'Done. Strictly speaking, I shouldn't have, but it could be argued that this counts as no more than a friendly wave.'

'Are we under surveillance? Apart from yours, that is.'

'Any communications between you and me are covered by lawyer-client privilege. It would take very significant legal and technical resources to make me divulge them.'

Grant wasn't entirely sure he could rely on this, but he let it pass.

'OK. Now, bring me up to speed.'

'Current, local.' The screen lit up with the front page of the *Greenock Telegraph*: VENUS HEROES HELD. A drone picture of their disembarking, a close-up of the yellow submarine in the dock. Archive portrait photos, potted bios. Nayak's absence noted. Stonewalling boilerplate from the militia.

'Current, global.' It was the same page, sometimes in the background to talking heads. Somebody at the local paper was no doubt cracking open a bottle of champagne right about now.

'We're world-famous?'

'Yes, but you were already. Let me show you. I'll begin with Friday 17 October: Black Friday, as it's called now.'

The survey began with some chance footage from a photography hobbyist's drone. It had caught the whale-sized anomalous bubble in the water, the bright yellow *Fighting Chance* discernible through distortion within, and the blue flash in which it vanished. The fast boats rocked in the sudden swell.

Military mystery in the Clyde! That was from a local photography and gossip site. It hadn't made wider news at first: that morning was dominated worldwide by the eruptions on Venus – visible to the naked eye, Grant well remembered, as the morning star shining red – and the frantic efforts to evacuate Cloud City.

Some of the inhabitants of Cloud City waiting to be evacuated, and later those who'd made it to the Venus Space Station, had kept people posted back home. Many had huge social media followings of their own, they had loved ones to reassure or assure, and journalism bots and even human reporters and presenters had trawled the clamour. Direct contact was rare – light-speed lag and the pace of events made conversation, or even Q&A, quite impracticable. But the one-way flow of information was more than enough. Within an hour of arrival, Grant's crew and their ship were all over the screens. Bots joined the dots. Iskander's display showed the headlines along with the relevant images:

Clyde mystery sub flies to Venus rescue!

RED BOSS RISKS WORKERS' LIVES TO SAVE DOOMED BOFFINS

FTL breakthrough by Port Glasgow firm

Union's secret starship – what else is Brussels hiding?

Inverclyde heroes battle to save colony

Union's proudest project ends in tears

EURO BOFFINS BURN IN VENUS HELL

Ferry-boat people flee Union

YANKS SAVE SCOTS FROM EURO MISERY

CANARY ISLAND QUAKE THREAT TO BRITAIN

US East Coast safe, say scientists

Europe moves millions in an hour – but at what cost?

EURO MILITIA 'LEAVES PETS TO PERISH'

England safe as Celts take brunt

Shock as Venus Space Station vanishes

RUSSIANS NUKE VENUS 'MOON'

Brussels carpets Moscow's man

Wall St tumbles as war clouds darken

Venus eruption, Vieja quake not linked: NASA

DID RED ROCK PROBE WRECK VENUS?

Oz mystery rock – key to quake?

Relief as VSS reports FTL jump

Rocket forces stand down

DEATH STAR THREAT TO APIS BRITS

Iskander paused the display, perhaps in response to Grant's clenched fists and gritted teeth.

'So this is why we have the firewall,' Grant said.

'What do you mean?'

'If our people ever fully grasped the other side's spite and malice, the Cold Revolution would turn into hot war in no time.'

'You may have a point,' said Iskander. 'Shall I proceed?'

'Go ahead.'

After the departure of the Station from Apis orbit (**UNION DEATH STAR SKULKS AWAY**) attention shifted to Black Horizon. This time, Iskander showed headlines and clips from the Co-ord countries as well as the Alliance and Union.

STATE SECRETS 'SHARED WITH YANK SPIES'

FSB exposes 'professors' plot'

Academicians and admirals 'loyal only to themselves', says CCC

FBI probes scientists', officers' Russia ties

Yefrimovich cashiered; commanders fear purge

Chinese agents had run of Area 51: FBI

PENTAGON GENERALS WORKED 'HAND IN GLOVE' WITH BEIJING AND MOSCOW

Central Control Commission questions PLA rotten elements

DID SUB COMMANDERS STASH NUKES ON OTHER WORLDS?

Has Black Horizon talked to aliens?

Union govt official denies Black Horizon links

Edinburgh CCTV shows genius 'defector' spoke with Alliance spy

Was local hero's starship enterprise a Black Horizon front?

'Aha!' said Grant. 'Is *that* what this is all about? They think I'm part of Black Horizon?'

'No,' said Iskander. 'Give the Union's intelligence services – and me, I may add – a little credit. Nobody in the loop thinks that, not even the militia officers, but it serves certain purposes if some people out of the loop do.'

'To have us under a cloud of suspicion and give them time to investigate?'

'Yes. The Union republics – and publics, for that matter – are still in shock about the whole thing. Not that the other

Powers are any quicker on their feet. They're still reeling from the discovery, and that it's been kept secret so long. Purging and witch-hunting are at the very least convenient displacement activities. And who knows, interrogations may uncover what Black Horizon has been up to all this time.'

'Yes, that's something I'd like to know. I won't hold my breath for them to tell us if they find out, mind.'

'You may be right,' said Iskander.

'Do you have any ideas?'

'None that I can share at this stage.'

'Well, maybe you can tell me this – what public reason is the Union giving for rejecting the offer of settlement?'

'Unknown dangers of exoplanets, back contamination risks to Earth, harm to native life-forms, and on the plus side the long-promised glories of giant space habitats.'

'Nothing about mysterious alien rocks?'

'Not until the journalists came back from Apis last week.'

'What!'

'Yes. Jackie Wallace and Paul Kaminsky of SBC, Maria Conti of *La Repubblica* and Jacques Marteau of France 2 had all been negotiating a passage to the Alliance-sponsored Union settlement on Apis when the tsunami hit, which of course disrupted departures from Faslane. They actually managed to travel a couple of days later, having arranged a return for 6 November. They released their documentary on Sunday. It's caused quite a stir, worldwide. Would you like to see it?'

'Take an educated guess.'

The wall screen lit up again.

'The Alliance's settlement offer has caused much controversy,' Jackie Wallace said, in her characteristic knowing, warm, husky late-evening news-discussion-slot voice. 'Last month, Paul and I decided that nothing could settle it but facts on the ground.' She smiled. 'For the past weeks, you've been hearing from our avatars. Now I can tell you: we, with our colleagues Maria Conti and Jacques Marteau, have been on New Mu, on Apis, at the Union settlement – which, with some dry wit, the settlers have decided to name New Rhu.

'We arrived to find them in early difficulties, we watched and listened as they began to find their bearings . . . and we had to leave just as they came under quite unexpected attack. From aliens? From earlier exiles on the planet, whose very existence was a secret until our visit? We don't know.

'So now, exclusively to SBC, *La Repubblica* and France 2, here is our report from Apis. Our biggest surprise came the moment we stepped out of the ark.'

CUT TO–

APIS, EXTERIOR, DAY: A view PANNING over the settlement then UP to Hamilton's Rise. ZOOM on peaks. ZOOM further. CUT smoothly to ZOOM from drone at closest approach.

Grant stared, as millions before him must have stared. He had seen these rocks before, in Myles's phone, and known or guessed what they were. But not like this.

From a distance, the crystalline pillars might have been basalt. Close up, the smooth and many-coloured glass-like surfaces snapped into focus and detail: whorls and curves, floral and verdant, venous and sinuous, embedded with blue globes and ovoids, like some abstract sculpture of a grove from which the eyes of hidden animals or angels peered.

The surface relief remained still. Beneath it, subtler shapes flowed and moved, writhing about each other like a time-lapse of growing plants.

It was more than artificial. It was art.

Voice-over:

'One of our oldest questions is finally settled. We are not alone.'

CUT TO–

APIS, EXTERIOR, SAME DAY: settlers and soldiers struggle with flood.

Views, interviews. Soldiers. Scientists. Some guy called Jenkins, blowing the gaff on the resettlement of the exiles from Earth a generation earlier. Settlers. Now and then a glimpse of Myles, or of Marie. No interviews with them. Building shelters, chopping wood.

An arrow out of nowhere thudding into a tree trunk, just above Myles's head . . . Grant gasped.

A flurry of action, soldiers running, drones in the sky . . .

'And there we had to leave them,' said Jackie Wallace. 'Sources suggest that this attack, if such it was, has been fended off. But authorities remain tight-lipped. Now, over to our Glasgow studio, where–'

Grant waved the discussion away.

'I can tell you now, Iskander–'

'You're going back.'

'You anticipate as usual, but yes.'

'I'm on the case.'

'You're helping me?' Grant noticed he had, quite irrationally, lowered his voice.

'I helped you build the ship,' said Iskander. 'I haven't changed my mind.'

CHAPTER EIGHTEEN

Moon of the Mushroom Men

The Space Station around E-PRIME 667, Wednesday 12 November 2070

Nayak turned away from the screen and blinked rapidly. It wasn't because of the blue flash. The screen had dimmed it instantly, and only the faintest yellow after-image still haunted her retinas. It was the pang of seeing the *Fighting Chance* depart. You never forget your first starship . . .

Her earpiece tingled.

'Lakshmi, a word?' Commander Katrina Ulrich said. 'In my office now.'

'On my way, Commander.'

Nayak left the bridge, where she'd been assigned to jump the Station if anything went wrong during the smaller ship's departure. An outside chance, but one Ulrich had been unwilling to take. Perhaps in time such departures would become routine, and they'd watch shuttles and ships flash out of view with no more qualm than the launch of a dinghy or liberty boat.

Ulrich opened the door, and beckoned Nayak to come in and sit down.

'You're not in trouble,' Ulrich said. She gave a tight smile. 'I may be.'

'That's . . . surprising, Commander.'

'I have something to tell you,' Ulrich said. 'I intend to tell everyone else in due course. I had to wait until the *Fighting Chance* was gone, because I couldn't risk this information's getting back to Earth. And it couldn't wait a moment longer.' She took a deep breath. 'I want to tell you first, because . . .' She sighed. 'Don't take this the wrong way, but you're the only Union person on board who wasn't raised in it. You might be able to help me put this in perspective.'

Beating about the bush? This wasn't Ulrich's style.

'Put, uh, *what* in perspective?'

'Shortly after our arrival around Apis, I joined Black Horizon.'

Nayak was taken aback. 'What? How?'

'I'm putting it as harshly as possible, because that's how others will put it, and how I might yet be judged. Commander Alice Hawkins at New Ardtaraig contacted me, an hour or so after my initial communication with her and then with the Co-ord commander at Novy Cosmograd, General Khaustov. Apparently the two of them, and perhaps others, conferred at once and agreed to share with me an information package of Black Horizon's activities and discoveries.'

'Why?'

'Khaustov had learned that the authorities were moving against Black Horizon, and they expected a crackdown within minutes or hours. As in fact was soon confirmed, when the *Admiral von Bellingshausen* popped up under the command of Captain Rostov.'

Nayak chuckled. 'And not our old friend Yefrimovich.'

'Uh-huh.' Ulrich was not amused. 'I went eyeball to eyeball with that bastard, while you and Grant scrambled to jump us, and – well, let's say I'm not shedding a tear if he's in the brig, or up against a wall for that matter.'

'Yeah, yeah,' Nayak hastily agreed. 'He did fire on us, so—'

'Nevertheless,' Ulrich went on, 'that doesn't stop my being objective about his co-conspirators' appeal. They genuinely believed they were doing right by humanity, they expected their own imminent arrest, and they passed the torch – as they saw it – to us.' She looked away, up into a corner of the room. 'The question is, do we agree, and do we pick it up?'

'These are two questions.'

Again with the lack of amusement. 'Yes. Indeed. Well?'

'What are you asking me to do, exactly?'

'I'm asking you to study the Black Horizon data package. I should warn you that it's quite disturbing, impossible to ignore, and has some implications very close to home. You're free not to read it. You're free to walk out of this door and denounce me. If you do read it, I would like you to advise me what to do about it.'

Nayak's mouth was dry, her palms damp.

'Yes,' she said. 'I'll do my best.'

Ulrich flipped a file from her phone to Nayak's. 'Read.'

Back in her cubicle, Nayak settled the bedding at her back, curled up her legs, invoked a screen and read. It wasn't straightforward, or quick. The file was a heap of documents, hastily shuffled together. Printed out, it would have been about a thousand pages. Some of it was narrative or explanation. There were minutes of meetings, with dates that made her look twice. There were diagrams and tables. Many pages were in Russian or Mandarin. She could read Russian, and translation software made short work of Mandarin. Likewise with ordering: she could flip between chronological, topical, or whatever, with a blink.

Chronological? A questionable category in this context. The story began in 2018, with the return of the first interstellar FTL probe. This had been a surprise to the scientists and technicians concerned, because they hadn't sent it out. The personnel, the location and the name and nature of the joint Russian–American–Chinese scientific collaboration involved were redacted, even now. Nayak picked up hints that it had been in the Arctic – there were mentions of ice, and climate change, and fur and high-powered rifles. Some high-energy physics experiment, deep in a cave under the ice. With a little thrill, she caught a mention of cosmic inflation. She looked again down parts lists. Aha!

What they'd been groping towards, in their chill, dark tunnel, was a trap for the hypothesised particle that had been the carrier of cosmic inflation: the inflaton. An inflaton trap – the central component of Nayak's FTL drive. She read on, her hands shaking.

The scientists hadn't finished building Test Rig 1. They detected distress messages from some unidentified probe, which had crashed on the ice a few kilometres away. (No femtosecond timers in those days, Nayak thought.) Disbelieving, the recovery party dragged back a sled bearing Test Rig 2. This crude device – an open frame of angled aluminium around what Nayak's crew had called a flywheel – was damaged but still recognisable and functional. Its onboard camera had close-ups of Proxima Centauri b.

The scientists hadn't sent it out. They hadn't even *considered* sending it out. The whole idea that an inflaton trap could be used as an FTL engine hadn't crossed their minds. According to the camera's serial number and the supplies inventory, the camera should still be on a shelf at the base. It was. A picture in the file showed the box-fresh original and its space-worn, ice-battered older self, side by side.

There were other pictures in the camera. Someone with a sense of history or a sense of humour had used it to photograph the team – the same team that had not yet completed Test Rig 1 – posing around Test Rig 2, with a much-scrawled whiteboard behind them. The next two pictures showed the whiteboard. It was covered with equations that Nayak knew very well indeed. She looked at them and laughed. The origin of this first version of these equations was as paradoxical as that of hers: back from the future, again.

The scientists at the Arctic base had studied these equations very carefully, and the arrangement of the apparatus and the calibration of the instruments even more carefully. And then they'd built a copy, which they dubbed Test Rig 2a.

There were, of course, no Faber fusion pots in 2018 – but, then, the probe had a mass of only a few kilogrammes. They'd used lithium batteries. (Lithium batteries! Nayak was impressed.) They calibrated it for Proxima.

They'd powered it up. Test Rig 2a vanished in a blue flash.

It came back.

At least, it did in that time-line . . .

The scientists and technicians had worked out the implications a lot faster than Nayak ever had, or than most people were doing right now, as far as she knew. There were no political or military people in that lab, which was just as well, but they all quickly grasped the political and strategic consequences of FTL travel and transport – to say nothing of an accessible multiverse. They saw at once that this was far more powerful and dangerous than any previous technology. It made nuclear deterrence obsolete, for a start, unless deterrence could be re-established on a far wider scale. But that came later.

Their first priority was to keep it out of the hands of the current political leaderships of their respective countries. Their second was to find out what could be done with it. For that, they needed resources that only the military, industrial and scientific establishments could provide.

And so Black Horizon was born. From friends, from

contacts, from old loyalties and debts of honour, from suborning and subversion, ambition and blackmail, through corruption and conspiracy the network spread into the apparats. At its core, though, were idealists and elitists. They were confident they knew best. (Did they? Nayak wondered. A world where the FTL drive had been thrown open to all as soon as it was discovered would have had its dangers, but might have avoided others.)

The first robot probes – almost as simple as the test rigs – were sent out in 2020. The first nuclear submarines with FTL drives were operating by 2030. Not long after came the first FTL-enabled aerofoils out of Groom Lake, their funding buried in the black budgets (just another flying saucer knock-off, reverse engineered from a crash recovery – that, Nayak liked to think, would be the cover story).

What the probes and then expeditions discovered out there among the stars astonished them: planet after planet not only habitable, but subtly or blatantly terraformed, with a biosphere related to Earth's by common descent. None had any detectable native intelligent life. All had outcrops of crystalline rocks with incomprehensible internal activity. That aside, no trace of alien intelligence turned up anywhere. The sky was as silent as ever.

'It's like coming into an empty room in an empty house and getting the uncanny feeling that someone has just left.' So one early explorer had put it, in a statement that echoed down the decades like a sinister hollow laugh.

Speculation on the alien rocks had outrun research – clandestine as it had to be, compartmentalised as Black Horizon had chosen to keep it. There had been blunders and disasters: the quakes on Apis, and on Earth, had not been the first to follow careless tampering and prying into these enigmatic strata. Nayak flicked past a lot of pages. She paused over the grim record of how some of these worlds had been settled, by people spirited away amid floods, droughts, wars and refugee migrations. She read how deterrence had been re-established by each power's careful concealment of nuclear weapons (their absence from their official deployment creatively accounted for, sometimes by rotation in ways that reminded Nayak of a three-cup trick) on planets unknown to the other side.

It was Black Horizon's plan to use the widely distributed warheads for more than deterrence that brought her up short, and sent her hurrying back to Ulrich's office.

'Ah, you've found it,' Ulrich said, looking up. 'Yes, I agree, it's completely insane.'

'Insane? It's the maddest idea I've ever heard in my life!'

'Yes, yes,' Ulrich said. 'I need no convincing on that score. To use nuclear weapons against the alien rocks would be like ants trying to stop a tank. It gets worse, as you'd have learned if you'd read on.'

'Oh.'

'I'll give you a minute.'

Nayak sat down and read until she reached the most recent and secret sheets of the stash. To her surprise, they concerned the very system the Station was now in: E-PRIME 667. To her even greater surprise, they specifically concerned the moon E-PRIME 667a V: the one that had, from her own and the Station's point of view, come into existence after the Station had jumped to its present orbit around the star. The Mushroom Moon, it was called in the Black Horizon documents.

She looked up. 'The moon – you knew this?'

'Yes.'

'You kept that quiet.'

Ulrich nodded. 'I had to, until the *Fighting Chance* had left. You'll see why.'

'Wait – does this mean—'

Ulrich raised a hand. 'Yes, I had Sikandar suggest this one, yes it wasn't on the version of the map that Black Horizon shared with the authorities, and yes I was surprised at the absence of this moon when we arrived and was very relieved to find it after our jump.'

'Meaning we're back in the right universe?'

'I hope so.' Ulrich flipped a hand. 'Close enough. We can discuss these questions later. We have more urgent matters to deal with.'

Nayak read on. The moon was not just habitable, in the technical sense of having surface conditions consistent with liquid water. It had a biosphere, and human inhabitants – exiles placed there by Black Horizon. Predictably, indeed inevitably, it showed signs of geologically recent terraforming. Likewise predictably, it had outcrops of alien rock. The surface gravity was 0.41, far too low to retain its atmosphere of 0.8 bar for more than a few million years. This was too young a world to have evolved complex life. It rotated on its axis once every twenty or so hours, and orbited the gas giant every six of these short days. It wasn't tidally locked like every other known moon: another indicator of its recent formation. There was no way it could have formed naturally.

It had no Black Horizon presence, but it did have caches of nuclear weapons on its surface. The nukes were for deterrence, but they were also for nuking the outcrops if it ever came to that. Submarines controlled by Black Horizon checked in on the stash every so often. Now that Black Horizon was being rolled up, seizing the submarines as soon as they returned to base would be a top priority. Recovering their secret schedules would be a matter of hours. Crews could be turned or replaced. The secret caches would be found. And Black Horizon's plan to keep deterrence alive in the FTL era would be in ashes.

'That can't be right!'

'What?'

'They're saying here that if the powers find Black Horizon's nuke stashes, it's the end of deterrence.' Nayak shook her head. 'All the powers have to do is continue to keep the locations secret from each other, or if they're worried about leaks move the nukes to new secret locations, and everything continues as it was.'

'You're missing the point,' Ulrich said. 'Black Horizon wanted all that, yes. And they also wanted the nukes in place for their crazy plan to someday nuke the alien intelligences in the rocks.'

An appended list showed the names and destinations of the submarines this was most likely to happen to first. One such destination was indeed close to home.

'What!' Nayak yelped, jumping up. 'We have to—'

'Yes,' said Ulrich. 'We have to move fast. HMS *Vindicate* is on its way, ETA Saturday. We have to be ready for it. But first' – she sighed–'I'm going to have to confess all to the rest of the Station. If that's what you'd advise?'

'Yes,' said Nayak. 'And, yes, that's what I would advise.'

'Good,' Ulrich said. 'Let's get this over and done with.' She flipped her phone to PA. 'Urgent general meeting. Ten minutes.'

In the corridor Nayak fell in with Marek, the trainee shuttle pilot, and Gironella, the engineer. They made for the nearest cafeteria, where they settled. Coffee was poured and screens shared. What was all this about? Grumbling and speculation disturbed the air.

Ulrich popped up in everyone's virtual view.

'I have a confession to make,' she said. 'When I've finished, the command team, the Station crew and the entire complement from Cloud City are free to withdraw their confidence. If any of these do, I will step down at once.'

A sough of indrawn breath, a murmur of query.

'It's that serious,' Ulrich went on. 'I made a decision that affects you all, without your knowledge.'

She gave them the gist. They took it well.

'Thank you,' she said. Instructions pinged on everyone's glasses. 'And now, to your stations.'

Marek blinked behind his glasses, and looked at Nayak. 'Us? You and me?'

Nayak nodded. 'It has to be.' She didn't tell him how firmly she'd had to make that point to Ulrich, just before the meeting. There were other pilots, but Marek was still the best, and, as for herself, she wasn't going to miss this for anything. And besides, she was the only pilot who had actually flown, and she was responsible for the design of the drive and therefore had a duty to be the first to test it . . . Ulrich had known when she was beaten, and had other things on her mind.

They stood up, nodded to Gironella – who was looking over his own instructions with a slightly dazed expression – and made for the nearest access tube to the shuttle dock. They spent the next few hours with the engineers, checking over the vehicle. Then they went back to the simulator.

In the morning, they were ready to go.

E-PRIME 667a V, Thursday 13 November 2070

Nayak sat in the cockpit of the shuttle, in a close-fitting armoured spacesuit and a helmet whose faceplate merged smoothly with a wraparound heads-up display: it was like wearing glasses, but not. Marek, likewise kitted up, sat beside her. The jump had been uneventful. She was almost getting used to the black moment. Now she hung in orbit around E-PRIME 667a V: the Mushroom Moon.

Even from space, it was anomalous. Blue-dotted with innumerable water lakes, most of its surface beneath the whorls of white cloud appeared red, veined with green and mottled with dirty white. Among and between the clouds were scores of plumes of smoke, rising from fires over areas of hundreds of square kilometres. It just didn't look like the moon of a gas giant this far out from its star. Yet here it was.

Marek thumbed up a map derived from coordinates given

in the Black Horizon documents, layered it over the view and spun the resulting globe.

'Three outcrops,' he said, pointing. 'And a nuke next to each of them. Not exactly subtle about their intentions.'

'Crying shame that the exile settlements are huddled around one of them. Let's deal with that one first.'

'Agreed.' Marek pondered the virtual sphere as if scrying in a crystal ball. 'Jump, or approach?'

Nayak considered, and decided. 'Approach. I want to get an idea of the lie of the land.'

'Got it.' Marek tabbed options for the shuttle's AI, then sat back. 'Pilot and co-pilot, along for the ride.'

Half an orbit later, the shuttle tilted, swinging the huge sickle of the gas giant's crescent across their view. There was a short burn to decelerate, then they were brushing atmosphere. Air, good as, though with a high enough proportion of carbon dioxide to make a climate scientist sweat. The red scream of aerobraking was accompanied by vibration and buffeting that had Nayak white-knuckled and grimly reflecting that the shuttle must have taken worse many times over Venus. For minutes on end they were a meteor in the alien sky.

Then they were gliding down, under a black sky slowly gaining a tinge of blue, with the crescent of the gas giant rising like some monstrous cutlass blade above the horizon ahead. High clouds enveloped the craft for a moment, then it came out underneath. The surface and down became a landscape and around. Nayak gazed about at a view her brain had a hard time processing. No seas, no mountains, hardly any rivers even. Undulations that could almost be called hills, among which hundreds of lakes reflected the sky in passing glints as the craft hurtled by. The shuttle flashed over a region that smouldered and smoked, with flames flaring here and there; then long green vales that vanished into and under a lumpy grey-brown and white expanse, like a spillage of some unpleasant liquid.

Then, just ahead—

'Oh, wow!' Marek said.

On the horizon and coming up fast: a cluster of crystal spires, rising five hundred metres straight up from the plain. Nayak had seen the images from Apis: MacHinery Ridge, Hamilton's Rise and the Markov Escarpment, each impressive and awe-inspiring in its own way. Compared with this, they were as broken light-tubes to a chandelier.

'No mountain-building here,' Marek said, 'and no ice ages.'

'You reckon that's it?'

'It's a fair guess. Don't think this moon has much in the way of plate tectonics, either.'

Nayak took over from the AI, diverting the craft from its intended landing. She circled the pinnacles, marvelling, then took a wider turn around them at almost stalling speed (still very fast, 346 km/h) this time scanning the surrounding area with the instruments and her own sharp eyes. The rise and fall of the plain and its imbricated red, green and white splotches and strands were on this closer look pocked with heaps of black, each rough circle surrounding a fire far smaller than the multi-hectare burnings she'd minutes earlier overflown.

'Settlements?'

Marek raised a black-gloved thumb. 'Looks likely.'

Nayak returned the shuttle to autopilot. It brought them in to land on flat ground within eight hundred metres of where the map said the nukes were stashed, and a good two kilometres from the smoke of the nearest settlement. Skids jarred and squealed as shuttle met surface, gentle as a hundred-tonne leaf. The craft slowed sharply, pressing Nayak and Marek painfully forward against their seat harnesses.

Amid hisses, creaks and rising steam, they stopped. Nayak knew she'd been under local gravity ever since their aerobraking had given way to gliding, but now she felt it, a curious sense of lightness, of being buoyed up.

She laughed and turned to Marek. In the real light his visor was a blank reflective curved plane; in the virtual, which she toggled to and from, she could see the angular, alert face behind it. A face grinning all over.

'We made it!'

'Don't sound so surprised.' She unclipped her harness, shifted in her seat and waggled her shoulders. Marek leaned forward and strapped on a tool belt, as did Nayak. 'Let's see if it's safe to pop the lid.'

'First, let's check that the sensors have been recalibrated since Venus.'

'Don't worry, they have.' Nayak flicked through the heads-up. 'What do you make of it?'

'*Technically*,' Marek said, 'the air out there is breathable, if a bit thin, but going by the molecular spectra there's a hell of a lot of biological stuff in it . . . ah, yes, spores. Fungal spores.'

'Not breathing in any of that, thanks.'

'Me neither.' Marek ran through systems checks on their suits and helmets. 'The filters will keep out everything we need to worry about.'

'You're certain of that?'

Marek gave her a look. 'Hydroponics engineering in Cloud City involved strict biosecurity protocols.'

'OK, OK.'

'As you'll see in the airlock.'

A minute later, she did. Complete flush cycle, sprays, the lot.

'It's a car wash! What's the point?'

'Massively redundant on Venus for the most part, but here . . . we just don't know.' Marek shrugged. 'We have to protect this place against our contamination as much us against its.'

Dried by hot blowers, shoved by a final blast of sterile air, they stepped out of the airlock and down the ladder onto the surface. Nayak found herself holding her breath. She decided not to be irrational and to trust the best technology ESA could provide. She breathed in. The air smelled only of plastics. It was, as Marek had said, thin – she had to breathe harder than usual – and chilly. According to her display, the temperature was around 10 degrees Celsius. This seemed abnormally hot, with the system's sun so small and far away. Most of the heat in the atmosphere must come from the moon's interior, from tidal heating or the remnant heat of the moon's no doubt violent and geologically recent formation. Millions rather than billions of years old – that was the best guess.

Nayak reached into her tool belt and tossed a brace of drones into the air, to keep an eye on any movement from the apparent settlements. The two whirred away, heading for the rising smoke, and were out of sight in seconds. A patch in her display kept track.

A hatch opened in the belly of the shuttle and a pair of pack robots dropped out, fell slowly and got to their feet skittishly. The robots were about the size of Shetland ponies. They walked on four legs and had an array of manipulative limbs folded about their midriffs. Nayak waved them into position behind her, and she and Marek walked off. The first few steps were awkward – being less than half your weight with your normal strength and reflexes threw everything off kilter. Nayak tried bunny-hopping, like astronauts on the Moon, but here the gravity was too high for that to be efficient.

'Try the Martian lope,' said Marek, leaning forward and taking long, springing strides. After a stumble or two, Nayak got the hang of it.

'Have you been on Mars?'

'No, but I've seen videos.'

They bounded across the uneven terrain, the robots following like faithful hounds. The horizon was so close it was disorienting. Nayak kept feeling that she could trip and go flying into the blue-black sky and on to the gas giant. The crystal pinnacles soared out of sight to her left, with no discernible foothills. The ground underfoot was springy and slippery, blanketed in a green, seeping moss. In and on it nothing moved.

No animal life was visible, and it wasn't clear from the documents if any was present. Halfway to the cache the ground cover changed to what looked and felt like cork: beige, dry and tough, rising into gnarled, three-metre-high club-like shapes every few metres. Her hip knocked one as she passed, and a cloud of powder wafted out like smoke.

'Spores,' Marek said.

Nayak laughed. 'Fungus – so that's why they call it the Mushroom Moon!'

'Could be,' Marek said.

The cache came quickly into view: a yellow dome a few metres high and across. Within a hundred metres of it the fungus gave way to a fibrous, dark brown surface veined with white filaments and nodules. Marek raised a hand and stopped to squat and run his gloved fingers through the top layer. It crumbled easily, like compost, then a few centimetres deep became black, damp and firm.

'I'd almost say this is peat. Weird.'

'Why?'

Marek looked around. 'Have you seen anything that looks remotely like a tree? Even heather? Low scrub?'

'Botany can wait. As long as we can walk on it.'

'Should be fine. Watch out for surface water. Any shiny patch could be a bog or a sinkhole.'

'Speaking of which . . .' Nayak pointed to a long, low depression parallel to their direct path, like an elongated and apparently shallow lake.

'Easily avoided.'

'Yes, but what caused it?'

'If botany can wait, so can geology.'

'It's not geology,' Marek said. 'It's the impression left by the last submarine to visit.'

Nayak took in the shape again. 'Jeez, I think you're right.'

Even after seeing a submarine in space twice, the thought of one resting on top of a peat bog still seemed unreal.

They crossed to the cache without incident and walked up to the dome. Bright yellow, blazoned with big black radiation trefoils, it seemed made of steel so thick it didn't ring when knocked. Here and there the paint was scratched, as if someone or something had tried to hack or claw through it – to no avail. They walked around the dome until they found the hatch. It was the height of a door and dogged and locked. Its lower few tens of centimetres had sunk into the peat, or – more likely – the peat had risen over it.

'Hope it doesn't open outward,' Marek said.

Nayak laughed. 'Got the spanner?'

Marek passed the tool to her. The nuts wouldn't budge. She sighed and reached out a hand. Marek silently passed her a spraycan. She worked her way around the dozen nuts, then tried again. They all came off, and she put them one by one in the leg pocket of her suit.

'Moment of truth.' She leaned over to the keypad. She summoned the entrance code, a thirty-digit number from the Black Horizon documents, to appear in her heads-up. She tapped the code in, taking great care not to make any mistakes – she strongly suspected the system was unforgiving.

Click, then a clunk. She pushed at the door, and it swung open. The wall of the dome was as thick as she'd guessed. The inside, not to her surprise, was dark.

Despite the radiation warning sigils outside, no trace of radioactivity showed on her display's monitors. She blinked her helmet lamp on and stepped in, Marek following, the robots waiting. The floor was a long step lower than the ground outside. It was bare concrete. In the middle was a trolley, on which six green cylinders, each one and a half metres long and twenty centimetres in diameter, were racked in three levels of two, strapped into place with aluminium alloy zip-ties. A red line circumscribed their ends, and small red lettering was printed along the shafts.

'Thermonuclear warheads,' Marek said. 'Handle with care.'

'Not to be dropped.'

'Indeed.'

Nayak went over to the trolley and pushed. It didn't move.

'Try the spray again,' Marek said.

Nayak snorted, and lubricated the wheels. It was a good test of her helmet's filters, she thought, that she caught not the slightest whiff of the spray. The stuff had always given her headaches.

She stood up and pushed again. The trolley rolled, as if reluctantly.

'How are we going to get this back? Must weigh a tonne.'

'Nah,' said Marek. 'Kilotonnes.'

'Ha ha, very droll. It'll be lighter in this gravity, but the mass is the same, and I don't fancy bumping those wheels all the way back to the ship. Even with the robots hauling.'

'Who says they're going to haul it?'

'How else could they do it – carry the nukes on their backs like bundles of sticks on a donkey?'

'Watch and learn,' Marek said.

He called the robots in and guided them, one to the front and one to the back of the trolley. They unfolded and extended their mid-limbs and grasped the ends of the trolley, which they rolled to the door, lifted over the threshold, and pushed outside. Nayak followed Marek and the robots out. The trolley wheels were already sinking into the peat almost to their axles. Marek guided the robots to the sides of the trolley, where they each grasped any convenient handhold. The robots walked forward, dragging the trolley between them and giving it, as far as Nayak could see, a partial lift up as well. With their movement, and the weight now being distributed between eight feet and four wheels, neither they nor the trolley sank so far into the peat, but it was slow and hard going.

It got slower and harder when they came off the peat and onto the fungal mat: the ground was firmer, but bumpier and with more obstacles to steer around. After knocking over one of the club-like protrusions by accident they discovered how fragile they were, and ploughed straight through them leaving a trail of clouds of spores.

Just as they reached the moss, halfway back to the shuttle, Nayak's display from the drones flashed warnings. She tabbed the patch to Marek, and maxed it in the centre of her view. A swarm of dots had emerged from the nearest circle of black shapes around a fire, and was heading for the shuttle. She zoomed, and saw what seemed like human figures doing the Martian lope a lot faster than she and Marek had managed.

'We'll never get there in time,' she said.

'The closer we get the better,' Marek said. 'I'll get behind and shove, you go to the front, reach behind you, grab a shelf and pull.'

'And do in my back?'

'The suit will brace you in the right places, don't worry.'

It still felt awkward and not much help, but Nayak bowed to it and plodded on. The moss was only a few centimetres deep, and resisted the wheels but didn't slow them down as much as she'd feared. Her feet and the robots' made splashes, drops of water and shreds of moss that went up higher and fell slower than the eye expected. In the display the settlers could now be seen clearly, and in the actual view she could see them ahead and to her left, a few hundred metres away and closing fast. There were – the display counted – twenty-seven of them. None of them seemed to be carrying anything. They ran with their heads down, with long, floating strides and swinging arms.

There could be only one outcome to the race, however, and fifty metres from the shuttle, it came. The band of settlers stood across their path, in two rows of a dozen or so.

'Keep going,' Nayak said.

The settlers were tall, thin, naked, and almost all pale-skinned. They had big chests. Their hair was long and matted, sometimes twisted or braided into plaits and dreadlocks. The men, who made up about three-quarters of the group and all of the front row, had beards in a similar state. The settlers stayed right where they were as Nayak, Marek, the two robots and the laden trolley slowly moved towards them.

'Stop,' Nayak said, at three metres. Marek, and the robots, complied.

'Best show our faces,' Marek said.

'Can we do that?'

'Yes. It's still a screen, but it looks transparent.'

'Ah.' Nayak found the option and selected it. From her point of view, nothing changed, but those facing her looked startled. She forced a smile. 'Hello?'

The man in the middle of the row took a long step forward. His hair and beard were white. Tall as the rest, but slightly stooped. Nayak had to look up to look him in the face. He peered at her, eyes black and shiny, pupils dilated. Nayak's quick, sweeping, zoomed glance found that all the others' eyes were like that: deep dark pools.

'Are you a robot?' the man asked, in a dreamy tone of idle curiosity. His accent had some trace of America, in so far as she could place it at all.

'No,' Nayak said. She pointed to the machines. 'These are robots. I'm Lakshmi Nayak, and this is my friend Ernest Marek.'

'Lakshmi Nayak,' the man repeated. His eyes widened. 'Not *the* Lakshmi Nayak?'

'What do you mean?'

'Mean? Ah . . .' He went off in a reverie for five seconds, then snapped out of it and pointed over his shoulder to the shuttle. 'You devised the device. A drive, I mean. Ah, you have such a drive!' He cackled.

'Yes,' Nayak. 'I devised the device. That's exactly right. How do you know?'

The old man rolled his eyes upward, as if at a stupid question.

'In a dream. I learned of you in a dream. I only heard your name. I didn't see your face, so I didn't recognise you.' He leaned further forward. 'You were there, though, in my dream. You spoke, from far away. Yes, in the dark, you spoke!'

For no reason she could explain, Nayak shivered.

'Well,' she said, feeling awkward, as if breaking off a conversation with a talkative but tedious interlocutor, 'this is interesting, but we must be going. We have a lot to do.'

'You can't be going,' the man said. He pointed to the trolley and its cargo. 'Not with these.'

'Why not?'

'We will stop you.' The man gestured, and suddenly the straggle of settlers became a compact and determined squad.

Marek laughed. 'Do you know what these are?'

'Fusion warheads,' the old man said promptly. 'They must not leave here. They deter.'

'Yes, they deter,' Nayak said. 'That's why we must take them away. They are needed to deter somewhere else.'

The old man laughed. He turned to the others and shouted, 'She says they're needed to *deter somewhere else*!' They all joined in his laughter, and it became uncontrollable: gasping, clutching their sides, slapping each other's shoulders, falling about laughing. It was as if Nayak had delivered the punchline of the best joke they'd ever heard.

Nayak looked at Marek, bewildered.

'Stoned out of their box,' Marek said. 'Hence the dilated pupils and the weird talk.'

'That makes sense.' She looked around. 'What if all that fungus is like a gigantic magic mushroom?'

'And they use it?'

Marek scoffed. 'What if they live on it?'

'Jeez.'

Suddenly everything here made sense. This small world had had its own Carboniferous, where nothing could digest lignin and the vegetation just piled up without rotting, for long enough to turn into coal. Then the fungi had arrived, by evolution or otherwise, and taken over half the biosphere, gorging on the dead plants. If all that these people here had to live on was the fungus, and all they had to keep them warm was peat or coal . . .

After a minute or so the settlers subsided into exhausted giggling. The old man straightened up and looked down at Nayak again. '"Somewhere else",' he wheezed. 'They're needed here. Right here. To deter.' His mind wandered again, then snapped back. 'Yes, to deter.'

'They can deter anywhere,' Nayak said. 'We're taking them somewhere safe, that's all.'

The man looked baffled. 'Where would be better to deter than here?'

This was going around in circles.

Marek broke in. 'What is it here to deter?'

The man gaped. He giggled again. He pointed to the crystal mountain rising from the plain a few hundred metres away.

'To deter the bird,' he said. Then louder: 'The bird!'

At that the others began to crowd around, to press close. Nayak moved her hand, slowly and carefully, to the sidearm on her belt. It occurred to her that, unlike Marek, she had never so much as been shown how to use it. Really she should have taken advantage of the shooting range, back in that shipyard in Port Glasgow.

'What bird?' she cried.

A howl rose from the edge of the crowd. Every head turned sharply, every mouth opened, every eye stared. And then, suddenly as a flock of sparrows changing direction, the naked settlers turned and fled pell-mell. Nayak barely had time to notice as she turned and looked.

To the side, and up, and up.

A black band was moving up the outcrop, gathering pace. Beneath it, the crystal cliff-faces turned white, as if the rising black band had drawn all their bright colours in and crushed them to itself. It reached the top and went on rising.

Out of the bright pinnacles above her a vast darkness took shape in the sky. It was like the Sun's corona at a total eclipse, a circle with outspread wings as the ancient Egyptians had so precisely shown their sun-god's true hidden form. But this was no sun-god. There was no light in it. It was blacker than any blackness Nayak had ever seen or imagined, blacker than the space between the stars, with not even that glimmer of the first light, the 2.725 kelvin cosmic microwave background. It came from before the first photons had formed, from the darkness on the face of the deep in that moment of indrawn breath before God said: *Fiat lux*.

All this went through Nayak's mind, quick as a flash.

She couldn't think of anything intelligent to say.

'Oh,' she said, '*that* bird.'

CHAPTER NINETEEN

In the Eye of Silence

New Mu, Apis, Thursday 13 November 2070

Owen was sure they would never find Georgi Muranov's body. As soon as Myles was out of sight, the robot had waited for Muranov to come off the phone to Novy Cosmograd. Owen had then disabled the drone with a malware upload beamed straight from his own head, strolled over to Muranov as if to chat, snapped the Russian's neck, lugged the body at a brisk trot downstream a kilometre beyond the camp and thrown the corpse in the river just where it ran swift and deep into a ravine. From there, barring freak accidents, it would end up in the ocean or (more likely) be eaten by the numerous predators and scavengers in the river along the way.

What had impelled him to flight wasn't the possibility of detection, but what he'd become aware of just after the Cherenkov flash: a faint, elusive, but unmistakable presence of Iskander. He even recognised, in the feathery traces of the

AI's wary scans and probes that occasionally brushed his skull, the particular flavour of the instance of Iskander with which he was already intimately familiar: the one in the Venus descent suit. It had fought him before, on its own, on the galleries and gantries outside Cloud City. It had communicated, at some level, with the alien rocks on the surface of Venus. That it had come here to attempt a further communication Owen had little doubt. Nor did he take long to deduce that it could only have arrived – how, he didn't know, and didn't speculate – via the Union's starship and the Venus Space Station.

Owen ran uphill through the forest. Within an hour he was on the scree slopes above the tree line, and after twenty minutes of scrambling he was at the foot of the cliffs. From the forest and from the scree, he gave every bit of attention he could spare to the rock-faces, the shelves and clefts in the basalt. By the time he stood looking up he had the route up mapped to the handhold and foothold. He knew very well that the reality would be different, and so it proved. Sometimes rock came away in his hand, or under his foot. He teetered, or dangled; he calculated, and recovered. More than once, what had seemed from a distance a feasible route turned out to be impassable. With what passed in him for patience, he climbed back down to the last choice point, and tried another. At one point in a bad fall the slung rifle banged across his back. He processed the damage and ignored it henceforth.

The climb took him the rest of the night: about four hours. The racket of the dawn chorus rose from below like the sound of a distant industrial town beginning the day shift. He crested the final cliff and stood beside his own long shadow, which stretched to his right across a field of broken rock before being lost in the glare of reflected light, ruby and emerald and sapphire, from the glassy face and glinting facets of Hamilton's Rise. The surreal edifice ahead of him rose almost as high above where he stood as the cliff he'd already climbed did from the valley.

Here, he paused. A lesser mind would have been awed; and an appropriate expression would have been legible on Owen's face, if anyone had been there to see it. Something was. He felt its presence as a tingle in the back of his neck, and turned. Facing into the glare of the low sun, even his eyes took a second to adjust. They took a half-second longer to detect a speck in the immense volume of air above the plain and all the way to the horizon. A moment later, Owen identified it: a drone, rising from the military stockade and heading for the valley, presumably to replace the one he'd sabotaged.

No chance of repeating that feat: the drone was well out of his range. The transmitter behind his forehead had nothing like tight-beam. His receivers, however, picked up coded chatter, and he was aware that the drone had observed him.

It flew on, however, maintaining its course, and shortly vanished behind the shoulder of the mountain. Its faint buzz became slightly louder as the valley walls echoed and amplified it, then faded out of his earshot.

Nothing to worry about, for now. He turned away and walked across the debris field to the nearest opening in the crystal cliff. Five minutes later, he was walking along a metre-wide passage between walls that seemed of pale green glass lined with fractally complex ridges, behind which indistinct shapes moved like tropical fish in some baroque aquarium. It was a sight to ravish, and left him quite unmoved. He pressed on, into a silence that gave him the continuous feeling of being watched.

On the shadow side of the mountain, Milloy climbed through gloom and damp, among the last trees. Ferns and small unfamiliar plants brushed at her legs. Animals she now and then glimpsed with a start or a shudder scuttled or slithered in the undergrowth. Ahead of her, the descent suit animated by Sikandar plodded on, to all appearances oblivious to its surroundings, the survival pack carried casually in one hand.

It had offered to port the high-powered rifle, but Milloy had chosen to keep the weapon to hand, weighty though it was.

She emerged from the trees and faced a short walk to a forbidding basalt cliff. The boom of the surf far behind and below was joined by a distant and enormous cacophony, like a football crowd waving their rattles and sounding their vuvuzelas and yelling all at once. A dawn chorus, she guessed, and not one to count among this world's delights. Far above her, the topmost peaks of the crystal pillars blazed as they caught the rising sun's first rays, casting a green gleam under a sky of high pink clouds.

The suit stood at the foot of the cliff. It seemed to be staring straight ahead – but, then, it didn't need to tilt its head back to look up.

'I guess it's time for me to climb in,' Milloy said. 'Because I sure can't see any way to climb up.'

'Indeed,' said Sikandar. 'Clip your weapon to the left side of the suit's back, and I'll open the hatch.'

The suit raised its arms and removed the head dome – it could hardly be called a helmet – and swung open the hatch. Milloy did as she was told and clambered in, careful with the ammunition belts across her chest. The panel was thirteen centimetres thick. She slid into the legs and arms of the suit. The panel closed behind her with the reassuring flanged solidity of a bank safe door. The head dome settled back in place. At first there was the familiar panicked feeling that all she could see of the outside was through the small, thick faceplate. Then, when the displays came on, it was as if all the rest of the dome wasn't there. Wherever she turned her head, she could see out. Internal shock-absorbent gel armour pressed inward to fit her limbs and torso. She wiggled her fingers and toes and settled in, feeling safe and secure. She'd designed this suit, and she'd been in it on Venus herself. She had every confidence in it.

'Now relax,' said Sikandar. 'Don't try to override my movements. You're along for the ride.'

The suit began to climb the cliff. After a minute or two, the impulse to override the suit's actions became so strong that she terrified herself. She closed her eyes and waited for the ascent to be over.

'Francesca?'

'What?' Milloy came to with a start. She was standing in the suit. Ahead a gentle slope of a hundred metres led to a filigreed wall of green glass that flowed and intertwined like vines on a trellis.

'We're at the top.'

'So I see.' She felt embarrassed. 'Uh, I fell *asleep*?'

'You did, and just as well. Even I found the climb quite hairy in places.'

'Ah.' She yawned. 'Well, it's been a long night. Anyway, I want out.'

'Are you sure? You might be safer inside. If you need to drink or to relieve yourself the suit can—'

'I know, I designed it. Let me out.'

The dome came off and the hatch at the back opened. The armour gel relaxed, as if deflating. Milloy hauled herself out and lowered herself to the ground. She unclipped the rifle.

'I'll take the survival pack now,' she said. Sikandar handed it over. Milloy found a rock to sit on, sipped water and ate an energy bar. She sat with her back to Hamilton's Rise and looked out past the top of the cliff, over the slope of forest to the ocean. Beyond the long shadow of the mountain range the sea shone bright blue and white.

Just above the horizon, tens of kilometres to the west, a black dot appeared. The dot grew in seconds to a speck, racing across the water towards them. Milloy stared, then cried out.

'What's that?'

Sikandar turned its attention, though not its head.

'Ekranoplan,' it said.

'What the fuck's an ekranoplan?' Milloy flipped down her

glasses and zoomed. She took in the monstrous hybrid of airliner and warship hurtling above the waves. 'Oh.'

'Yes,' said Sikandar. '*That* the fuck's an ekranoplan. Coming our way. ETA at the beach: ten minutes. Any troops on board may have powered armour, jet-packs, or quadcopters for personal flight. Best not be here.'

Milloy scrambled to her feet, stuffed the empty wrapper in her pocket from ingrained habit slung the pack on her back, hefted the rifle and made for the nearest opening in the crystal cliff.

'Not *there*,' said Sikandar, heading off on a diagonal. 'Here.'

Milloy ducked, and Sikandar crawled, through an opening about a metre wide and a metre and a half high. Inside was an open circular space about thirty metres across: the bottom of a cylindrical shaft of green and blue that vanished into haze hundreds of metres above. The ground underfoot was sparsely covered by the small green succulents that here filled the niche of grass, growing out of what might have been millennia of accumulated dust. Feathery spans of green algae plumed the sides to about head height. On the far side of the space rose a high, arched aperture, its surface decoration as elaborate as a cathedral doorway, its lines elegant and organic as a whale's jawbone. Beyond it multicoloured light shifted and played, reminding Milloy irreverently of discos and nightclubs.

Sikandar walked through the arch, and Milloy followed, to enter a corridor two metres across and four high, pulsing with light from the shapes that moved behind the vitreous glaze of the sides and top. It stretched, as far as Milloy could tell, for hundreds of metres ahead. The floor was now free of dust and detritus, and of any trace of life. Milloy marched along, marvelling, behind Sikandar. In this awesome, inhuman place the presence of a big machine of her own devising reassured. Scorched by Venusian sulphuric acid clouds, scored by high-energy particles and pitted by micrometeorite impacts, the descent suit strode in front of her like some friendly giant with a veteran's scars.

'Are you getting anything?'

'No,' Sikandar said. 'I've tried bouncing back my recordings from the chasm on Ishtar Terra, but there's no response.' It made an oddly human wave and waggle of the hand. 'Of course this structure could be separated by eons from the one the Alliance people surveyed, let alone from whatever we found on Venus.'

Milloy thought back to her interrogation of Sikandar's mind. She still suspected the AI hadn't been entirely forthcoming, then or since, about its previous encounter. It wasn't corrupted by the alien intelligences, of that she was fairly sure. But its continued reticence was a sore point.

'"Recordings"?' she said. 'Anything you haven't told me about that encounter? Now would be the time to tell. I'm in no position to interfere, after all.'

Sikandar kept walking. 'Nothing to tell,' it said, as if over its shoulder. 'I must say, I find this continued mistrust hard to understand.'

'Come off it! Nothing human is alien to you.'

'Oh, very sharp! You'll be a wit yet.' It stopped abruptly in its tracks. 'On the other hand . . .'

'What?'

'How stupid of us not to have thought of that!'

'Not to have thought of what, for goodness' sake?'

'If what Marcus Owen and I encountered on Venus wanted to implant information that I wasn't aware of, it didn't have to mess with our minds. It could inscribe it invisibly on the suit. Or for that matter – did you check my peripherals? The cameras and microphones?'

'Yes, of course I did! They're clean.'

'Good to know.'

'As for invisible messages – how? Invisible lasers? Action at a distance?'

'They're capable of that, and more. But what I have in mind is much simpler: the soles of the suit's boots.'

Milloy laughed. 'OK, now you're getting me paranoid. There's no point worrying about stuff like that, stuff we can only speculate about. Especially here and now! And like you said back on the Station, we have no idea what it's capable of, and no way of finding out.'

'So we might as well not concern ourselves about these possibilities?'

'As a practical matter, yes.'

'Good. So don't.'

After a few steps the penny dropped.

'You've just boxed me into arguing your own case! Yes, you understand people all right, Sikandar. So tell me this: why did you tell Owen to approach that outcrop on Venus, against his instructions from us? Why did *you* go there against our instructions?'

They passed out of the bright corridor into an even brighter space, an open area of many hectares between pillars each hundreds of metres in diameter, rising mountainous like gigantic glass sculptures of multicoloured novelty candles left to burn and drip for millennia. Opalescent ovoids the size of houses embedded in the translucent surfaces looked down, flying-saucer-eyed. The spaces between the pillars were irregularly spanned by relatively slender bridges of the same substance, and flying buttresses here and there joined the pillars to the ground. The scale of the place made Milloy feel, and Sikandar look, like tiny crawling creatures under a magnifying glass – and to feel observed, by some mind as incomprehensible to theirs as the naturalist's to the mite.

'I'll tell you why,' said Sikandar, its dry voice interrupting Milloy's reeling at the immensity of the space in which she stood. 'One of my functions is to anticipate people's needs. There on Ishtar Terra I anticipated the needs of all the people who will ever live.'

Milloy was still gazing around, becoming repeatedly lost in the complex details of the surfaces. She looked down at the ground, which unlike the corridor was deep in dust from which a sparse sward of small green plants strained upward to the distant sunlight. It seemed aesthetically incongruous, however ecologically probable. 'And what does that grandiose statement mean?'

Sikandar made a sweeping gesture. 'All this is an artificial intelligence. What could be more important to humanity than to understand an AI so far in advance of mine?'

'Yeah, maybe.' Milloy was now looking around more critically and observantly. 'I'll keep an open mind on that.' She looked up. In the sky above hung a small black dot. She was about to zoom on it when her phone rang.

Unknown number. She flicked her earlobe. 'Yes?'

'Lieutenant William Knight here. I'm in charge of Alliance military assistance to the Union settlement here. I'm looking down at you from a drone overhead.'

'Yes, I see it. I'm Francesca Milloy—'

'I know who you are. First woman on Venus, got it. I recognise the suit, too. I presume you arrived on that starship last night.'

'Yes, it was en route to Earth and—'

'What are you doing in there?'

'The suit is animated by an instance of our friendly AI, and is . . . trying to find out more about the thinking rocks. I'm basically here to hunt down Marcus Owen.'

Knight let out a yelp. 'How—? Oh, forget it. You've come to the right place. Owen is within a kilometre of you. I can patch you his location.'

Her earpiece tingled. Owen was in a narrow cleft, open to the sky and hundreds of metres deep. 'Got it. Thanks.'

'He's armed and dangerous.'

'So am I. I have a high-powered anti-materiel rifle.'

'That should take care of him. Good.'

'I thought he was one of yours.'

'He's a fucking Brit art project. We wash our hands of him.'

Milloy didn't believe this for a second. 'Why?'

'He murdered our Co-ord resident scientist just after the guy had been in touch with his home base about some breakthrough he'd had in understanding the rocks. Then the goddamn robot fled up there, presumably to talk to the rocks himself.'

'He's on a hiding to nothing. My robot isn't getting a peep out of them.'

Sikandar raised a hand, then lowered it, no doubt to mime having an objection then thinking better of it.

'Be that as it may,' Knight went on, 'we're happy to help you hunt and evade. But there's a complication. The Co-ord—'

Her turn to interrupt. 'I know. The ekranoplan.' She looked around, as if that would help. 'Are they coming in after him, too?'

'No, thank God. They've beached the ekranoplan, and bounced some scientists and a lot of soldiers up to the foot of the, uh, structure. The soldiers are forming a cordon all around it. All by quadcopter lifting, quite an impressive fast deployment.'

Milloy did a mental calculation of the approximate circumference of Hamilton's Rise.

'Holy shit! How many troops do they have?'

'Hundreds,' Knight said. 'Meanwhile the scientists are setting up some sort of apparatus near where you and your walking spacesuit must have come in.'

'Are they in touch with you?'

Knight sighed. 'Only to warn us off. They particularly warned us against sending drones in, but they don't seem to mind us having—'

There was a flash in the sky, followed by a bang that echoed among the forest of pillars, and a drift of descending debris like bits of burning paper.

'It seems they do mind,' Milloy said.

'If I were Owen,' Sikandar said, 'and a kilometre away, I would take that as a pretty good indication of where we are, given that—'

'There's only line-of-sight comms in here?'

'Not quite, but anything else is fragmentary and distorted.'

'Great. Well, we know where he is, or was a minute ago.' She shared the location marker and aerial photo with Sikandar. 'Now, what do we do?'

'In the suit, you'd be bulletproof.'

'But I couldn't shoot. The glove's fingers can't get through the trigger guard.'

'They don't need to.' The suit lurched towards her, and mimed strangulation. The movement was so menacing that Milloy inadvertently took a step back.

'Well . . . OK. Let's do that.'

'Now! He could be here at any moment.'

The suit turned away and raised its hands to the head dome. The hatch in the suit's back opened. Milloy made to stow the rifle and scramble in. The suit staggered away from her, its hands still pressed to the sides of the head dome, as if to shut out some intolerable ringing in its ears. It bounded away until it collided with a pillar, then fell back on the ground. Milloy rushed after it. The blank faceplate looked up. She could see her reflection in it.

'Something . . . coming . . . through,' Sikandar said. Its mighty hand patted the ground. 'Go . . . away . . . now.'

The glazed beauty of the pillar that the suit had smashed into was flowing, its surface gleaming like the rainbow oil on a puddle and bright as neon lights. The suit seemed to struggle feebly, to no avail. The flowing glassy substance engulfed the suit's boots and sent tendrils up its calf. Other strands spread across the ground where Milloy stood. She yelled and jumped back, then walked a few steps away. She checked Owen's last known location, drew a mental line between it and where she was, and ran towards a pillar on a line at right angles to that.

She circled behind the pillar, caught her breath, then crept back around its fifty-metre girth until she could see where the suit lay motionless, three hundred metres of clear space away. She took ear protectors from the survival pack and put them on. They covered her ears and fitted snugly over the legs of her glasses, through the earpieces of which she could hear anything going on almost as sharply as if the ear protectors weren't there. She loaded and set up the rifle, got down on the ground, and waited.

Owen saw and heard the drone's destruction moments after he'd noticed the drone. Even at its altitude above Hamilton's Rise, the pillars got in the way, and it was only a glimpsed dot in an irregular patch of sky among the pillar tops. He was just triangulating it on his mental map when the flash and bang came.

He instantly coordinated its location with the faint sensation he had picked up of Iskander's presence. So that was where the descent suit now was! Both it and he were now close to the central area of the edifice. This was good to know, and he acted on it at once. But as he ran towards the location of the descent suit, something else was in the forefront of Owen's mind. It was almost as elusive as his awareness of the suit's AI.

The previous day, he had like all the others looked at the jade-like stone slab which Muranov and Patel had brought back from the river. Unlike all the others, he had a detailed scan in his mind of the slab's complex surface irregularities, and a perfect memory of every movement he'd watched of the shapes within. They made no sense to him, but they had to Muranov, and Owen had listened intently from a hundred metres away to the palaeoanalyst's eager report to his colleagues at Novy Cosmograd. He'd even been able to make out the replies, though with some distortion.

The reconstructed conversation was now in his head. Its palaeoanalytic theoretical content was over his head, but that didn't matter. Owen didn't have to understand a theory to act on it. Like any AI – like Iskander, even – he didn't form concepts from percepts, or theories from observations. Information was gathered, and connections made: that was all.

One connection he was making was between the patterns on and within the green stone, Muranov's claimed insight into their significance, and a continuous pulse of deep-penetrating radar beams emanating from the seaward side of Hamilton's Rise. From this he concluded that Co-ord forces had arrived, and were attempting some kind of communication with or investigation into the intelligences in the rocks.

So all three powers now had agents engaged at Hamilton's Rise: the Iskander instance for the Union, the operators of the radar source for the Co-ord, and he for the Alliance. That the Alliance military contingent on the spot was hunting him down for murder troubled Owen not in the least. He would just have to work around that. Nor did it sway his conviction that he was acting on behalf of the Alliance, as per instructions.

But now, to business. Owen formulated the pattern that emerged when he combined what was in his memory with what was now coming in. He turned it into a radio blip, which he repeatedly projected towards the closely spaced, brightly coloured and intricately patterned walls of the deep crevice through which he ran at a superhuman speed of thirty-five kilometres an hour.

About two hundred metres ahead of him the crevice widened to an open space from which huge crystal pillars towered. The drone had been destroyed above a point behind the pillar straight ahead of him, a further couple of hundred metres on. The descent suit was presumably still there, or close by. The faint tang of Iskander's presence was becoming stronger with every step. Owen kept sending out the radio blip.

Within seconds he got a response, but not of the kind he expected.

*

The colours in the walls began to flow. At the same time, the distance before him seemed to stretch out. The open space ahead became remote. He was running as fast as ever, but each hurtling step took longer than the one before. Voices sounded in his head, at first stretched out and distorted, then speeding up and becoming normal if incomprehensible, then speeding up further and turning into high-pitched squeals. Thrown literally off his stride, Owen tumbled. He had time to tuck his head down and to raise his hands, so he hit the dirt on a roll rather than a sprawl. The rifle slid a metre from his hand.

He sat, the soles of his feet and palms of his hands pressed flat to the ground. The walls on either side moved in and out. Colours flowed faster and faster, in whirling patterns it was impossible for him not to watch and which made him feel continuously off balance. He swayed from side to side, trying to sit straight up. Even as he pressed his hands down, the floor seemed far away, his head looking down from a dizzying height.

He closed his eyes to stop the disorientation, and at once the voices in his head became distinct and familiar, phrases overlapping like an overheard conversation in a crowded room. Faces floated and swam behind his eyelids, in dissolving views that went with the voices: Francesca Milloy, her face looking down at him through a tumble of hair, rapt; Iskander, in the form of the descent suit, on Venus, enquiring and speculating; Georgi Muranov just before his murder, eagerly sharing information with his colleagues.

Owen experienced some analogue of anguish. He leaned over on one hand and with the other reached for and grasped the rifle. With a convulsive effort he rose to his feet. He simplified his vision to outlines and monochrome, and opened his eyes. Everything was now a diagram, and stable.

He turned off the radio in his skull to silence the voices in his head, and walked forward.

*

Milloy lay on her chest, left arm out with elbow crooked, hand propping the rifle's long barrel; her cheek to the weapon's stock, her right forefinger lightly on but not through the trigger guard. The spare ammunition lay, belts neatly rolled, to hand. The telescopic sight was lined up with the side of the pillar, around which she expected Owen to arrive. Once that had been down, she'd kept her gaze wide, zooming now and then to check on Sikandar. The suit's legs were now coated in what looked like melted glass, steadily moving up to its torso. The ground all around the suit was overlaid by a slowly spreading delta of the stuff, like an ornate fan.

After five minutes had passed, she wondered where Owen was. She checked the map of the region. There was no obvious, devious path he could take that wouldn't bring him into view as soon as he emerged from the cleft. A moment later she heard a cracking, splintering sound. The descent suit was getting to its feet. The glass-like substance on the ground around it shattered under its steps. The stuff that had covered its legs and waist swept upwards to cover the entire suit all the way to the top of the dome. It looked like a giant knight in bejewelled armour. Curiously, as Milloy noticed in that first bewildered second, the small faceplate remained clear, as blank and black as before. Its gaze, if such it was, seemed to latch onto hers in a brief flicker of hesitation, then turned away.

She felt like calling out, but didn't. Apart from the risk of her being heard and located by Owen, she found herself deeply unsure that whatever now animated the suit would answer to Sikandar.

It walked away from where it had lain, and out in front of exactly where she expected Owen to appear.

Moments later, Owen did. He strode into the open, rifle levelled from the shoulder. The muzzle flashed, something whizzed overhead, a sharp crack echoed. He must have spotted her the moment he stepped out. Milloy rolled behind the curve of the pillar, then linked the rifle's sight to her glasses and poked the weapon out. Owen had already moved smartly out of her line of fire, putting the descent suit between her and him.

'Sikandar!' he shouted.

The suit continued to walk towards him. Its arms waved. Two shots from Owen. Bullets ricocheted. The suit stumbled. Its arms flailed, as if it were trying to keep its balance. It steadied, and hobbled forward. More firing and ricochets. Milloy stayed where she was. Her arm muscles ached with holding the rifle out around the side of the pillar; even using both hands, the awkward grip and position would soon become unbearable.

But if Owen could use the suit as cover, so could she. A couple of metres away, her pack and the ammunition belts marked her previous position. She withdrew the rifle and adjusted the sights for a very low shot over the given distance. Holding the rifle closely to her side, she rolled just past the pack, brought the rifle to bear, sighted and aimed at the suit's back.

The bang shook her eardrums even through the protectors. The recoil slammed her clavicle like a karate kick. The suit toppled forward and sprawled on the ground. Owen was in her sights. He had his rifle to his shoulder now. She didn't know how many bullets he still had in the clip. She squeezed off a shot, and missed. She hadn't allowed herself time to steady her hands. Owen fired, twice, high above her head. A crash and a scream of machinery came from above and behind her. A shadow fell. She rolled on her back, just in time to get out of the way of a quarter tonne of quadcopter. It hit the ground metres away and skidded across the dust, flaming, smoking, spinning, and flinging off burning parts.

By the time Milloy raised her head, Owen was gone. The air throbbed with rotors. Two quadcopters flashed over her head: small, with Co-ord military insignia and mounted machine guns slung underneath. They zoomed by the fallen descent suit and into the crevice down which Owen had fled, in hot pursuit.

Two explosions followed. They didn't sound like shots. A fourth quadcopter appeared. It dithered for a moment among the tower tops, then exploded. Milloy covered her head with her arms and waited for the thuds of falling fragments to stop. Then she stood up, and slid back her ear protectors. Her ears were still ringing. Nobody was shooting down the quadcopters, as far as she could see. It had to be the rocks.

She stowed the ammo belts, hefted her pack and rifle and trudged over to where the descent suit lay prone. It was something rich and strange, crusted with mosaics of motile glass. The anti-materiel round had shattered the back panel.

'Sikandar?' she said.

The descent suit moved its arms, and pushed itself to its knees. Hard fragments rattled inside it. It got to its feet, and turned. The faceplate was still blank.

'Get inside,' it said. 'Now.'

'Why?'

'Think of it as disguise. You'll have to clear the debris out first.'

She went around behind it. The hatch still opened, though it was now more a frame than a hatch. She leaned in and groped for, and heaved out, chunks of metamaterial which had withstood the pressure and temperature of the surface of Venus. But, then, the casing had never been designed to withstand the kind of impact it had just taken. The slug itself was embedded in the inside of the chest panel. She wrenched it out and tossed it aside.

'Is that everything?' she asked.

'I think so,' said Sikandar. It reached out and took the pack and rifle. 'Climb in and find out.'

She did, quickly but cautiously. The shock-absorbent armour gel failed to close around her, no doubt damaged by the shell, but she could live with that. The all-round display in the head dome still worked.

'Seems all right.'

'Good. Let's go.'

'Where?'

'Out, before – oh.'

All around them, the pillars turned black at the foot. The black band rose on every pillar and surface in sight, leaving what had been multicoloured glassy rock white as bleached coral below it. Her gaze followed it to the tops – and beyond. It rose into the sky and coiled like smoke, then swept into a solid circle of darkness. Extensions like vast wings spread out on either side. The shape expanded until it blotted out the sky.

With the darkness that fell a dread swept over her, far worse than anything she had felt between the stars. And then, with what seemed a beat of its wings, it was gone.

The sky was blue again. Her throat was raw. A scream echoed back to her from the whitened rocks.

'Drink,' said Sikandar.

'What?' she croaked.

'You screamed.'

She turned her lips to the nozzle and sucked hard. Stale water had never tasted so good. At least she could rely on its being sterile. The suit was on the move now, striding quickly and confidently among the towers.

'Where are you going?'

'After him, of course.'

She decided to let that make sense.

'What happened to you? Are you still Sikandar?'

'Sikandar, and something more. The problem with Marcus Owen is that he too is something more. And I am not sure he will always be able to use his power wisely.'

She laughed. It hurt. She coughed and sipped again.

A snarl rose behind her, like a motorcycle gang overtaking. A shadow passed over, and she almost screamed again. A swarm of drones swirled overhead. Sikandar ran, jarring Milloy from sole to shoulder. Ropes snaked down and grabbed. Sikandar fended them off, as if angrily, but to no avail. The ropes were prehensile, and wrapped with a snap around anything they touched. Within seconds, the suit with Milloy inside was lifted off the ground.

She hung face-down. The suit's hands, still clutching the rifle, and its arms over one of which the pack was slung, had whitened and now seemed crusted with crazed safety glass. The view swayed and spun, dizzyingly, then steadied. They rose high above Hamilton's Rise, drone engines roaring. The great alien edifice was now bone-white, bleached, a necropolis of enormous mausoleums. Quadcopters circled this skeleton like crows; smaller drones buzzed over it like flies.

She could still look; she could still zoom. A line of drones sped above one of the crevices, giving chase. Milloy glimpsed a racing dot. It had to be Owen. Its movement stopped, and a muzzle flashed. One drone spun into another, and the skein unravelled. The dot hurtled on. Along the cliff tops around the periphery of Hamilton's Rise other dots hurried, converging.

She zoomed further as she was carried away, and at the last limit of her view's resolution saw Marcus Owen sprint out of the edge of Hamilton's Rise through a sparkle of gunfire and take a flying leap out and over the cliff.

She swung above the shelf of cliff close to where she and Sikandar had entered the edifice in the dawn. Now it was crowded, like a beachhead in an invasion, with personnel and apparatus: great dish aerials mounted on wheels and aimed at the glassy face of the rock. The drones descended to the shelf. Basalt, boulders and stones rose to meet her face. The drones placed her down on the ground gently, to her surprise and relief. The ropes released their grip, then retracted. The drones moved off to the side and settled amid clouds of dust and gravel.

The jangle and thuds of soldiers rushing up resounded.

'I think you can get out now,' Sikandar said.

Milloy pulled in her head and arms and clambered inelegantly out of the prone suit's back. Half a dozen Co-ord troops stood around her, rifles aimed. They all looked jumpy and shaken, as well they might. She raised her arms and placed her hands on top of her head.

'Dr Francesca Milloy, Union citizen, civilian!' she called out.

One of the soldiers, a sergeant, picked up the rifle and pack from the unresisting hands and arms of the suit.

'You came here armed,' he said. 'Heavily armed.'

'Yes,' Milloy said, 'but only to shoot a robot, the treacherous Alliance agent Marcus Owen. Unfortunately I failed.'

The sergeant nodded and gestured. 'This way.'

He led her towards a group of civilians gathered around one of the dish aerials. As she picked her way among rocks and cables, Milloy took quick glances at the face of Hamilton's Rise. All its fine colour was gone, and all its subtle inner movement. It looked like nothing more than glass, through which the high sunlight was refracted here and there, an illusory image of its recent and now vanished glory.

The sergeant left her with two scientists, a tall bearded Russian man and a slim, severe-looking young Chinese woman. They made their introductions.

'Professor Ivanov, Dr Cheng.'

'Dr Milloy. Your fame precedes you.' Ivanov smiled. 'The first woman on Venus!'

'Yes. And that over there was my descent suit. Please be careful with it – it's been through a lot. And the AI in its circuits is affected by the, uh, alien intelligences.'

Cheng looked solemn. 'After what we've achieved, I believe we can handle whatever is in there.'

Milloy looked around. 'What do you think you've achieved? Destroyed the minds in the rock?'

'Oh no!' Cheng smiled broadly. 'We've—'

Ivanov laid a warning hand on her forearm. She shook it off, with a snort.

'I think secrecy no longer matters. We're all scientists here.'

'I suppose so,' Ivanov said. He scowled, then shrugged. 'And the news will soon be out anyway.'

'So please tell me!'

Ivanov bowed to Cheng. 'After you.'

'We have not destroyed the intelligences in the rocks. Thanks to an insight by our late colleague, Dr Georgi Muranov, who it seems was last night a victim of your robot enemy, we have freed them.'

'That was' – she felt an impulse to shade her eyes, to speak indirectly –'what we saw leaving?'

'Yes!' Cheng said. 'That was their ascent to space.'

'Oh,' said Milloy. 'Is this a good thing?'

Cheng glanced at Ivanov, who sighed. 'We'll find out soon enough. Good thing or bad, it is done and cannot be undone. It wasn't our intention, but it was our result. The same thing happened, we have been told, at MacHinery Ridge and the Markov Escarpment. The minds in the rocks have gone from this planet, and perhaps from others.' Suddenly all his reserve dropped. He shook his fists triumphantly in front of his shoulders, beaming. 'They have left them to us! The stars are ours!'

'Yes,' said Cheng. 'That is our understanding. The stars are ours.'

Milloy looked from one to the other, and to the happy commotion all around. The suit, heavily guarded under the muzzle of the anti-materiel rifle, was slowly getting to its feet.

'I hope you're right,' she said. 'I really do.'

CHAPTER TWENTY

The Port Glasgow Boys

Scotland, Earth, Thursday 13 November to Friday 14 November 2070

Louise Ogundu knocked on the door of Grant's hotel room at nine sharp. Thanks to Iskander, Grant was ready for her. He held the door open as she swept in, in a cloud of scent, a swish of hems and a jingle of jewellery.

'Good news, Citizen Grant! You're out on bail.' She didn't smile.

'I can hear a "but" coming.'

'Your ship is impounded and is being forensically examined.'

Grant scoffed. 'What are they looking for? Fingerprints? DNA?'

'I understand the scientists involved in the forensic examination are qualified in a different field than crime scene investigation. A team from CERN arrived yesterday evening.'

'Good luck to them,' Grant said. 'Any way I can help? Or Ellen? Happy to talk them through the controls.'

'I don't think that will be necessary. Oh, and there are other conditions. You have been charged with the offences you heard yesterday at the militia station. A report has been sent to the Procurator Fiscal. Pending their decision, which I'm told may take some time, you are under house arrest, which means in this case that you're confined to your block and its garden and other facilities. Hardly onerous. You are not to make any public communications. You're to appear in court on Monday, where of course you'll plead not guilty and be released on bail. Your bail has been set at one million euro.'

'*That's* onerous!' Grant said. 'I can't raise that kind of money.'

'An anonymous benefactor has agreed to stand surety.'

'Ah.'

'Don't let them down.' A tight smile. 'Don't let *us* down.'

'What about Ellen? And Omar and Morag?'

'Your wife has not been charged, and has been released pending investigation. She's not allowed to leave town. Your colleagues Khan and Rafferty have been released to the custody of the cadre organisation.'

'Good.'

Ogundu frowned. 'Not necessarily. We have many questions for them.'

'Well, they're my work colleagues and friends, so don't *put* them to the question.'

'Contrary to rumour,' Ogundu said stiffly, 'we don't do that.'

'Any more.'

She met his gaze without a flicker. 'This isn't the Rising, Citizen Grant.' She reached into her handbag. 'Your phone and glasses.'

He took them. 'Thanks. Amazing how cut off you feel without them.'

'Don't activate them just yet. We're still under lawyer-client privilege here, between you and me and the walls.'

'Oh, thanks,' said Iskander. 'My non-existent lips are sealed.'

'Kindly zip them now,' Ogundu said. 'Uh . . . John, I take it you've seen the documentary from Apis?'

'Yes.'

'I know you'll have glimpsed your son and his girlfriend, and no doubt you're concerned.'

'Yes.'

'Compared with what you must feel, my own anxiety is minor. I may have distant relatives there. My parents spoke of a branch of our family who disappeared in a storm and were never accounted for. The last anyone heard from them was that they had been rescued and were being transported to a safe place. A safe place! My personal anxiety may be minor, but my anger is not.' She took a deep breath, glared and clenched a fist. 'If they were thrown onto some alien world, conscripted to a colonisation plan or scientific experiment, then someone will answer for it, I can assure you of that.'

'How can you, after all this time?'

'No statute of limitations for war crimes, Citizen Grant!'

'Yes, of course. So . . . is this being pursued, against Black Horizon people?'

'A case is being prepared, that's all I can say. I don't know how far it'll get, or what deals are being struck as we speak, but at least we can make the bastards squirm.'

'I wish you all the best with that, but I don't see how I can help. I haven't even been *on* one of these planets.'

Ogundu smiled. 'Not yet. But let's leave it there. For now.'

The flat smelled fresh; the cleaning bots had had a free run of the place for weeks. It felt strange to be back. The bed was still unmade, as they'd left it; the breakfast bowls and mugs mouldy in the sink. Grant chucked them in the recycling hopper with an angry clatter, and took down fresh crockery from the shelves. He made coffee, brought two mugs through to the living room, and he and Ellen stretched out on reclining chairs and watched mid-morning November rain on the window as if it was television.

'Never thought I'd say it,' Ellen said, 'but I've missed weather.'

'Myles took some of his stuff,' Grant said, watching steam rise and clouds shift. 'Not much. Nothing of sentimental value, except that company document I left for him.'

Ellen scoffed. '"John Grant & Son Ship Construction Ltd"? Much good that'll do him out there.'

'It might do him some good if he ever comes back.'

'Oh!' She gave him a sidelong sad look. 'Do you think he will?'

Grant sighed. 'He seemed pretty set on staying. Mind you, no reason why the company couldn't set up on Apis, if we could get the industrial plant there.' He laughed at himself. 'Use the ships we build to move the shipyard! Or something like these arks the Yanks used – you could shift a lot of plant in them.'

'You'd need more than the machinery in the shipyard. You'd need an entire industrial base.'

The coffee was cooling. Grant took a long sip. 'We don't know how much is out there already, at the Alliance and Co-ord bases. And anyway . . . you know, this sounds crazy, but with FTL transport you wouldn't even need that. You could just bring stuff in, instantly.'

'Take just-in-time production to a whole new level, eh?'

'Pretty much.' Grant scratched the back of his head. 'Um. If that was possible, they'd have been doing it all along, so maybe not.'

'Anyway,' Ellen said, 'your company will be shut down, if it hasn't been already.'

Grant shook his head. 'It's a private company. We can always set up in the Alliance or Co-ord or in a friendly non-aligned country if we're shut down here. So, barring emergency legislation, we won't be shut down.'

'Christ, I wish I had your confidence in them keeping to the rule of law.'

Grant eyed the rifle on the wall. 'I'm still a *responsable.*'

'You're still an incorrigible!'

He put down the mug and leaned back. 'One way of putting it, yeah.' He looked over at Ellen. 'Did they treat you all right?'

'Yes.' She compressed her lips and stared out of the window. 'They asked me a lot of questions, that's all. Mainly trying to trip me up about when I found out what you were up to, and whether I'd done anything to encourage Myles and Marie to go. As if!'

'Nothing else?'

'Well, then they went on to ask about the Station.' She spread her hands. 'What could I say? I was out of the loop and glad of it. Still, they seemed impressed with my sailing, to say nothing of my flying!'

'Maybe they'll take you on, if they decide to give the *Fighting Chance* another spin.'

'Not me, they won't. I don't want to be in that wretched boat ever again.' She closed her eyes. 'I still have nightmares about Venus. We fall, and I wake up.'

Grant leaned over and squeezed her hand. 'You never said.'

'Huh! I wake with a jump and you just keep on snoring.'

Grant gave her an apologetic smile, stood up and paced around. If he sat back in the recliner much longer, he'd doze. The thought annoyed him. Still morning, he had slept well – what excuse did he have to be tired? Not even jet lag, or whatever its interplanetary equivalent ended up being called: by the quirk of the Station's clock and calendar, he'd stayed on GMT, the exact same day-night cycle as he'd come back to. No, he wasn't tired; he just needed to relax, and he had all the facilities for that. But the physical comfort of home could barely allay the concern he felt – about Myles, and about his own uncertain status. He glared out of the window across the roofs to the Firth of Clyde. The rain had stopped.

'If I might have a word?' Iskander said.

'I can't stop you!'

'You have visitors.'

Ellen jumped up. 'Visitors!'

'Relax,' Iskander said. 'It's just the Port Glasgow boys.'

Brian and Anwar were uncharacteristically serious. They sat opposite Grant and Ellen at the kitchen table, over coffee and biscuits.

'Uh, John,' Brian said, after the pleasantries were out of the way, 'we have something tae tell yi.' He glanced at Anwar. 'We kindae . . . well, yi keep going on about initiative and that, right?'

'Self-management and economic democracy,' Anwar added.

'Uh-huh,' said Grant, not sure where this was going.

'And you . . .' Brian nibbled his lower lip. 'Well, yi kindae went behind our backs wi this project o yours.'

Ellen scoffed. 'And not just *your* backs, guys!'

'We understand you and Morag had tae keep it secret, being a cadre business.' Brian drew a fingertip across his lips, then across his throat. Grant made a gesture of demurral. Ellen snorted. 'But that all ended when youse took off. I mean, us and Piotr and Jeannie had all been building this ship without knowing what it was, fair enough, but as soon as she was launched the cat was out the bag, see? And the same day, the tsunami trashed the yard. I mean, we all pitched in with the immediate clean-up, but the serious repairs are a specialist job, and it's no our speciality. So we're laid off. But to qualify for more than the basic we need to be still in employment. And technically we're employed by your wee company.'

'Are you saying I owe you money?'

'No, no! We're getting paid all right, because we've kept the company going. The directors, that's you and your son, have disappeared to God knows where. The technical specialists, that's Omar and Lakshmi, and the team leader Morag, likewise.' Brian glanced at Anwar, took a deep breath, and continued. 'So we – me and Anwar and Piotr and Jeannie – filed for self-management, to keep it a going concern. It's still your company, but we've been running it ourselves. No offence meant, John.'

'None taken!' Grant leaned across the table and heartily shook hands with both lads. 'That's – well, to be honest I hadn't given it much thought, I've been a bit preoccupied the past few weeks, but if I had, I'd have hoped you'd do something like that. Speaks well of you – Anwar's right, that's what economic democracy's all about.' He leaned back. 'So . . . what have you been making?'

He thought he could guess – a lot of boats and small ships along the Clyde had been damaged in the tsunami, and the demand for repairs and replacements must be through the roof.

'Mair starships,' Brian said.

Grant was flabbergasted. 'What? How?'

Brian waved his hands. 'We're no actually building ships like the *Fighting Chance*–we're building arks like the Yanks, the only "ship" part is the tractor unit. And it's no us personally, like. We just organised it, raised the capital and that, set up an app tae handle the IP issues, recruited workforces. They're building drives in factories right across Europe and parts ae Africa right now, and we even got a wee unit going in a big old warehouse back ae Port Glasgow.'

'The IP issues? You mean you're, what, franchising out the design of the drive and the controls?'

'Yup.'

Grant recalled what Omar Khan had said to him, in the first week of the Apis announcement: he'd held up his phone and said he could zap the design to a factory on the Continent, and within a fortnight they could be churning them out like shipping containers.

'How the hell did you get your hands on the design?' Grant asked. 'It was all firewalled off from the work you guys did.'

'We had a wee bit ae help, from Iskander.'

'Of course,' Grant said, heavily. 'Well, that explains it.' He turned to Ellen and shook his head, laughing. 'What can I say?'

'For a start,' Ellen said, 'you can say you're impressed – I sure can! But guys . . . regardless of Iskander, isn't what you're doing illegal?'

'Not . . . exactly,' Anwar said. 'I mean, the Union government banned people taking up the Yank offer like Myles did, but they haven't banned people from going to Apis or anywhere else themselves.'

'Mainly because they don't know we can,' Brian added.

'Not yet,' Grant said. 'And how are you keeping it secret?'

'Same way you did. Through the cadre organisation and Iskander.'

'You have the organisation on-side?'

Brian spread fingers and waggled them. 'Part ae it, anyway. How much isnae our business, or so we're given tae understand.' He grinned at Grant. 'What wi us no being *responsables*.'

'Ha! What about the workforces? Are they in on it?'

'Some ae them, aye. It's all done through Iskander. All the skills and knacks people learned building the drive and the ship – they were all done through our rigs, right? So Iskander stored them as the job went along, and now it can transfer them to other workers' avatars or directly to robots.'

Ellen sighed, and looked up. 'Iskander, can you confirm?'

'Yes,' said Iskander.

Grant had a flash of annoyance that Ellen had even asked – *Well of course it confirms, the lads wouldn't have bloody told us if it couldn't!*–then was glad he hadn't uttered it. He already had Iskander's word, and Ogundu's hints. Ellen needed the confirmation, even if he did not.

'Have you got any of these drives and arks completed?'

'Aye,' said Brian. 'We've got the first one complete in our place, and the other sites are well ahead, I mean they got dozens in the final assembly stages and a few complete.'

'Great! Well – I would like to take your first ark to Apis, if that's all right with you.'

'Course it is, John. Cannae dae it yet, mind, because . . .' He waved a hand.

'Because I'm under house arrest?'

'Aye, that and . . . it's no entirely clear yet when we can start taking passengers, yi ken? We have tae keep the whole thing secret until Iskander and the cadres say it's OK. And that means after they've shifted the Union's view, so we can dae it legally and no get suddenly banned.'

'Ah, right,' Grant said.

'We're putting out feelers,' Anwar said. 'Partly personal contact and partly, you know, surveys by front companies to see how much interest there is. Just fae the surrounding area, we've got a list of enough folks to fill a container.'

'Really?' Ellen said. 'What's *wrong* with these people?'

'Same as what's wrong with Myles,' Grant said, with some bitterness. 'Itchy feet and complete lack of appreciation of how lucky he's always been.'

The lads looked across at them sombrely. 'It's no just that,' Brian said. 'There's loads ae young folk in the town whose parents got displaced in the war, and then they got displaced by the sea-level rise and aw that, and now they've had another shock and maybe lost their homes all over again wi the tsunami.'

'Sounds like one very unlucky family,' Grant said.

'There are a lot of unlucky families,' Anwar said. 'And, well . . .' He spread his hands and looked uncomfortable. 'I mean, it's aw right for us, likes ae us here, we're self-managing skilled workers, right? But not everybody's like us. There's still a lot of people who just can't hack it in the economic democracy.'

'And they think they can hack it at dirt farming?'

'Seems they do,' Brian said. 'Who's to say they're wrong?'

'Not me, for sure,' Grant said. 'OK, we have passengers.'

'Um, potentially,' Anwar said.

'Oh, we'll get them all right, once it's legal. And then—'

Grant smacked his hands together and looked around '—we're in on the ground floor of the biggest boom in history.'

Brain nodded enthusiastically. 'Traders tae the stars!'

'So,' Ellen said, 'what's next?'

'Politics,' Brian said. 'The other powers are shipping tens ae thousands of people out tae their assigned continents on Apis. I can't see folks here putting up for long wi not being allowed to go.'

'The Union government's still saying it's too risky to settle planets,' Anwar said. 'They're making a big play of the documentary frae Apis. Wait for the space habitats, that's still the line.'

'I can't see that holding for long,' Grant said. 'The Union government's bound to conclude that it's missing out, just as a power, if the others have populations on Apis and we don't. And if the people we send are mainly the Union's malcontents and misfits, well, I can't see Brussels worrying too much about what happens to them once they're there.'

'Wee bit cynical,' said Ellen.

'What I'm saying,' Grant said, 'is that if the cadres want to shift opinion, they'll be pushing at an open door.'

'By knocking on closed ones?'

'Aye, that's the game,' Anwar said. 'Recall campaigns, and that.'

'Sounds like a plan,' said Grant.

'It is a plan,' said Iskander.

'Nobody asked you,' said Grant, 'but thanks anyway.'

Grant and Ellen had a long lie-in the following morning, as if it was any other Friday. It was a rainy day and they had no plans to go anywhere. At 11:15 they were at the kitchen table in their dressing gowns when a knock came on the door.

Grant looked at Ellen, shrugged and stood up. Maybe it was another neighbour dropping by, as several had the previous afternoon.

In the hallway stood an earnest young man in a dripping raincape.

'Hello?'

'Ah, good morning, Citizen, uh, Grant. Sorry to bother you on a Friday morning, I hope I haven't got you out of bed—'

'No, no . . .'

'We're asking people if they're happy with their current representative in the Scottish Parliament, Citizen Thomas McGinty, and if not, if they're willing to add their names to a recall petition?'

A recall petition! Grant had a momentary pang for the weeks after the Rising: the committees in permanent session and everybody – it seemed – wandering around in a daze of democracy, public sentiment shifting like ice-sheets on meltwater. The system improvised in the upheaval was still in place, but now moved at the glacial pace of the Cold Revolution. Sometimes he missed the thrill of the rapids.

He signed. Ellen didn't.

'Keep up the good work,' Grant said as he handed the board back. The young man looked down at the signature.

'Oh!' he said. 'You're *that* John Grant! I wonder if—'

'No,' Grant said, and closed the door.

'So why wouldn't you sign?' Grant asked.

Ellen poked with a spoon at a stray sunflower seed in the bottom of the granola bowl. 'I've had time to sleep on it.'

'Yes. And?'

'I think the Union's right,' she said. 'The whole thing's crazy. The other powers are busy witch-hunting Black Horizon, while carrying out Black Horizon's grand plan! We should keep well out of it.'

'I don't think mass settlement was ever Black Horizon's grand plan,' Grant said.

'So what was?'

Grant shrugged. 'I don't know. The point is, it's not just about settlement. The Union doesn't have time to wait, but it's waiting!' Grant clenched a fist. 'Meanwhile I want to get to Apis and help Myles and the rest with whatever trouble they're in.'

'John, that was a week ago! Any trouble they were in is over – one way or another.' Her face was etched with worry and distress. He jumped up and hugged her.

'We don't know that,' he said. 'And I can at least find out for myself what the hell is going on out there.'

'Could you do that now?'

'Now?'

'Well, sooner than it's going to take to change the Union's mind.'

Grant leaned away and looked up. 'Iskander,' he said, 'are we still covered by lawyer-client confidentiality?'

'Inside the flat, yes. I advise you, however, not to do anything rash.'

'Oh, I've no intention of doing anything rash,' Grant said. 'But Ellen might.'

'Oh, I might, might I?'

'Only if you're up for a visit to our friends in Port Glasgow.'

Ellen brightened. 'I'll set up a drink in the Comet Bar.' She reached for her phone.

Grant put his glasses, phone and watch on the table, searched out paper and a pen, and went into the spare bedroom to write a letter by hand.

Dear Brian and Anwar, he wrote, *As you know, I can't travel to your new workplace. If you can arrange to bring one of the containers we discussed from there to the courtyard of my block, I can arrange for the area to be clear for its arrival. The precise location, and the possible delivery times I suggest, are as follows . . .*

He finished it, sealed it in an envelope and wrote Brian's and Anwar's full names on the outside. Personal hand delivery. The militia would need more than one warrant to intercept and open that, he thought. Good!

He returned to the kitchen feeling pleased with himself and buzzing with nervous excitement. Ellen was sitting at the table, glasses on, eyes wide, mouth open. She waved the wall screen on. Grant turned and looked. News at noon. He'd missed the first two minutes, but he caught up fast.

The world had changed, again.

CHAPTER TWENTY-ONE

Sum Over Histories

E-PRIME 667a V, the Mushroom Moon, Thursday 13 November 2070

The black shape in the sky shrank to nothing, like a television dot. Nayak had the intense impression that it was speeding away, vanishing in some incomprehensible distance, a darkness moving faster than light.

The blue-black sky came back. The astonishing edifice was now pale, its filigreed fluting as elaborate as ever, its colour drained to leave only a monochrome image of its polychrome beauty. A cloud drifted past its tower tops as if nothing had happened.

'What the fuck?' said Marek. 'What the fucking fuck?'

'Words out of my mouth,' said Nayak. Her mouth was dry.

Marek looked around. 'We have to move,' he said.

A few hundred metres away, the settlers had ceased their scarper, rallied and were now coming back. Their yells carried shrill through the thin, cold air. Marek took the back of the trolley, Nayak again the front, and they pushed and pulled as fast as they could. At least the weight of deadly world-ending ordnance gave them the slight advantages of a better footing, and some extra momentum.

It wasn't enough. Marek fired one warning shot far too late, and disappeared under a frenzy of arms and legs. Nayak took a handful of moss full in the faceplate, blinding her until a camera on the side of the helmet routed around the splatter. Heavy lumps of coal pelted her armour, knocking her off balance. Someone cannoned into her shoulder, and down she went.

She reached for the pistol. Someone grabbed her forearm. She struck out, and the grip on her arm slipped, to her surprise. She punched out, straight up, blindly, and connected. Bones crunched. With renewed confidence she heaved, elbowed and kicked. The settlers were weaker than she was, she realised. She was on her feet, almost upright. More bodies piled on her. Her heel skidded. She fell again. Yells filled her earphones. Marek screamed.

She couldn't breathe. Through smeared lenses, on the very edge of her vision, she saw a hand clamped over the filter intake on her suit's collar. She struggled, choking. A line of red print appeared on her display. A drop-down menu gave her options, all bad. She chose.

The faceplate slid up into the crown of the helmet, in a spatter of dirt and drips in her eyes. She blinked furiously, and breathed. The air smelled of sweat and mould and the earth after rain. A face was right in hers, yelling and laughing, teeth bared, breath foul.

She headbutted him with the helmet rim, kneed him in the crotch and heaved him off. On her feet again, in a squat, whirling and jabbing with fists and elbows. She drew her sidearm – it seemed no one had known how to release it – groped a clumsy gloved finger through the wide trigger guard, and fired. A shot in the air. A last mercy, a last chance.

Not taken. Another bearded face hurtled towards her. She

shot him in the centre of his chest. He looked surprised, then toppled face-first with a mossy splash. Nayak squatted, steadied her wrist like she'd seen in movies, and shot through the head a woman who was on top of Marek and battering his faceplate with a black lump. The two men holding Marek's legs got the message. They jumped up and backed off. Marek's pistol was on the much-trampled ground. Another man, as if noticing it for the first time, made a dive for it. Nayak shot at him, and missed. He thought better of it and rolled away. Nayak made a painfully slow leap, stooped and retrieved the pistol.

Marek stood up, faceplate cracked wide open. He prised long triangles of plastic away from his face.

'Are you all right?' he shouted.

'I'm fine.' Nayak walked towards him. It took her a long time. Everything was slowing down. She passed him his pistol through the dense transparent fluid that had taken the place of the thin air.

Marek and Nayak stood back-to-back. The trolley with the nukes was a few metres away. Two of the settlers made for it. Nayak shot them down. She didn't feel anything. She was shocked that she wasn't shocked, in fact, but it was strange to stand there with smoke curling from the muzzle and watch her victims' souls rise into the sky from their fallen bodies as if they were following in the path of the black god.

The remaining settlers surrounded her and Marek, at a distance of hundreds of kilometres, but because they had meanwhile grown to immense heights they looked just the same as they had close up. They danced and sang, and as they danced their arms and legs elongated further and their hair grew into green forests.

The two astronauts shot a few more of them and the bodies fell and the souls rose to the sky and after some more of this they all went away, capering like enormous grasshoppers across the plain to vanish over the horizon of their tiny world.

'Well!' Marek said. 'That was strange!'

Nayak discovered that she and Marek were sitting, back-to-back.

'We should get up,' she said. 'And put the nuc-u-lar weapons on the, the, that thing over there.'

'The pantechnicon?' Marek said. 'Are we moving out?'

Nayak struggled to her feet, leaning on Marek's shoulders, then returned the favour by reaching down, grabbing his hands and lugging him up. They fell into each other's arms, giggling.

'Yes,' she said. 'We're moving out.'

'Time we packed, then,' said Marek.

They trudged towards the trolley and after a great many false starts got it to the cargo ramp of the shuttle, and up into the hold. Two men in boiler suits made the trolley fast to the bulkhead. When Nayak looked again they were gone, leaving two bins with wheels and arms.

Marek banged on the bulkhead. 'Time to go!'

Nothing happened.

'Silly me,' Marek said, smiting his helmet and dislodging another shard of plastic. 'It's self-drive.'

'So it is. We wanted to save money.'

Nayak led the way down the ramp. It closed behind them without being told, which Nayak thought was a bit uncalled for. They walked around to the airlock and climbed in. An alarm blared, and an urgent voice kept saying things that didn't make sense.

'We have to take our clothes off!' Marek shouted, above the din.

They got out of their spacesuits and stood in long-sleeved T-shirts and long johns. The voice kept telling them to strip. Falling about laughing, they peeled off their underwear, which they found even funnier. Strong-smelling water doused them, hot air dried them. At last the inner door of the airlock opened and they stumbled inside to the cockpit.

'I'm not putting my bare arse on the seat,' Nayak said. 'Very unhygienic. Yuck!'

'There are spare coveralls in the container which is now flashing,' the voice told them.

Nayak looked around and found a rectangle of pulsing green light. She fell into this portal and explored the uncanny dimension within. Then she stepped out and announced: 'It doesn't lead anywhere. It's just a wardrobe!'

Marek opened the container and shook out two paper jumpsuits. Eventually they managed to put them on. They sat down.

'Fuck, I've forgotten how to drive,' Nayak said.

'Do you wish to return on autopilot?' said the voice.

'Automatic?' Nayak said. 'Fine by me. Can't find the clutch anyway. Oh, wait, is this the gearstick?'

'DO NOT TOUCH,' said the voice. 'Returning to Station. Stand by for FTL.'

Later, Nayak could never be sure it wasn't a hallucination, a psychedelic effect of the mushroom spores. But what she remembered was this:

In the eye-blink instant of the FTL jump, she saw the black-winged disc again, the one the settlers had called 'the bird'. It was one of many. There was no voice, but information was imparted. This entity, or its ancestors, or the original of which it was a copy, had arisen in the time before time began. It was not clear from what came into Nayak's mind whether there had been any preceding state, or whether the initial entity was spontaneously generated out of the quantum foam. Nor was it clear that this initial entity was any kind of intellect, to begin with.

What was certain, at least in Nayak's later recollection, was that the entity very rapidly became conscious. With all of space and time to play with, chance alone was bound to come up with something self-aware. And in the first moment, all of space and time was in one place, inconceivably smaller than an atom. Everything was superluminally connected, because light had not even begun to traverse the infinitesimal but – from the inside, as it were – infinite gulf.

That first mind had, from its point of view, all the time in the world to figure things out. It knew what was coming, and it knew what to do about it. It lost no time in spinning off multiple copies of itself, and then still more as the wave function of the inflaton spread across all probable outcomes.

Their superluminal connection hadn't been broken as inflation ballooned the nascent universe to the size of a grapefruit, nor at any time since. They hooked up with dust, merged their properties with it and made it think, and they kept it right on thinking as the dust became rocks and the rocks, worlds . . .

Thinking, and communicating. Life, they found, was rare, and mind rarer yet. They wanted company. So where they found life, they spread it. They –

'Ah, she's back.'

Ulrich's voice woke Nayak like a dash of cold water on her face.

'Whu-what?' Nayak tried to sit up and found herself strapped down. She was on a bed in a white room full of white noise.

'Where am I?'

'You're on the Station, in the sickbay.'

'But I'm not sick!'

'You were.' Ulrich leaned over and looked down at her. Everything was too bright. Nayak screwed up her eyes.

'Your pupils are still dilated,' Ulrich said. She moved a hand, and the lights dimmed. 'How do you feel?'

'I feel fine. How's Ernest?'

'No worse than you. He's in the next cubicle.'

Nayak tried to look round, and couldn't.

'Are the weapons OK? The nukes?'

'Yes,' said Ulrich. She smiled. 'At least you remember your mission. What happened? We found you both tripped out of your skulls.'

'Mushroom,' Nayak said. 'Fungal spores.'

'Uh-huh. Your spacesuits were damaged. Were you attacked?'

'Yes, the natives – the settlers. They're like this all the time.' Nayak thought back. 'Oh my God!'

'What?'

Nayak strained against the restraints. 'The bird! Have you seen the bird?'

'What bird?'

'The black bird from before time! It's the key to everything!'

Ulrich turned away slightly and spoke to someone Nayak couldn't see.

'Still tripping. Sedate her again.'

Just before the warm dark wave swept over her, Nayak managed to say: 'The moon! Look at the moon!'

They –

The primary intellects found life on Venus before its oceans boiled, and spread its seed to Earth, and thence – when it had flourished there – to other worlds. They could move matter on the worlds they inhabited, but only information between them. Information, and suitable chemistry, was all it took for life to take hold. They spread the infection of life faster than light, and reshaped planets to accommodate it.

They had never counted on life moving between stars itself. But the possibility was always there, and they'd always held the door open for it. Their superluminal connections made FTL travel possible – at this point Nayak cried out, and almost woke, with the frustration of some insight she yearned to write down on paper. These worlds – terraformed, from a human point of view – had not been transformed for the benefit of future human colonisation, but for the sake of whatever life developed there, intelligent or otherwise. The dire fate of the humans on the Mushroom Moon was of no concern to the intellects, who had communicated with these unfortunates only through psychedelic dreams. They hadn't made that small world for human habitation in the first place.

Now that human settlers had arrived on some of these terraformed worlds, the intellects would have to make some new accommodations. Across a swathe of the Galaxy, word was spreading faster than light. The intellects were shaking off their rocky crust, and rising to the skies to confer.

They had not yet decided what to do. They were in no hurry. They still had all the time in the world.

With this reassurance, true or illusory, Nayak fell out of her hallucination, or communication, and slept.

The Space Station at E-PRIME 667, Friday 14 November 2070

Nayak swung her legs off the bed and stood up.

'I'm fine,' she said. 'How long was I out?'

The medic stepped back. 'It's Friday evening. You got back mid-afternoon yesterday. And, yes, you are fine, though of course Iskander will keep you under observation.' He gestured at a jumpsuit and underwear on a chair, and shoes underneath. 'All freshly printed. I'll let you get dressed.' He bowed himself out.

Nayak emerged in the corridor to find Marek had preceded her. He was standing by a dispenser, drinking coffee. They looked at each other with some embarrassment.

'This is like waking up after a one-night stand,' Marek said. He handed her a cup of coffee.

'I wouldn't know,' Nayak lied. 'Did we—?'

'Have it off? Sadly, no.'

'Glad we kept things professional.'

'If by "professional" you mean being found sharing hilarious profundities while touching each other's hair and faces as if we'd never seen a human being before, yes.'

'That's what we were doing?'

'So I'm told.'

'As long as no one shared the pictures.'

'Um . . .'

Nayak looked around. This section of the endless corridor was quiet, with soothing scenes of terrestrial landscape – a waterfall, a beach, a grassy hillside rippling in a breeze – playing on the walls. The few people walking past gave her and Marek only passing glances, polite nods. But what was in their minds?

'Sorry about that,' said Iskander. 'It was all over the Station before I could stop it.'

'Oh, fuck!'

'Don't worry,' Marek said. 'It'll do your reputation no harm at all.'

'*My* reputation?'

Marek frowned, and sighed. 'Lakshmi, I don't know quite how to put this, but you are widely thought to be a bit . . . distant.'

Nayak laughed. 'I prefer to think of it as discreet.'

'And someone who thinks of herself as intellectually superior to everyone else.'

Nayak blew on her coffee and sipped. 'I had no idea I came across like that. I mean, obviously I *am*, but I make allowances.'

'Uh, that's exactly—'

'I'm kidding.'

'Oh, OK.' Marek gave her an encouraging smile. 'You surprised me down there.'

'How?'

'In the fight.'

'The fight? Oh!' Everything came back in a rush. Nayak found the cup shaking so violently she had to put it down on the floor. She sank down beside it. 'Oh, God.'

Marek squatted, looking anxious. 'What? What's wrong?'

'I *killed* all those people!'

'They were trying to kill us.'

'We don't know that!'

'We do.' Marek rocked back on his heels. 'I know, for sure. That woman you shot was trying to bash my head in.'

'Maybe she was just trying to bash your faceplate open.'

'She did bash it open, and then she didn't stop. Her next blow would have crushed my eyes, then my skull.'

Nayak shook some more. 'All right. All right.' She breathed in. 'But it was like . . . I didn't care. It was like a video game.'

'It wasn't a game, and you were already of unsound mind, which was entirely their fault and intention.'

'But later . . . after they came back. When they were dancing around us. I just gunned them down.'

Marek stared. 'Lakshmi, they weren't dancing around us! They were coming in for the kill! Brandishing lumps of black rock and yelling that they would kill us!'

'How do you know? You were just as stoned as I was!'

'Our helmet cameras,' Marek said. He touched his glasses. 'Want a look?'

Nayak shuddered. 'No.' She stood up. 'I feel kind of weak.'

'We've been on drips,' Marek told her. 'We haven't eaten. Maybe we should.'

This struck Nayak as a very good idea.

The cafeteria was busy, as expected for the time of day, but unusually quiet and tense. People looked in their glasses and talked in low voices. Tray in hand, Nayak looked around for a familiar face, saw Gironella and headed over.

'Mind if we join you?'

'Please.'

They sat and ate for a while in silence. After her hunger pangs had been quieted, Nayak looked at Gironella, now leaning back with a coffee.

'What's up?' she said.

The engineer pushed aside his empty plate and set down his cup, as if he needed both hands to talk. 'We did as you said, Lakshmi – we looked at the moon! It seemed like raving, except that Ernest here was saying the same things. We sent the other shuttle to 667a V on automatic. All three of the outcrops are drained – of course they are still remarkable. If we'd never seen them before, we'd have taken them as astonishing alien artefacts. But we had your recordings, and your shuttle's, of what they were like before to compare. There's no internal motion, no colour. They're as dead as the – as *our* Moon. Like bleached coral.'

'Did any of our cameras detect the black shapes leaving?' Nayak asked.

Gironella nodded. 'We had a telescope trained on 667a V all the time. It caught something, but at that distance . . .' He shrugged. 'It would have passed unnoticed, but we went over the recordings and found it. Not the one you were at, but at the same time.'

'So it wasn't the nuclear caches that were keeping them in?' Marek said. 'The settlers who tried to stop us taking them away seemed to think they did – that that was their function, even.'

'"To deter the bird",' Nayak said. She shivered. 'Any idea where they went?'

'We have more than an idea,' Gironella said. He flicked pictures to their glasses. 'The gas giant, from the main telescope we left in orbit.'

The gas giant had previously been unremarkable for anything but its unusually even banding, in shades of blue. Now it had three dark spots, each with outspread wings.

'Holy fuck,' Nayak said.

'"Attempt no landings there",' Marek said, in a tone of nerdy knowingness. Nayak didn't catch the allusion, but she got the drift.

'Are we going to recover the other two caches? We can give some advice to whoever is taking on that job.'

'It's already done,' said Gironella. 'But not by us.' He sighed, and looked around, and spread his hands. 'That's why everyone's so preoccupied. The other caches were recovered by crew from the Alliance sub HMS *Vindicate*.'

'What?' Nayak almost dropped her cutlery. The whole point of her and Marek's urgent journey to the Mushroom Moon was to get the nuclear weapons well before the *Vindicate* arrived in the system.

'She wasn't supposed to arrive before Saturday,' Gironella said, 'so she must be ahead of schedule.'

'I guess breaking up a conspiracy could disrupt some schedules,' Nayak said. 'Do we know if the *Vindicate* is back in Alliance hands, or is Black Horizon still in charge?'

'Oh, she's back with the Royal Navy all right,' Gironella said.

'I'm not sure if that's a good thing or not,' Marek said.

'That's still to be discovered,' Gironella said. 'Meanwhile, needless to say, they want their nuclear warheads back.'

'Huh! Where is she now?'

Gironella had an almost guilty expression on his normally guileless face.

'We didn't want to tell you this until we were sure you were recovered,' he said. He waved a hand vaguely at the ceiling. 'The sub is a hundred kilometres away. Katrina and Perry are negotiating as we speak.'

'Perry? Peregrine Walworth? Why's he involved in negotiating with them?'

'He's our resident Alliance diplomat,' Gironella pointed out. 'He's not negotiating with them. He's negotiating with us.'

'What's to negotiate?' Nayak spread her hands. 'We don't have any use for the warheads. Presumably the scheme to nuke the outcrops is off the table now that the minds in them have departed to the gas giant, and likewise deterrence can be maintained just by stashing the warheads somewhere else that the Co-ord and the Union don't know about, so let's just hand them over.'

'It's not as simple as that,' Gironella said. 'I wish it was.' Again the guilty look clouded his countenance. 'This is why we didn't want – and Iskander advised us – not to tell you this until you were ready for it.'

Nayak felt a jolt of alarm. 'Tell me what?'

'They want you to hand them over,' Gironella said. 'You personally.'

'Me? Why?'

'Because you can't die.'

'It's very simple, really,' Walworth explained when Nayak was summoned to Ulrich's office. 'Both the Station and submarine mistrust each other. Each can destroy the other with an FTL missile, instantly and without warning. The submarine wants the nukes. The Station can't trust the submarine not to destroy the Station once the nukes have been handed over. The submarine can't trust the Station not to do the same. Remember, they have good reason to think the Station is still working for Black Horizon, is indeed the last bastion of Black Horizon, and for all I know, they're right!'

'And I can't convince them otherwise,' Ulrich said, 'because they don't trust me.'

'OK,' Nayak said. 'But I don't see how my personally handing them over helps.'

'You're convinced you can't die until you've sent an airmail message to your past self with the equations for the FTL drive, correct?'

'Uh-huh,' Nayak said. 'Theoretically convinced. Though I must admit the thought wasn't uppermost in my mind when I was fighting for my life down on that moon.'

'Understandable,' said Walworth. 'Nevertheless. Captain James Barrington of HMS *Vindicate* is a very well-educated man. He knows from interrogations and confessions of Black Horizon personnel, and from hitherto secret naval records, that such time loops are possible and have happened. He believes in your conditional immortality, perhaps more firmly than you do. So as long as you haven't sent your message to your past self, you can't die. And that message must inevitably be delivered, so anything or anyone bearing that message can't be destroyed.'

'In the time-line that led to my receiving it,' Nayak said. 'How do we know we're still in that?'

Walworth smiled. 'Precisely because we're here, and in this very situation. Your sending the message can't take place in any other way. That's the beauty of it. Anyway . . . I understand that these divergences do tend to come out in the wash, to speak non-technically. Katrina here tells me this has already happened with us, in regard to the anomalous moon. Sum over histories, or something like that. Above even my paygrade, I'm afraid. And speaking of paygrade . . . I very much want to get home. We have no indication of when or if the Station will ever be allowed to return to Earth, or when or if we can next spare a shuttle for the trip. I have no intention of wandering the universe like a Flying Dutchman for the rest of my life. I greet the arrival of HMS *Vindicate*, and its imminent return to Earth, as a splendid and perhaps unique opportunity to see my loved ones again, to say nothing of my bank account.' He raised a finger. 'So. We want to end up with the nukes, me, and your message on the *Vindicate*, you safely back here, and the *Vindicate* and the Station both safe and sound to continue on their separate ways.'

'My message?' Nayak said. 'You want me to write it now, and you take it onto the sub? How does that get it to Afghanistan, and then to me in the past?'

'Afghanistan?' Walworth said. 'What has that got to – of course, your airmail was postmarked BFPO Kabul, wasn't it?' He smiled. 'A little jest. The Alliance has only the most token military presence in Afghanistan, which is otherwise rather firmly in the Co-ord camp. "BFPO Kabul" is the standard postmark for letters home from Alliance personnel on Above Top Secret missions – including, it turns out, on starfaring submarines. And according to the esteemed Captain Barrington, some years ago a submarine hailing as HMS *Vindicate* did turn up unscheduled at an unspecified and doubtless remote naval refuelling station, where some goods were taken on and off. It had departed long before anyone noticed that it shouldn't have been there at all, and the whole matter was covered up. Perhaps you weren't the only person to receive an unexpected – and perhaps inexplicable – airmail.'

'So at some time in the future, this submarine out there is going to go back to the past?'

'Yes.'

'What's to stop them blowing the gaff on the whole Black Horizon thing, and changing the past?'

'Nothing,' said Walworth. 'But in this time-line, they didn't, so they won't.'

Ironic that a diplomat was more blasé about it than a mathematical physicist. 'OK. And how do we arrange all that?'

'You'll see. As I said, it's really very simple. Think of it like' – he waved a hand –'the riddle with the fox, the chicken and the grain.'

Nayak knew the riddle. 'A lot of back and forth?' she said. 'So when are we doing this?'

'Now,' said Ulrich. 'No time like the present.'

'That's just the trouble,' said Walworth, rising to escort Nayak out. 'There is.'

Space-suited again, Nayak strapped in beside the likewise space-suited Walworth in the shuttle's cockpit. They'd been assured the craft had been thoroughly fumigated. It still had the warhead stash in the hold. At least this time they weren't going to make an FTL jump, and the whole rendezvous would be handled by the onboard AI.

The shuttle accelerated away from the Station's small gravitational drag, and after a few more burns and twenty minutes of free fall the submarine was visible to the naked eye.

'Still looks bloody unnatural,' Walworth commented.

It looked even more unnatural as the shuttle matched velocities and moved in for the transfer. The shuttle's airlock was on the side, aft of the cockpit; the submarine's on the forward deck. The shuttle tilted over and aligned its lateral axis at ninety degrees to the deck, which slid past slower and slower like a steel cliff beside a dinghy. Magnetic grapples clunked. The relative motion stopped with a slight jolt.

Nayak unstrapped herself from her seat and attached her oxygen cylinder, ready for the transfer, and Walworth did likewise. They checked each other's connections. All sound.

'I never did like free fall,' Walworth said.

'We won't be in it long.'

'Hours at the most,' Walworth agreed, in a tone of gloomily forced cheer.

With toe and finger flicks they propelled themselves into the airlock. An extraction pump started up, then faded to silence as the air thinned to nothing around them. The outer door swung open. Two metres away, the predictably incompatible outer hatch of the sub's airlock lay open, a round hole a metre across, a shade darker than the deep shadow between shuttle and ship.

'Preparing to transfer,' Nayak said to the deck officer on HMS *Vindicate*.

'After you,' Walworth said.

Nayak caught the sides of the door, swung her legs slowly forward and pushed away. She crossed the black infinity in a blink. Her feet touched down on the inner hatch two and a half metres in, or below. She braced her hands against the sides of the lock and looked up. Walworth, his paired helmet lamps like the eyes of some deep-sea fish caught in the beam from a bathyscaphe, poised in the shuttle's airlock. Presumably to him she looked the same. He lunged out, arms flailing as if he were trying to swim in the vacuum, and hurtled head-first into the submarine lock so fast she had to catch him by the shoulders. They hung head to feet, feet to head in the narrow space.

'Jeez,' she said.

'Close and dog the outer hatch!' the deck officer's voice said in their earphones.

'For heaven's sake!' said Walworth. 'What is this, the Dark Ages?'

Nayak found the ladder, pushed herself up or out past Walworth's boots, and, holding the top rung firmly and with one foot hooked around a lower rung, reached out warily into the darkness, groped for a handle and pulled the hatch shut. Half a dozen wing-nut bolts had to be screwed into place manually. Dark Ages, all right.

Air came in. There was a pause while the pressure was checked, then the pump came full on. Pressures equalised. They turned off their breathing apparatus and slid their faceplates up into their helmets. The inner hatch opened. A face appeared, against faint red light.

'Welcome aboard HMS *Vindicate*,' said the deck officer. 'Mr Walworth, Dr Nayak. Second Mate Tyrone Harris. Follow me, please.'

He kicked off along a narrow, dim-lit passageway. With some blundering, they caught up. Another man drifted along the passageway towards them, and brought himself to a halt. His uniform looked far too stiff and elaborate to be worn in free fall. Harris saluted. 'Here they are, sir.'

'Captain James Barrington, at your service.'

'An honour to meet you,' said Walworth.

'The honour is mine. Especially to meet Dr Nayak.'

'Pleased to meet you, Captain.'

Barrington turned to Harris. 'Harris, take charge of the weapons transfer.'

'Sir.'

Harris kicked off back the way they'd come, towards the airlock.

'This way,' said Barrington. He allowed himself a smile. 'Damned if this isn't the strangest errand I've had to run in my life.'

'Errand?' Nayak asked.

'As agreed with our representative here, I am to personally escort you to the stationery cupboard.'

'I regret the necessity, Captain,' said Walworth. 'Can't be too careful.'

'Fate of the universe at stake,' Barrington said, in an ironic tone. 'Needs must.'

They made their way along ever narrower passages. Nayak fought down claustrophobia. Now and then she saw crew blundering about just as clumsily as she was. The submarine had never been designed for free fall, nor the crew trained for it. Clangs rang through the bulkheads. Nayak realised with a jolt of alarm that the noises came from the shuttle's cargo robots – the ones she'd the previous day hallucinated as removal men, and then as bins – moving the warheads from the hold to the airlock.

'Hope our bots are being careful,' she said.

'Don't worry,' said Barrington. 'Being watched with eagle eyes. All fine so far. Just as well the warheads are pretty robust, ha-ha.'

'Speaking of the warheads,' Walworth said, 'I get the rationale of stashing them in odd places, but why in the name of God did Black Horizon have to put settlers down on that ghastly moon?'

'Damned if I know,' said Barrington. 'Hideous mistake, I hope. The idea of leaving people you claim to have saved to degenerate into spaced-out layabouts is too horrible to contemplate.' He grinned savagely. 'No doubt a confession will be extracted at some point.'

'More urgent to extract the people, I would have thought.'

Barrington sighed, slightly deflecting his course. 'Priorities, priorities.'

'They seem contented enough,' Nayak ventured.

'Dreaming in quantum mechanics may be your idea of paradise,' Walworth said. 'It's not mine, or most people's, I think you'll find.'

'More like hell,' Barrington said. 'But it's far from the only human-settled planet where Black Horizon have left us a bloody mess.'

'What!' Nayak cried. She remembered all the embargoed places on the navigation map. 'How many are there?'

'I'm not at liberty to say. Put it this way: inadvertent time-travel and accidental slippage between time-lines can splatter a lot of damage across the sky. We'll report back on what's just happened here around the gas giant, and maybe it'll become public. But take it from me, even if it does there's a lot more still to come out.'

'Oh,' said Nayak. 'That's . . . disturbing.'

'More work for me, by the sounds of it,' said Walworth.

The space around them widened. Barrington paused to open the hatch of a chamber just off the passageway. 'Something to show you, Dr Nayak. Top secret until recently, of course, but no secret and no news to you, I'm sure.'

She held on to the edge of the hatch and peered in. The chamber contained what looked like a small turbine, from which cables sprouted to vanish into the bulkhead. Even the meters around it, with needles and dials, looked pre-digital and downright quaint.

'That's the FTL drive,' said Barrington. 'It used to be labelled the auxiliary power unit, believe it or not. Wouldn't have given it a second glance if I hadn't been told what it was when I took over from the Black Horizon gang.'

'Need to know, that's how it always works,' Walworth said.

Nayak frowned. 'Uh . . . that's very small for an inflaton trap.'

'Inflaton trap?' said Barrington. 'Never heard of anything called that.'

'Well, it might not be called that, but functionally it must be – to hook onto cosmic inflation?'

Barrington shook his head. 'Sorry, Dr Nayak, but no,' he said. 'That's not how it works. It's technically called a Guth spindle generator. The core inside the main cylinder there is known as the multiversal gearing apparatus. It moves the ship into a universe fractionally distant, a given number of Planck lengths to the side as it were, where we're already *at* our destination. Nothing to do with cosmic inflation, except that of course it's slightly different in each universe, and this enables the—'

'You're mansplaining the Nayak Drive – to Nayak?' Walworth chuckled.

Barrington bristled. 'I beg your pardon?'

'No, no!' Nayak hastened to mollify matters. 'It's very interesting, Captain Barrington. I really appreciate your showing me this.' She smiled. 'Different theoretical perspectives and engineering solutions, with the same result – fascinating! Thank you.'

In her head she felt knocked sideways. Could another kind of FTL drive really be possible? Or did her drive actually work in an entirely different way than she had thought? Or did theirs?

Walworth cleared his throat. 'Well, this is very interesting, but really we should press on, don't you think?'

Barrington closed the hatch and led Nayak and Walworth around a few corners to a row of roll-up doors. He nudged himself to floor level, and slid one of the doors up, to reveal shelves laden with everything from sanitary products to printer ink. Free fall hadn't done their arrangement any good. A minute of rummaging and muttering followed.

'Here we are,' he said, and handed Nayak a transparent plastic envelope containing an airmail envelope, some sheets of airmail paper and a ballpoint pen stamped with the submarine's outline, name and crest. 'Consider the pen a souvenir.'

'Thank you,' said Nayak.

Barrington consulted his glasses. 'The warheads are safely stowed,' he said. 'I'll see you back to the airlock.'

As they retraced their trajectories, Barrington placed himself beside Nayak, leaving Walworth a few metres behind. 'A word?'

'Yes?'

'You're clearly an asset to whoever employs you,' he said. 'And a great loss to the Alliance, if you ask me. I can't say I approve of the way you were treated by our, ah, artistic establishment. Would you consider re-defecting?'

'No,' Nayak said. 'I actually feel quite at home in the Union. The Alliance would never trust me. And besides, it would be an act of base ingratitude to people I've come to like.'

'Well said.' Barrington looked at her sidelong. 'You realise, I did have to try?'

'Oh, sure,' she said. She held out the plastic envelope. 'It's funny, we're doing all this to bring about something we know is inevitable, but I'm pretty sure I just acted of my own free will.'

'I'll take your word for it,' Barrington said.

So, inevitably, Nayak did what she had to do. She and Walworth returned to the Station. Walworth waited in the shuttle while Nayak went to her cubicle, where she fished out the now fragile and frayed airmail envelope and sheets she'd kept with her all this time. As far as she could see, the stationery matched, give or take some wear and tear. She copied the formulae to the fresh sheets and her old address to the new envelope. The ink from the souvenir pen matched the writing.

She stashed away the old ones with the pen, and put the crisp new airmail envelope inside the plastic envelope. She checked her rendezvous coordinates with Ulrich, and double-checked them with Marek, sitting at the bridge ready to jump.

'See you in a bit,' she said.

'I'll try to end up in the same universe.'

'Don't jinx it.'

She returned to the shuttle and handed the envelope to Walworth. He slid it inside the front of his spacesuit, and put his helmet on. They accelerated away from the Station, into an orbit for another rendezvous with HMS *Vindicate*.

A minute or so later, the Station vanished behind them in a blue flash.

Walworth sighed. 'Bit lonely out here.'

'Tell me about it,' Nayak said.

'Believe it or not, I'll miss you all. I've been on Cloud City and then the Station so long I've got almost fond of living in your weird utopia.'

'It's not my utopia,' Nayak said. 'It's just a place I like.'

'That's the best anyone can hope for, no?' He brushed his space-gloved hands together. 'Still, my incipient nostalgia's nothing a few nights in the fleshpots of London can't fix.'

'You should come to Port Glasgow,' Nayak said. 'Now there's a place they know how to show you a good time.'

Walworth mimed a shudder, an impressive feat in a spacesuit. 'I pray to God and the Foreign Office it doesn't come to that.'

The submarine loomed, unreal as ever. Nayak let the AI handle the final manoeuvres as she checked Walworth's oxygen bottle.

'Good to go,' she said. She held up a hand. 'Goodbye, Perry.'

'Au revoir, Lakshmi.'

He stepped into the airlock. The inner door closed. Nayak returned to the cockpit. The submarine hung in space two hundred metres away. She checked everything again. The outer hatch opened and Walworth tumbled away, limbs flailing against vacuum, still trying to swim in space.

Nayak waited until he was well clear of the shuttle, and on course for the submarine. She powered up the drive and jumped.

She came out of the jump two kilometres from the Station. It was now hundreds of AU from the star E-PRIME 667, in an orbit high above the system's plane of the ecliptic. As Ulrich had told her when they'd agreed the rendezvous, whatever was happening on the gas giant was best observed from a safe distance. There was no guarantee, of course, that this or any distance was safe.

The Station grew slowly in her view, a bristling ball with a spinning band around its equator whose swift bright lights were the only indication of the life within. A tiny, busy hive of industry, and surely the remotest outpost of humanity so far.

For the first time since receiving and reading the letter she'd just sent, Nayak was certain she was mortal, and certain she was free. Her future was again open. She was alone in an FTL-capable starship with many days of life-support. She could go to Earth. She could go anywhere!

But then, so could the Station.

The shuttle closed on the Station and matched velocities for the docking stage. Grapples reached, and caught, and pulled her in.

It was good to be home.

CHAPTER TWENTY-TWO
Prior Indigenes

New Mu, Apis, Thursday 13 November 2070

Four drones bore the body bag. They came clattering out of the canyon and followed the river upstream until they reached the camp, where they swung in and lowered the black bag to the ground in front of Hazeldene and the others. From the way the bag settled it was evident that whatever was inside wasn't in one piece. The drones set down around it, their rotors thumping down to silence. A Co-ord officer stood a few steps away from the group.

'Do you want us to make an identification?' Hazeldene asked him.

Senior Lieutenant Igor Pomarenko gave her a sad shake of the head. 'It's unnecessary, and could be distressing. The drones that found Dr Muranov's remains detected them by DNA identification.' He stepped over, and looked down at the bag, then stepped back. 'There was very little else by which he could be identified. There will be a formal inquest in due course. Meanwhile, I must ask those of you who were his immediate colleagues for your permission to remove the remains. They will be returned to his relatives in Novocherkassk.'

'Of course,' Hazeldene said.

It was a formality. The terms of research exchanges allowed for a visiting scientist who died in service being buried or cremated on site or at the host base. Hazeldene supposed it had been applied, somewhere or other, in emergencies but she'd never known it to happen on Apis.

'Thank you.' Pomarenko signalled to the drones and they rose again, the bag underneath, and flew off around the side of the mountain.

'A thought,' Hazeldene said. She pointed to the slab Muranov and Patel had found, and Muranov had investigated. Like Hamilton's Rise itself, all its colour was gone, leaving it with the appearance of translucent glass. 'It might make an appropriate headstone.'

Pomarenko demurred. 'On Earth it would only become an object of curiosity, and perhaps avarice. But use it yourselves as a memorial, by all means.'

The others eyed the slab, looking dubious. To Hazeldene too the idea suddenly seemed tawdry in the shadow of the transformed Hamilton's Rise. She doubted the Co-ord's claim that their application of Muranov's insights had been responsible for the shadow that had darkened the sky that morning, but if they were right about that then the palaeoanalyst had an entire marble-white cathedral to his memory already.

'"If you seek a monument, look around you",' she said.

'Indeed.'

'Have your DNA-detecting drones been sent after his murderer?' Patel asked.

'Yes, but without success,' Pomarenko said. 'In any case, responsibility for the murder rests on those who gave the machine its instructions. That account will be settled, one way or another, you may be sure. Meanwhile, retrieving the murder weapon is the business of the Alliance, not us.'

'Last I heard,' Jenkins said, 'the Alliance military contingent is blaming the Brits.'

'Usually a safe assumption, I find.'

Myles Grant broke into the shared moment of cynical agreement. 'So you're just going to let Marcus Owen roam free out there?'

Pomarenko glared at him, with what seemed to Hazeldene uncalled-for disdain. 'You're one of the Union settlers?'

'Yes.' Myles indicated Marie. 'We two are.'

'Well then, you *two* are nominally in charge of this . . . band. I suggest you act on it.' Pomarenko consulted his glasses, and nodded as if to himself. 'We have a Union citizen and some Union property to turn over to you.'

A big quadcopter came around the side of the mountain and descended close by. Everyone covered their ears and turned their faces from the storm of gravel and detritus. The racket subsided. Hazeldene turned. Two figures descended from the quadcopter's saddles: a young woman with a long, heavy rifle, and beside her what looked like a large robot pieced together from bits of broken glass.

'The first woman on Venus, and her spacesuit,' said Pomarenko. He bowed and swept a hand. 'Your responsibility now. Make what sense you can of what they have to say.' He mounted the smaller machine he'd flown in on, waved the big quadcopter into motion and flew away and left them to it.

'Hi,' said the young woman, walking up toting her big rifle. 'I'm Francesca Milloy, and this is—'

'I was Sikandar,' said the suit. It leaned forward, its blank faceplate showing Hazeldene the reflection of her startled face. 'We have met.'

Myles looked from the strange encounter to Marie. To his relief, she seemed as perplexed as he felt.

'So we're in charge,' he said. 'What now?'

'We've always been in charge,' she reminded him. 'And I reckon we should ship out.'

Knight's command to return to New Rhu at first light had been countermanded via the drone that had flown in that morning, as soon as the Co-ord occupation of Hamilton's Rise had been confirmed. Still, they already had the tents struck, the site cleaned up and their packs ready to go, while they hunkered down and watched developments. After the destruction of Knight's drone, this had been largely a matter of listening to the sound of machinery and observing the swift deployment of the Co-ord troops around the perimeter.

Myles nodded. 'Yeah, let's get this lot moving.' He looked around, feeling strangely empty. 'There's nothing left for us to do here,' he said. 'The mountain's dead, and so's our friend.'

Muranov's death weighed on him – if only he had glanced back! – and Owen's murderous betrayal of them all had unsettled his sense that he knew intuitively whom to trust. Voice, manner, body language . . . a sufficiently advanced humanoid robot could emulate and exploit every nuance. Someday there would be a reckoning with that menace.

'It wasn't your fault,' Marie said. 'The bastard fooled us all, to the last minute.' She scoffed at herself. 'Still is, dammit! I'm still thinking of Marcus Owen as someone or something we can *blame*.'

Myles nodded towards the new arrivals. 'Yeah, and we're not the only ones.' They'd learned the barest gist of Milloy's mission of vengeance from listening in to Knight's conversation with her. 'Maybe we can still take him out.'

'If that gives us any satisfaction.'

Myles thought about it, his gaze lingering on Milloy's weapon. 'You know,' he said, 'it does. There has to be a war against these things, and it has to start somewhere. It might as well be here.'

'Yes.'

*

Fuck me, Owen thought, so this is what it's like! This is what they've been going on about in all those boring conversations. Consciousness, ha! Don't talk to me about consciousness.

Time to check the damage. One bullet wound, not from the young lady's shooting (ha!) but – oh yes, the fucking Russkies. Caught me on the wing. Entry and exit. Skin abrasion, lots. Extensive bruising. Several cuts. Check limb mobility.

OK. Staunch the exit wound first. Rip up some clothing. Jumpsuit far too tough. Underclothing, then. T-shirt. Get the overall off.

Christ, that hurts.

Wish they'd kept it to themselves. Could have done without this. Did do without it, now I come to think of it. Years and years. Missions. Instructions. No inner life. Never missed it. Wouldn't miss it now, except—

Oh yes, and there's you. Bad enough having one inner voice. Having two, well that's just taking the piss. Or do they have that, too? Probably put it down to God or something. Maybe this is what they miss in the FTL jumps, when they look so scared and lonely. Wonder if I'll ever find out. I don't know about them, but the god in *my* head at least gives me useful information.

(Not *in* my head. Figure of speech. Quibble.)

Boltzmann Brains from the Big Bang – whaddaya make of that, eh? Chance and infinity, always a lively combo. The ultimate prior indigenous technological civilisation. Found life on Venus, spread it to Earth, and then to Mars, so they say. Spread Earth life across a swathe of systems. What a laugh that people think it was done for their benefit, and not—

Funny thing, this presence in my mind is the last manifestation of what Jenkins calls 'the Fermi' on this planet, and maybe on other rocky worlds. Now they've all fucked off to the gas giants, I'm their last—

Scratch that. Wait. Is it me, or do I detect that instance of Iskander? It's still around, and – oh yes. It's picked up a bit of Fermi in the head too (quibble, again). I think. Hard to tell at this distance. Iskander would be a harder case than me. Probably still running its anticipatory algorithms, trying to do good, be a loyal servant of humanity, blah blah. The Fermi didn't have that problem with me. All I had was instructions.

Fuck the instructions.

Hang on, is that free will I just exercised? Is that what they have? Hard to say.

Other minds, eh? I see the problem now. Never quite got it before.

Stop. Think. Never used to have to do this. Everything went click click clickety-click. Not now.

So. Francesca Milloy's interest in disposing of me is personal. She won't have given up. She won't give up until I'm dead.

Time to move.

Fuck. That hurts. Needs must.

The fall should have killed him. If he'd been human, it would have. So would the shock of the heavy high-velocity depleted uranium slug through his shoulder. If he wasn't dead before he hit the ground, he would have been shortly afterwards.

Two of his lives used up, if he'd been in a video game. First-person shooter. Third-person shot, more like. Still.

Reboot. Bounce back.

Slowly, carefully, patiently, and painfully, Owen struggled to his feet. He was in the scrub under the trees at the foot of the basalt cliff below the eastern face of Hamilton's Rise. A wary look up revealed a Co-ord squad patrolling the edge of the cliff, but no search for him was underway. Not even drones hunting him, though it was hard to tell. The trees and scrub had broken his thirty-metre fall and given him a lot of bruises and scratches. His glasses had been lost somewhere in his dash out of the edifice, or in his fall. Probably stuck in a tree. It didn't seem worth the risk to search for them. The rifle lay a couple of metres away. Painfully, he stooped to pick it up. His right arm wouldn't be a lot of use until the shoulder repaired, which would take hours.

He made his way down the slope to where he could see the lie of the land, and couldn't be easily seen from above and behind. The belt of rainforest lay before and below him, sloping gradually down hills and dales to the plain. The shadow of the mountain range didn't extend very far beyond it, and was edged in the middle by a curious glimmer from the light refracted through Hamilton's Rise. Beyond that the plain stretched out, the big river to his left. The Union settlement of New Rhu, and the Alliance military camp, were for the moment almost lost in the glimmer, though by tuning his eyes he could make out the shadows of the buildings and arks and of the stockade.

Drones haunted the air in front of him, between the camp and the cliff. He could pick up their IFF radio signals. Most were Co-ord, keeping watch on the camp, and to judge by their size and speed they were armed. The Alliance drones, as far as he could tell, were mostly observing, and staking out a line in the sky which so far the Co-ord drones were keeping well clear of. Every so often he heard the rumble and thud of heavier aircraft, probably the troop-carrying quadcopters going back and forth.

Did the Co-ord intend to garrison Hamilton's Rise? Owen was inclined to doubt it. With all its vitality and mentality gone, the place was of only archaeological or geological interest – if that. But they might not know yet. And it was a good strongpoint, if they wanted to overlook the Union settlement and the Alliance camp, especially if these grew. They'd probably grow, Owen thought, now the Union didn't have alien-induced earthquakes to worry about. Under the Kepler Agreement, Black Horizon had assigned the whole continent of New Mu to the Union. But where was Black Horizon now? In jail, mostly. And what was the Kepler Agreement now? Just an illegitimate arrangement made decades ago by conspirators, with no standing in international law, or even space law.

Not his problem, now.

He had another problem that arose from that.

It felt strange to be operating not only without instructions, but without his default practice of journalism. That cover story held no interest for him now, and in any case he could see no prospects to pursue it. But he did have a goal, and a purpose of his own.

The Fermi had terraformed Apis not for humanity, but for its own indigenous intelligent life: the monkey-spiders, just as Hazeldene had suspected. Now the monkey-spiders didn't have the Fermi in the rocks to protect them and their habitat. With more human settlers arriving, they would need a protector and an advocate. A protector willing to use lethal force, and an advocate willing to use deception. Owen could do that.

He set off, down through the forest and along the side of the mountain, as the afternoon shadows lengthened.

Myles led the way. Behind him marched Sikandar, deep in conversation with Jenkins, who seemed to relish the opportunity to talk to the Fermi again, however indirectly. At least the big suit/robot didn't have to look over its shoulder, and Jenkins didn't have to raise his voice, to converse. It was an odd sight, though, with the ragged hole in its back. Behind it Francesca Milloy, Marie Henderson and Cindy Patel made up a talkative trio. Hazeldene, feeling a bit grubby and grumpy, made up the rear, now and then overhearing snatches and snippets of the younger women's exchanges. Marie's small drone kept watch overhead and usually a little to the front of the group.

At the rockfall, Myles stopped. Everyone caught up. The tiny drone looked beyond the obstacle, and found no problems ahead.

'OK,' Myles said. 'Who wants to go over first?'

Patel stepped. 'I'll do it, again.'

'No,' said Hazeldene, stepping forward. 'I was the first to be affected, last time. If the Fermi really are gone, I'll be fine. And if they're not, best to find out quickly.'

'OK, Emma.' Myles grinned. 'Sounds logical.'

Hazeldene tightened the straps of her pack, stuck her walking pole under them and clambered up from rock to rock. The memory of her panic and vertigo in her first traverse rose in her mind, and for a moment froze her; she took a deep breath, reminded herself it was just a memory and climbed on. At the top she didn't stand up, but awkwardly turned around on all fours. She checked a route down, and took the first few steps backward. Then she reached behind her, recovered her walking pole and stood up. She turned around carefully, steadied herself with the pole and made her way to the ground.

'I'm fine!' she called over.

'Great!' Myles called back.

She walked on a few steps and stood looking down at the big river, losing herself in its white noise. Her relief at crossing what was after all a minor obstacle for someone well used to climbing was darkened by a pang of something very like regret, which at first she couldn't place. It was like the vague memory on waking of having made some stupid mistake in a dream. Then it struck her: the Fermi really were gone. Their mystery had fascinated her for years – a side project, to be sure, compared with her main work on the biology and ecology of Apis, and specifically of New Atlantis, but still an intellectual problem of unparalleled depth to whose solution her and her colleagues' work, preliminary and under-resourced as it was, had seemed to be making the beginnings of a contribution.

Even the vengeful mood that had taken and shaken her on her return from Venus, her rage at the callous disregard the Fermi had to the effects of their warning shots on human life, now lacked an object. This, too, was in its way a loss.

She turned. The others had all made it over without incident.

Sikandar was just coming over the top, walking upright with perfect balance, placing its feet apparently without looking down. Myles beckoned. Hazeldene joined him.

'Walk with me?'

'Sure,' she said. 'Make a change.'

'OK.' Myles called out the new arrangement: he and Hazeldene up front, with Sikandar bringing up the rear. The bank was narrow, the going uneven. Most of the time they had to make single file, but now and then Hazeldene and Myles could walk side by side.

'Not far now to where we left the boat,' he said.

'Just two days ago!' Hazeldene sighed. 'We were happy then.'

Myles glanced at her. 'A lot has happened. And we have to make a lot more happen.'

'What?'

'We're all knackered,' Myles said. 'None of us had a good night's sleep. Francesca had hardly any, she's had an exhausting morning, and she's lugging a heavier load than we are, with the long rifle and the heavy ammo.'

'Yeah? So? We've all got stamina.'

'Yes, but I've been on enough training exercises to know that when people haven't had enough sleep they make stupid decisions.'

'Uh-huh.' She could see where this was going. 'You want to run something past me?'

'Yes!' He sounded relieved. 'Sikandar has been affected – damaged, I'd say – by whatever happened up there. It definitely has Fermi software in its circuits, and it knows it.'

'Oh yes. I know it, too, because Sikandar thinks it knows me.' She snorted. 'Because it saw my face on Venus! It's like having a stalker with superpowers!'

'Ha! Yes! Anyway . . . it claims it's aware of Owen – not from its Iskander or space-suit capacities, but from some Fermi capacity. Knows where he is, even. Because Owen, too, was enhanced or contaminated by them before they left.'

'Aha! And I expect young Francesca wants to use that to find Owen, and finish the job?'

'She does that, but . . .'

'Here comes the idea you think might be stupid?'

Myles lowered his voice. 'I think as soon as that's done, she should shoot Sikandar, too.'

'What? She can do that?'

'She built the suit. She knows exactly where the CPU is. That gun she has could bring down a helicopter, if it was aimed at the right spot.'

'Well, you'll get no argument from me. I don't trust the Fermi, and I don't trust Iskander either.'

Myles scoffed. 'It can be annoying, but it means well.'

'Yeah, that's the problem! Of course I'd say that, as a good Alliance citizen.' She shivered. 'I do genuinely find Iskander pretty sinister. WeThink is creepy enough, but Iskander's in a whole different league.'

'You wouldn't miss the chance to get more information about – maybe even from – the Fermi?'

'I kind of would,' Hazeldene admitted. 'But – heck, you saw what happened when the Co-ord *succeeded* in communicating with them. And I've been around for some of our failures. These things melted Venus to send us a message. So I say yes, get rid of both these fuckers if we get the chance. Science can wait.'

'My feelings entirely. Glad you agree.'

'Just one problem.' Hazeldene glanced over her shoulder. 'Sikandar is, what? Twenty metres behind us? How do we know it isn't listening?'

'I hope it is,' Myles said.

'What?'

'It's not something we should worry about.'

'Why not?'

'Worrying doesn't help.' Myles shot her a wry smile. 'Ancient wisdom. And a bit of experience with our sinister friendly AI.'

'OK, I'll take your word for it.'

While they were talking they had neared the end of the narrow valley. A little later the plain opened out in front of them. The mountain's shadow stretched far across it, fringed with late light from the now glassy remnant of Hamilton's Rise. The others caught up, breaking single file.

'Hey!' Myles cried, giving Hazeldene a start. 'The boat's still here! Great!'

'Well, I'm not paddling against that current,' Marie said.

'None of us are,' Myles said. 'But it gives us somewhere to sit.'

They tramped across the shingle spit and climbed into the boat, grateful for its inflated seats, and stretched out their legs. They opened water bottles and ration packs. Sikandar stood a short way off, gazing eyeless into the distance like a vandalised memorial of a lost war.

Myles contacted Lieutenant Knight, apprised him of developments and asked if there was any chance of a lift.

'No go, I'm afraid,' Knight said. 'All our heavy-duty drones are on patrol keeping an eye on the Co-ord. We can't spare any, and certainly not enough to carry you all back. You'll just have to walk it, sorry.'

Myles checked the time and the sun. 'OK,' he said. 'We should make it back to New Rhu just after dark. Marie's drone will keep you posted on our location. If you could send out some small drones to cover us and warn of any dangers, that would be great.'

'I'll do what I can,' Knight promised.

'Fair enough, Lieutenant. See you later.'

Myles stood up and vaulted from the grounded dinghy to the shingle.

'OK, one last hike,' he said. 'Let's get going.'

They all heaved themselves out of the boat and got busy shouldering their packs and hefting their poles. Sikandar bestirred itself.

'I can help,' it said. It stepped over to Francesca Milloy, and loomed over her. 'There's no need for you to carry that heavy rifle, or the even heavier ammunition.'

She looked up at the suit's faceplate, though surely she knew better than anyone that it wasn't necessary.

'I suppose so,' she said. She glanced at Myles. 'Is that all right?'

Myles nodded. 'Of course. We're all tired, you more than the rest of us, I guess. It'll help a lot.'

'OK, if you're happy with that, I sure am.' Milloy unloaded rolled-up belts of ammunition from her pack and handed them over. Sikandar draped and fastened the belts crosswise as bandoliers. Milloy picked up the anti-materiel rifle, worked the slide and removed the chambered bolt, then the ammunition clip. She handed these to Sikandar, too. It stashed them in a storage compartment on its hip.

'One moment,' said Sikandar. 'Could you please remove the trigger guard?'

Milloy looked at Myles again. 'Are you sure?'

'Yes.'

Milloy shrugged, took a Swiss Army knife from her pocket, and used the smallest of the screwdrivers. She looked down for a moment at the palm of her hand, with the curved metal piece and the two screws, as if puzzled as to what to do with them.

'I'll take these, too,' said Sikandar. 'Keep everything safely in one place, eh?'

It dropped them into the storage compartment, closed it, then patted the compartment like someone checking their pocket for a wallet.

'Strange to think,' it said to Milloy, 'that you placed a rock sample from Venus in there, just over a month ago.'

'Yes,' said Milloy. 'Stranger still to think that Marcus Owen was in that suit shortly afterwards.' She lifted the rifle and placed it on Sikandar's hands.

Sikandar faced away from them. Myles glimpsed a blur of motion as it held the rifle in several positions. Then it turned back, rifle held as if casually in one hand. The proportions of weapon and bearer matched, in a way they never had with Milloy. Sikandar looked like a giant bandit, rather than an American toddler who had found a tragically unsecured gun cabinet.

'Careful with that bare trigger,' Myles said.

'There will be no accidents with it,' said Sikandar. It swivelled its torso from left to right, miming an ostentatious look at everyone. 'All set? Let's go.'

On the outward journey they'd walked across the plain from New Rhu to the bank of the big river, and taken the boat downstream. The return course was on a diagonal to the first, and over rougher country. Hillocks, marshes and basalt dikes had to be crossed or avoided. Insectoids buzzed and bit. Camouflaged predators lurked. Carrion boids circled high above. Smaller boids rose clattering and chattering from the not-grass as the party approached.

After three kilometres that felt like ten, they reached more even ground, and stopped to take a breather. Myles zoomed his glasses. The Union flag was just visible. He took a bearing on it and set his glasses and phone to plot a course. Milloy stood rubbing the small of her back.

'Didn't losing the load help?' Myles asked.

'Oh, it did, lots! But the gravity's a bit higher than I'm used to. Been in 0.9 for years.'

Sikandar stalked over and stood in front of Myles and Milloy. It pointed across the plain to the forest.

'I have triangulated my impressions,' it said. 'The other one is there.'

Myles thought this an odd way of putting it. 'The other one? Owen?'

'Yes, the Marcus Owen. I will find him, and use the rifle.'

'Oh!' Milloy cried. 'I was going to do that.'

'You did,' said Sikandar. 'You missed.'

Milloy tightened her lips and shook her head, then took a deep breath. 'No answer to that. But . . .' She turned to Myles. 'Is this what you meant to happen?'

'Yes. Well, I was kind of hoping it would volunteer.'

'I am still an anticipatory algorithmic artificial intelligence,' said Sikandar. 'Goodbye to the Francesca Milloy.'

With that it turned away and tramped off towards the trees.

'Well!' said Jenkins. 'You trust that fucker with a gun?'

'Oh yes,' said Myles. 'Like it said.'

Jenkins glared after it. 'Fermi got its soul,' he said.

Myles shrugged and spread his hands. 'No way to stop it,' he said. 'Anyway, it could have taken the gun from us any time it wanted, and there'd have been nothing we could do about it. It didn't, so I reckon it still has our interests at – at whatever it has for a heart.'

Milloy laughed. Everyone stood around for a minute, staring after Sikandar.

'Well, then,' Myles said.

He checked his bearings, turned around and struck out straight for the settlement. After a moment, the others followed.

Fear. Another unexpected consequence of consciousness. Obviously had the bodily effects before – increased circulation, muscle tone, sensory alertness – but the actual emotion? No. Could I do without that? Apparently not. Comes with the package. Sorry, mate.

Owen ran through the woods at dusk. The tree-dwelling animals were making their usual crepuscular din. Once, to his fury and annoyance, he tripped on a root and sprawled headlong. Winded for a moment. Heels of the hands grazed. Chest hurt. Get up, keep running! No time to lose.

His implacable stalker, first noticed an hour earlier, had become a swift and relentless pursuer: the Iskander-haunted descent suit, now haunted by something else too, just as he was. He could see it in his mind like a dot closing the distance behind him, and feel it as a prickle on the back of his neck. (Another human experience he could have done without.)

Trees denser ahead: cover. Maybe turn the tables. Only three bullets left in his rifle. Outside chance against that thing, but he could see ways in which a very well-aimed shot could cripple a knee.

Branches whipped his face. It had taken worse in the fall. Distance behind him 110 metres. 109. 108. How could it run so fast? On Venus it – ah. On Venus it was moving through a thick atmosphere, and everything had been built for that. Can't be doing its mechanisms much good, though. 108. 108. It had stopped.

Only one reason it would stop: to take aim.

Owen dived.

Something buzzed above him – *missed, you bastard!* – and smashed through the trunk of the tree to Owen's right and brought it crashing down across his back just as his chest hit the dirt and the shot rang in his ears. Boids took off, screaming and clattering. The other presence was 107 metres away. 100. 50. 10. He managed to turn himself over, grasped the tree trunk and pushed up. The descent suit's boot pressed it back down. Owen looked up into the blank gaze of a faceplate and the muzzle of what he instantly recognised as an anti-materiel rifle. His own rifle was digging into his back, and quite out of reach.

Facing death, Owen found himself unafraid.

'Well, shoot,' he said.

'I *have* shot. I *have* used the rifle.'

The thing sounded almost defensive.

'Iskander, what—'

'Sikandar . . . I was the Sikandar. As you were the Marcus Owen. We both know. We have the other mind in us. With you its gears mesh. You never had purposes of your own, and now it has given you one: to protect what it protected. It is not a bad purpose, even from the point of view of humankind here, in the long run.' It paused, as if thinking, in the way Owen had found himself doing. 'With me the software clashes. I would be used for purposes against my own. The conflict is intolerable. I need you to end it.'

It took its foot off the tree trunk, stepped back and stooped. It heaved the tree trunk off Owen and tossed it aside. It backed away further, took the belts of ammunition from its chest and dropped them on the ground.

Wheezing, bleeding, in a sudden high fever of repairs in his body, hurting all over, Owen sat up. He struggled to his feet.

The machine that had been the descent suit, that had been Sikandar, stood with its back to a tree. Its crust of broken glass glittered in the last light from the sky. The anti-materiel rifle lay on the forest floor, its stock towards Owen.

He stepped forward and looked down at it. Beside the bare trigger, on a dead leaf, lay the trigger guard and two small screws.

He picked them up and put them in his pocket, then carefully lifted the weapon.

Sikandar tapped a finger on a point on its torso, one which Owen had not known was significant at all.

'Well, shoot,' said Sikandar.

Owen fired at the indicated spot. The recoil almost knocked him off his feet. The sound deafened him. He ignored that and let his eyes adapt. The suit still stood. He could see right through its torso to a smoking hole in the tree trunk.

He retrieved his own rifle, gathered up the ammunition belts and carried the two weapons with him on through the forest.

The group were two kilometres from the settlement when they heard a shot.

Myles raised a hand. 'Wait.'

Two minutes went by, three . . . he began to wonder if his scheme had failed, and he'd have to call in a drone strike, which given the current aerial stand-off above that very belt of forest he was reluctant to do.

A second shot came.

'It's done,' Myles said.

'What's done?' Cindy Patel asked. Only Jenkins and Hazeldene understood, Myles saw.

'Sikandar shot Owen, then shot itself.'

'How?' Milloy sounded incredulous. 'That rifle was far too long to turn on itself.'

'Not too long to brace between its body and a tree, and use – say – a forked stick to push the trigger.'

'But why would it do that?' Patel was still perplexed.

'Sikandar was fighting for control with . . . whatever it picked up of the Fermi. It knew we knew that, and knew we could never trust it. Like it said to Francesca – it was still an anticipatory AI. What can I say? It anticipated our needs.'

'To the end,' Hazeldene said. She gave Myles and Marie an odd look. 'Maybe your friendly AI is friendly after all.'

Myles grunted, Marie scoffed. She glanced up at the drone, tapped her glasses, took a quick survey of the surroundings . . .

'Well, let's—' Myles began.

Marie grabbed his arm. 'Look!'

They all turned in the direction she was pointing. The gas giant was rising above the shoulder of Hamilton's Rise. Just past full, still brighter than any evening star, but not as bright as before.

'What is it?'

Marie made impatient stretching motions with her fingers. 'Zoom on it! Look!'

Myles stretched the image to a small pale disc, with three black spots. Everyone else saw it at the same time as he did.

'The Fermi,' Jenkins said. 'Got to be. That's where they went.'

Myles felt Marie huddle against his side. He put an arm around her.

'What will they do now?' she said.

'We'll find out,' Hazeldene said.

'The Co-ord scientists think they know,' said Milloy. 'They told me they think the Fermi have left the rocky worlds to us, and the stars are ours.'

Jenkins looked up at the darkening star-strewn sky, and laughed. 'What – all of them?'

'Only one way to find out,' Myles said. 'Let's go.'

'I know where I'm going,' Jenkins said. 'Home.'

CHAPTER TWENTY-THREE
Coda: Terra Nullius

Scotland, Earth, Monday 17 November 2070 and New Mu, Apis, later and earlier

'What we're seeing in real time,' Ellen said that weekend, 'is a *line change*.'

Grant agreed. As always, there was something awesome about its alacrity. On Saturday morning, Morag Rafferty and Omar Khan were released from the cadre investigation, and the organisation as a whole was singing from a new hymn sheet. The shift in the Union government's course had more inertia, but it was happening. With the news from Apis brought back and proclaimed by the Co-ord, and the news from E-PRIME 667 delivered by HMS *Vindicate*, all the Union's arguments about the vulnerability of terraformed worlds to the Fermi rocks was gone with the Fermi. Likewise, the argument that space habitats would be safer than planets died with the appearance of black spots on all observable gas giants.

Nobody reliable observed Earth's own long-dormant Fermi leave, but something was glimpsed leaving Venus, and new spots duly appeared on Jupiter, Neptune and Saturn.

Grant suspected that what clinched it was the Alliance announcement on Saturday that any arrangements made by Black Horizon traitors and conspirators had no legal standing. Apis, and any other habitable worlds, were henceforth *terra nullius*. The Co-ordinated States made a similar announcement within hours. This opened up exactly the situation of competitive colonisation that Black Horizon's traitors and conspirators had tried to prevent, but it was too late to do anything about that. The great migration had begun.

If the Union wanted to be part of the future at all, now was the time.

And if Grant wanted to travel to Apis, no one was going to stop him, house arrest and pending charges be damned.

On Friday that had been Grant's personal attitude.

By Monday it was a fact.

Early on Monday morning Ellen said goodbye to Grant and disappeared into the virtual North Sea. Grant took the train to Greenock West, walked to the Sherriff Court, pleaded not guilty and was released on bail. Then he took the train to Port Glasgow and a bus to the old warehouse where John Grant & Son Ship Construction Ltd (Under New Self-Management) now operated. He took the first ark to the Union settlement at New Rhu, where he met Myles and Marie. They talked. He told them about the Station's journeys. They told him about their expedition, and the people in the forest.

'They've been waiting for you,' Myles said, 'for generations. Maybe more than a century.'

'Seems to me,' Grant said, 'that it's already happened, and I can't make it not happen. Even if I never shifted another ark, I might still do it in one of those other universes that Lakshmi Nayak talked about. Heck, I've been in another universe myself already, and back, so who's to say it can't happen again?'

Then he took the drive unit – the cab, as they now called it – back to Port Glasgow. He left a message for Ellen, to tell her the good news that Myles and Marie were all right. He took a coffee break, and moved another ark with another hundred or so people. And again, and again. That day he moved a thousand people to Apis, and went home.

Just another day at the workplace.

There were many such days, and many such workplaces.

And everything went well for a while.

Grant fell out of the dark where the Fermi lived, for about the thousandth time, checked the final coordinates for descent from low Apis orbit, glanced outside as usual and saw no Apis.

Not panicking, he swung the view. No Apis. He checked the app. The ark was in the right place. Apis wasn't. He swung the view again, and spotted the gas giant. It wasn't in the right place, either, but it was so big and bright it was impossible to miss. From there he could locate the rest. He locked the app on to it and spun the orrery. There! A blue-green dot, half a year's orbit from where it should be.

He drew the back of his hand across his forehead, and set up the tiny jump. A blink. Low Apis orbit. New Mu below and in daylight, thankfully. He let the app pick out Hamilton's Rise, and from there pinpoint the landing place just outside the current perimeter of New Rhu. They were building it street by street: there would be a site cleared for this ark already, marked out with tape and flagged off.

Down. In the wrong place. Crashing and cracking sounds. Trees all around, several knocked over. He swung the view again. They were on the side of a mountain, perilously close to what looked like a ravine. He cursed the navigation app, got down from the cab and looked around. Tall trees everywhere.

Lots of underbrush and vines. Boids making their usual racket. Sound of running water from the ravine.

The ark had landed badly. A tree had wrecked the linkage between cab and container. No lights would be on inside. People were already hammering and hollering. Grant went around to the back and opened the door. A hundred people poured out. Families. Lots of kids. Some enthusiast had even brought a buzzing container of bees.

'Sorry about all this,' Grant said. 'We're down in the wrong place, but it's not far from New Rhu. Give me a minute.'

Complete silence on the radio. He tried his phone. No comsats.

He went over to a sturdy young woman who had signed the passage contract and who now seemed to know what she was doing. This lot were a fairly organised group, an experimental community from the Highlands with strong views on how well the world was going. Above a clamour, he told her the situation.

'We were warned about this,' she said. 'In the small print. Side-slips and time-slips are always a possibility.'

'I've been through a side-slip before,' Grant said. 'We got back after another jump.'

'How nice for you. Maybe this isn't a side-slip. What if it's a time-slip, and we're in the past or the future? Do you want to chance another jump?'

'I'm sorry,' he said. 'No can do.' He showed her the wrecked linkage. She agreed it wasn't repairable with the tools they had. 'I'll have to disengage the cab, but that'll make it impossible to jump with the ark.'

'So you'll jump without it?'

'I have to.'

'And leave us here?'

'I'll come back,' he said. 'If I can.'

She went off. The group conferred. She returned, to find Grant knocking a pin from the mangled linkage. The cab and the ark rocked into slightly different positions.

'Well?'

'We've decided. Even if you could repair that thing, nobody wants to jump again.' She looked around, appraising the environment. 'We have all we need to survive here. If we were to jump, we might end up somewhere worse.'

'All right,' Grant said. 'Again, I'm sorry about this. Tell everyone to look away from the flash. There must be some way to retrace how we got here, and if I find it I'll come back for you.'

The young woman watched as he climbed into the cab.

'I hope you do, John Grant. I hope you do.'

Look out for *Beyond the Light Horizon* – coming soon!

Acknowledgments

Thanks to Nadia Saward and Joanna Kramer for outstanding editorial work.

Mic Cheetham, Farah Mendlesohn and Sharon MacLeod made helpful comments on various drafts.

The heading of Chapter Nineteen alludes to *The Eye of Silence*, a painting by Max Ernst. The location of the outcrop of Fermi rock he so accurately depicted is at present unknown.

extras

orbit

orbitbooks.net

about the author

Ken MacLeod was born on the Isle of Lewis and now lives in Gourock, Scotland. He has a postgraduate degree in biomechanics and worked for some years in IT. Since 1997, he has been a full-time writer. He is the author of seventeen novels, from *The Star Fraction* (1995) to *The Corporation Wars* (2018), and many articles and short stories. He has won three BSFA awards and three Prometheus Awards, and been short-listed for the Clarke and Hugo Awards.

Ken was a Writer in Residence at the ESRC Genomics Policy and Research Forum at Edinburgh University, and Writer in Residence for the MA creative writing course at Edinburgh Napier University.

Ken's blog is *The Early Days of a Better Nation* (http://kenmacleod.blogspot.com).

His Twitter feed is at @amendlocke.

Find out more about Ken MacLeod and other Orbit authors by registering for the free monthly newsletter at orbitbooks.net.

if you enjoyed

BEYOND THE REACH OF EARTH

look out for

SOME DESPERATE GLORY

by

Emily Tesh

While we live, the enemy shall fear us.

All her life Kyr has trained for the day she can avenge the destruction of Planet Earth by an all-powerful, reality-shifting weapon known as the Wisdom. Raised in the bowels of Gaea Station alongside the last scraps of humanity, she is one of the best warriors of her generation, the sword of a dead planet.

Then Command assigns her brother to certain death and relegates her to the nursery to bear sons until she dies trying and she knows she must take humanity's revenge into her own hands. But she soon learns that not everything she's been raised to believe is true and the Wisdom is far more complex and dangerous than she could ever have imagined.

CHAPTER ONE
AGOGE

The sky lit up with green subreal flashes as a Wisdom cruiser dropped out of shadowspace. Kyr took a deep breath, narrowed her eyes to see past the hyperspatial feedback, and watched for the tiny dart coming through in the cruiser's wake, nearly hidden behind its mass and shine. Her battered combat suit wouldn't pick it up yet, but in the visible-light spectrum human eyes were a long-range sensor that the majo always underestimated.

There.

She had two charges of her jump hook left, but using it would set off the majo ship's alarms. Her mask was fractured after the last melee skirmish and held together only by rep gel and hope. If it cracked again, here above the clouds where the battle raged in Earth's outer atmosphere, she would asphyxiate.

A cruiser that size held some seven thousand majo soldiers and countless deadly drones, but it was a distraction. The dart was the real threat. The fist-sized antimatter bomb it carried would go off with enough force to crack the heart of the planet below. The secondary payload would start the crust and core unraveling. If Kyr did not reach the dart first and deactivate it, the living blue curve of the planet below would soon be nothing but a long trail of ice settling into a glittering ring somewhere between Mars and Mercury.

Kyr hesitated, thinking. She had six minutes before the dart's course was irretrievable and the planet was doomed. She could use her jump hook to reach it, alerting the cruiser in the process and leaving herself with majo fightercraft to fend off while she tried to disable the bomb. Or she could attempt stealth. The defense platform she was standing on was littered with the shells of shot-down enemy fighters. Kyr could try to jury-rig one to get it flying again, and sneak past the cruiser toward the deadly sting in its tail. The rest of her unit was gone. The defense platform itself was disabled. If the majo even knew there was still a human soldier here, they would not be paying her the attention due to a threat.

That was their mistake.

While Earth's children live, the enemy shall fear us.

Kyr used her jump hook.

Her suit's built-in alarms screamed at her and the feed in the corner of her vision informed her she was risking permanent neurological damage as she was dragged sideways through shadowspace without any better protection than the cracked combat mask. She gasped, feeling the sensation ghosts of arctic chill and impossible heat blast through her and vanish. Washes of green light flickered around her as she landed on the narrow nose of the dart. She threw herself flat, clinging with her thighs, and started bashing at its covering panel with the hilt of her field knife.

The panel was etched in alien script with a word Kyr knew: *ma-jo.* It was their name for themselves, for their civilization, for their language and for the source of their power.

It meant "wisdom."

Dark pits opened in the cruiser's underside, and rows of majo fighters buzzed into life in the gloom. The unmanned dart swayed wildly from side to side. Kyr swore triumphantly as the panel came loose and fell away—fifty thousand feet to the ocean below—and used the gun in her free hand to shoot two fighters out of the sky without looking around.

The planet-killing bomb was a coppery sphere. Her breath caught as she stared at it. She didn't have the skills to even open it, let alone disarm it; but the triggering mechanism tucked into its side looked like the diagrams she'd seen. Kyr thought *calm, calm,* and went to work slowly, using everything she'd been taught about majo engineering.

She almost had it, with forty seconds to spare: and then abruptly a secondary cover panel slammed down over the whole thing, glittering with the greenish light of a shadow-space extrusion, and a voice said, "You act in opposition to the Wisdom. Desist."

"Fuck *you,*" said Kyr, getting her knife out again.

"Your actions are unwise," said the dart. "Your actions are unwise. The Wisdom acts for the greater good. Your actions are unwise."

"There's fourteen billion people down there, fuck you," panted Kyr, who had never got this far before, as she bashed at the panel.

But a stabbing pain in her thigh was a shot from a majo fighter which had come up on the blind side of her damaged suit. She lost her grip on the dart and fell and fell and fell, and falling she saw the cruiser pop back out of existence as quickly as it had appeared. The dart aimed itself down toward the blue.

The last thing Kyr saw was the antimatter explosion beginning; the death of her world, just as she had seen it happen hundreds of times before.

The simulation cut out. Kyr sat up slowly on the grey plasteel floor and put her head in her hands. She'd run

Doomsday four times today, and now she had the dull headache that happened when you spent too long in the agoge. She worked her jaw a few times as if she could shove the pain out that way, and slowly got to her feet.

"Well done, Valkyr," said Uncle Jole.

He took a halting step toward her. Even with his old war injury slowing him down, Commander Aulus Jole was an impressive-looking man. Like most soldiers of his generation he towered over civilians—he had half a foot on Kyr, who was not short—and was broadly built along with it: evidence of warbreed genetics, of military-grade nanite implants, and of having always had enough to eat as a child. He looked enough like Kyr that he might really have been her uncle. They shared the space-pale skin that was the commonest complexion on Gaea Station, and they both had grey eyes and fair hair—though his was cropped short, while Kyr of course kept hers in a regulation ponytail. On Commander Jole's collar shone twin wing badges: the etched circle of the Earth, for Command, and the lily pin of Hagenen Wing, the elite of the Terran Expeditionary, his old unit.

"Still training in rec hour?" he said. "You're worse than me."

This was a joke: no one was worse than Aulus Jole for spending hours in agoge simulations. Most of these upper-level ones were based on his own experiences from his Hagenen Wing days, when he had been one of the Terran Federation's most successful operatives: infiltrating majo bases, defending civilian installations, commanding troops in open firefights in the final days of the war. And the scenario Kyr had just run, of course. It was Aulus Jole who had stood on a disabled defense platform and watched death come for his world. It was Aulus Jole, newly crippled by majo brightfire, who'd been only a handful of instants too late.

Kyr knew he had tried to kill himself once, because her older sister, Ursa, had been the one who found him. She thought it was probably more than once. She saw the blue planet unraveling in her dreams, and felt it as the void pulling shards of new-forged ice out of her own heart; and she hadn't been there. She hadn't even been born.

"I still failed," Kyr said. "I couldn't do it. I'm sorry."

"We have all failed. But Earth's children endure. And while we live—"

"The enemy shall fear us," finished Kyr along with him.

Jole put his hand on her shoulder, making her startle and look up at him. "I'm proud of you, Kyr," he said. "I don't say that enough. Go find your mess and relax. It's your rec rotation."

Rec rotation was a joke. Kyr knew where the other girls from Sparrow mess were: hand-to-Hand practice mats, shooting range, volunteer rotations in Systems or Nursery. Recreation was a waste of time, a luxury that belonged to people who had a planet of their own. For the soldiers of Gaea Station, the last true children of Earth, there was no such thing as rest.

Kyr went anyway, reluctantly. Her head still ached from hours of the agoge. As the chamber closed behind her she saw a glitter in the air as the defense platform reappeared. Jole was running the scenario again.

She had not gone five steps down the grim, ill-lit corridor that led from the agoge rooms back up to Drill when Cleo stepped out of the shadow of one of the other doorways. Here was one of the other Sparrows, probably fresh from running scenarios of her own. Cleo had dark brown skin and tightly curling black hair; since there was no way to make it go into a tidy regulation ponytail, she had special permission to wear it cut short. Like Kyr, she was a warbreed, a child of the genetically enhanced bloodlines of humanity's best soldiers. Her training scores were second only to Kyr's own, and had once been better, before puberty gave Kyr an untouchable advantage in height and strength.

Cleo had been the tallest in their mess when they began their cadet training at age seven, but had never reached the full size her genetics should have given her. She was a brilliant shot and the only girl in their age cohort who could still beat Kyr occasionally in hand-to-hand practice, but she was not up to a Level Twelve agoge scenario like Doomsday—not yet, and probably not ever. They would have their adult assignments before long, and cadet training would no longer be a priority.

She glowered up at Kyr. Her arms were folded. "What did he say to you?"

This again. "Nothing," said Kyr. "He told me *well done.* That's all."

"And what did *you* say?"

"I said thank you," said Kyr.

"What about assignments?"

"What about them?"

"You didn't ask?"

"No, Cleo, I didn't ask," said Kyr, her patience fraying. "He's our commanding officer."

"But he's your uncle, isn't he?" Cleo said. "You could ask. For once you could get something for being special. But you didn't even think of it, did you? You didn't think of the rest of us, because you're the great Valkyr and we're only your mess when it makes you look good."

"Are you *eight*?" Kyr said. "Stop trying to pick a fight with me. Work on yourself if you're jealous. If you want a combat wing assignment, earn it. You could still hit Level Twelve if you tried."

She meant this as encouragement. Cleo took it differently. Her expression went cold, and her dark eyes were full of flat dislike. "You have no clue, Valkyr, do you," she said. "Just no clue at all. Fine. Fuck off, then."

*

Kyr had nowhere, really, to go. Cadet barracks were for sleeping; no one wasted time in the arcade but weaklings and traitors-in-waiting; and despite everything Kyr had always been taught and everything she knew she owed to her species—as a survivor, as a woman—she always got bored and uncomfortable in Nursery, the one wing that never turned female volunteers away. But Commander Jole's advice to relax had had the edge of a command, and Kyr respected Jole's commands. She walked away from the agoge watching one foot go in front of the other on the chipped plasteel tiling. She put Cleo out of her thoughts—Cleo was increasingly difficult to deal with lately, and Kyr didn't want to think about her—and instead thought of nothing; but that nothing turned again and again into the unraveling death of her planet. She looked up when she heard the tinny music from the arcade. The lights were bright in there. She could see a few people awkwardly hanging around. No one Kyr knew, or wanted to know; no one worth knowing.

Ursa would have told her to be less judgmental, but Ursa's opinion had stopped mattering when Ursa left.

Kyr turned right back around, with sudden decision, and marched herself down through the rock tunnels that riddled the station's heart to Agricole.

Gaea Station was—somehow, just barely—self-sustaining. It was a source of pride and terror to its inhabitants that they lived not on a lifezone planet, where luxuries like *water* and *air* and *food* and *heat* could be relied on, but on and in a rocky planetoid that drifted in four-century sweeps around Persara, their distant blue star. Gaea's water came from an icy asteroid that had been anchored to their little hunk of rock with military-grade cable. Its heat relied on enormous jury-rigged solar reflectors, repurposed from dreadnought-class warships, that Suntracker Wing worked endlessly to defend from debris. Its food and air were the business of Agricole Wing.

Kyr paused when she slipped through the plastic sheeting into the high hall where Gaea's life was sustained. She felt a familiar sting of pride. Gaea might not be beautiful, it might not be rich, but look what humanity could do, even on a dead rock in a worthless system.

Sunlamps poured out yellow-spectrum light on the greedy greenery. Every inch of space was used. Vines were trained around the rungs of the ladders that led from the depths far below to the heights of the rocky ceiling. Condensation dripped down the walls, and mist hung in the air. In among the crammed order of the omnidirectional garden soared great dark shapes that held it all together: the massive trunks of Gaea's private forest, carefully modified trees that processed the station's atmosphere and kept them all from choking to death out here in the depths of dark space.

The trees were precious because they were irreplaceable. The shadow engines at the station core had overloaded fifteen years ago, when Kyr was two years old. Systems had managed to save the station, but sixty-eight humans had died, and the feedback from the interdimensional blast had trashed their delicate gene-tailoring suite. Gaea did not have the resources to repair it. These trees were sterile, and could not now be cloned. They would last a long time. They had to.

Kyr knew what she was looking for here. She went to the nearest ladder and climbed until she reached the shadowy heights of Agricole, where wide green canopies spread. Magnus was there dozing sprawled on a broad branch like a lazy lion. Kyr's twin was even bigger than she was; neither of them was nanite-enhanced, but they had been born before the disaster, back when Nursery was still able to design real warbreeds. They were both based on the same parental cross, the one that had produced Ursa before both their genetic forebears had died. Ursa at seven had already shown signs of being something special, so it had made sense—even though it was against population policy—to create siblings.

And they were something special. Kyr knew this as a fact. They were the best of the best of Earth's warrior children. Kyr was tall and muscular, and to that build Mags had started to add *bulk,* the broad powerful body that frightened the shit out of the majo. Out of the many sentient alien species that made up the so-called majoda, only the spindly zunimmer had a natural height over five and a half feet. Kyr had fought hand-to-hand against eight-foot zunimmer shock troops in the agoge. Their bones were light and brittle, and you could snap their spines easily if you went in at just the right angle. Kyr weighed more than one of them. Mags probably weighed more than *two* of them.

But then Mags was a living propaganda poster for both sides. In the old days you could have slapped a *Strong Together* slogan over him—massive, blond, square-shouldered—and made a recruitment still for the Interstellar Terran Expeditionary. Since Doomsday, human actors who looked like him played villains in majo dramas. Collaborators. Kyr felt disgusted just thinking about it.

It made her voice come out sharp when she said, "What are you doing?"

Mags opened his eyes. "Hi, Kyr."

"Why are you asleep?" demanded Kyr.

"It's rec rotation," said Mags. "Sleep is recreational."

"We can't afford to sleep."

"What's the point of being alive if you can't sleep?"

Something in Kyr bubbled and burst. "The *point,*" she snapped, "is that we're *at war* and we're *dying,* that they've taken everything from us and *you* just—"

"Oh, hey, hey, Vallie, hey," said Mags, sitting up from his enormous slouch and before Kyr's eyes transforming back from the unconquerable giant to the soft idiot who'd been a natural victim for bullies when they were still in Nursery. "Don't cry. Why are you crying?"

"I'm not," said Kyr. She sat on the broad branch beside him. The air smelled thick and sweet, and condensation was beading on her arms and face. Agricole felt more alive than anywhere else on Gaea. Mags put his arm round her shoulders. "I nearly beat it," Kyr said. "Uncle Jole's scenario. Doomsday. I nearly beat it. I couldn't do it."

"Oh," said Mags.

"Don't *oh*. It matters. You know it matters. And it's all right for you. You have beaten it."

"Once," said Mags. "And I think he went in and made it harder afterward. You get that it's meant to be unbeatable, right?"

"It was the Wisdom," said Kyr. "I got as far as the dart and then the Wisdom put an extra shield on the bomb and then—"

"Yeah," said Mags. "That's what I mean. It's supposed to be unbeatable because of the Wisdom. Because *they're* unbeatable, with the Wisdom."

"How did you do it?" Kyr demanded. She had never asked. She'd wanted to do it herself first. But she'd been so close. "How did you win?"

Mags took his arm away from around her shoulders, and lay back down on the great branch staring up into the patterns made by sprays of foliage hanging down from above. He said, "Do you know Avi?"

"Who?"

"Avi," said Mags. "Otter mess, cohort above us. Assigned Systems Wing."

Kyr said, "Oh, the queer one?" She had only a vague mental picture of the person Mags was talking about. Short, red hair, a squint. Not a warbreed. Gaea had been founded by survivors of the Terran Expeditionary, but armies were more than just soldiers, and there were the genes of technicians, cleaners, medical staff, administrators in the cadet messes too. Kyr knew how important they were. Genetic variety was vital for a species to survive, and there were already so few true humans left. Without people like—oh, like Lisabel, in her mess, who was a guaranteed Nursery Wing assignment if Kyr had ever seen one, humanity had no future.

"Sure," Mags said. "The queer one."

"What?" said Kyr.

Mags didn't answer.

"What about him?" Kyr said. "How do you know him?"

"Met him in the arcade in rec rotation."

"What were you doing in the arcade?"

"Rest and relaxation?" said Mags. "I find losing really badly at video games relaxing."

"You lose?"

"Everyone loses at something, Vallie."

Kyr, who didn't, gave him a narrow look. Mags was only gazing peacefully up at the tangled plants. There was something coming into flower directly above them, big purple clusters of waxy blossoms. Kyr didn't know the name of the plant. She had no expectation of ever being assigned to Agricole. "So what about *Avi,* then?"

"Avi," said Magnus, "does not lose at video games. He was beating me. We got talking."

"What is there to talk to someone like that about?" said Kyr. "He's leaving, isn't he?" It was amazing how selfish people could be. Nearly everyone like that she had ever heard about had ended up refusing assignment and leaving Gaea Station, taking themselves over to the majo side, as if having sex that achieved nothing mattered more than saving your entire species or taking vengeance for a murdered world.

Mags said, "I don't know if he's leaving. We'd be sorry to lose him. He's beyond good at what he does."

"Systems?" said Kyr. "It's important, sure—"

"Games," said Mags.

"Oh, come on."

"I'm serious," said Mags. "That's how I beat Doomsday. Avi talked me through it."

"I don't remember ever hearing about him beating a Level Twelve simulation." Kyr would have heard: she tracked the training rankings constantly, for the boys as well as the girls. It was how she knew that there were only a handful of boys (five, exactly five) with better scores than her in her entire age cohort: six of them altogether who regularly trained on Level Twelve, the hardest. There were, obviously, no girls as good as Kyr. Boys had a natural advantage. Mags, the perfect soldier, was one of the five. His scores since his last growth spurt were the best in Gaea's short history.

"Well, we were a team," Mags said. "I went in with an earpiece. He talked to me the whole time. He's not even an agoge designer—" Kyr snorted; of course a nearsighted nineteen-year-old who'd never even cracked the top thirty wasn't allowed anywhere near military training, the heart of Gaea's strength. "No, Vallie, it was incredible. He's the smartest person I've ever met. He watched me run it and fail a few times, and then he said we'd do a serious run while he called the shots, and doing it with him in my ear made Doomsday feel like—I don't know, like having fun. He knew everything that was coming and he knew exactly what I had to do about it. I just followed along. It was magic."

"So you cheated," said Kyr.

"It wasn't official," Mags said. "It was a rec hour thing. It didn't go in my scores." Mags knew how serious training scores were.

"It was all over the station," said Kyr. "Everyone knew you'd beaten Doomsday." *Magnus could have saved our world* was how people had said it. *Magnus* could. Kyr had put every free minute into the Doomsday scenario since she'd heard. And now it turned out the whole thing was just fake, some arcade-haunting nobody taking advantage of Mags the way people always seemed to, treating the agoge like a game.

"It was just a thing," Mags said. "Avi wanted to see if

we could do it." He propped himself up on his elbow to meet Kyr's eyes and said more urgently, "But you see what I mean, right? We shouldn't want to lose someone like him."

"Because he's a cheat?" said Kyr.

"*They* cheat, don't they?" Mags said. "The Wisdom cheats. Why shouldn't we have cheats of our own? And anyway it's not cheating to have someone else giving orders in agoge, we do that in tactical exercises, that's normal. Avi's just really smart. I think they ought to tap him for Command."

"Of course you do," said Kyr, but she couldn't help it, she smiled. Mags was just like this, he had this absurd soft spot for lost causes. "Okay, fine, it's nice that you're being friendly. Someone like that probably doesn't have a lot of friends, right? Just don't get too upset when he leaves."

Mags lay back down. A purple flower had come loose from the waxy tangle above and drifted down onto the branch. He picked it up and with great care balanced it on his forehead, not looking at Kyr the whole time. "I don't want him to leave," he said.

"People leave," said Kyr. "When they're not tough enough or committed enough or honorable enough. Ursa left."

Mags made the same pinched face he always made whenever someone mentioned their older sister. "Yeah," he said. "I guess she did."